Marathonarium Anthology
Volume II

Marathonarium Anthology
Volume II

Edited by Stephen Zimmer

Copyright © 2025 by Seventh Star Press

All rights reserved. No portion of this book may be copied or transmitted in any form, electronic or otherwise, without express written consent of the publisher or author.

Cover design: Olivia Pro Design

Cover art in this book copyright © 2025 Olivia Pro Design and Seventh Star Press, LLC.

Editor: Stephen Zimmer

Published by Seventh Star Press, LLC.

ISBN Number: 9798290226941

Seventh Star Press

www.seventhstarpress.com

info@seventhstarpress.com

Publisher's Note:

Marathonarum Anthology Volume II is a work of fiction. All names, characters, and places are the product of the author's imagination, used in fictitious manner. Any resemblances to actual persons, places, locales, events, etc. are purely coincidental.

Printed in the United States of America

First Edition

Table of Contents

Introduction..................................1

When the Clock Strikes Null Time by Annette Miller............5

Night and the Perfect Blue by Zevon Price.....................23

The Pixie Job by Kathy L Brown................................53

A Spark of Necromancy by Teri Kay Jobe.....................75

Burden of Duty by Brian Ronk...................................101

The Muskogee Kid by Lisa Mildon............................115

Blood for Blood by Clayton Barnett............................133

Space Junk by Grathew..141

The Spider in the House of Chosroes by Joseph M. Isenberg.....165

The Kotaran Mission: A Weapons of Legend Tale by S. D. Croft..183

A Tale of Tails by R.N. Warren..211

Redemption's Secrets by Randi Perrin..........................247

Why Can't You See by Abigail Christine Cahoe..........287

Following Jack by Carma Haley Shoemaker..............295

The Bank Robber and the Beer Belly by Marian Gosling.....327

Publish or Perish by Alisa Childress................................345

Pawn to King Four by Ana Maria Selvaggio..................365

Author Biographies..437

About the Editor..447

About the Imaginarium Convention..........................449

Introduction

Welcome to the second Marathonarium Anthology! The short stories that you find in this anthology are the result of a creative journey that began at the Marathonarium II Workshop, held on the eve of the Imaginarium 2024 weekend, on Thursday, July 18th, of 2024.

The workshop brings together writers of many styles and genres, and the initial phase involves a marathon writing session of three hours in length. All of the participants are encouraged to tell the story that they want to tell; there are no restrictions on genre, there is no common theme, nor are there any parameters on the voice the story must be told in.

This project reflects the spirit of the Imaginarium Convention, whose mission statement is, "To foster and inspire imagination, one creative at a time. Create and make your world everything you imagine it to be." The Imaginarium embraces celebrates all forms and genres of creative writing, and this anthology reflects that.

The Marathonarium was conceived by award-winning author and editor Sandy Lender, who helmed the first one as editor back at Imaginarium 2023 (with the release of Marathonarium Anthology, Volume I, taking place at Imaginarium 2024). It was a great honor to take on the

Editor Stephen Zimmer

position of editor for the second Marathonarium, and it has been my sincere focus to deliver a volume that continues the excellence demonstrated in the debut year. Sandy set the foundation for something truly unique and wonderful, and I have done my best to build upon that excellent beginning.

As the editor of Volume II, I chose to allow a larger group of writers to participate. Writers were also given greater flexibility in the size of the final stories, resulting in a wider range of story sizes found in this volume.

I have really enjoyed working through all of the stories in this anthology and helping all of the authors see them to the finish line. The participating writers demonstrated great attention to the craft of writing as well as the art of storytelling. They have my gratitude for their hard work and creativity. The result is a group of tales that will entertain, captivate, provoke thought, stoke the imagination, thrill, and engage the readers of this book.

It was a great experience, and I am looking forward to July 17th, 2025, when the creative journey for the Marathonarium Anthology, Volume III begins!

Onwards and Upwards!

Stephen Zimmer

Editor

Welcome To The Marathonarium, Where Your Imagination is the Foundation

When the Clock Strikes Null Time
by Annette Miller

Dust swirled in the air, making Lynn Porter shield her eyes against the man-made tornado. The helicopter landed and the man she waited for stepped out carrying a large, leather briefcase. His suit jacket, draped over his arm, waved in the strong wind. He waved to the pilot, signaling to take off, as he hurried over to her and extended his hand.

He pushed his short brown hair off his forehead. "Dr. Porter I assume?"

She shook his hand and smiled. Strands of blonde hair swirled around her face as she tried to tuck them behind her ears. Her jeans, white shirt, and hiking boots were covered with dust from the surrounding desert. The helicopter's arrival had only raised more to land on her shoulders and legs.

"Dr. Christopher Matthews, I'm glad to finally meet you." She directed him toward the large, white building behind them. "Your expertise will be invaluable to solve a particularly bad problem."

They walked inside and Chris shook out his jacket,

trying to remove some of the sand clinging to it. "I didn't expect so much dust out here."

Lynn chuckled. "You did land in New Mexico, after all. Dust is one of our major exports."

Heading out the front door, they got into a waiting car. "You never said what the problem is you're having out here."

"I'll explain more when we get to my lab."

They rode in silence, and Lynn could feel Chris's eyes on her for most of the trip. She inwardly groaned and grabbed the jacket she'd left in the car. She'd hoped he wouldn't be another one of those men who thought that because she had a pretty face, she couldn't be in the top of her field. Once they got to their destination, he'd understand the scope of what she needed him to do.

She snuck a quick glance at him, thinking he could have the same problem she did. Christopher Matthews was incredibly handsome, with light-brown hair and blue eyes. A square jaw, broad shoulders, and a tie hanging loose around his neck. He didn't strike her as the suit and tie type, any more than she was the skirt and high heels type. They were scientists who belonged in labs and out in the field trying to understand the mysteries of the world around them.

The car stopped and she got out and waited for him to join her. He hesitated and stared at an area off to his right. A small yard with a fence looked out of place without a house in the middle of it. He walked closer and stared. The grass was green to about halfway up, and then nothing. No grass, no weeds, no flowers; nothing living anywhere at all near the center.

"What happened here?" he asked.

Lynn walked over to him and stared at the area. "That's what you're here to help us figure out. Let's get inside and

When the Clock Strikes Null Time

we'll talk."

Two armed guards stood at the entrance of a two-story building. They wore army uniforms, and more soldiers patrolled around the perimeter of the building. Lynn took out her ID badge and waited while they scanned it. Chris gave them his driver's license, and they entered it into their handheld computer.

They entered the lab, and a small man in a lab coat hurried out of a side door to greet them. "Dr. Matthews, I'm Dr. Medlin, head of the research staff. When Dr. Porter told us you were coming, we all were very relieved. Your knowledge will help us retrieve one of our colleagues from a dangerous situation."

Chris raised an eyebrow and glanced at Lynn. "I hadn't been told about any danger here. Is this why the Army is here? I didn't know of any military experimentation. Are we safe?"

"The soldiers are here because they've funded this whole thing." Lynn hung up the jacket she hadn't worn. "Yes, we're safe. We're far enough outside of the radius to not be affected." She walked to her desk and picked up a pile of papers. "What has happened here must remain classified. Government money funded this operation, and they are serious to keep it hush-hush. What has happened needs to be buried and forgotten."

Chris hung up his jacket and perched on the edge of the desk. "You still haven't said what occurred out here. I have to admit, the more you say, the more intrigued I become. Tell me what happened and how you think I can help."

Lynn handed him the papers. "Here. Read through these later." She walked away and spun around. "My father, Dr. Edwin Porter, has discovered time travel."

Chris shot to his feet. "Time travel has proven to be

impossible."

"Until now," she said. "Unfortunately, something went wrong with his experiment. He's trapped in a null time field."

He rubbed his chin. "I know of your father's work. He'd been laughed out of every college and university in the country. Even the government proclaimed for years they wouldn't fund his research. I guess he found a way to change their minds. How did he discover time travel?"

Lynn began to pace. "It was kind of a fluke accident. He'd been working with ley lines here in the desert. I'm not sure exactly what components he had with him in his lab. We had a huge storm last week. When lightning struck the roof of the house, it and my father disappeared."

He glanced toward the window. "The empty spot in the yard outside. The house used to stand there?" She nodded and he walked over to her. "What happened to the grass?"

"Anything organic dies inside the field. My father can't leave the house. We've tried to think of how to get him out before the house disappears completely."

"The house isn't there now," he pointed out.

She nodded. "I know. The house can only appear between the first stroke and the last stroke of midnight. Between those twelve strokes, it's not yesterday, it's not today, and it's not tomorrow. It's null time. Only then, the house appears."

"So, we only have twelve seconds to retrieve him."

"Last night, it was only eleven. The house began to vanish before the last stroke. Those papers are his notes of what he's tried to get out." She laid her hand on his arm. "Chris, we're running out of time to save him."

"But if nothing organic can leave the field," he shook the papers, "how did you get these?"

"He's been using different things to put the papers in.

When the Clock Strikes Null Time

You know, tin foil, coffee cups, beakers, anything he can find."

"Good idea." He glanced at her and smiled. "Your father is a smart man."

Lynn took to pacing in the lab, her assistant and Chris watching her. "We need to stop the time decay or find a way to safely get him out. Your work with ley lines is well known. Until you proved they existed, most people thought they were complete mumbo jumbo. Those lines have the power to make time travel possible."

"Or to make null time exist, to destroy anything living."

She stared at the floor. "I can't lose my father to something like this. Do you think you can help us?"

"I'll be honest with you, Lynn. I really don't know." He glanced through the papers in his hands. "I didn't even think a situation like this was possible."

"Dr. Porter, why don't you take Dr. Matthews to get some dinner. I'll monitor the energy fluxes until you get back. When midnight approaches, you two can go out and see what's going on with the house."

"All right." She turned to Chris. "Would you like to get something to eat? We're in for a long night."

He smiled and pulled her arm through his. "I thought you'd never ask."

She drove them to the small, nearby town and parked in front of a steakhouse. Noise and laughter drifted to them from the open door and Chris laid his hand on the small of her back and ushered her in. They were seated at a back booth and stared at the menus on the table.

"I did bring my research with me," he said. "After hearing what I'm up against, I'm not sure how helpful it will be. I've never run into this kind of problem before."

Their food was set in front of them, and the waitress

hurried off. "My father talked about you a lot," Lynn said. "Apparently, you were one of his favorite students when he taught back east. I was almost jealous of you, but he assured me I would always be his best and favorite student."

Chris was quiet for a moment. "I thought you might have been talking about him when I got asked to come out here." He took a sip of his water and traced a circle in the wet ring on the table. "A lot of the students thought he was a crackpot, but I found his theories interesting. We used to have a lot of, let's say, spirited discussions about different aspects of energy and what it could actually accomplish. You know, he encouraged my study of ley lines."

"I know." She pushed the remains of her food around on her plate. "He suspected they might be the catalyst to make time travel possible. He wouldn't tell me what else he planned to use, claiming scientists were like magicians. No one could know all the secrets of what they did."

Chris laughed. "That sounds just like him. I'll say it again. Edwin is a smart man. I'm not sure how he got himself into such a bad situation."

They paid the check and walked out to her car. "If you know my dad, when he gets a thought, he's like a dog with a bone. He can't let it rest until he's poked, prodded, and proved it to death." She sat in the driver's seat and stared out the windshield. "We've got to save him, Chris." She turned to him, tears glistening in her eyes. "We've got to."

He laid his hand on her shoulder. "Don't worry. We'll save him, and we'll do it long before time runs out."

They were silent on the drive back to the lab. She led him down to the break room and poured them each a cup of coffee. She sat and looked at the clock, feeling it tick away the minutes of her father's life. As much as she wanted time to hurry so she could show Chris what happened, she

When the Clock Strikes Null Time

also needed it to slow down and give her a little more time to hope for a miracle.

"When do we go outside to see the house?" he asked.

"I try to get out there around eleven-forty-five. He can stand on the porch, but not leave the shelter of the house."

He folded his hands on the table and leaned forward. "Tell me again exactly what happened."

She took a deep breath and let it out slowly. "Dad was working in the lab in our house. He said he'd discovered the missing element to make time travel possible. He told me he'd tapped into one of the ley lines under the house. The night he turned on his machine, we had a terrible storm. I'd never seen so much lightning out here before."

Chris took out a pad of paper and took notes on everything she was telling him. "It appears to me whatever element he found drew the lightning to the house. If it hit at the right moment, like when he tapped into the ley line, that could explain everything."

She shook her head. "But not why it kills anything organic around it."

They lapsed back into silence, the only sound the loud, echoing ticking of the clock over the door. Finally, the time had come to go outside and see the phenomenon for themselves. She walked to the lab and wrote out a note and wrapped tin foil around it, making a strange ball. Lynn grabbed her coat and handed Chris his jacket.

"It's always chilly at night, but around the site, the air is a lot colder."

At eleven-forty-five, they stood at the fence and waited. Soon, the clock in the town chimed the midnight hour. The air rippled and slowly a small house began to appear. She stepped closer and Chris grabbed her arm.

At her nod, he let go and followed her up the walkway.

Annette Miller

At the edge of the live grass, she stopped and bounced the tin foil ball in her hand. When the house fully appeared, the door opened and an older man with white hair and the beginnings of a scraggly beard appeared.

"Lynn, go back. I can't stop the surge from spreading," he shouted.

A wind picked up and whipped her hair around her face. "It's okay, Dad," she yelled back. "We've got help now. We're going to stop this and save you."

On the tenth stroke, the house began to waver and fade. Lynn pitched the ball at her father, who caught it and stepped back inside, slamming the door just as the house faded completely.

"I thought you said we had until the eleventh stroke right now," Chris said. "And if the null field is expanding, more than just your father's life is at stake."

"What can we do?" She stared at the empty spot where her father had been a moment before. "This isn't my field of study."

"Let me go over his notes thoroughly. I may find something all of us missed."

They walked back to the lab, his arm around her shoulders. Lynn knew the chances of saving her father were getting slimmer all the time. "I don't think we're going to save him, are we?"

"Like I said, I think the whole world is at stake now. If the field continues to grow, it may consume the whole planet. We may have to try to duplicate his experiment."

"But if we don't know what he was working with, it will be impossible."

They walked inside and hung up their coats. "Get some rest, Lynn. We'll tackle this first thing in the morning. There's not a lot we can do tonight."

When the Clock Strikes Null Time

"You're right. We have some quarters here for visiting scientists. I'm in the one down the hall and to the right. You can take the room across from mine. There's no one there at this time."

"Good night, Lynn, and don't worry." He leaned over and kissed her cheek. "We'll find the solution, I promise."

***

Lynn woke to bright sunlight and stretched.

Only ten chimes last night. The null time grew shorter and shorter. How long before the house faded entirely?

She got up, showered, and dressed, all the time thinking Chris would have a solution. After all, he'd studied ley lines for years. Her father bragged about him all the time. He'd wanted his daughter to meet him for a long time, kidding her about having genius grandkids. She would always smile and roll her eyes and tell her father she was married to her work. Now, she hoped he'd be around for any grandkids she may give him.

She walked to the break room and found Chris there, already studying the pages laid out on the table. "How long have you been up?" she asked.

"Since around five. I never sleep very long when there's a puzzle to solve." He picked up one page and frowned, before writing on his notepad. "I can't understand where your father went wrong. He took all the necessary precautions. The chemicals he used are some of the safest compounds around. He only tapped a little of the power in the ley line under his house."

Lynn leaned over his shoulder. "Then, the only explanation is the lightning. That storm came out of nowhere. None of us expected it to hit so close by. When we discovered it hit the house, we weren't sure what to do.

Annette Miller

We thought the house had been vaporized, but at the first stroke of midnight, it appeared, and faded by the last stroke. Is there anything you can do to reverse what happened?"

He threw the papers on the table and sat back. "I don't know. If it was the lightning that set this in motion, we'd need a bolt to hit at just the right time, with the same amount of power as the first one. That's going to be the tricky part. I'm hoping we get everything right."

She slumped down in the chair opposite him and rubbed her eyes. "It sounds like you're saying there's no hope at all. Because of my father's obsession with time travel, the whole world is going to be sucked into a null time field and be destroyed."

"I admit, the odds aren't good, but we at least have a small chance to put things right. We need to get a message to your father." He shuffled through the papers and found the one he wanted. "We've got to plan this right. We need him to conduct the experiment in the exact same fashion he did the night of the accident. If we can come up with a way to duplicate the lightning surge, we can stop the null field and save Dr. Porter."

"I believe the military was working on some big generator to study the effects of lightning on surrounding things like trees and houses. We could use that to simulate the strike that started the null field." She shook her head as a frown creased her brow. "There's a lot of variables in that plan. Even if we can duplicate everything perfectly, down to the microsecond, can we be sure it will work? We may only have one shot at it. If we fail in that one attempt..."

"I know," he said softly. "But it's all I can come up with. We have to duplicate the experiment. Do you think your father can do it on his end?"

She shrugged. "I don't know. It depends if he has

When the Clock Strikes Null Time

enough of what he needs. We'll have to ask him tonight." She glanced at the clock. "It's a long time until midnight."

He smiled and stood. "Then let's get to work. Call your military contacts and let them know what needs to be done."

She walked to her desk and picked up the phone. "General Deering, we may have a way to stop the null field." She paused and looked up at Chris. "We'll need the new lightning generator your scientists are working on." She waited while he spoke. "Yes, I know it's only experimental, but General, if we don't stop the field from expanding, the whole world could be in danger." She jumped to her feet, gripping the phone tight enough to turn her knuckles white. "I am not a hysterical female and I don't appreciate the insinuation."

Chris gestured for her to give him the phone. "General Deering, this is Dr. Christopher Matthews. What Dr. Porter is telling you is true. This null time field is beginning to expand. I suggest you listen to her and give her anything she needs to stop this from becoming a cataclysmic situation."

He handed the phone back to her and grinned as she rolled her eyes. "Yes, General, he's the specialist you let me call in. Dr. Matthews studied with my father and he's the best qualified to help with this problem. So, send me the generator before the world pops out of existence. We plan to duplicate the experiment my father was working on." She scowled. "He told you multiple times this experiment was dangerous. I know. I was there at his meeting with you. Messing with time is never a good idea, and now we're all paying for your pompous attitude. Let us fix this mess and save my father. Oh, and General, never call me a hysterical female again, or you'll see how hysterical I can really get."

She slammed the phone down and Chris burst into laughter. Her frown slowly faded, and she chuckled before letting the huge laugh building inside her escape. She fell back in her chair and swiveled it back and forth. She wiped her eyes and the two of them stared at each other for several silent minutes.

"Thank you. I needed that," she finally said. "I didn't really need your input with General Deering, but I appreciate it all the same."

"I guess the general is old school and thinks any crisis a woman brings up to him is just a small thing blown out of proportion."

She nodded and picked up a pen to make notes on what to tell her father. "I don't think that man was ever young. He thinks only men have good ideas and know what they're talking about."

Chris leaned his arms on her desk. "I guarantee you, none of us know what we're doing."

"You don't have to tell me." She gave him a sly smile. "I figured that out for myself."

He stood. "I'm going to read over your dad's notes some more. I'll come get you when it's time for lunch."

She nodded and began to form a note to give her father in the coming midnight. She prayed Chris's plan would work. So many things could go wrong. They were working with forces none of them truly understood. She'd only heard her father mention ley lines in passing and never gave them much thought. How ironic she needed to know more about them now, to save not only his life, but the life of everyone on Earth.

The two of them worked through lunch, and around six, Lynn went to the break room and knocked on the doorframe. "I think we need to get some dinner. We worked this whole day away. We need to get ready for tonight."

Chris stretched and rubbed the back of his neck. "I

When the Clock Strikes Null Time

didn't realize it had gotten so late. Your father's notes are interesting. I have a better understanding of what he was trying to do with his experiment." He pushed all the papers into a messy pile and stood. "Let's get some food. You mentioned dinner, and now I'm hungry."

They went to the same restaurant as the night before and ate without saying much. Each was lost in their own thoughts as to what else they needed for their sketchy plan to work. Too much could go wrong, and not enough could go right. Neither wanted to contemplate the consequences of failure. Failure meant no more planet, just an empty hole in space.

When they returned to the lab, Lynn went to her desk while Chris headed for the break room and gathered his notes. On the way back to Lynn's office, Dr. Medlin hurried out of the observation room.

"Dr. Matthews, I'm on my way to get Dr. Porter. There's been an energy surge."

Chris hurried into the room and stared at the computer screens spitting out numbers in rapid order. He waited until Dr. Medlin returned with Lynn. From the data he was seeing, they might have less time than they initially believed. The null field had expanded more, which meant they'd have less than the ten chimes the previous evening.

"What's going on, Chris?" Lynn said while Dr. Medlin hovered in the background, wringing his hands. "Dr. Medlin said things are getting worse."

"He's right." He pointed to one of the screens. "The data here shows the null field has gotten larger since last night. We're running out of time. The Army needs to get that generator here no later than two days from now. We have to stop the field as soon as possible. The longer we wait, the stronger it will get. That will make it harder to close."

Lynn wrapped her arms around herself. "I have to tell my father this. Let me add to the note and see what he says. I'm sure he'll want us to try anything we can to stop the null field from expanding."

She hurried back to her office and opened the note she'd written. She added what they'd just learned and knew her father would do his part to make their plan work. All they had to do was get everything coordinated at the same time. And therein lay the hardest part of the plan. She glanced at the clock. Eleven-forty-five. She took a deep, shuddering breath and slowly released it. Time to go. But would this be the last time? When would the Army's generator arrive? She ground her teeth at the delay. *It had better get here soon.*

"Chris, it's time," she called.

The two of them went to the site with two guards behind them. After being apprised of the seriousness of the situation, they'd been ordered to keep the two scientists safe. The clock began to chime, and the house faded into existence. Her father stepped out, his shoulders more slumped, his steps slower, and his cheeks more hollow than the last time she saw him. Being trapped in the null field had worn him down more and more.

"Dad, read this right now," Lynn yelled as she threw the tin foil ball.

They waited while he scanned the note. The clock chimed nine and the house began to fade. "I have enough," he shouted as his voice grew faint with the disappearing house.

Lynn stared in horror at the grass. The dead lawn reached almost to the fence now. The null field had grown exponentially since the night before. How much longer did her father and the world have? From the looks of things,

When the Clock Strikes Null Time

they had three, maybe four days. *General Deering had better get off his olive-drab butt and get us the generator soon.*

***

Later, the next morning, a large, Army transport truck pulled up in front of the lab. Chris and Lynn walked out as the soldiers began to unload a crate at least seven feet high and eight feet long. Two men in suits climbed out of the cab and walked over to them.

"Is that the generator?" Chris asked. He glanced at Lynn, whose shoulders had sagged with relief. "We were wondering when it would get here. We're running out of time."

One of the men held his hand out and Lynn and Chris shook it. "Yes, it is. It should give you the same voltage as the lightning that hit the night Dr. Porter disappeared. We're the head designers of the generator. We were told to give you all the assistance you need."

"Thank you," Lynn said. "We're hoping the generator will stop the null time field from expanding and save my father."

Chris whistled as he walked around the box. It was taller than his own six-foot-two inch height. "I knew it would be big, but I didn't consider it would be large on this kind of scale. Here's hoping it will be enough."

One of the men smiled and nodded. "We're sure it will give you the power you need."

Lynn directed it to the side of the lab, closest to where the null field was expanding. They watched a bird land and instantly disappear. They looked at each other and continued directing the generator placement. The situation was becoming worse, and she could only think of it as a catastrophe on a cosmic level.

Annette Miller

Back inside, Chris led her to a map. "I found the ley line Dr. Porter must have used. I think he didn't realize this is one of the stronger ones in this region. He's going to have to tap into the same line if we're going to make this work."

"Should we do this tomorrow night? I'm going to need to tell him when, so he can do the experiment, and we can use the generator at the same time." She rubbed her arms, fighting off an internal chill. "We really need this to work."

He pulled her in for a tight, brief hug. "It will. We'll have everything planned down to the second. Your father is a genius. You are as well. Add in me, and this null field doesn't stand a chance."

"I'm glad you're certain this will work. Even the butterflies in my stomach have butterflies."

As the time grew close to midnight, Lynn took her next note as she stood farther back. The null field had made it to the fence. She grabbed a rock and wrapped the note and tin foil around it. When the house appeared, she threw it as hard as she could, sighing in relief when it landed at her father's feet. As he gave her a thumbs up, the house faded on the seventh chime.

"I know which ley line to use," he called, his voice barely above a whisper. "I'll be ready at the same time as before."

Back in the lab, she paced as Chris watched. "We lost two chimes tonight from last night. We have to consider we may lose three tomorrow night. If our plan doesn't work, I'm afraid that will be it, and we'll be out of time."

"You're right. I've had the same thought myself. We have to try it tomorrow night."

She stopped her pacing and turned to him. "Dad said he has enough of the compounds and knows which ley line to tap into. We have the lightning generator and the team

When the Clock Strikes Null Time

who knows how to use it. It's definitely a do-or-die for real tomorrow."

***

The next day was spent in preparation for that night. Chris found the ley line and directed the scientists how to tap into it. The lightning generator would need more power than the lab could supply. Ley lines had almost unlimited power. They could run the generator and Edwin Porter's experiment at the same time.

Lynn laid her hand on Chris's shoulder. "Look."

They turned to see the fence fall in on itself. The null time field had grown even more that morning. They didn't want to wait until midnight, but that was the only time the house appeared. Neither of them could sit still all day. Neither wanted to eat. They went over the data coming in on the screens in the observation room. They went over Edwin's papers multiple times. They ran through the plan again and again.

At eleven-forty-five, scientists and Army troops gathered outside. The field had grown larger, giving the air around it a wavy, shimmering look. Each person held their breath as the clock crept closer to midnight.

Would their plan work, or would the world be doomed?

The clock chimed one, and the house appeared. Two, and flashes of light started in what Lynn knew was her father's lab. Three, and Chris raised his hand. This was it. The clock chimed four and started to fade.

Chris dropped his hand, the signal to turn on the generator. They all shielded their eyes, and a deafening crack filled the air.

Lynn squinted to watch the bolt strike the house as the same light filled the lab windows. She felt Chris's arm go around her shoulders. Smoke filled the yard and drifted around them, obscuring the view of the house. Several minutes passed before the light dimmed and the smoke cleared enough for them to see. Lynn held her breath as Chris's grip on her shoulders tightened.

The clock chimed twelve as they all waited to see if the plan was a success. As the last of the smoke drifted away, she couldn't believe what she saw. The house stood there, slightly scorched, but whole, and not faded. The front door opened, and her father came out. He was hunched over, and thick coughs wracked his body.

Lynn reached up and gripped Chris's hand, squeezing it as she waited to see what would happen. Edwin Porter staggered down the few steps to the yard. He looked around and straightened up. He took another couple of cautious steps. When he was no longer in danger of disappearing, Lynn ran to him and flung herself into his arms.

"Dad, you're safe!" She kissed his cheek and held him tight. "I was so afraid I wouldn't be able to save you. I'm so glad we got you out in time."

"I worried about me too, my girl." He held her close as they walked back to the cheering crowd. "I feared I'd never see you again."

Chris shook Edwin's hand. "I'm glad we got you out, sir." He grinned. "But please never do anything like this again."

"I promise, but only if you date my daughter."

Chris smiled as Lynn looked up at him. "It's a deal."

Night and the Perfect Blue
by Zevon Price

Avery had spent the last three days searching. That was what she did, after all. Nothing officially, of course. She didn't have an office or a business card. Things like that turned into liabilities in this kind of work. No, what she did, she did on the down-low, and the lower, the better.

She was beginning to think this job might be digging turnips in Hell. It was turning into one of the hardest jobs she had ever done.

Her employer had shown up at the dive bar she liked to inhabit. It was dark, it was quiet, it was a filthy little hole in the wall that helped facilitate her line of work more than one would initially think.

She only noticed him because he was the exact opposite of someone who would ever step foot in a place like this.

She knew nothing of fashion above thrift and chain stores, but even she could tell this guy was loaded. You didn't get a suit like that at a strip mall. It looked like something a movie star would wear in a flick about high-stake corporate shenanigans. The haircut went along with it, and there was no way his hair was naturally that shade of black. It didn't look bad. It just didn't look natural. Even jet-black hair had some variation when the light hit it. But not his. His hair was shiny, uniformly black, like the brightest part of a raven's wing all throughout.

The more she looked at him, the weirder it got.

He was handsome enough, in that too-much-money-golf-country-club-and-McMansion way, all slick and polished and just a bit too much to be old money; but there was something about him that hung askew. He was probably her age, mid-thirties or so, but he looked like an easy mid-twenties, with his tanned skin and smooth features. None of that impending crow's feet and hair starting to gray at the temples like she was beginning to notice in the mirror. His tan was even and deep, and now that tanning beds were out of style, she assumed he was probably into some outdoor sport. Only, there were so signs of tan lines or the redness of sunburn anywhere. She bet if she could have gotten him down to his skivvies, (a thought she found more than a little repellent) that he would have been the same uniformly caramel color all over, with the same lack of variation of his hair. His teeth were the blinding white of toothpaste commercials and as evenly spaced and uniform as tombstones in a modern cemetery.

It was his eyes, though, that she couldn't stop staring at.

They had no color. No color at all.

"You're staring at me again," he said, smiling at her behind his coffee cup. She blinked and jerked, startled. She was used to weirdos. In this line of work, you had to get over that hangup quick, but this was the second time he had called her out.

"Sorry," she muttered, forcing herself to look away. It wasn't just that his eyes had no color. He had all the eye

Night and the Perfect Blue

parts: the pupil, iris, sclera, even the tiny veins at the corners that seemed even redder than they should have been. But the sclera had absolutely no color at all. They were as clear as quartz, although someone like him would probably prefer the analogy "clear as diamonds."

"I know, it's quite disconcerting." He cast his gaze demurely down at his hand resting on the scarred tabletop between them. The ruby in the gigantic signet ring he wore winked up at her like Satan's eye. "I usually wear sunglasses, even at night, but this seems like the sort of place where that might not be the best sartorial choice."

A dive bar like this, with patrons like these; mostly good-old boys and the hard-bitten women who put up with their bullshit, would likely take to him like gasoline to a block of ice.

That was also the second time he had busted out the big vocabulary. The first time it had been when he asked if she would "be able to ameliorate a problem for him," and then he stared at her as if waiting for her to ask what "ameliorate" meant. It instantly got them off on the wrong foot. She might be from the sticks, she might be living over a shitty bar, and she might be working crap jobs for crap money, but she wasn't stupid. Lower class didn't mean lower intelligence. She had the feeling he was much more impressed with himself than most other people were.

"Probably a good idea," she said. "Getting your ass beat in the parking lot might ruin the lines of that pretty suit you're wearing."

Something flickered across his face, an emotion too quick for her to catch and name, but she hadn't given him the reaction he had wanted, and that was more than enough for her.

Her curiosity over why a guy like him would come

into a place like this, looking for someone like her, was quickly waning. She needed money. Hell, when didn't she need money? But she didn't like him. It was more than just his weird crystalline eyes and off-putting self-satisfaction. There was a vibe coming off him that she couldn't name and it made her skin crawl.

He reminded her of the time she had been young, back on her grandfather's little hobby farm, down by the tiny pond off the pasture. She had been turning over pieces of wood to see what sort of creatures she could uncover. She found the bright red salamanders she liked and even a family of field mice that scurried off into the weeds. But when she turned over a piece of burning hot sheet metal and uncovered a coiled copperhead, the same stomach-chilling dread she'd felt in that moment filled her now.

"You don't like me very much, do you?" he said.

His bluntness caught her off guard, with the bottle of Coors halfway to her lips. She studied him for a moment before sitting the bottle down, untouched.

"Not really, Mr. Maddox. No."

"It's simply Maddox, please." His smile widened, but it was just one corner of his mouth that stretched back, and it never reached his eyes.

"Look," she said, wanting to get this over with. "I don't think I'm the person you want—"

"Fifty-thousand dollars."

She stopped mid-sentence, the rest of it thrown completely out of her mind. She stared at him stupidly.

"I beg your pardon?"

"I want to pay you fifty-thousand dollars to do something for me."

It didn't make any more sense than it had the first time. She was used to weird jobs and weirder payments. Her

Night and the Perfect Blue

apartment, shitty as it was, was payment for helping the bar owner with one of his own problems. It beat sleeping in her car, and sometimes the bar cat was friendly enough to visit and patrol for mice. Who cared if the roof leaked or if the bathroom was haunted by the ghost of the old man who had fallen in the tub and died there back in the sixties?

"I'm not sure what it is you think I do," she said.

That amount of money would be life-changing, and for that very reason she didn't trust it. To someone like him, it might be like change in the couch cushions, but she could think of nothing she could do for him that would be worth that amount of money.

"You can find things. I need you to find something for me."

A dozen possibilities ran through her mind, all of varying degrees of illegality. He was looking for an ex-wife. A custody dispute, maybe. Or maybe he wanted her to hunt down the ghost of a relative over an inheritance spat. Maybe he wanted her to search for the meaning to his life. She always turned those jobs down. Sure, she could do it. Pretty easily, actually, but that wasn't her place.

One thing life had taught her was to know her place.

"It's nothing as bad as that," he said again, with that knowing smirk. God, she was beginning to hate him. She had never had such a visceral reaction to anyone before, not even the asshole car salesman who had sold her the rust bucket Toyota she was driving right now.

"Yeah, I don't think this is going to work." She was down to her last twenty bucks, and it had to last until payday. The coffee shop had cut her hours again and she was still waiting to hear back from the frigging call center, and she would rather bare-knuckles brawl than do that kind of work again. Some things in life were worth selling your soul for.

She had the feeling this wasn't one of them.

"You're not even curious what I want?" he said, surprised. It seemed like a genuine human emotion, but he had to spoil it by saying, "For fifty-thousand dollars, you could at least humor me."

"You can shove that fifty grand up your well-tailored ass, pal," Avery said, letting all her contempt for him show.

He let her get halfway around the table before he said, "I've offended you. I'm sorry."

Again, it sounded like a genuine human emotion, and that was the only thing that made her pause. Avery looked down at him to find him staring at her with those strange, clear eyes. His expression was guarded, but at least that mocking superiority was gone.

"Please, sit down. Hear me out, at least. If you don't like what I have to say, I'll pay you for your time and we can go our separate ways."

Reasonable, and an apology to boot. She had a feeling it actually meant something from a guy like this.

Begrudgingly, she sat, still wary, but willing to listen.

Maddox leaned forward, his head lowered and his hands clasped on the table between them. When he finally looked at her with those clear, crystal eyes, she saw what that smugness and sarcasm had been masking. She found herself infinitely preferring them to this.

"I want you to find me the perfect shade of blue."

She wasn't sure if she had heard what she thought she had.

"That's it?"

She didn't mean to sound so surprised. Maddox flinched, then pressed his lips together until they were bloodless lines. He took a breath and held it, and she had the feeling he was fighting the urge to hurl this table, and

Night and the Perfect Blue

possibly her with it, across the room.

"Yes." He drew the word out between clenched teeth, so much that it sounded like a hiss. "Yes, that's it. Entirely. I need you to find the perfect shade of blue."

It wasn't the strangest request she had ever heard. Avery had been asked to find everything from a grandmother's lost recipe to the last word whispered by a man who died all alone in the South Dakota wilderness. The weirdest thing she had ever searched for had been the twin of a man that had died in utero, and she had to step into an alternate timeline to do it. But this? A color? And for him to be this tightly wound over it? No, there was something else here, something he was hiding.

"Yeah, no," she said. "I don't think I'm going to be able to do this for you."

"Why not?" He was almost whining now, like a child. "I need your help. Do you know how hard I've searched for this? I *need* to find this."

"Why?"

Avery had just broken her own most important rule. Never ask why. Never get that involved. Ultimately it didn't matter why. It usually didn't help her accomplish her tasks, and it just entangled her more with the people she wanted the least to do with. Getting any closer to this guy seemed like the worst possible thing she could do, but she had never seen a need like this, so naked and intense and scary.

"I can't tell you." He averted his quartz-clear eyes. "I just... please. I need your help and I can't find it on my own. I've been searching for—" His jaw snapped shut and his furtive eyes darted to hers. He'd almost given something important away.

"Okay," she said, before she lost her nerve. "I'll find your color blue."

Zevon Price

"The perfect shade of it," he said quickly. "It has to be the perfect shade."

She nodded, waving him off. She'd already gotten that part. "For fifty thousand dollars."

He didn't even flinch or hesitate when he nodded.

"And you have to tell me the reason why you want it so bad."

That stopped him mid-nod. "I told you—"

"Those are the terms. If you don't like them, the door is over there." Avery hooked her thumb over her shoulder. She caught the eye of Zach, the bartender, who had been surreptitiously watching them this entire time. He'd taken a shine to her since she helped him with his problem, which was figuring out why his bar sometimes shifted into an entirely different dimension just long enough for someone to ransack the place, raid the liquor shelves, and rob him blind. He had been on the verge of torching the bar for the insurance money when he found her through a friend of an acquaintance, and he had been protective of her ever since.

"Yes." The word came out a hard exhalation. "All right. But only after you find the color. I'll tell you then."

She mulled it over, feeling the sense of deep water rising around her. She wasn't naive enough to think this was going to be as easy as finding a simple color. Blue was everywhere, after all, but she wanted to know why that color, why that particular shade, was so important to him.

That settled, Maddox dropped her a check for twenty thousand dollars, and then handed her five more in cash in an envelope. Then he left with a briskness in his step that might have looked like confidence at first, but became a slithering retreat the more she watched him. He opened the door to the blistering daylight outside, his figure silhouetted against the stark yellow sunlight of a delirious afternoon

Night and the Perfect Blue

before the door closed again, leaving them in musty, air-conditioned gloom.

"You better cash that before he puts a stop on the check," Zach said, wiping down the spotless bar. The rest of the place might be a shit hole, but that bar was clean enough to perform brain surgery on.

She laughed and left to do just that, after paying her tab down and giving him the three-month's back-rent she owed.

***

Later that night, she lay in bed under the squeaking ceiling fan, sweating in the late July hell of a southern summer, thinking of how much of an idiot she was for accepting this job.

The bar was winding down, last call purging the die-hards out into the street where they yelled and laughed and stumbled off to parts unknown. Quite a difference from the tree frogs screaming out her bedroom window when she was growing up in her grandparent's tiny back bedroom, waiting for the sun to come up. Waiting for the chance to get the hell out of there, back then just as much as now.

The bar had one of those old-fashioned neon signs, the kind that hung off the side of the building, flickering like a firefly to attract patrons. Red and green and yellow. Red for the silhouette of the woman's red dress, yellow for the stylized blond hair, and green for the name of the bar. Sally Anne's Bar, although there was not, and had never been, a Sally Anne as far as she knew. Across the slant of her ceiling, she watched the green flicker to red, and the red and yellow change to orange as they ran across one another, just above her head.

Weird how there weren't many blue neon signs. Most of the colors she could think of, from Mickey D's golden arches to Target's red bullseye, were bright shades of red and yellow and orange. The strip club down the block had a big pink neon sign over the door. The Sucker Club, with a giant electric-pink lollipop for a logo. She had once read in Tennessee Williams's play *A Streetcar Named Desire* that Blanche Dubois preferred paper lanterns because they hid the garish reality of her ruined youth behind a softer pink facade. She guessed the patrons of the strip club preferred their fantasies bathed in pink neon for much the same reason.

Red.

Green.

Why was Maddox looking for the color blue? What significance did that hold for him? Why did he need it? How could she even bring it to him? It was one thing if it were something tangible, like a watercolor or the particular shade of paint on a car. She could present him with a tube of paint or steal a car, but she didn't think he was looking for something that basic. By what she had read in his expression, by the desperation in both his voice and those crazy clear eyes, she didn't think it was anything that basic, or he would have found it by now.

Red.

Green.

She slung her arm across her eyes to block out the light. She could hang a blanket over the window, and she would if it wasn't four-thousand degrees outside and the ceiling fan wasn't a relic from the Vietnam War era. A sleep mask might work if she could stand the thought of having something tight over her face. She could barely stand to sleep under a thin sheet, claustrophobic as she was.

Red.

Green.

Night and the Perfect Blue

The colors edged around her arm, pressed against her closed eyes, and were insistent as cicadas' screams. It had to be getting on to two a.m. now. Another sleepless night, apparently, while she tried to keep from thinking about Maddox's desperation and what would satisfy his need for the perfect shade of blue.

Red.
Green.
Black.
Finally.

She took her arm away from her face, already sweaty, and stared at the ceiling. Ambient light from the street was still there, the dull orange from the sodium lights the city kept promising to replace with new energy efficient ones and never got around to doing. A faint gleam of bright, antiseptic white from the all-night laundry down the street.

There wasn't a shade of blue anywhere in this room, save for the darkness itself, where it crouched in the corners furthest away from the light.

Avery sat up and leaned against the headboard. She stared into the darkness, trying to differentiate the various shades and shapes of things. When she was younger, when she lived with her grandparents, way out in the middle of nowhere, the nights had seemed full of shades of blue. Dark blue, midnight blue, that faint pale lavender that eased into blue as the sun rose over the mountains. The bright, blinding blue that palaces of white clouds inhabited, the ones she always pretended she was an exiled princess trying to return to.

The August blues, faded by the heat like the old flag hanging from her grandfather's work shed, pale and dusty and turning to the gray of ashes.

September blues, for the handful of days when the sky

seemed so painfully, uniformly blue that it hurt her eyes to look at it too long, right as the trees began to burst into flame and burn into autumn.

But here, all the darkness was stained red by the neon and the streetlights.

She flopped back on her pillow and once again stared at the water stains on the ceiling.

Fifty thousand dollars could do a lot. It could get her out of here. She could start over, pull a life together that wasn't barely scraping by. She might be able to get back to some place with more green in it. A place with dirt for a garden and a yard for a dog. She might be able to put down roots again, instead of drifting around like a windblown piece of trash.

That money could help her pull together the tattered edges of dreams she had had a long time ago. Might give her something to dream about again, rather than just keeping her head down and trying to push through day after week after year. Those were good, tangible, practical things, and only a drop in the bucket compared to the enormity of the task in front of her.

That was how she found herself, three days later, exhausted and on the hunt for something she wasn't even sure existed.

Avery had tried all the obvious places. Several different craft stores, looking at paints and crayons and fake flowers. On a trip to the drugstore, she looked over the hair dye, thinking of the time she dyed her hair bright orange just for the hell of it, as she studied the various shades of blues and purples and even the blacks with blue undertones. Pretty colors, but none of them had jumped out at her.

A painting caught her attention in the window of a junk store. The sign above the door with its jingling horse

Night and the Perfect Blue

bell proclaimed *Antiques,* but one step inside showed that to be a lie when the smell of rancid mold and ancient cigarette smoke all but smacked her in the face and demanded all the money in her purse.

In the brightness of the sunlight outside, the blue sky in the background of the pastoral painting sitting in the window seemed like it might be a possibility, but inside, under the janky store lighting, it turned out to just be another cheap, faded print of an old red barn standing sentinel over a field of yellow wheat. She thanked the store owner, who looked crestfallen over losing a potential sale, and stepped back out into the blistering heat.

She squinted up at the sky. Faded blue, like the painting in the store window, a heat haze bleaching the world like a skull under a desert sky. She wiped her forehead with her forearm and started off again.

***

Blue was the rarest color found in nature. She read that, squinting at the busted screen of her phone, when she ducked into a coffee shop to escape the heat and regroup after another fruitless day of searching. Ignoring the press of patrons and the pervasive scent of scorched coffee, she read about natural pigments, color wavelengths, and the physics of light while a cup of overpriced burnt coffee cooled next to her elbow.

Blue was the rarest color found in animals, too. At first, she thought that couldn't be. There were blue parrots and fishes and those poison tree frogs from the Amazon, but after falling down a rabbit hole of research, she realized there really just weren't that many animals sporting the color blue compared to other colors. According to one website from a bug nerd who specialized in butterflies and moths, there was only one species of butterfly that actually produced the color blue within its own body, a tiny and innocuous little butterfly called an obrina olivewing.

Strange how it was the only butterfly to create blue rather than reflect the blue wavelength, and it hadn't even been named for that phenomena.

Maybe this was the color she had been searching for? She was already thinking of how she was going to get a specimen from South America.

"You'll know it when you see it," Maddox had said with maddening certainty, and for a moment she was certain she had found it. But when she clicked on the picture, she knew instantly that, while pretty, this wasn't the color she was looking for.

She went back to her research.

Even blue eyes weren't really blue. Clicking yet another link, she found herself reading about the Tyndall effect. Humans didn't have naturally blue eyes. It was caused by light scattering when it hit particles suspended in a layer of fluid inside the eye. She got bogged down a bit in the particulars, the headache she had been nursing all day intensifying as she read, but she grasped the gist of it. There was actually no blue pigment in blue eyes, simply certain light waves refracting against particles. The density of those particles determined how many of those wavelengths were bounced off the eye. The denser the particles, the bluer the eye.

Back on the farm, she had been enchanted by the blue jays. Raucous screamers, they brawled with the crows and the hawks, screamed blue murder every time someone came near their nests, and tormented her grandfather every time he went outside to work the fields. She had loved the bright flashes of color from their wings, a beautiful, icy blue, and

Night and the Perfect Blue

had always been disappointed when she found the feathers they left behind lacked that bright, vibrant color. Only now did she know why that was. Like human eyes, the color of their wings was actually refracted light. It was the shape of their feathers that gave them their unique color, and not the color itself.

Blue existed without existing at all.

She put down her phone then, ignoring the cold cup of coffee and the waitress giving her the stink eye, and stared out the window at the lengthening shadows outside on the street and marveled that something could be without being.

***

The waitress finally chased her out of the coffee shop and back into the misery of late evening. She walked the streets as the faded blue gave over to the sunset. Pollution from the industrial plants on the western outskirts of the city gave the sky an artificial, almost Hollywood glamour as it rolled through its repertoire of reds, oranges, pinks, and finally faded to a purple verging on royal blue that swept over the sky like a magician's cloak. There was too much ambient light for stars, too much light pollution for true darkness, and what was there was again stained red from the streetlights.

It should have cooled down once the sun set, but it was still miserably hot. Sweat dripped from the faces of people she passed, and crescents of it ringed the underarms of the t-shirts of several teenagers hanging out on the street, looking for something to do.

Avery was starting to get desperate. She had forgotten to eat again today. Even if she hadn't been squirreling her money away, to possibly make her getaway after she found Maddox's elusive blue, she would have forgotten because of the all-consuming focus on what she was beginning to think was a fool's errand.

Maddox might even be doing this for a joke. Rich people did things like that sometimes, right? She couldn't even begin to think of what kind of joy he might get out of sending her on a wild goose chase, but it was preferable to thinking about the soul-breaking need in his eyes as he described this perfect shade of blue; and his absolute refusal to explain why he needed it.

By nine o'clock, her feet were screaming in agony and the hazy edges of the headache she had been fighting all day had become a full-blown migraine. Head down, eyes squinting against the lights blinding her from every street corner, she looked for relief and found it in the one doorway on the street that didn't have any sort of light surrounding it. Not a neon sign, not even a handwritten one on the door to tell her what it was. She didn't care. She just needed to get out of the light, away from the red and orange, the noise of traffic and people who were yelling and laughing and shouting into cell phones.

The door was heavy and solid wood, almost twice as tall as she was, with heavy brass door handles elegantly curved in deference to Victorian aspirations. She shouldered it open and threw herself into a vestibule that was barely large enough to turn around in. She closed the door behind her, and the silence was absolute.

So was the chill. It shocked her enough to take her breath away. Compared to the unbearable heat outside, it was like plunging beneath a glacier.

She knew what she had stumbled into without having to look any further than this room. She had once again stepped into one of the liminal spaces, without even looking for it.

Night and the Perfect Blue

For one mad moment, she thought about flinging the door behind her open and fleeing into the carnival of the street, migraine be damned. But she wouldn't be here without a reason. Liminal spaces seldom opened themselves up just for the hell of it. They showed themselves for a reason, and that reason had to be on the other side of the doors leading deeper into the building.

Stay in a place like this long enough, though, and she might not be able to find her way back out of it. It had happened to people like her before, the ones who hesitated too long on thresholds and found themselves lost. There was nothing else to do but go forward.

She touched the handles of the doors in front of her, leading to whatever was on the other side, and took a deep breath. Unlike the doors leading in from the street, these opened without a whisper of sound.

She stepped through into an elegant bar that would have looked perfectly at home in a 1930s gangster flick. Lots of gilded gold, Art Deco designs, plush white carpet, and black and white tile.

She was in a speakeasy. And dressed like a 90s grunge reject.

The bar itself took up the center of the room, a giant horseshoe shape of golden gilt and black lacquer. Bottles upon bottles of liquor stood in crystalline ranks in front of the gigantic mirror that reflected the bar back at itself.

The bartender stood in the center of it like a captain helming a cruise ship. She was tall and slim and dressed in a men's tailored vest over a crisp white shirt, and her dark hair was a slicked down Lulu bob. She was drawn in shades of black and white with the exception of her lips, which were as red as a bloodstain on white tile. She eyed Avery with obvious distaste.

Zevon Price

"You're supposed to be here." It might have been a statement or a question. She had the cultured, mid-Atlantic accent of old Hollywood, and a chipped right bicuspid, completely at odds with her polished exterior.

"I guess I am," Avery said. "Can I get a drink?"

Looking more put-upon than if Avery had just straight up solicited her, she blew out a breath and then brought a glass out from beneath the bar. "What's your pleasure?"

She started to ask for her usual, then changed her mind. "I'm feeling a little daring this evening. What do you have that's blue?"

A thin, black eyebrow rose over her equally black eye. "I beg your pardon?"

"Surprise me," she said, inspired. "Make me whatever you want, just as long as it's blue."

Like Maddox, her expressions were mostly unreadable, but the bartender begin mixing her drink with decidedly more enthusiasm than she had greeted her with.

Avery took the moment to look around and get a feel for the place. She had hoped, with the liminal space inviting her in the way it had, that she might step through the door and find exactly what she was looking for. Rich blue tapestries, carpets, maybe a peacock motif. But this place was happy to run in the theme of black and white, maybe as a callback to the old movies it seemed to be aping.

She should have known it wouldn't be that easy.

The patrons were happy to keep to themselves, although she caught a few furtive glances when the watchers thought she wasn't looking. She couldn't even begin to guess who they were, or what they might be up to, and didn't want to know. You didn't walk into a place like this by accident. Either you already knew about it, or it wanted you here.

Light glinted over the various bottles behind the bar,

Night and the Perfect Blue

some seeming to wink at her as if inviting her to have a closer look. So she did. Various whiskys and spirits, gins, tequilas and rums. She spotted a bottle of black vodka among the ranks, as well as blue curacao. Pretty, but not the color she needed.

And it was a need now. Maybe not as all-consuming as the one Maddox possessed, but one that had taken root in her all the same. She had dreamed of blue every night since she met him, of the skies above her grandparent's farm, and of the Mustang of the guy who had taken her best friend to the prom and broke up with her right after. She had dreamed about picking blueberries with her grandmother, and the stark blue veins under the paper-white and tissue-thin skin of her hands stained purple with the juices.

Staring at herself in the mirror every morning after the nights she chased her memories until she awakened, exhausted in the yellowed light of morning, she saw haunted eyes staring back at her that had been bright blue when she was a child, but had faded to the color of old denim in the years since. She tried not to see the blue-black circles underneath them. Broken capillaries from hard nights, but even that blue wasn't really blue. The broken blood vessels bled red under the skin, and the bruising was simply another color masquerading as blue.

The bartender set her drink in front of her. She startled, having forgotten where she was. Dangerous in a place like this.

"It's pretty." She admired the play of light against the ocean blue of the cocktail. It even had a gradient to it, a bluish-green at the top, fading into what looked almost purple at the dregs. "What is it?"

"Does it matter?"

"It might," she said, but didn't push the issue. While

the drink was pretty, it wasn't what she was looking for. But no sense pissing off the bartender until she at least figured out what had brought her here. Avery took a drink, and barely kept herself from spitting it all over the bar. It tasted like turpentine, and it burned the whole way down.

"Oh my God," she strangled out, once she was certain her organs weren't going to evacuate her body through the nearest available orifice. "That's awful."

"You said you wanted something blue. You didn't say it had to taste good."

The bartender wasn't quite smiling, but it was there in her eyes in the way the curve of her lips only hinted at. Quite the opposite of Maddox, whose eyes remained as empty as a broken glass bottle while his mouth had spread in a smile almost too wide for his face.

The joke had been entirely at her expense, and she was sure she'd be breathing fire for the rest of the night, but there was no sense making a scene about it.

"You're here for Mads, aren't you?"

Avery blinked the tears out of her eyes to find the bartender staring at her with that unreadable expression she had worn when she walked in.

"If you mean a weirdo with a color fetish named Maddox, yeah, I am. I take it that means I'm not the first."

The bartender looked away. "Not even close."

She picked up a towel and began wiping down the bar, but she didn't seem like she was closing down the conversation, so Avery decided to press her luck.

"What's your name? Mine's Avery."

The bartender gave her a sardonic look that stated quite clearly she hadn't asked and didn't care, but finally capitulated and spat out a petulant "Louise."

"Nice to meet you, Louise." Avery saluted her with the

Night and the Perfect Blue

drink and took another swallow to show she was a good sport.

"Why don't you go over there and talk to Nate. He might have a story to tell you, if you have the time."

She glanced over her shoulder in the direction Louise pointed. The tables had a decent mixture of men and women, some drinking in pairs, while a few others had congregated in groups. At the far end of the room, up against the wall, were a row of booths tucked out of the way. They were all empty except for one, and the man hunched over a bottle with his hands folded as if in prayer around it looked like the worst sort of drunk to meet in a bar. A maudlin one.

Avery hiked an eyebrow in query. Louise shrugged and went back to wiping down the bar. It wasn't her job to make Avery do anything. She was just here to keep this little pocket of liminality doing what it was supposed to do.

Sighing, Avery slid off the barstool and crossed the room, feeling the stares of the other patrons hitting her back the whole way. The guy didn't look any better close up. She had pegged him as mid-to-late twenties at a distance, but he was obviously much older than that. At least old enough for regrets to mean something. Gravity pulled at the corners of his mouth as if trying to drag him to the ground. He didn't even look up when she stopped in front of his table, her shadow covering him like nightfall.

"Louise at the bar said you might have a story to tell me, if I have the time. I've got the time, so can I buy you another drink?"

It took him another few seconds to pull himself away from wherever he was in his mind and squint up at her. He had a few days' growth of stubble on his face, and his eyes were the green of a sickened sea. He blinked, long and slow, eyes flitting from her face up, and then down again.

Something cranked to life in his eyes, a slow widening and realization.

"Do you have red hair?"

It was the last thing she expected him to say, and it took her a moment to regroup. "No, sorry. It's brown."

"Oh." That animation flickered out again, leaving behind something that seemed disgusted with itself. "I thought it might be red."

He returned his attention to the beer bottle in front of him. He hadn't told her to leave, though, so she slid into the seat across from him and leaned forward.

"Why red?"

"Huh?" He didn't look up.

"Why did you think my hair might be red? Colorblind?" She ventured it carefully.

Surprisingly, he started to cry.

Nothing accompanied it. Not blubbering sobs or sniffing. Just fat tears rolling from his eyes like water off a melting glacier.

"She had red hair," he said, so softly at first she wasn't sure she heard him correctly.

"She?"

He nodded, still not looking up. The tears dripped off the sagging line of his jaw and splashed onto the backs of his hands. "She had the brightest red hair I'd ever seen. Like it was on fire, always. Even in the dark, I swear I could see it, burning like a flame."

The corner of his mouth turned up, an awkward smile painful to look at, an expression trying to be born and dying before it could take its first breath. "She'd always laugh when I said that. Said I was silly. I just…"

A ragged sob caught in his throat.

Avery glanced across the room at Louise, who

Night and the Perfect Blue

steadfastly refused to look at her. She continued to wipe down the bar, and none of the other patrons were interested in getting even tangentially involved.

"I can't see it anymore. I can barely remember what she looked like, but I remember that color. Only…" His expression twisted in agony. "Only I can't see it anymore. I know what it is, but I can't see it."

His head snapped up. His eyes were wild with pain and misery. He fixed his stare on her face and grabbed both her hands in a bone-crushing grip.

"Do you know what that is?" he said. "A red so bright, so strong, you can't look away from it? A color you can't see anymore, even though you know what it is? I had it once, and it was all I could see. I saw red everywhere, and he told me he could take all that pain away, but then he took that, too, and now I can't see it, even though I know what it is." His voice rose sharply like a keening howl. "Don't you *understand?*"

She opened her mouth to tell him she had no idea what he was talking about, and to back the hell out of her face, but this close to him, she saw her reflection in his eyes. His eyes were the same color blue as the veins in the backs of her grandmother's hands, and she was adrift in that color.

She had always clashed heads with her grandmother. It was just the way of the women in their family, she'd heard later, from other relatives when she finally came back home for the funeral. She only stayed for a week, just long enough to see the casket go into the ground and settle affairs. Then she ran again, down the road, down the highway, away to anywhere that wasn't that small homestead tucked between two mountains that were older than bones.

It was the first time she had been back in over a decade. When she had finally had enough of living in a place that never moved, where nothing happened, where everyone fought so hard to keep it from happening, she had thrown her luggage into the back of her car and left while her grandparents were gone to church.

Her grandmother had admonished her for not going with them. She stood in the door of Avery's bedroom wearing her favorite dress, a simple thing of gingham blue checks, and told her to have the house cleaned by the time they got back, because they were expecting the preacher over for lunch. Avery gave them enough time to get to the church, and then she roared out of town in a car the color of aquamarine. She left without a note or a way to contact her. She wanted to get good and gone first, so they couldn't find her and drag her back before she was settled and secure.

It was over a year before she called them. She sent them a letter once, to let them know she was safe, but she hadn't put a return address on the envelope. Her grandfather had asked if she was safe and if she needed money. She told him she was safe and she had money, even though she was broke and sleeping in her car.

Her grandmother refused to talk to her. She refused to talk to her every time she called thereafter. Her grandfather would tell her in his gruff but soft voice not to worry, she would come around eventually. But even after Avery settled into a job and a place to live and put down tentative roots, when she finally broke down and told them she had moved to Memphis and sometimes sang in a bar and was working on getting somewhere in life, her grandmother still refused to speak to her. She sent letters that went unanswered, too. The one time she sent money home, that one came back "Return to Sender," with the check still inside.

It was three months after her grandfather died before she even knew about it. She had called several times that

Night and the Perfect Blue

week and no one picked up, and she was beginning to think the worst. Her aunt had answered the phone on the morning Avery decided that if no one answered, she was going to do what she had sworn she never would and go back home to find out what was wrong.

Her grandmother couldn't forgive her for leaving, not even enough to tell her that her grandfather had passed. Peacefully in his sleep, her aunt had assured her, and also that she would tell her grandmother she had called.

It was the last time Avery called home.

Another five years passed. The band fell apart, her music dreams died unmourned, and Avery stumbled quite accidentally into her new life of finding what couldn't be found. She always waited for the phone call that never came.

Until one day, it came.

It was the same aunt again. Her grandmother had been sick in the hospital for a couple of months. She had fallen into a coma. Avery needed to come home.

She packed her suitcase and she, finally, went home.

She didn't notice the color of the sky that day, or the painted hospital walls, or the flimsy cloth gown covering her grandmother's emaciated body. She was covered in tubes like an insect half-wrapped in a spider's web, her freckled skin showing through the wispy white hair clinging to her scalp, half-dead and barely hanging on.

"She might still wake up," her aunt had said, standing in the doorway, holding Avery's hand between hers. "Go on in and speak to her. It might do you both some good."

Avery went inside, not seeing the pale walls, or the cracked plastic chair that looked like it belonged in an elementary school. She sat next to her grandmother with the sky beyond the window so hazed with humidity it was almost white, and the mountains seemed to disappear in the distance.

She tried to speak, but she could think of nothing to say that they hadn't already said. Not with words, but with the silence that had stretched between them for over a decade.

The machines beeped and hummed. A little blue line blipped across the screen, keeping time with her heartbeat. The plastic tag around her bony wrist had her name written on it in blue ink.

The veins stood out, so bright blue under her skin, like rivers that had carved valleys between the tendons on the backs of her hands. Like the creek that ran through the valley where she had lived since she was eight years old, when her mother dropped her off on her grandparents' front porch with the promise she would be back after her shift at work, and then never returned. Her eyes had been blue. Avery barely remembered what she looked like, even though her grandmother said they were the spitting image of one another.

It was remembering the blue of those veins in that cold, motionless hand, that had her recalling every time the color blue had been in her world. The sky overhead, and the river in the valley. Bluebirds and jays in the trees. Blueberries so heavy in the bushes that one year they made jams and jellies and cakes and pies and still had so many left over that the taste of them even now made her slightly nauseous. Her grandfather's denim overalls, that he always wore when working in the fields, or on the old car he always said he would restore and take them all for a drive in one day, the way he had taken her grandmother out for their first date.

The walls of her bedroom had been a deep, dusky blue, like twilight rising over the hills. She had worn a blue dress to prom, a hand-me-down from a cousin she hadn't really liked, but she had needed a dress and that was the one

Night and the Perfect Blue

she got.

And it was the blue of her grandmother's eyes, so bright with unshed tears when she held Avery on the front porch of her tiny blue house, while Avery bawled her eyes out waiting for her mother to come home. Her eyes had been so bright then, so full of sadness and fury and grief that the color seemed as if it would spill from her eyes and drown the world.

It was the same look Avery imagined every time she called home and asked to speak to her. She imagined her grandmother standing in the kitchen, staring at that phone, defiant and proud and disappointed and unable to bend.

Avery yanked her hands out of Nate's grip so hard she dragged him halfway across the table. She knocked the bottle he'd been guarding to the floor in her escape and glass shards scattered in all directions. They crunched under her boots as she ran for the door, only to find herself in the restroom instead, staring into the mirror at a woman surrounded by ghosts.

Unlike the bar, the lights in here were stark fluorescence and flickering at the right cadence to send her migraine screaming to the front of her brain. She staggered to the sink and turned the cold tap wide open and let the sound of the water splashing into the basin drown out the noise in her mind.

Too many memories. Too much noise. Too much she wanted to forget.

She braced her hands on both sides of the sink and bowed her head over the water, eyes closed against the light. It should have been red, gold, and green spinning and crashing together like universes exploding.

But behind her eyes, there was blue. A blue so bright it hurt to look at, a sky so wide she couldn't see one end from the other. Her whole life had been blue, and she had forgotten that.

"He's going to want that."

Avery stared up at her reflection in the broken mirror. Two different Louises stared back at her, her expression closed down, but her eyes pensive and hard. When had the mirror broken? Had she done that, or was it like that when she came in?

"He'll have to kill me to get it." How had she forgotten all that? Where had she buried it so deeply that it hadn't even existed before this moment?

"If you give it away, then it won't hurt anymore," Louise said, almost reasonably. "What you want is already gone. It doesn't exist anymore. Why not let it go?"

How could something exist and not exist at the same time? Like light refracting color, creating blue where it didn't exist. She could put that pain to rest and never even know she'd ever felt it. Let it go forever.

Let it go, and lose that perfect shade of blue.

She pushed past Louise and stumbled out of the restroom and into the bar.

She found herself in the street again, with no recollection of how she had gotten there.

The migraine hadn't gone away. Like always, it intensified everything. Every sound, cars honking and people laughing, stabbed agony into her brain. A woman screamed as someone grabbed her from behind. Her scream shattered into a shrieking laugh as the man swung her round in a circle, her blue skirt spilling out like a wave to drench the street.

A motorcycle roared by, a streak of liquid metallic midnight that only barely squeaked through the intersection before the light changed to a red all but swallowed by a

Night and the Perfect Blue

scrolling bank billboard behind it. It splashed the bright neon blue of the company logo onto the street before it scrolled over to the faces of a laughing couple who presumably were approved for whatever loan the bank was hawking.

She swung away from it and found herself looking into the window of a florist where she was certain the door to the speakeasy had been only a moment ago. Inside, surrounded by arrangements of red roses and pink carnations and bright orange and yellow Gerbera daisies, was a vase filled with blue irises, their bearded heads the royal blue that monarchs had once forbidden anyone but themselves to wear.

Drowning in the richness of hues against the blinding fluorescent lighting, she looked skyward for relief and caught a flash of heat lightning as the thunderstorm that had been gathering all week finally began to coalesce above her.

In that flicker of light, she glimpsed the blue of the sky above. It was as deep and impenetrable as the deepest parts of the ocean, the blue becoming deeper until it became the pure black emptiness of space.

Of nothingness. Nonexistence.

Existing without existing. Being without being. It was nothing; and it was everything.

It was all there, and it had always been there. She just hadn't allowed herself to see any of it for so long. She was drowning in water that didn't exist, in the color of that nonexistent water, and she didn't know how she was going to keep it from killing her.

The only thing she knew, in that moment, was that this color belonged to her.

It always had.

She realized then what Maddox had given away, and what he was trying to get back. She had seen the red of

Zevon Price

Nate's lost love in the ruby Maddox wore on his hand. She remembered those clear, empty eyes, and thought of her grandmother's eyes again, the way they had been the day Avery became hers.

She couldn't let him take that. He couldn't possibly understand what it meant. He could only wear it like cheap ornamentation, to hide whatever he had given away that had made him what he was now. He could reflect it, but not what it *meant*.

That color belonged to her. It was everything she was, and now that she had it again, she would hold onto it until the light went out of her own eyes forever; and that blue became black like the sky above.

The Pixie Job
by Kathy L Brown

Already, I wasn't liking this pixie job at all.

I'd travelled that cold October morning in the fall of 1924 to see Angus McKirtle, ready as I'd ever be for my first investigation of—let's just say—special problems. For money, that is. Investigating for money.

A rich man in a poor town that he'd named after himself, McKirtle operated a rinky-dink lead mine in a county owned by the nation's largest lead producer, St. Joe Mining. Perhaps McKirtle's operation was too small to notice—the village remote and the mine, as I was soon to discover, a technological throwback to 1890 or thereabouts.

Whatever the reason for his independence from Big Lead, I'd high hopes of a good payday. Lord knows I needed the money. I'd spent my last dollar on the one-way train ticket, relying on the job to pay enough to get me home.

The locomotive paused long enough to deposit me at a once-white clapboard station labeled "McKirtle." It's peeling paint revealed the place was once called New Penzance, a reference to the Cornish roots of the people around here. A hundred years or so ago, back when the bosses decided to really make a go of lead mining in southern Missouri, they'd imported boatloads of Cornish miners to tell 'em what's what. And a good job they'd done; lead mining made a lot of people rich.

The train was gone before I'd even stepped off the platform into the dusty street. Gray film covered the town and muted the leaves, by rights at their most colorful. A rotten-egg odor hung in the air, slightly offset by smoke from burning leaves. Not a soul was out and about to ask for directions, but I soon found I didn't need any. A splendid, if spindly, gray house, covered in turrets, widow's walks, and round, stained glass windows perched atop the village's highest hill. It had to be McKirtle's place.

A knot of people milled about the mansion's front gate. They commenced pointing and mumbling amongst themselves when they caught sight of me. Most were down-and-out looking men, carrying placards with slogans I couldn't make out. By the time I was close enough to read their picket signs, I didn't need to.

"Scab," muttered a young woman, child clinging to her skirts. She was handing out meat pies—pasties the Cornish folks around there called them—to the picketers.

"Sean Joye, ma'am." I tipped my hat to her. "Likewise, I'm sure."

"Hey, there, brother," one old gent caught my arm. "Rethink your course. The mines ain't healthy for your sort."

I took the bait, of course, and turned on him. "And what sort would that be?"

"You appear to be what they call, in mixed company—" he indicated the woman, "a replacement worker." His tone had shifted from cajoling to threatening, an effect reinforced by the other men crowding around us. "All we done was ask for the new safety equipment, like they got at St. Joe's. And

The Pixie Job

a wage increase—it's been over two years. We were about to vote an action against McKirtle, and he shut down the mine. No warning at all."

"No quarrel with you have I." My accent can get a bit thick when I'm in a tight spot. "But by Jesus, Mary, and Joseph, I ain't fixing to work in no mine."

"You're breaking our picket line, even going in his house," said the geezer.

I wondered how—and why—a boss would lock out his miners, but let it be. "And ain't I telling you I'm not a miner. Just a visitor to your man."

"It ain't a social call, for sure, Paddy," said one of the younger men. "Look at you."

Well, that was rich—a Cornish "Cousin Jack" disparaging the Irish. And I looked presentable enough. If I'd given it any forethought, I'd have pretend to be an American. I'd about decided to bop him in the nose and run for it when barking and shouting commenced from the yard.

"Let the man be or I'll set my dogs on you." A portly gent accompanied by a couple of Irish wolfhounds stood on the big house's steps. The three of them growled.

The picketers growled back but retreated across the street.

"I remember the day you started working in this mine as a breaker boy," said the old man who'd first grabbed me. "We took in your ignorant Scottish ass. Taught you the business."

"Aye, and now it's my business."

"We want to work, sir," said another man. "Just give us better equipment, the battery lamps at least, and we'll be right back in number seven shaft again."

The woman scooped up the child and trotted away,

calling over her shoulder, "Not without a living wage, they won't be setting foot in your death trap number seven."

However, the men weren't quite as ready for an out-and-out brawl with their erstwhile guvnor. Quiet one and all, they retreated to their pasty eating and my verbal abuse; "Burn in hell, scab," being about the only remark I can repeat here.

I scooted through the mansion's gate and across the lawn without really having much of a chance to decide if I wanted to take a job for a boss facing a labor action. But with every step toward the house, I felt more and more sick. No, I didn't like the pixie job at all.

***

"I'm Sean Joye," I said as we stood in his foyer. "Mrs. MacSweeney said you was having a problem here with your house. Can you tell me the details?"

"Let's not waste time on idle speculations. It's pixies," he rumbled as he led me into the house, the two wolfhounds sniffing me up and down as he yacked about his business, his town, and his life story.

The dogs must have liked what they smelled—perhaps the tuna sandwich I'd carried in my pocket half the day. One of them stood on his hind legs, paws on my shoulders as he gave me a big, wet kiss. The other rubbed his head against my hand until I got the idea; I was to be stroking his ears. "Who are the good boys?" I had to say. "Sure are you now." I wished I had something for them, but I'd eaten the sandwich on the train ride.

"Brian, Tobby, heel." McKirtle said. "Leave the man be, for Christ's sake. Mr. Joye has important work to do." He left me while he settled the dogs somewhere in the rear of the house.

The Pixie Job

Angus McKirtle was a great windbag of a Scotsman, and yet I concluded right quick that there was much he weren't telling me. Like how he was so sure his household troubles were due to pixies, rather than haunts, mice, or—I dunno—disgruntled employees.

I made myself at home looking about his office, a room just off the foyer. A couple of uncomfortable-looking chairs stood against a wall decorated with faded, old-fashioned, cabbage-rose wallpaper. A broad oak desk took up half the room—open ledger books and stacks of papers covered its surface. With lines clean and construction solid, it brooked no more nonsense than its owner himself.

A respectable number of books, all on topics like geology, engineering, law, and the like, lined a shelf at ready reach from the desk's swivel chair. McKirtle was an educated man, but no scholar, and not given to reading for pleasure. *At least, not in here,* I cautioned myself against jumping to conclusions. Work time was work time. It remained to be seen what play meant to him.

I thought perhaps the frame photographs could tell me something of the man, but they were all work, too—not a wife or child in the lot. No, just a younger McKirtle, cutting ribbons and shaking hands with other swells. A couple of the pictures featured laboring men in stained dungarees and headlamps, shovels and picks hoisted over their shoulders. The workers appeared to have met some production goal or other, although their dour faces didn't match any celebration that might be going on in the head office.

I looked a little more closely. These weren't even all adult men; smaller figures sat cross-legged in the front row. Children. And there was a couple of shy ones, Lord, not much taller than my toddler nephew, barely visible and hanging back behind one of the men. A man who could have been McKirtle, forty years ago. I guess that oldster wasn't lying; it seemed McKirtle had indeed started out as a miner.

Nothing in the office explained McKirtle's insistence on a pixie infestation in his house. Cursing my landlady, Mrs. MacSweeney, at least in my heart, for sending me here, I waited for him to come back so I could resign before I'd even properly been hired.

When he finally returned, he looked surprised to see me. "What, not out pixie hunting yet? I told you, the basement." He bustled behind the desk and took his seat. "Be gone. Be gone."

I tried yet again to get a straight answer out of the man. "Mr. McKirtle. Please. What makes you think you've got them about? Not likely, here in America."

He glowered across an acre of desk. "The cleaning lady back at my city house—"

"Mrs. Charity MacSweeney," I said.

"What? Oh, yes, I suppose. She says to me—" Simpering like Mrs. Mac in her cups, he continued, "You must meet me lad, Sean. He's Irish, but one of the smart ones. A faerie man back in the old country. A wise woman's grandson."

Some of that might be true, I suppose. But I'd wanted nothing to do with the fae back at home and still didn't here in America. Yet I regularly found myself on the other side of the veil. I was living in Mrs. Mac's drafty attic, and I imagined she'd set me up with this job with hopes I'd pay for my lodging.

"Look here, young man. Do you think me a superstitious fool? I've seen the evidence, plain as day. There's a pixie about—possibly several—and I want them gone."

"If you do have—the good folk—about, you're not

The Pixie Job

doing yourself any favor, talking about them aloud. And what do you propose I do with them, assuming they can be caught? I take 'em away, they're like to come back. Kill them?" I'd no earthly idea how to kill a faerie. A good way to get cursed for life, if I wasn't already, but I wanted him to think this scheme through a bit more.

"Well, death seems a bit extreme." McKirtle glanced over at the photo of his younger self. "Look here, young man, I employ dozens of men and boys in my mines. I pay for a job and expect it to be done. You're the expert. Figure it out."

"I haven't taken the job, and you haven't paid me. And it looks like those men and boys outside want a bit more than whatever it is you pay them now."

McKirtle's face dropped. I could see, at least, the old man behind the mask. "I'm begging for help, Mr. Sean Joye. And I don't often go hat in hand to anyone, let alone a mick."

That was obvious. He was terrible at asking for help. Every word made me less inclined to listen to his story.

"But I will pay you. And well."

Oh, yes. Payment. I recalled I didn't have enough coin for one of those tasty meat pies, let alone my train fare home.

"I don't know where else to turn. Perhaps I've made a few errors in judgment. I'm…I'm not used to that. Won't you at least try? Look around with your Sight or whatever tricks you learned from your grandmother."

What in the world had Mrs. Mac told him? Surely a highly embellished version of a few passing comments I'd made about my granny. I tried talking to him low and calm. Like to a child. Or donkey. "Sir, it would help if you could tell me about this evidence. Exactly what have you seen?"

Kathy L. Brown

"It's obvious," he shouted. "All the signs are there. The thumping, the knocking. At all hours, day and night."

Actually, it weren't obvious. McKirtle's so-called evidence could mean several sorts of ghosts, spirits, and fae creatures or, more likely, the striking miners up to a bit of sabotage. But something about his bleary, bloodshot blue eyes tugged at my heart.

Or maybe it was the fistful of cash he promised.

"Sir, you've got yourself a deal."

***

While the alleged pixies had wreaked havoc all through the house for a solid week—tearing up featherbeds, curdling milk, and ringing the servant bell pulls at all hours of the day and night—they mostly frequented the basement, knocking on the rafters and banging on the steps—'Twas no end to their noise.

McKirtle's household staff had quit, and he hadn't been able to keep as much as a scullery maid more than a few hours since then. He grabbed an electric torch and escorted me to the basement.

The space was dark as pitch, mildew and overripe fruit odors hanging on the chilly air. I walked smack dab into a large icebox crowding the stairs. "Don't you got lights down here?"

"You know the cost of running electric wires into an old basement like this?" McKirtle tisked, but handed me the torch, and I made a show of snooping about. I played the light over the low ceiling and corners; the floor was dirt, and the walls rough field stones interrupted by shelves and a rickety wooden door opposite the descending staircase. "What's back there?"

"Just the coal cellar. Come over here, lad, here's some

The Pixie Job

evidence for you. Look at this. He directed me to pools of water under the icebox. "The little devil's footprints, right here." The prints looked more like they'd been made by some small animal than any fae creature.

At last, he left me to it. As soon as I was alone, I sat down on the basement stairs with a sigh. Had Gran ever said anything about pixies? I'm sure there'd been stories. Some sort of Cornish sprite, I was pretty sure. Were they the ones so fond of cream?

"And what've I got myself into now?" I muttered, lighting a cigarette. "I wouldn't know a pixie if it bit me on the arse." As if I'd conjured it, a sharp nip attacked my backside, and I whirled around. "What the feck—"

I heard a skittering and shined the electric torch behind the steps but saw nothing that could bite. No, nothing there but a few basementy sort of odds and ends. A large wooden fruit crate gave me an idea. Most likely an animal was down here, rather than a fae creature. Maybe if I caught it, McKirtle would be satisfied. Its capture would show a good faith effort on my part and perhaps loosen his tight grip on that cash.

And ease the poor man's mind, of course. I had to wonder how a respected businessman, living in America most of his adult life, had become so obsessed with pixies. I was missing something, for sure.

The crate looked likely for a box trap. So, I went back to the kitchen to scare up a bit of twine and a saucer of cream. I about spilled it stumbling back down the stairs but managed not to fall. I dragged the box out from under the steps and set it up in trap position. Whatever I'd heard skittering under the steps was now hissing. I shone the torch in its general direction but saw nothing and only heard a bit of scrambling about behind the basement debris.

Kathy L. Brown

Possum? Raccoon? I've spent more time in the woods with bootleggers than I care to admit and find America to be full of wild animals that you sure wouldn't want to find in your house.

A strong sense of being watched overtook me as I fiddled with the box, and I looked up to see glowing eyes from across the room. I wondered if I had a big enough crate but felt pretty confident of my possum theory.

There weren't no servants around to stop me from raiding the kitchen, so I figured I'd just go make myself a sandwich while I waited for ole bright eyes to fall for the trap. But as I made for the stairs, the trap's twine seemed to wrap itself round my ankles. I stumbled, and as I fell something threw me through the now wide open coal cellar door. I landed in a great heap of coal, and my box trap flew in right behind me. The door slammed behind us both. We were treated to slurping sounds and laughter as the possum enjoyed the dish of cream.

The door was, of course, latched. I stared at the box. It stared back at me. *Just a minute there.* Possums don't laugh, I was pretty sure, and the box agreed. The shock of the whole situation seemed to wake me up, in a way. I'd been going about this all wrong.

I'd survived the war listening to my gut, my intuition, whatever you call it. Of late, I'd found that sense was good for something else. Magic.

Just last night I'd read a cantrip that might help me, and while I tried to recall it, I could hear my quarry prowling about. I peeked through a knothole in the door's pine planks. What I saw was light. Not much, kinda shadowy, but some light. Enough to tell that whatever haunted the basement weren't no possum.

The light came from a small figure—more rightly it

The Pixie Job

came from his headgear—who stood in the center of the room, guzzling down the cream as bold as brass. He might have come up to my knees, but I knew he weren't a child; his beard was too long and red. He had on an old-fashioned oil cap lamp, and his clothes were raggedy and thin.

My haunt theory was right out, and I'd never thought trooping faeries to be in the frame, but many sorts of small, household imps plague folks: grogoch, far darrig, brownies, and the like. If McKirtle has caught sight of this little fella, pixie weren't a bad guess, particularly as McKirtle had been lived in this Cornish settlement for a long time and likely heard their favorite tales.

"Hey, I've got some more cream here for you in my... pocket." The pixie couldn't possibly be that stupid, but I could think of nothing else.

He laughed and threw the empty dish at me, shattering it against the coal cellar door.

"I swear," I said. "Just want to talk to you. Never met your tribe of good people. Pixie, is it?"

"And ye ain't met one now." He strode across the space, "But here's a clue, ye ignorant lummox. Perhaps ye can reason with himself." He rapped smartly on the door that divided us, then he commenced an unholy ruckus, tapping up and down the basement stairs.

I took the opportunity to make a bit of a racket myself, prying off a few loose door slats, enough to squeeze through, at least. All the while I worked to free myself, I wondered what he meant, denying that he was a pixie. Now the fae are prideful and prickly; mistaking a redcap for a gnome, say, was the worst sort of insult. The old folks will tell you abundant rules about salutations, titles, and to avoid talking about the fae. If you must, always say "good people." And labeling a supernatural creature by the wrong species could land you in a world of hurt. This critter denied he was a pixie. I'd better figure it out, and right quick, as well as grovel in apology.

By the time I got out he was long gone. I could hear him moving throughout the house, slamming doors and tossing crockery hither and yon. With all that hullaballoo, I expected McKirtle to come fire me, lickety-split. While I waited, I thought more on small, domestic fae. Gran hadn't talked about British sprites and spirits so much. I wished I could question those miners a bit. Hell, maybe this fae weren't Cornish at all; he'd just latched onto these miners for some reason.

Sometimes figuring out a puzzle goes best if you work on a different problem. Such as how the creature had gotten into the basement in the first place. I think better on my feet, so I prowled around the basement, looking high and low with the torch, and let my conversation with the little fellow sit on the back of my brain.

Which was hard; he was rap-tapping across a radiator, sending a vibrating gong into the boiler. On my second pass, I saw a small opening in the wall, peeking out from behind a shelf of Mason jars. "He dug his way in," I murmured to myself, barely able to think for the noise. I shouted, "Leave off the knocking, you wee little… little…"

My brain fog lifted, the sun came out, the birds sang. I had him. "You wee little tommyknocker." Tommyknockers were a sort of Cornish fae, a pixie cousin twice removed, perhaps, who frequented mines. Some say they guard the miners, others that they lure them to their dooms. Probably a bit of both, knowing the ways of the fae.

It likely made no difference that I'd figured out his tribe. But I felt the proper faerie man for the first time. I got down on my hands and knees, shifted the jars of

The Pixie Job

tomatoes and green beans off the shelf, and shone the torch down the hole. It was a neat little tunnel with smooth dirt walls and miniature timber bracings. The tommyknocker, elven protector of miners, particularly Cornish miners, everywhere, had tunneled his way into the basement. But why?

Steps marched down the basement stairs and a voice rang out, "A fine job you've done, to be sure. They're ten times worse than ever."

I enjoyed shining the torch in McKirtle's face as I did my best to brush the coal dust and spider webs off my only decent suit coat. Impossible. I just smeared the muck around. I gave it up as a bad job half-done. "Don't you mean 'him?' Your mine's good folk is a tommyknocker? Or do you know for a fact there're more? Shut up in that shaft number seven, perhaps?"

A new voice floated down the stairs. "The others are too stubborn." The knocker'd been eavesdropping. "Won't come out until you make the mine safe for your human crew."

"Is that what this ruckus is all about?" I said.

"They're lying about down in the shaft, half-starved and thinking Slim here actually cares about them."

"I do care," McKirtle said. "And I gave you amply warning to clear out."

I figured Tommy and his friends were both hungry and cold down in the mine shaft, which reminded me of a granny story. While pixies went about in raggedy clothes, just like this tommyknocker, that's the way they want it. If you gave them proper clothes, they'd clear out, insulted.

I pulled McKirtle away from the stairs and whispered, "You happen to buy any of that safety equipment the miners are on about?"

"No, of course not." He thought for a moment. "Well, we ordered some samples to look at, but...it's just not in the budget."

I gave him some side eye.

"You wouldn't understand."

"Show me the samples."

McKirtle shrugged and led me out of the house and through the backyard to a small copse of gray, sickly trees, behind which lay a rutted dirt road. I thought Tommy was trailing behind us, darting from shadow to shadow. "Must not care for the daylight," I thought. I filed that bit of lore away for future reference.

We followed the road past a couple of industrial buildings to a shack built up against the hillside. "St. Barbara Lead Mine Co. Shaft 7" proclaimed the weathered, peeling paint. McKirtle pointed to an adjacent shed. "In there," he said. "But don't be thinking I'll reopen. Can't afford it, not with the changes they want. It's not just better lantern caps, not by a long shot."

McKirtle has lost the fire in his eyes somewhere along the way. He rubbed his hands through his hair. "Just get the rest of them to come out?" He held up one hand, as if to stop me from arguing with him, though I'd not said a word. "But I can't have the buggers living in the house with me. Too noisy. They've got to move on. Over to St. Joe's mine. Out West. I don't care."

"'Tis the noise bothering you?" I asked. "Not your own guilt?" I held out my hand, and he surrendered a key without looking me in the eyes. I opened the padlock and hoisted the iron bar blocking the door. "You use iron for all your barriers?"

"Aye," he said, "What of it?" As McKirtle elbowed past me into the supply shack, I felt Tommy, perhaps grown

The Pixie Job

bold with the iron barrier gone, brush against my legs as he followed the boss in.

"The new cap style is in that crate over there," McKirtle said. They sent a couple of sizes."

The shed was full to the brim with mining gear of all sorts, as well as a changing room for the workers. I grab one of the old cap lanterns off a shelf in a cubby labeled "Kellow, Ted." Meanwhile, McKirtle opened the crate to show me several battery-lamp caps along with brochures touting their many advantages and the prices. I gathered them up.

"What're ye doing, Faerie Man?" a voice hissed at me from the shadows. "Ain't enough for all the miners."

McKirtle shook his head. "'Tis the worst day in the worst year of my life."

I'd no advice for the man, so, laden with the new battery-lamp caps, I headed toward the mine. "You coming?" I called out to McKirtle. He sighed and followed me.

Tommy now walked with us openly. "Where's ye going, Faerie Man?" He tugged on my coattail. "What're ye up to?"

I stopped. "I'm sorry I called you 'pixie,' earlier. 'Twas quite ignorant of me. Now, you gonna show us your friends? Or do I have to find them myself?"

"Ye should be sorry." He looked up at McKirtle. "And himself knowing better."

McKirtle wouldn't look at the little fella, instead addressing me. "You're an outsider, Mr. Joye. I thought it best to draw no more attention to the mine and its problems than necessary."

"You thought wrong," I said, then turned to Tommy, brandishing the bottle of cream I'd grabbed from the icebox on our way out of the house. "I'd say they need a snack by now."

He sighed. "Ye be too big for my tunnel. I'll find ye in the mine." And with that, he vanished into the shadows.

A lean-to entry shack marked the mine entrance, a place for the supervisor to shelter from the rain and snow and blow a huge steam whistle at the start and end of shifts. McKirtle unlocked a heavy iron gate that barred the way into the mine itself, and I followed him into a deep, bone-chilling cold.

The few electric light bulbs overhead were dark. "You cut the power, I suppose?"

The old skinflint shrugged. "A penny saved is a penny earned." We lit the lanterns on our miners' caps and followed the donkey cart rail tracks deeper into the tunnel. The sound of water dripping was constant echo in the dark.

"Tommy?" I called. "Hey, where are you?"

"His name's not Tommy, you ignoramus," McKirtle said.

"Well, we ain't been properly introduced."

But we heard knocking on the timbers up ahead and saw the dim light on what I sure hoped was the tommyknocker's own cap. *Like chasing a will-o-wisp.* That generally ended in a bog-soaked death. Or transportation to Faerie. I could hear my heart pounding. And Tommy knocking.

The tunnel narrowed and sloped downward. I took to picturing the hillside above me, the weight of the earth bearing down on the sketchy-looking timbers. *Weren't these miners picketing about unsafe working conditions?*

Up ahead, the light bobbed along, getting fainter and fainter. "Wait up, will ya?" Tommy didn't stop, and I quickened my pace, McKirtle panting alongside me. When we caught up at last, the little man was standing at a T-intersection.

"It's that way," he pointed at a lift cage suspended in the air by a rusty chain.

The Pixie Job

Brilliant. Of course his friends would be down in the shaft. This was a fool's errand, and I was the fool. The problem with quitting then and there was I didn't have any confidence in my ability to find my way out. "You been keeping track of all the twists and turns he took us on?" I asked McKirtle.

He snorted. "I know this mine like the back of my hand."

"Which we can't rightly see in the dark." But we trudged forward into the tiny wire cage. "Where's Tommy?"

"Isn't he in here?" McKirtle shone his lamp all about, half blinding me. "Naughty bugger."

"What's his game?" I said.

"Hard to say. The tommyknockers can be vicious when crossed."

"Really? So why did you cross them?"

McKirtle mumbled something about things being complicated but swore he could find the other knockers without Tommy's help.

Thank all the saints in heaven, the lift functioned as intended. As we clanked to the bottom of the shaft, I could heard the knockers' voices. "Well, that was the lift, plain as the nose of ye face," said one. Another voice replied, "Don't mean the boys are coming back to work, now does it?" They squinted when my light hit their faces, two bearded, bald-pated fellows, huddled together. "Aye, who's there now? A miner come back to work are ye?"

"No, I'm not," I said as I approached. I'm Sean. Working for old McKirtle here. Today I am, at least. We brought you some provisions." I held out the bottle of cream.

"Hello, boys," McKirtle said, choking on the words. "Good to see ye again." I couldn't tell if emotion or lead dust had closed his throat.

"Who's this now?" said the one with the curly beard. "Young Slim, ye are? Ye ain't so young anymore."

"Aye, nor slim." McKirtle patted his girth. "But 'tis I."

I looked from McKirtle to the two tommyknockers, then back at McKirtle. "You've met these blokes before?"

"Met us," said the gray bearded one. "He were a particular favorite of ours, when he was a lad. We looked out for him special, so young and stupid and all."

"Hey, I weren't—" McKirtle said.

"At first ye would just about walk off a ledge or drown yourself in a pool every day before breakfast. There weren't enough pasties or milk in the whole town to pay us for our care of you, child," said Curlybeard, "but we did it, anyway." He smiled and took a long chug of cream then handed the bottle off to Gray.

"Look here," I said, seizing the moment. "We got something for you." I prayed I was right about tommyknockers' quirks. I held up one of the battery-operated lamp helmets, switched it on, and offered it to Curlybeard.

He snarled and backed away.

"For you. A gift from Mr. McKirtle, for your years of hard work."

"It's time to move on now," McKirtle said. "This mine is played out."

That was news, and news that went a long way toward explaining his behavior.

McKirtle offered a cap to Graybeard, who'd flung down the bottle and looked ready to run and hide somewhere. "I gotta sell the company to St. Joe for whatever I can get."

Curlybeard looked like he couldn't decide to attack me or not, and Graybeard just burst into tears and snatched the cap from McKirtle.

The Pixie Job

"How dare ye," Curlybeard said, putting an arm around Graybeard's shoulders. "Look at him, ye heartless brute." But his eyes were rivetted on the cap I offered: his hand reached out, then he'd pull it back. But within seconds, he'd go for it again, watching the cap's light as I waved it about.

At last, he grabbed it out of my hand, and they melted away into the shadows. "Plenty of work for ye, over at St. Joe's," McKirtle called, "or even out West in the silver mines."

"Now was that so hard?" I guess I was crowing a bit over my brilliant plan.

"You think I didn't tell 'em to move on, straight away? No, them lot's loyal to the miners. They insisted the boys would come back soon enough."

"So, ye've done it, eh?" Tommy had snuck up behind us. "After everything we done for ye. Gave them...clothes." He spit on the ground.

"You don't like it, you can leave, too." I said.

"Oh, I'm leaving." He giggled. "But ye ain't hexing me first."

"I do thank you. Tell 'em—tell the others," McKirtle said. "I just can't keep the mine open. It's not good business."

So he told himself, anyway. I can't say I believed him about the mine being worked out. And to run a safe operation would cost a pretty penny, I was sure.

"A blight on ye and thy house," said Tommy. And then he was gone.

I jumped up and ran toward the lift. "We've got to catch him before he burrows his way back into your basement."

McKirtle, right behind me, panted. My cap lamp started to flicker, and just as I reached the lift, a loud rumble shook the tunnel. "What did I tell you?" McKirtle said. "They're vicious when crossed." His lamp had grown quite dim, and

I could barely see his face.

We stuffed ourselves in the car and strained together against the pulley system. *Would the lift chain hold?* It alternatively shrieked and moaned, but we made it to the upper level and fell out of the car, which plunged back down into the dark. I heard it crashed far below, but we were already sprinting through the low, narrow tunnel, McKirtle in the lead. The air was thick with dust, and we coughed as we ran. Drips of water plinked in our faces and a knocking sound drummed from somewhere. Perhaps off to my right, but it was hard to tell. "Don't you hear that noise?"

"The way out is forward," McKirtle called over his shoulder. I could no longer even see a dim light from his lamp or my own. "Those scamps know all the crevices in and out, and likely made a few more in their spare time." I followed his voice and prayed McKirtle remembered the way. I heard another pair of knocks, up ahead this time, I was pretty sure. Question was, if it was Tommy, did he aim to lead us out? Or confuse us?

I decided to think positively for a change. "Perhaps we can beat him to the house." I'd lie in wait with a new cap in hand, ready to gift it as he emerged from his little basement tunnel. He'd have no choice but to take it. The good people love rules, and them was the rules. I hoped. I heard more knocking, behind me this time. "Are you sure you're going the right way?"

"I am," McKirtle said, his voice echoing in the dark. "We should be seeing some light by now, but maybe it's already night." I heard a thump and McKirtle softly swearing. And soon learned why.

"Just as I feared." McKirtle was on the ground where he'd fallen against a pile of rubble. That earlier rumble was the tunnel collapsing.

The Pixie Job

"The knockers generally this dangerous?"

"No, but they're vindictive little buggers." His voice seemed unnaturally loud in the dark. "I should have seen this coming. I didn't know what to do when they wouldn't leave. Figured they'd pout for a bit then move on to a bigger mine."

I lit a cigarette, noting I had five matches left in the box and that I really should conserve them. But I offered him the pack. "They seem quite loyal to you."

"Aye." Smoke glowed in my sputtering lamp light and curled around his face.

"What's that?" I thought I heard knocking; maybe even a voice. "Is he coming back?"

McKirtle tapped on the fallen rock in a deliberate pattern, mimicking the sound I'd first heard. He snubbed out his smoke and leaped up to grab bits of debris and toss them aside. "We're trapped back here!" he shouted. To me he said, "Get a move on—clear the way." The other side of the rock pile transmitted more coded taps, and we could hear several voices. The blessed sounds of rescue.

***

After several hours of excavation, we crawled out into the night to warm ourselves by a fire, wrapped in blankets and sipping hot coffee served by the miners' wives. The miners were jovial, energized, and pleased with themselves. I'd spied not a hide nor hair of the tommyknocker who'd collapsed the tunnel. McKirtle stared into the fire, long and hard.

I nudged him with the toe of my shoe. "They saved your life. You gonna reopen?"

He continued his contemplation. At last, he said, "No. I can't. This operation—it's doomed, don't you see?"

"Their 'strike' ain't hurting you at all, is it?"

"Oh, there's hurting a plenty, but the company's already dead. They'd best apply over at St. Joe."

"You think that's where the tommyknockers went?"

"I can hope, though I don't know that a modern operation would suit them much."

The knockers, like the miners, were more likely scarred by his betrayal, the broken faith between them, than work conditions. But I kept my thoughts to myself. McKirtle still hadn't paid me.

A Spark of Necromancy
by Teri Kay Jobe

The orange glow of the flames approached quickly. To the left, Valerie looked at him in fear. "What are we going to do?"

"I don't know!"

Indecision blocked any coherent thought. Their escape routes were cut off, and no one else remained in the area to help. There was no time. There were no options. Death approached fast, bright, and hot.

He reached out and wrapped an arm around Valerie to shield her, though he knew it was a futile effort. Together, they knelt on the ground. His back got warm, then hot. Unbearable.

Valerie started to scream. As heat turned into pain, he put a hand over his head. Instinct pulled him to draw on the untrained magical power he possessed. The air around him cooled and the pain lessened. Valerie's screams lessened to crying.

Did minutes pass, or mere seconds? Time no longer had meaning. The bright flames around them diminished. Valerie was silent. He knew the true danger had passed, but he did not let go of the magical power surrounding them.

He shifted his weight, but Valerie did not move with him. She slumped against him, unmoving. He looked down. She looked unharmed. A faint line of magical energy flowed from her chest into *his hand, sustaining the shield he had conjured.*

"No..."

She shouldn't be connected to his power. He hadn't even tried to connect her to his power. He was trying to protect her. He released his hold on the magical energy and the line connecting them dissipated.

She remained unmoving.

"No!"

He laid her down and shook her shoulder. This was not what he wanted. His world lay dead on the ground, not from flame, but from him. He had become the thing he wanted to run away from. The thing he feared.

He was a necromancer.

His power came from the essence and energy of the life around him, and it didn't care what the source was.

"Valerie! NO!"

***

Vincent woke to the sound of his own sobs as he finally wrenched himself out of the nightmare. He took several deep breaths and tried to redirect his mind away from the images that had been haunting him for the last seven years. At least he hadn't been screaming this time.

After several minutes, he got up and got dressed. He knew it was pointless trying to get back to sleep. His room was still dark, but there was a faint glow in parts of the sky outside his window.

Out in the dormitory hallway, the magical lanterns were mostly dark, with just a couple on a dim setting so anyone walking through didn't run into the walls. Vincent walked the familiar halls and stairs out of the dormitory, into the fresh air.

Outside, the chill of the pre-dawn air nipped at his face and arms, but it was welcome. Vincent found that chill to be

A Spark of Necromancy

helpful on nights like these. It cleared his mind and helped chase away the ghosts of the past.

The paths to the garden and menagerie were hard to see, but he knew them well. He learned long ago to navigate them in darkness deeper than this.

As he walked, he continued to redirect his thoughts. *What happened was a long time ago. It wasn't your fault. It was the magic doing everything it could to protect its wielder.* It was the mantra that the healers of the Association of Wizards had taught him to say many years ago. He remembered being forced to repeat them over and over in years passed. It had happened so many times that even though he only believed one of the statements, he still repeated them under his breath.

At the very least, it kept the healers and other Association members from hounding him. The words themselves never helped. The only thing he felt was true about them was that the event happened long ago. Seven years, to be precise.

Seven years, six months, and thirteen days, Vincent thought, doing the math in his head.

His feet carried him around the edge of the gardens, and he stopped, listening for the sounds of scurrying in the taller grasses. It gave him something constructive to focus on. There was a difference between the grass rustling in the soft breeze, and a mouse scurrying between the blades, looking for food in the dark.

He finally heard what he was listening for and sent a tiny orb of magic toward the sound. The scurrying stopped. Vincent bent down and within a few moments had found what he had heard. A mouse, lying dead in the grass. He gently picked it up and walked on.

A few minutes later, he arrived at one of the habitats of the menagerie. All of the Association members were responsible for helping to care for the animals here, and most had favorites. Vincent stopped in an area with several large trees and sat down at the base of one of them. He scanned the branches above him, looking for the owl that lived among them. He hooted softly, knowing the bird to be curious and somewhat territorial.

Sure enough, within a minute, a silhouette appeared on one of the branches. The large owl bobbed its head, looking down at him with curiosity and disdain. Vincent held up a hand, the dead mouse lying on his flattened palm.

The owl bobbed its head again, then swooped silently down through the air, talons outstretched. Vincent watched as the owl grabbed the mouse from his hand before pulling out of its dive and returning to its branch. It bent its head, taking the mouse from its talons and gulping it down. The bird puffed out its feathers and hooted.

"At least you appreciate what I can do," Vincent said quietly.

The wizard and the owl sat in their respective places for some time. Eventually, the owl began preening itself, giving Vincent the opportunity to admire it even more. It was a creature that relied on death to live, something that Vincent deeply understood. Almost every living thing needed death in order to thrive, just like owls ate mice. But the mice ate seeds and snipped off blades of grass to make their nests. Even plants grew better when they were fertilized with the waste of animals or the rotting vegetation of other plants.

Vincent had once heard it said that necromancers had the most lively gardens because they understood how to take advantage of these principles of life, but it was hard to practice this in the Association gardens, where everything was tracked and recorded. Even minor changes in the proven routine were frowned upon.

A Spark of Necromancy

Daylight had fully arrived when the owl suddenly stood straight on its branch and turned its head around to look at something. Vincent followed its gaze and saw someone else approaching. He stood up as the owl took off from its perch and flew out of sight.

"I thought I would find you out here," the newcomer said.

"Good morning, Kaddrick," Vincent said, stretching out after sitting still for so long. "I'm surprised you're up so early. Or were you too busy 'flirting' last night that you didn't go to bed at all?"

Kaddrick waved away the insinuation. "Does it matter? I've been looking for you. You weren't in your room, so I came out here. I had an idea I wanted to run by you. Shall we walk?"

Vincent fell into step beside Kaddrick. He was half a head taller than Kaddrick and a couple years older, but they had joined the Association at the same time.

Kaddrick was also the one who had helped him the most in the past year, to overcome the worst of the nightmares.

"Is this going to be another harebrained idea that will get us into trouble?" Vincent asked. "I'm still getting suspicious looks from some of the older members for the last stunt you thought up."

"No. This one is serious. You know how long we've both been in the Association. Most of the other members have found homes for themselves by the time they've been in this long."

Vincent felt a slight heat rise in his cheeks, but didn't say anything. Most Association wizards established their own residences within five or so years of being accepted into the ranks. Vincent was the most senior member currently living full time in the dormitory.

Kaddrick went on with no indication that he had noticed Vincent's discomfort. "Well, I recently did some work for a baron off to the west. It was relatively simple work, but he thought it was impressive. I managed to get him to give me some land in return!"

"Land?" Vincent asked, not quite understanding why Kaddrick was telling him this. "How much?"

"Most of a valley, actually. Best of all, no other wizard has lived there before!" He looked at Vincent, a big smile across his face. "It's magically untampered with!"

Vincent gave a half-smile in return. It was a wonderful thing to acquire. Such a space could be molded to a wizard's taste and desire without needing to worry about prior enchantments or traps. It was something young wizards could usually only dream of. A boon given to those who were driven and determined. Not ones who tried to suppress their powers. Vincent did his best to keep the disappointed longing out of his voice, with minimal success. "That's great, Kaddrick. I'm happy for you. You'll be able to do whatever you want."

"We," Kaddrick said.

Vincent tilted his head in confusion, and Kaddrick blushed.

"I'm sorry Vincent, I didn't mean to make it sound like I was just bragging to you. I know things have been hard for you, and I've been thinking about it a lot lately. No one here really knows much about how to properly cultivate necromancy, since many of the great necromancers didn't leave notes or journals, and those who only barely understand it just think it's bad. I admit, I don't fully understand it myself, but I want to help you, and now that I've got my hands on a piece of land…"

He paused, redness deepening on his face.

A Spark of Necromancy

Vincent waited, nervousness spreading from his chest to every inch of his body. Their friendship often had awkward pauses like this, but the gravity of the possibilities presented by what Kaddrick now had made the seconds of silence stretch into minutes. He didn't want to think that Kaddrick was so selfless that he would let a necromancer share a space with him unsupervised, or that their connection was that deep. But part of him wanted it to be so, and he needed to hear the truth of it, so that he could silence that thought before it took hold and crushed him with disappointment.

"Spit it out, Kaddrick."

Kaddrick, usually so suave and eloquent, stuttered. "W-will you...I mean...do you want to help me turn it into a proper wizard's residence?"

Vincent stopped and stared at Kaddrick. "Are you serious?" he whispered. "This isn't some joke or prank?"

Kaddrick quickly shook his head. "Shit, no! I wouldn't do that to you. I want your help. You're better at caring for the garden and menagerie here than I am, and this would let you make one of your own. You'd have free reign to experiment the way you want to and learn how to master your power away from the eyes of the Association."

Vincent stared off into the flowers of the gardens around them. "I wouldn't have to be careful. I could experiment with whatever I wanted to find what worked best..."

"Exactly!"

"...and there wouldn't be other people who I could hurt accidentally."

It was several seconds before Vincent realized the silence had stretched out again. He turned around to see Kaddrick looking at him with an odd expression. It wasn't pity, but a sad understanding. He reached out and touched

Vincent's shoulder.
"That's right."

***

Vincent stood on the edge of the cliff looking down at the valley. It was quite a bit larger than he had expected, and it had his mind whirring with excited ideas. It was already green with vegetation, a large stream ran through it with several pools of calm water, and there was so much room!

"What exactly did you do for the Baron to earn *this?*" he asked.

Beside him, Kaddrick shrugged. "Honestly, it was nothing. I lifted a curse that had been placed on his bedchamber."

Vincent raised an eyebrow. "Who placed the curse?"

"His wife."

Vincent tore his eyes away from the valley to give his companion a shrewd look. He was about to ask more questions about the incident, but then thought better of it and started laughing. The most likely scenario was that the Baron's wife had cursed him to be unable to *perform* in the bedchamber, probably due to a real or suspected affair with another woman. Assuming the Baron was a prideful man, then the gift of such a perfect bit of land for lifting that particular curse made sense. Whatever the truth was, it surely couldn't be more amusing than that.

***

Vincent sat at his desk in the dormitories, writing his letter of intention to take up residence away from the Association.

A Spark of Necromancy

The work he and Kaddrick had already done in the last month to make the valley an adequate home for a pair of wizards had gone remarkably quickly. There was still a lot to do, like setting up the garden, but it was something to look forward to.

It was all going so well.

A knock on the door made Vincent start, leaving a small ink blot in his usually neat handwriting. It was nothing that couldn't be fixed magically, but it put Vincent on edge. It didn't help that he wasn't expecting anyone, and unannounced guests were rarely a good thing in his experience. He opened the door, and the annoyance was immediately replaced by a wave of anxiety washing through him. Standing in front of his door, was Judith, the Senior Healer of the Association.

"Good morning, Vincent," she said.

"Judith! I, um, wasn't expecting you."

The healer put on the small smile that never reached her eyes. "I know this isn't the time for our usual appointments, but I heard you intend to leave the dormitories for an outside residence and I thought we should talk about it." She gestured towards the inside of Vincent's room as she spoke, then walked in without waiting for an invitation.

It was all Vincent could do to simply step aside and let her pass. He felt all of his insides begin to shrivel as though a seed of acid had been planted in his gut. *No... he thought, I'm so close to being free, please don't take this away from me...* He closed the door and swallowed, his throat dry. Turning, he saw Judith had already sat down in the chair at the desk. He walked to the bed and sat on its edge automatically, as he always did during her regular visits. He had to make a conscious effort to keep his expression neutral.

"So," Judith said once Vincent was settled, "I understand

that you intend to leave the Association dormitories, is that right?"

"Yes."

"And you'll be sharing your new residence with another Association wizard?"

"Yes."

"I heard that other wizard is Kaddrick Meadowlark."

Vincent nodded.

Judith raised an eyebrow. "Hmmm."

The silence began to stretch out. Vincent fought to keep his breathing at a normal pace. Something was off. He could feel it, and it was igniting the first embers of panic in his chest. After another ten seconds of silence, it became too much. Hoping he sounded as mildly curious as he was trying to, he asked "Is something wrong?"

Judith made a clicking sound with her tongue, then said in a quiet voice, "Do you really think this is the best move for you right now?"

The panic burned a little hotter. *I knew it...* "What do you mean?"

"Given your history, I am concerned about your well-being. Here with the Association, there is always help if you need it. Out there," she gestured at the one small window, "you wouldn't have anyone to turn to if you had another… episode."

Vincent managed to redirect a little of the panic he felt toward anger at the insinuation, which helped to keep his voice calm. "I haven't tried to hurt myself in over a year. Besides, I won't be alone. Kaddrick will be there if I need someone to talk to."

Judith's expression darkened. "Yes…Kaddrick," She glanced at the door as though concerned they were being overheard, then leaned forward and lowered her voice further. "We've been keeping an eye on Kaddrick. We believe he may have ill intentions."

Vincent tilted his head in honest confusion. "Ill intentions?"

"Yes. He has always been headstrong and opinionated. We think he may be trying to establish an opposition to the Association, and sway you toward that same rebellious path."

The accusation would have been funny if she hadn't been trying to prevent him from leaving the dormitories. As it was, it only confirmed what Vincent had been afraid of throughout the conversation. *No, it's not Kaddrick you're worried about, it's me. You're afraid of what I'll do with my necromancy if I'm not under your thumb!*

Vincent did his best to outwardly look like he was shocked by her words, while inwardly he desperately tried to think of a way to turn the situation around. If he said nothing, he would be forced to stay in the dormitories. Even though he had been telling himself that leaving wasn't all that important, he realized just how much hope for the future had built up in him at the prospect. Having that chance ripped away now would be crushing, demoralizing, untenable.

I CAN'T let that happen! The panic flared.

"If you're worried about Kaddrick," Vincent said, the effort of keeping his tone calm making the words come out very slow, "maybe I can help."

Judith tilted her head to the side. "How?"

"If I'm living with Kaddrick, then I would be able to watch him. Being away from the Association, it would be just as difficult for you to watch him as it would be to monitor me. I could be your eyes at his residence."

Judith raised an eyebrow. In his current state of near-panic, Vincent couldn't tell if she was honestly considering the idea or preparing to reject it outright. *This is your only chance! All or nothing. Give her just a little truth mixed in with the lies and she might believe it.* It wouldn't matter if she saw how desperate he was if he failed.

He plunged on, his words coming out faster now. "I am loyal to the Association. You especially have helped me through so much. If it weren't for your guidance and counsel, I wouldn't be here now. I'd be dead. I owe you and the Association my life. If that hasn't earned my loyalty, then I don't know what would. Let me return that kindness by helping you now."

The silence stretched out again. Vincent's heart beat so fast in his chest that he thought it might burst. Judith's eyes regarded him with some judgement he couldn't read. He wanted to swallow again, but resisted the urge.

Finally, Judith spoke, almost to herself. "I suppose it would be a benefit to have an extra pair of eyes on Kaddrick, but I still have concerns about you." She paused, then refocused her attention on Vincent. "We shall compromise. You will keep your arrangement with Kaddrick, however, your room here will also be retained. Once a month, you will come back here for a few days to report what you observe about Kaddrick and to meet with me, so I can be sure you aren't getting lost in your darker thoughts."

"Very well," Vincent agreed, trying not to sigh in relief. "Thank you for the opportunity to prove my worth to the Association."

As soon as Judith left, Vincent curled up on the bed, his face buried in the pillow to muffle any sound he might make as he let the panic he had been suppressing run its course. It didn't take long, given that the conversation had been generally successful. Partial freedom was better than none

A Spark of Necromancy

at all. But once the panic subsided, Vincent felt something pull at his insides that wasn't panic, but wasn't relief either.

It was guilt.

***

Three months later, Vincent and Kaddrick sat at the kitchen table in the house the two of them had built. In addition to the normal rooms every house had, this one also contained a large laboratory and library. The grounds surrounding the house were still mostly wild, but they had made lists of plants and animals that would be most useful to their styles of magic. This evening, they were supposed to be drawing up some initial designs for the gardens, something Vincent had fantasized about being about being able to do uninhibited many times.

Even so, it was hard for Vincent to focus. He would be traveling to the Association the following morning for another round of interrogation, probing questions, and "sharing information" about Kaddrick. Each time his monthly visits to the Association approached, Vincent felt a pit in his stomach. Once again, he would be forced to tell Judith and other high-ranking Association members about every little odd thing his friend did. How could he have been so selfish as to get himself stuck in this nightmare?

"Vincent? Vincent!"

Vincent looked up, realizing too late that he had been quiet for far too long. "What? Sorry, lost in thought."

Kaddrick glanced down at the parchment under Vincent's hand. "You've been staring at a blank page for over an hour. Are you alright?"

Vincent's anxiety, already triggered by the prospect of going back to the Association the next day, began to rise even further. Kaddrick could read him in a way Judith and the rest of the Association couldn't. They all saw him as a future evil necromancer, a potential threat that needed to be closely monitored. Kaddrick saw him as a person, a friend who happened to be a necromancer.

A friend Vincent had betrayed by agreeing to spy on him.

"Just a lot on my mind," He said. "I hate these Association visits."

Kaddrick's eyes narrowed. "Even when you were living there all the time, it didn't bother you this much. Ever since we left you've acted off every time you have to go back there, and it's getting worse. What's going on? What are they doing to you?"

Something in the way Kaddrick asked the question broke the walls Vincent had put up inside himself. He wasn't asking for personal gain, or to get information he could use against the Association. He was asking out of genuine concern, something Judith seemed incapable of.

You have one friend, Vincent thought, *and you betrayed him.*

This couldn't continue.

"I...I'm sorry," His breathing was getting ragged, the anxiety he already felt becoming fuel for panic. There was no way their friendship would survive this. Kaddrick would kick him out of the valley, and he would have no choice but to return to the Association. What little freedom he had from them now would be gone. But that thought hurt less than the idea of continuing to lie to the only real friend he had. "It was the only way they'd let me go."

"What are you talking about?"

"They didn't want to let me leave. Judith said the Association members think you're going to start a rebellion against them. That you're trying to get me to join you. But they're just afraid of me. Of what I might become. So I said

A Spark of Necromancy

I'd spy on you for them."

Kaddrick's eyes widened. "What?"

Vincent's words were spilling out faster and faster, his voice cracking. "I panicked! It was the only thing I could think of to convince her to let me leave! I agreed to spy on you, to tell them everything you've been doing...I betrayed you!"

He was gasping for breath now, fully engulfed in the burning panic. Every second that passed without a word from Kaddrick was a confirmation. It was over. Tomorrow's trip to the Association would be his last. He'd have no friends, and no hope of ever mastering the magic he was good at.

He couldn't keep sitting at this table. He had to move. Had to leave.

He pushed away from the table, but something held his hand down. He blinked, focused. Both of Kaddrick's hands were over his own.

"Hey, hey!"

Kaddrick quickly scooted his chair closer and moved one hand to Vincent's arm.

"Vincent, look at me. You are my friend. We can get back to the spy thing in a minute. What's important here is that you didn't betray me. Being forced into this situation isn't betrayal, it's coercion. The Association is shit! Of all its members, you are the only one I fully trust. Nothing you said has changed that, I promise. Come on now, deep breaths."

They stayed that way for several minutes until the panic subsided and Vincent could breathe normally again. Kaddrick stepped away to make tea, putting an extra spoon of honey in Vincent's cup. Vincent picked up the cup and took a sip. It was hot, sweet, comforting.

"Did you mean it?" he asked. "That our friendship

hasn't changed?"

"Every word." Kaddrick said firmly.

Vincent shook his head "I don't know what to do. I can't keep spying on you, but the Association won't let me stay here if I don't."

Kaddrick thought for a moment. "Hmmm...It's not really spying if I'm telling you what to tell them."

Vincent stared at Kaddrick. "I don't understand."

Kaddrick smiled. "When you go back tomorrow, tell them you found out that I'm putting up a magical barrier so that no one can physically or magically enter this valley, or scry on it from a distance, except the people I choose."

Vincent almost dropped his teacup. "You can't! That will make them even more suspicious!"

Kaddrick nodded. "Yes, but it will also make you indispensable, because you are the only person that I am going to allow in for the moment. I'll put up the enchantment while you're gone. When you come back, meet me at the top of the southern rim of the valley. Once the magic is placed, I'll have to escort you in the first time you return. After that, you'll be able to come and go as you please. Tell them all of that."

"Are you sure this is a good idea?"

"Of course! Regardless of whether they are more concerned about your necromancy or my rebellion, *I've* been suspicious of *them* for a while, so I finally decided to do something about it. In fact, you can tell them that too."

He paused.

"Of course, if you don't want to do that, you could just stay here and not go back at all." He put up a hand to stop Vincent's protest. "I'm serious. I don't want you to feel obligated to put yourself in danger by continuing to go back there. It's true the Association would probably overreact and try to hunt us down if we stay away, but you would be safe here, at least for a while. The magic would protect this place until we figured out something else. If worst came to worst, we could just run. We could go somewhere far away from here and never look back."

Vincent looked down at his tea as the possibilities swirled through his head. What was the right choice?

Is *there even a "right" choice anymore?*

"Take your time," Kaddrick said. "You don't have to decide now. I am still going to set up the barrier enchantments tomorrow, even if you decide to run away the next day. Whatever you decide, whether to stay as we are, hide, run, or..." he laughed, "actually start a rebellion, I will stand by you."

Vincent stared at his tea, a drink made by plucking leaves from their source of life and boiling out their essence. Maybe that was why it was comforting.

He was free to choose his future. He didn't want to go back to the Association, but staying away would mean he would be looking over his shoulder for the rest of his life, expecting to see them pursuing him. It would be a constant ache of anxiety, wondering what would happen once they finally found him. But going back meant playing the exact same game they did, spewing lies and half-truths, just like Judith did to him.

But the thought of lying to Judith didn't hurt the same way that lying to Kaddrick did. As long as he could keep his true emotions hidden from them, something he had been practicing for a long time already, it might work. It was a game he thought he could play. After all, he had already done it once, and earned partial freedom from them. What could he do with more practice?

Vincent nodded once, then drained his remaining tea

in one gulp. It was still hot, almost to the point of burning. The feeling spread down his throat, and radiated out into the rest of his body. He looked up to see Kaddrick staring at him with a surprised expression.

Vincent smiled. "Let's see how long it takes them to realize we're using their own games against them."

***

It turned out that they were able to play the game quite well. Kaddrick's instinct that the Association would want to keep a pair of eyes on him was right. They were alarmed by the sudden move of putting up a protective barrier around the valley, but impressed that Vincent had told them about it. It further solidified their trust in him, something Vincent hadn't expected. They even agreed to let him return to the Association less frequently, to keep Kaddrick from becoming suspicious.

Vincent had never been happier, which made the next two years fly by. He was free to experiment with whatever plants he liked, even dangerous ones. Understanding the interactions between certain flora and even some fauna came easy to him, and he could work here without worrying that disapproving eyes were watching him. He could combine poisonous mushrooms with regular flowers and not be scolded. He released rabbits into the valley and foxes to hunt them, instead of seeing them separated and purposefully fed on a schedule. Whether they lived or died was up to them, and that freedom made their usefulness in spellcasting that much more potent.

Freedom didn't mean Vincent was careless, however. He kept careful notes on which plants worked best together, and which needed to be kept apart. He noted the animals that were already living in the valley before bringing in new ones, making sure that the balance of life in the valley was kept, and not tilted too far in any one direction.

Of course, Kaddrick helped every step of the way, but his understanding of why Vincent did what he did with the garden was never as deep. But his grasp of the structural needs of a wizard were very acute. Kaddrick was responsible for further improving the house in the middle of the valley, and for maintaining the defensive spells that would keep the valley hidden from other Association spies. Of course, Vincent helped with these endeavors, and they deepened his own understanding of other aspects of magic he was less proficient with.

Everything that was done in the valley helped Vincent to keep moving forward. As his abilities increased, he realized that his nightmares were less frequent. Even when they did happen, they were not as powerful or disturbing. The guilt he felt whenever he thought about his sister Valerie never fully went away; but as his power grew, new thoughts occurred to him. He was a necromancer, after all, and control over death was what he understood best.

One winter, while Vincent and Kaddrick sat in front of the fireplace of their home, Vincent finally gave voice to his thoughts. "Kaddrick, do you think that, with enough care and preparation, that one could speak with the spirit of someone who died?"

Kaddrick thought for a few moments. "Ghosts exist, but not every person who dies becomes one, so theoretically the spirits of everyone else who isn't a ghost have to go somewhere." He looked over at Vincent. "What are you thinking?"

Vincent stared at the flames crackling in front of him, the pleasant heat of the tame fire reminding him of the searing pain of an uncontrolled inferno years before.

"There's someone I need to apologize to."

***

Vincent went over the components of the ritual one more time.

The words he needed to speak were written down in the book he now carried. He had memorized them weeks ago, but it still felt better to have them written down in front of him. Lit candles were set at the corners of the laboratory table. On the table itself were five other items. Four of these were set to the points of the cardinal directions, each about twelve inches apart. An owl feather and a tuft of mouse fur sat on the north and south points, while a death cap mushroom and mint leaves sat on the west and east points. Life and death balanced in all directions. The last item, placed carefully at the center of the others, was a small fox he had carved out of wood. It hadn't belonged to her, but foxes were her favorite animal, and they reminded him of her.

Kaddrick came in, closing and locking the door behind him. "Is everything ready?" he asked.

Vincent nodded, going over the list again in his head. "I think so. If all goes well, the whole process shouldn't take more than a couple minutes."

Kaddrick joined him at the table and patted his shoulder. "It's going to be fine. You've done everything you can to prepare. What's the worst that can happen?"

Vincent didn't notice the genial attempt at reassurance and simply answered the question. "Yes. Everything should be right. The very worst that can happen is that I accidentally kill us both and summon a horde of malicious dead things into the valley."

Kaddrick made an odd noise and Vincent turned to

A Spark of Necromancy

see his friend staring at him with a slack-jawed expression. It dawned on him what he had just said. "I mean, it's highly unlikely, just possible," he said quickly.

"Right...well, let's hope that doesn't happen then."

Vincent nodded and started going through the list yet again, making subtle adjustments to the objects on the table. A combination of anticipation, anxiety, and nerves coursed through him. While the worst outcome was unlikely, simple failure was not. What he was about to do was the most powerful necromancy he had ever attempted. Even a small mistake could mean that nothing happened, and all his preparations were for nothing. Or it could kill him outright.

Kaddrick seemed to sense his hesitation. He put a hand on Vincent's arm. "Hey, you're the best necromancer I know. I'll be right here if anything happens."

Vincent wanted to point out he was the only necromancer Kaddrick knew, but decided against it. Instead, he took a deep breath, nodded, and opened his book to the marked page. "Stand back. I don't want to pull you in by accident."

Kaddrick did so, but kept his attention on the proceedings.

Vincent held the open book in his left hand, raised his right hand over the items in the center of the table, guided his thoughts to her, and started to read out the spell.

As he spoke, the candles flared a little brighter, while everything else dimmed. He felt the latent magical energy in the room around them being channeled through the candles, to the items, and up into his hand. From there, it spread through every part of his body. It began to concentrate at a point just below his stomach, filling him with an odd combination of nausea and arousal.

He didn't have time to dwell on the sensation. His

vision was blurring, the edges going dark as though he were in a tunnel. He couldn't see the words on the page anymore, and recited the last two lines from memory, fighting his body's instinct to panic and stop what he was doing.

As soon as his spoke the last word, the point of energy in his lower abdomen swelled and he felt himself being yanked forward.

***

He stumbled, but somehow managed not to fall, even though the table hadn't caught him. The table wasn't there. In front of him was an open grassy meadow. The sky was as black as the darkest night, with tiny stars drifting about in the sky. Despite this, the rest of his surroundings were perfectly visible, as though bathed in twilight. The meadow extended in all directions until it disappeared in dimness, the grass a little less than knee-high. Several large, leaf-covered trees stood in various places around the meadow. A gentle breeze made the grass and leaves rustle. Sometimes it sounded more like barely audible whispers.

He could feel the presence of spirits here, hundreds of them. The spirits of those who had died. But instead of feeling afraid, it occurred to Vincent that he felt calmer than he had in a long time. The low and almost constant pressure of barely controlled anxiety and other emotions was gone. He could think clearly without effort. He hadn't felt anywhere close to this level of calm since before...

Remembering his purpose here, he said aloud, "Valerie."

In front of him, appeared a girl no older than sixteen. Her long hair, the same blonde color as his, was tied in a braid that hung over the front of her right shoulder. Her slight frame did not detract from the sense of confidence she held in her posture. She was exactly the same as he

A Spark of Necromancy

remembered her.

She smiled at him. "Hello Vincent."

"Hello Valerie. I don't think I have long, but I came here to find you and apologize."

Valerie tilted her head to the side. "What for?"

"For what I did to you during the Trials to join the Association."

She gave a resigned nod, and reached out a hand to him. He copied the gesture. He wasn't surprised when her hand passed through his, causing it to feel like he had dipped it into an icy lake. She looked a little disappointed, but recovered quickly. "I don't blame you for that. You're my brother. You were trying to protect me. If you hadn't acted on instinct and called on the magic you have, we would have both died. What good would that have done?"

"That doesn't make it right."

Valerie shrugged. "Right, wrong, it doesn't matter. It simply is. Besides, you've managed to get here. You've learned to control the magic you have and use it the way you want to. That's an accomplishment many others can't claim."

She was right. She was always right. Maybe he had just needed to hear her say it.

For the first time since appearing in this place, Vincent's emotions started to get the better of him, making his voice quiver. "I miss you."

Valerie smiled again and took a step forward. She wrapped her arms around him, careful not to actually make contact. Even so, he felt the cold drifting off her. He returned the delicate embrace with the same care she had shown.

After a moment, she stepped back. "You know I'll be here if you need me, just promise me one thing."

"Anything."

"Don't kill yourself by accident just to see me."

He laughed a little, grateful for the reminder. *She's always right.*

"I promise."

Not looking away from his sister, he willed himself backwards.

***

He couldn't see. He didn't know which way was up. His lungs were burning.

He gasped for air as he felt himself falling. Pain flared at several points on his left side as they made contact with something solid. The ground?

He felt his body being moved by someone other than himself. From far away, but getting closer, someone was calling his name.

"...cent...Vincent? Hey, are you in there?"

The world was getting brighter and coming back into focus. He was in the laboratory. The table was above him, which meant he was lying on his back on the floor. Kneeling at his side was Kaddrick, looking at him with concern.

The calm and control he had felt in the meadow was fading. Replacing it was a choking haze of jumbled emotions and the familiar flare of panic. He knew it would consume him soon, but he also knew it would eventually burn itself out. It always did.

"Are you okay?" Kaddrick asked, seeming a bit panicked himself. "Did it work? What can I do?"

Vincent's vision blurred as tears filled his eyes. The first of many, no doubt. He rolled onto his side, closer to Kaddrick, ready to ride out the rising inferno inside him. As his breath started to get faster, he grabbed onto the last remnant of the fading sense of calm. He wanted to give Kaddrick some kind of reassurance while he still could.

He said, "It did. Just stay with me. I may not look it in a minute, but I'll be okay when the panic passes. I'll tell you all about it then."

Burden of Duty
by Brian Ronk

Sir Mykel stepped into the throne room as King William shouted at his ministers, "That is the fourth village in as many weeks! Why has no one been able to take this monster down?"

No one noticed him as he walked in, even though he had never been there before. He didn't look out of place, just another man dressed in armor.

"Sire, five squads have been killed hunting this creature," a noble stated. "It hasn't been for lack of trying."

The nobles stood together in small groups, around the chamber, and Sir Mikel walked through them towards the front. They allowed him through, as the king's anger had spread them out.

"Then send more than one squad at a time!" King William yelled.

This was why he had come. A threat to the kingdom to be destroyed. The rumors had reached him a week ago.

"I will hunt it down." Sir Mykel's voice echoed inside the metal of his helmet and reverberated in the stone hall.

He could feel the gazes of everyone turn to him. And

what would they see? A man in dented armor with a worn traveling cloak and a sword. He knew he was not impressive to look at, but that didn't matter. This monster had killed people, and it needed to be destroyed.

The look of disbelief and dismissal on King William's face was obvious. "A single man take out the monster?" He waved his hand and shook his head. "Fine, take care of it."

Sir Mykel bowed. He knew the king didn't believe him. He had grown immune to people's doubts. Their thoughts didn't matter in the long run. "All I need is for someone to point me in the right direction."

The king sighed. "Captain, have one of your men point the way for..." The king looked at him with a frown.

"I am called Sir Mykel, my lord."

The king sighed again, like he was wasting time. "Have a guard point *Sir Mykel* in the right direction." He could hear the dismissal in the king's voice.

"I will bring the head when it is dead." At that, Sir Mykel turned and left.

As he walked out, the nobles whispered as the king began talking about the destruction caused by the monster again. Sir Mykel ignored it all.

***

Sir Mykel breathed evenly as he readied his sword for the next attack in the dance of death, the breaths sounding hollow and empty in his helmet. He felt no nervousness or fear. Between years of experience and a holy blessing given long ago, he was confident of success. The monster before him had been created through foul magics and had to be destroyed.

A manticore.

It moved one of its massive paws, the claws scraping

Burden of Duty

through the dirt, as it watched his movements with yellow eyes. This creature was an amalgamation of multiple beasts: the head and body of a large tawny cat, with a humanoid face, a venomous scorpion's tail, wings from a roc, and the curled horns of a mountain goat. There were rumors that it could breathe fire, but that hadn't been his experience. This one approached the intelligence of humans, but seemed to have the pride and avarice of dragons.

Sir Mykel found the monster in the fields outside Gladebrook, the most recent village to be destroyed. The manticore bled heavily from multiple wounds, the most grievous from Sir Mikel's first strike. He knew that he would have trouble if the creature took to the air.

He found the creature was near a barn, so he leaped onto the creature's back from the second floor, and severed both wings. Their battle had raged for an hour since then, and Sir Mykel was not bleeding, despite the blows he had taken and the dents and tears in his armor.

He charged forward, blade held low, swinging upward as he got close. The manticore roared and swiped at him.

Experience allowed Sir Mykel to anticipate the attack, and the claws narrowly missed him. The second attack caught him, knocking him to the ground three body lengths away.

Rest. It was a whisper in the back of his mind as he lay there. "No," he responded as he looked at the crystal-clear, cloudless sky. The armor groaned as he moved to stand. He didn't check for injuries, as he knew he wasn't hurt or bleeding.

There was no pain. No fear. And he still had too much to do.

A thump alerted him to the presence of the manticore before he could rise. It landed in front of him and stopped him from moving by placing its paws on his arms. It leaned back, and the barbed tail stabbed through the armor into his chest. He gasped as the tail pulled out, revealing a bloodless hole in the armor. The manticore released his arms as it sat back, the golden eyes staring down at him, daring him to continue and promising death.

"Is that all you have for me?" he growled. There was still no fear, or anger. His sword lay on the ground under the body of the manticore. "You don't live as long as I have and not learn other tricks." He stood and quickly determined his next attack before he moved.

Sir Mykel charged forward, avoiding the claw that swiped at him, and grabbed the chin fur under the creature's head and pushed up, revealing its throat.

Leaning his shoulder back, Sir Mykel thrust forward with his free hand pointed like an arrow with all the force he could. There was a moment of resistance before the hide broke, and his armored hand pierced through. The creature made a noise, but that reverberation allowed Sir Mykel to find its throat, grab hold, and rip it out.

Sir Mykel backed up and watched the manticore as it bled out, ready to attack again if necessary. But the creature collapsed to the ground, dying. As the twitching of the body slowed, Sir Mykel retrieved his sword and stepped up to the head. With powerful strokes, he hacked off the head of the manticore.

He took a breath and leaned against the body. The hollowness of the sound was only matched by the silence around him. He felt no satisfaction in a job well done. No contentment. No justice in the destruction of a creature that had killed so many innocents.

It was a job, nothing more, nothing less.

Weariness slammed into his soul. Visions of monsters

Burden of Duty

and evil men flashed through his mind's eye. *You can relax now.* The whisper in his mind was discarded immediately. He didn't have that luxury. He patted the body, "This would have been a lot harder if it had been mixed with dragon blood."

Sir Mykel stood and looked at the hole in his armor. "I guess a replacement is what I will ask for as a reward. I hope my cloak covers the hole."

***

The gathered nobles and council members were silent as Sir Mykel walked in with the bloody, severed head of the manticore. King William stood at the dais in the back of the room. "Sir Mykel, you have done what no one could!" He spread his arms as he continued. "You must be repaid. Anything! Name it, and it will be yours."

Sir Mykel pulled the cloak tight and listened to the whispers from those gathered. King William's offer was more than there was any reason for. The people would be concerned that he would ask for something extravagant. If he asked for something that would upset the political balance, the king would have trouble refusing. Sir Mykel had seen these situations arise before, and they would again.

He bowed and spoke. "I'm afraid that your ministers fear that I could bankrupt the kingdom, King William. But I only ask for two things. A new sword, and new armor to replace my broken equipment." He revealed a glimpse of his armor beneath his cloak, before hiding it again. And then drew his battle-damaged sword, which he placed onto the ground.

The king blinked, surprise evident on his face. "Easily done, Sir Knight. But you don't want anything else? I am offering anything."

Sir Mykel nodded. "I understand. I require nothing else," he said simply.

The king frowned. "Would you run the risk of insulting the crown by not accepting a reward?" He held out a hand, and a beautiful young woman stepped forward. "I am even prepared to offer the hand of Princess Melody, my only daughter, in marriage." The princess's eyes flashed as she glanced at her father, but she said nothing, and kept her face calm.

Sir Mykel bowed low, sweeping his hand forward, and stood again. "King William, you honor me. But I have lived for a long time. I do not intend to insult you or your reward. I understand the depth of your offer. But your daughter does not need an old man to be her husband. She deserves better than me." The flat tone of his voice carried through the hall, unwavering and consistent. He was not bragging or boasting, just making a statement.

The king finally nodded. "I will take you at face value, Sir Mykel. Although I'd like to see your face, to take you at face value," he replied with a small smile. There were chuckles from the councilors.

"My code does not permit me to remove my helmet, King William. I am sorry."

The king smiled further, and waved his hand. "You have strange codes, Sir Mykel. Well, if you will not allow me to give you my daughter's hand, then a sword and armor it is. You may visit the armory to pick your reward." He spread his hands out. "And we will hold a feast to celebrate the destruction of that vile creature," he said, pointing to the head. "Sir Mykel, please stay to celebrate, at least."

The knight took a breath, the sound echoing in the armor. If he was annoyed or excited at the request, he did not show it in his reply. "I will stay as long as I can, King

Burden of Duty

William. There are other things I need to do."

***

He found himself slouched on a bench in an area they called the Queen's Garden. Exhaustion permeated his body, sapping him of strength, and threatening to destroy him. "I need to keep going," he whispered. "It doesn't matter if I'm alone. I have to go on."

Sir Mykel stood, the new armor making a soft creak. The new sword was on his hip, bound with twine to prove that he hadn't unsheathed it while he was at the celebration that evening. The king had also granted him a new cloak that was edged with purple. This was a royal gift, and he thanked the king for it, knowing that it wouldn't last as well as his traveling cloak.

Earlier in the day, he had seen Princess Melody and her retainers walking through the garden, talking. They had ignored him, although he caught them watching him multiple times. This evening, he was enjoying the beauty of the gardens and staying away from people.

He stopped in front of a rose bush, which was filled with white blossoms. The blessing spoken over him so long ago repeated in his mind, *You will have the strength you need to complete your quest.*

"Are you enjoying yourself, Sir Mykel?" Turning, he found that Princess Melody had silently approached. "I thought that the champion of the kingdom would be drinking with the others in the hall."

"I don't enjoy the rich food and drink of nobles." He shrugged, indifferent. "It does not agree with me. Too long on the road." He turned to the roses that he had been looking at. "They are beautiful." He looked back at her. "I don't make time to relax. I move from one event to the next."

"Thank you. My servants and I spend much time tending the garden. But we are not as good as my mother was." She sat down on a nearby bench. "Sir Mykel, you are an enigma. You are offered anything, even the hand of the princess, and you turn them down? Saying that you are too old?" She waved her hand towards the castle. "There are dozens of old men in there right now who would jump at the chance. Your only request is armor and a weapon to replace your broken items. Nothing more. Why?"

"I need nothing else, Princess."

Princess Melody leaned back and laughed in disbelief. "Then there is that. You act like you did nothing great. I've seen men and women boast for lesser feats. So many are cheering you on. I've heard many women asking where you were, wanting to throw themselves at you. Many of the men in there are jealous while they praise you." She paused and frowned. "Yet you don't seem proud, excited, or any other emotion. You might as well have stepped on an ant."

He took a seat on an opposite bench. "This is a job, my Lady. Nothing more. Over the years I have been offered crowns, the hands of hundreds of women, and wealth beyond measure. I have turned it all down. That is my duty. There are evils to remove, wrongs to right. The lands are filled with never-ending problems." He looked off at a tree in the center of the garden. "In the morning I leave for the next issue to tackle."

The princess laughed, the tone was long, and harsh, not matching her beauty at all, he thought. "Sir Mykel, you must be careful, otherwise it would sound like you are proud and boasting." She shook her head and scoffed. "Men are confounding creatures. Do you know that? You talk of honor and duty. And you admit that you don't even relax."

Burden of Duty

Melody folded her arms. "I demand you tell me why."

Sir Mykel was about to deny her request. *Tell her. Let someone understand.*

He hesitated for only a moment, but that was enough for him to reconsider. "So be it. Let me tell you a story."

"When I was a young man, I was married to a wonderful woman. We had a child, a young boy." He paused, remembering. "At that time, there was a bandit terrorizing the lands. His band swept through, killing and pillaging. There wasn't anyone to do anything because of the chaos of the time.

"We were simple farmers. One day I traveled to a neighboring village to trade for some supplies. We needed some more seed that season, I think. While I was there, a survivor came running into the village, saying that there had been an attack by the bandits on my village."

He felt sadness and grief rising. He took a breath, and steadied himself.

"I rushed home, and found everyone dead. My wife, my child, the hired hands. Everyone. I found one survivor, an old man who had been ignored. Tens of people killed. All the supplies and food had been taken." He took another breath. The sadness and anger he felt were foreign." I spent days burying everyone with help from other villages. I was in a deep grief, but I needed something to do, or I would have died myself. So I gave myself a task. Bury my family and my friends and my neighbors.

"While I did this, I found a sword. I stowed it out of the weather until I was done with my task. And after that week, I picked it up. If anyone saw me, they said nothing.

"I was consumed with sadness, anger, and every other imaginable emotion. I almost lost myself to them. But when I picked up that sword, I found another focus. Revenge.

Justice. Retribution.

"I was only a farmer, but even a farmer can learn a new skill. So I traveled, practiced, and listened to rumors. When I finally found the bandits, I had been practicing for weeks.

"The first kill was truthfully the hardest. I almost lost my resolve after that. One of the bandits was in the tavern that I stopped at. Once it was done, I took his armor and searched for my next target.

"The rumors said that there was a ghost killing the bandits. I would add to my armor and replace anything that was broken as I went along. Soon, the bandit lord had enough, and hunted me down." He shrugged. "I killed him, and found my vengeance."

"Who was this bandit? I would think that I would have heard of him, if something like that happened." He could see concern on her face.

"He is long dead, as I said. And in a kingdom far from here. You wouldn't have heard of him."

Princess Melody frowned. "That may be, but I am concerned. Who was he?"

A feeling of annoyance crept in. He breathed again, calming himself. "It was during the War of the Drakonids. His name is forgotten by all but me."

The princess frowned. "The War of the Drakonids? Is that when the dragon Thyal'draemok ruled the lands under the Dragon Gate with its hybrid dragons?"

Sir Mykel nodded in response.

She laughed and shook her head. "We call that the Wyrm Cataclysm. And that was hundreds of years ago. That dragon was killed by the Wyrmbane Mage."

Sir Mykel shrugged, pushing aside the annoyance. "You wouldn't believe that I met the Mage, either. He gave me a blessing to help me finish my quest. I suspect he was really a

Burden of Duty

prophet." Something was kindled inside, something that he hadn't felt in centuries. Pride and the desire to prove himself. "I also killed King Aelron the Mad. Caeros the Usurper. The dragon Kaelsting. And more. I saw the aftermath of the Cataclysm. I saw those draconic hordes flee when their master died and the Dragon Gate was formed. I spent time killing many of them before leaving those lands."

Princess Melody frowned. "Aelron was killed by Thomas of Oakvale. Caeros by someone called The Wanderer in the histories. And Kaelsting? The legendary Lord Jorge. Well, Saint Jorge now, I hear."

He nodded again. "Yes."

"That would make you hundreds of years old," she snapped. "Is that why you don't want to take off your helmet? Because you are so old and wrinkly?"

"One of many." He stood, feeling frustration and anger gnaw at him. "I grow weary of this conversation. I need to leave."

Princess Melody stood and cried out, "No!"

Sir Mykel was taken aback. "No?"

"You will show me your face. That is my request."

"I already told you my story. I refuse, Princess." He took a step to move around her, and she moved in his way again. "Princess, I will not. That is that."

"I demand it. I can at least see the face of the man who saved my kingdom and refuses to marry me. That is the least that I deserve."

"You deserve nothing of the sort." The reply came out as a growl, and he felt anger rising. He stopped, and took a breath. "Princess, again, I refuse. Good night." He turned and began walking away.

Suddenly, the princess shrieked, and he felt the weight of her land on him as she leaped onto his back. Her hands grasped the helmet and yanked before she dropped to the ground.

"Ha!" she laughed as she looked at the helmet. "I told you I..." She stopped as he turned to look at her.

He was seeing red in his anger. Snatching the helmet back, he placed it on. "You might be the princess of a kingdom, but that gives you no right!" he roared.

"Where is your head?" Princess Melody whispered, stepping back. "There was nothing there."

"I am nothing but a spirit in armor these days. A force of nature that seeks out evil and destroys it. I don't feel anything. Now leave me alone!" He spun and started to walk away again.

"You are lying," it was soft, and he almost missed it.

He stopped to look at the girl. "You don't know me."

"You lie. You do feel. You are angry. I can see it. A crimson light is leaking from your armor." She stepped forward. "Why don't you admit it?"

"Why do I need to explain myself to a spoiled child?"

Princess Melody looked at him for a moment. Then she walked forward and hugged him. "It's okay to feel."

Memories of his wife and son flooded back. When had he last been hugged?

When she released him, he stood there. He held up a gauntleted hand and looked at it. "If I feel, I won't be able to keep going. I need to complete my quest."

"But you completed your quest. You avenged your family. You aren't living, just a spirit in a suit of armor trying to forget the pain." There was concern and understanding in her face.

"There is evil..."

"That is the job of the living. You have done enough. Do you remember what it is to be happy? To rest? To be

Burden of Duty

proud of what you have accomplished? You have done more than any one person could. You are a spirit." She smiled. "You have earned your time of rest. If anyone has earned a time in the unending glory of the Holy One, you have." She placed a hand on his gauntlet. "Go see your wife and son. Haven't they waited long enough?"

Princess Melody watched as something broke in the man. A sob escaped his spectral lungs, and became a cry of pain. The glow that she saw inside the armor shifted between multitudes of colors. And then abruptly stopped. The armor that held the great hero collapsed to the ground, and the helmet rolled to her feet.

She knelt down and picked up the helmet, feeling a wave of emotions wash over her. She wasn't sure if that was from Sir Mykel disappearing, or her own.

A little while later, she heard footsteps, and her father's voice. "Melody, have you seen...?"

Princess Melody stood and rushed to hug and hold her father. "Are you alright? Isn't that Sir Mykel's armor?" He gently loosened her grip to look at her better. The tears were still flowing. "Where is he?"

There was only one word she could get out, in-between sobs.

"Home."

***

The garden had a new feature within a week. King William had argued against it, but as this was the purview of Princess Melody, his vote only went so far. Stones had been piled around Sir Mykel's sword, which was stuck into the ground, creating a small mount. His helmet had been placed on top of it. She had a plaque commissioned as well.

The days since she talked to Sir Mykel were emotional.

The whole experience troubled her. She hoped and prayed that he found peace. She believed he did.

She woke that morning with a dream fresh in her mind. Sir Mykel had been sitting on a bench, on the shore of a crystal-clear lake next to a woman and a man. Princess Melody approached in the dream, and Sir Mykel noticed her and smiled.

"This is my wife and son," he told her. The smile on his face was infectious. "Thank you, Princess."

The Muskogee Kid
by Lisa Mildon

Dan cussed under his breath as he pulled up to his trailer in his dusty, red Ford pickup. Eyeing up the ancient white Cadillac that was parked already in front of his home, he muttered angrily, "Jesus Christ, she beat me home?"

As he slid out of his truck, jangling his keys absent-mindedly, Barbara stepped out on the front porch and smiled.

She said, "Have another busy day at the store?"

Dan looked up and grunted, mostly dismissing the white-haired woman. "Same-o, same-o," he barked. "I see you're eager to see my rugged face."

As he walked through the door, Dan dropped his keys into the rusty, orange ashtray by the door. Grabbing a beer from the fridge, he chugged down the first few swallows. Barbara gave him a reproachful look. He moaned, "I know, I know. Less booze, more water. But it's cold, and I'm parched."

Barbara, continuing to eye Dan, "You sure you should be drinking that with your meds? You know your doc wouldn't approve."

Dan plopped down in his ratty, brown recliner and grimaced. Gulping the last few swallows of his beer, he sat with a scowl on his face, not answering her. After a few minutes of silence, he added, "I don't need you harping on me about my health. I don't need a nurse, a wife, or a busybody. Why can't you just leave me alone?"

Coming out of the kitchen, Barbara frowned and said, "Look, you know very well you need someone to at least come to check on you. You're all alone. Don't you get lonely—"

Dan interrupted , "I see people all day long at the hardware store. When I get home, I just want some peace and quiet. You know?"

"Ugh, I do understand. But since you and Ellen split, and you never see your daughter, Diane, you must feel a bit lonely," Barbara said.

"I…DON'T…NEED…ANYONE!" Dan barked. "Now or ever. Now leave me to my beer," he added, moving towards the kitchen again.

"Okay, Dan. Drink your beer. I'll be by tomorrow. Do you need me to bring anything? Fritos, bologna, maybe a salad?" she smiled.

That comment seemed to melt a small chunk off Dan's shoulder. He turned and chuckled. "Okay, bring some greenery to make the doc happy. I'd rather have my fried bologna sandwiches, though."

"Salad it is. I'll even bring some of my homemade Ranch dressing for you to drown the lettuce in," she laughed.

"Now, off you go. I need some quiet time," Dan said as he nudged Barbara out the front door.

The Muskogee Kid

***

Dan shook his head as he watched her old car go down the driveway. He often wondered why she kept coming back to check on his grumpy, old ass.

Hell, I don't need nobody. Ellen showed me that, he thought. As he polished off another beer, Dan, at first, hesitated, then fixed himself a whiskey and sat down in his old recliner. Since his last doctor's appointment, he had started second-guessing himself.

That quack thinks I have signs of Alzheimer's? Yeah, I've been a bit forgetful lately. That's just the whiskey talking, he thought.

Flipping on the TV, he sipped on his whiskey until he found his favorite channel, the Western channel. "Wild West, all day, just like the real West," as the commercial blared.

Dan glazed over a bit and started thinking about the "old" days, as he put it. He didn't like to think of the past, but it often crept into his mind after a few drinks. The ol' whiskey was the worst to trigger it.

He and Ellen were sitting around the table, planning their first real family vacation. A rafting trip down the Colorado River. What better way to keep cool in the summer and have some fun, too.

"Don't you think Diane and Jim are a bit young for rafting?" Ellen asked Dan. "The river can get a bit treacherous."

"Nah, they both know how to swim. And this isn't Jim's first rafting trip, remember? He went with his church group last summer," Dan said.

"That was a float trip, hardly a river rapid. And I know even some adults have drowned while rafting," she said.

"We'll all be fine, don't you worry," he said.

Those words kept echoing in Dan's head. He shook his head as he looked down at the whitening knuckles surrounding his glass. *We should have never gone...*, he thought.

***

"Honey, will you help Jim and Diane with their life vests? I just want to make sure they're on securely," Ellen yelled to Dan at the river site. "I'm going back to the car for some sunscreen."

Dan looked at his children. He motioned for Diane, his nine-year-old, to come over. "Let me check your vest, or your ma will kill me." Dan tugged on all the straps and made sure the buckle was firmly seated. "Okay, Jim, you got yours all sorted?" he asked his twelve-year-old.

"Yeah, Dad, I'm good. Let's go!"

Ellen, slathering on the gooey, white cream on her face and neck, asked, "Are we all set?" Dan agreed and began helping Diane into the first raft. Ellen walked up to the second raft as her son was almost seated. Dan and Ellen untied the rafts, and off they sailed.

***

Dan took another swig of his drink and adjusted the volume of the TV. A single, silent tear had formed in the corner of his eye.

Muttering to himself, "I should have checked, I should have just checked."

***

As the river flow picked up the pace, so too did everyone's excitement. That was until, floating around the bend, they all came upon some violently moving rapids.

"Dad! It's getting rough!" Jim yelled.

The Muskogee Kid

"Hold on, everybody! We're gonna have to ride this one out!" Dan barked.

Both rafts were being tossed in the river like nature's own wild rollercoaster. Both Dan and Ellen were paddling wildly to keep control of their rafts.

Just as Ellen thought she had better control, they were catapulted into the air, Jim flying out the back. His life vest popped open as he sailed across the churning water.

Diane screamed in the back of her and her father's raft as she held onto the ropes attached to the boat. Dan, seeing his son launch off the raft, screamed in a weak attempt to guide Jim to safety.

Both Dan and Ellen managed to get to the side of the river as the flow slowed down. Scrambling to tie their rafts to a fallen log, both hopped out and began running back up the river, yelling for Jim.

"Jim! JIM! Son, where are you? Swim to my voice!" Ellen screamed.

Dan, thinking he saw his son's blue shirt, dove into the river, swimming against all hope to retrieve his son. "Jim!" Dan splashed and dog-paddled around, looking for him.

Then, a bone-chilling scream from Diane was heard. "Daaaadddd!" Both Dan and Ellen looked and saw Diane pointing to something. Ellen began running towards her daughter as Dan swam like an Olympic swimmer.

He saw a glimpse of blue. "I'm coming, hold tight!"

Ellen screamed as she dove in. She could see Jim's shirt, his face in the water.

Dan and Ellen, reaching Jim almost the same time, grabbed their son and began pulling him towards the shore.

Pulling him onto the bank, Dan saw that his son wasn't breathing. He began chest compressions, breathing into his mouth and praying in the same breath.

Lisa Mildon

"Come on, Son, you can do this! Breathe!" Dan croaked in between compressions. "Breathe, damn you!"

It must have been thirty minutes…or it felt like it. Ellen grabbed Dan's arm and sobbed. "He's gone…he's gone…gone."

Dan stopped and looked at his son's lifeless body. He grabbed him and cried out loud, "No, no, no, no, no…!"

***

Dan grimaced as he took another swallow. She should have checked on him. Ellen was in charge of her raft. He died because of her.

But as his gut cramped and ached, he knew it was all his fault. *I should have checked his vest…I should have swam faster…maybe I should have done CPR longer…*

***

Dan and Ellen were arguing for the umpteenth time. Dan had become a shell of himself. Sullen, bitter, barely speaking, spacing out, except when they fought.

"Dan, why don't we go to the movies? Just you and I? We could use a little alone time," Ellen asked.

Dan spewed, "I don't need any time; I just want my chair and a good drink to chase the day away."

"You never talk anymore; you don't even leave that chair after work most days. Some days you just sit there staring off in space. It's like living with a brick wall. Cold, lifeless, and thick!" Ellen yelled as she slammed the front door.

"Leave! I don't need you!" he roared as he dropped into his chair.

The Muskogee Kid

***

Diane walked into the kitchen while her father was making a drink. "Hi, Dad," she said.

Dan mumbled to himself, looked up, and glanced at his daughter. "Hello," he quietly mumbled and continued fixing his drink. Diane frowned and walked out.

***

Dan often looked away as his daughter approached. He couldn't look her in the eye. He was so ashamed that he couldn't save her brother. He no longer knew how to interact with her, so ignoring her was his default reaction.

***

Dan, nodding in and out of consciousness, passed out as his glass dropped to the floor. On the TV, a gunslinger was readying his hand to reach for his holster and draw before his opponent drew first.

***

Dan lifted his head up from the gnarled saloon bar. Smacking his dry mouth around, after what was obviously too many drinks. *Man, my mouth is like cotton,* he thought as he looked around the old saloon. As his eyes focused, they flew wider, once he realized he wasn't home in his chair.

Dan looked down at his clothes. Gone were the gray polo shirt and well-worn khaki pants. In their place were a rather crinkled brown shirt and faded denim, along with a pair of dust-encrusted cowboy boots. "What the fuck?" Dan said aloud as he stumbled off the barstool.

A balding man with an untamed, thick mustache walked over to him, polishing a glass. "I see you've risen from yer drunken stupor, mister."

"Wha..?" Dan looked pale, and his eyebrows rose slowly. He shook his head again, in an attempt to wake up. "Where am I?"

"Uh, mister, that must have been some moonshine you polished off. I told ya not to sample it. Them Foster boys do like to make it strong…and boy, does it burn!"

Dan, bewildered, looked down at his watch, which was nowhere to be found. *I must be dreaming…passed out again in front of the TV,* he thought.

"Mister? You okay?" the bartender asked.

Rubbing his hands over his face, Dan shrugged and figured it was a dream. *I'll just go along for the ride,* he thought.

"Yeah, I'm okay. I'm just not too familiar with this town…" he half-asked.

"Dry Gulch?"

Dan nodded. "Yeah, Dry Gulch." He didn't feel like drinking too much, but this dream made him feel hungry. "Where can I get me something to eat?"

"Why right here, mister. I've got some beans from yester-dy and a chunk o' bacon on the side. Lemme get that served up."

The bartender placed before Dan, on the countertop, a bowl of beans in a dark, viscous gravy with a crudely chunked-up piece of ham. "Dig in!"

Dan spooned in the first bite, eyeing it with caution. "Mmm, not bad." He started shoveling in the rest. As he slurped down the last few bites, he heard bells ringing.

"What's that? What are the bells for?" he asked as he scraped the bottom of the bowl.

"Oh, that's the school bell. Dry Gulch just built a

The Muskogee Kid

school a few months back. It'll be time for the young'uns to get some learnin."

***

The bells were chiming in Dan's head. He groaned, "Yeah, yeah."

Barbara, using her key, unlocked Dan's front door. "Dan? Didn't you hear me knocking and ringing the doorbell?"

Dan was still slumped over and staring at the floor.

"Dan? Dan!" Barbara ran over to him, slouched in his chair. His eyes glassed over; she shook him violently, trying to wake him up. Dan slowly blinked his eyes after a couple of minutes, his eyes coming into focus on his familiar friend.

Half-slurring, "Yeah, I'm awake, I'm awake."

"Dan! Did you pass out again? Or was it you spacing out? You had me scared seeing you there slumped over with your eyes open. I thought you'd met your maker!" she chastised him.

"I'm fine. I just fell asleep watching Westerns again. You don't need to get all worked up. I'm okay," he said.

Barbara picked up the grocery bag she tossed to the side. "I brought you a salad. It has sliced chicken and the fixings. And some of my Ranch dressing. Please try not to bathe in it," she said as she placed the items in the refrigerator.

"You really worry me sometimes. I'm afraid I'll come in and see you dead from a heart attack or stroke. You never check in with anyone."

"Bah! Thanks for your concern, but I'm alright. I'm tough as nails. I don't need anybody looking after me."

"Have you talked to Diane lately?" she asked. "I'm sure she'd be so happy to hear from you. You should really let her know what your doctor said. This diagnosis isn't a joke."

"No! You know I haven't. She and I haven't spoken in years," he retorted. "She doesn't care about me…and that's that."

"Fine. I just think it's time you reached out, open up a little. It's time to heal, Dan. You need to think about the future. I may not be here forever to care for you."

"It's past time for all of that. My life is how I like it. Quiet…I'm a lone wolf."

"Okay, Dan. I'll leave your wolfy self to howl. I'm off for the weekend," she said as she gathered her things. "Do try to eat something healthy, please."

He half-smiled. "Yeah, yeah. Thanks, Mom!"

***

After pottering around in his garden, Dan thought he deserved a reward. *See, I do mess around with veggies…I just don't eat many of them.* He chuckled at his own quip. *I think it's time for a little reward for good behavior.*

He went to the refrigerator and began to reach for a beer. "Nah, I deserve the good stuff." He closed the fridge and got out a glass.

I know I need to take these "brain" meds and stop with the booze, he thought as he rolled the glass in his fingers.

Decanting his favorite whiskey, he poured his normal portion, paused, and smirked. "Maybe just a little taster." He filled his glass.

Sipping on his drink as he sat down in his favorite seat, he grabbed the TV remote and switched on his Westerns. "Oh boy, John Wayne! I love the Duke!" Dan fully reclined his chair and continued to sip on his whiskey. He began nodding off but jerked awake. "Ooh boy, I need to finish this off before I spill it." He chugged the last of his drink and faded off into sleep.

The Muskogee Kid

***

Dan awoke in a small room. It had a simple, spring twin bed and a small bedside table with an empty glass turned over. A washbasin on a simple pine dresser was at the wall, across from his bed. His clothes piled neatly next to the dresser.

Pausing, he noticed the clothes were the crumpled brown shirt and denim jeans he dreamt of the previous night. Looking around, he realized he must have been in an old inn. He was dreaming again.

"Hell, another dream?" he muttered. Getting dressed, he wondered if he shouldn't have taken his alz meds with his whiskey. *Guess I better see what's going on*, he thought.

He stumbled down the wooden stairs, only to see a familiar, balding and mustached bartender. "Well, glad to see you're up and about, mister," the bartender said. "I knew you'd be plum tuckered out after yesterday."

Dan tilted his head and asked, "What was yesterday?"

"Boy, you did whack yer head good. That fool boy trying to rob the bank hit you on the back o' the head. Knocked you clean out. But you went down a-swinging."

Dan, looking a bit bewildered, asked, "Did I stop him? What happened?"

"No, but you put up such a ruckus that the sheriff came a-running. He arrested him before he got out of town." The bartender mimicked a few punches in the air. "You might'a kept our bank open a little longer, that's for sure."

Dan, realizing he didn't know the bartender's name, quipped, "What's your name again? Guess I was hit pretty hard."

"Jack's the name. But you can call me friend. Cause a man that helps a man out has got to be a good one." The bartender smiled.

Dan rubbed his head. He could feel a large knot on the

back. He winced. *Ouch! That does smart!*

"You been such a help around these parts the last few months. I sorta feel bad charging ye for the room. Tell ya what, I'll knock off a nickel from the rate. You deserve it."

Dan started wondering just how far ahead his dream had skipped. He shrugged and figured he'd play along again. It was kind of fun, anyway.

***

After finishing up a bowl of Jack's famous beans, Dan decided to explore his dream world. "I think I'll see what trouble I can get into," he told Jack.

Stepping out of the saloon, Dan saw a dusty road with wooden buildings lined up on either side. Dan could see the new schoolhouse at the north side of the road. It was obvious it was a fairly recent build, as the paint was still fairly white and not bleached out like most of the other buildings in Dry Gulch. He remembered Jack saying the school marm was a younger lady. Maybe he could see if he could help her out…or at least have a look at this fair lady.

Strolling up to the dusty, white, one-room building, Dan could see a pair of eyes peeking out behind the curtain. He smiled slightly as he walked up to the door and raised his hand to knock. Before his fist hit the wooden door, a chestnut-haired woman opened the door with a start. "Oh my!" she gasped.

Dan took a step back and nodded his head. *Might as well play the part right.* He took off his cowboy hat and said, "Howdy, ma'am. I'm fairly new to town. Thought I'd see if you needed any help. Maybe a rusty hinge or loose board to fix on the school?"

The young woman, in her late thirties, Dan guessed, would be past her prime in the Old West, but she was still

The Muskogee Kid

a beauty, even with a couple of laugh lines around the eyes. "Well, not at the school, but I do have a bit of mending on my barn," she said. "You're that fella, Dan Jenkins, right? You've been sure helpful to the townfolk."

Dan smiled and put his hat on. Sticking out his hand, "That's me. But I think a formal introduction is in place. I don't recall your name, ma'am."

"Oh," she smiled, tilting her head to the side, "I'm Sarah. Sarah Sawyer. The schoolteacher, as you can see."

As they shook hands, she said, "If you're serious about wanting to help, I really could use a handyman at the place. Jed, my son, tries. But he's too young to do much. He's determined to be the man of the family since Ben died."

Dan, startled by the last comment, said, "I'm sorry, ma'am…"

"Sarah, call me Sarah," she interrupted.

"I'm sorry about that, Sarah. I didn't mean to bring up sad memories."

"Oh, that's all right, he's been gone some three years now. Me and Jed are doing just fine now. How about I fix you a nice lunch, and you can do some fixin' for me?"

"That sounds like a plan, Sarah. Shall I come by tomorrow, first thing?" Dan asked.

"That will be just fine. We'll be looking for ye," Sarah said.

Dan headed back to his room at the inn. As he walked, he thought about Sarah. *She was so nice. Such a gentle smile.*

Part of him was fully aware of this Western dream world, yet another part instinctively played the part of the handy drifter looking to settle down. He sat on the edge of his bed, considering the situation as the pit of his stomach lurched.

It's either the beans I ate or…something else. I need to just lie down for a bit. Dan stretched out onto the old cot and quickly dozed off.

***

Still sitting in his favorite chair, Dan stared out blankly. He didn't know if his mind was short-circuiting, the booze was finally catching up to him, or maybe...God forbid...the Alzheimer's was catching up to him. He sat frozen in his chair until a familiar voice pierced his blank stare.

"Dan! Dan! Can you hear me?" Barbara yelled as she shook Dan.

Dan blinked and slowly turned his head. Still feeling like he was in a fog, he shook his head as his eyes focused on his caregiver's ashen face.

"Huh? Stop shaking me!" Dan bellowed.

"Dan, you were just sitting there staring in space. I banged on the door and finally found my keys. I kept shaking you. I thought you had a stroke...wait, have you just been sitting there in the same clothes all weekend?" she asked.

"Wait, what day is it?" Dan asked.

"It's Monday," She said.

Have I been sitting here since Friday? Wasn't I in Dry Gulch? Wait, what?

"Dan? Are you ok?" asked Barbara. "Should I call your doctor or an ambulance?"

She would never believe me...I don't believe me...what's happening to me?

"No, I'm fine. I was just having a lazy weekend. Been napping, that's all," he said.

Barbara eyed him, her brows knitting. She pulled out her blood pressure cuff. "Let me take your BP just to make sure."

"Fine, fine." Dan stuck out his arm as she wrapped the

The Muskogee Kid

cuff around it.

"Well, not bad. It's 130/75, so it doesn't look like it's that. I should really call your doctor," she said.

"See, I'm fine. Don't worry yourself. Just set up my meds and be on your way," he said as he looked at his watch.

Barbara sighed and walked to the kitchen. Dan, still sitting in his recliner, looked down at his rumpled clothes, as memories – or was it hallucinations? – flooded him of his Old West dream.

Was it a dream? Is this what I have to look forward to? Hallucinations? Delirium? But he couldn't stop thinking of Sarah Sawyer and how alive he felt.

"Dan?" Barbara asked.

"Huh? Oh sorry, guess I was daydreaming." Dan said.

"Ok, your meds for the week have been set up in your pill case. I brought you some chicken salad sandwiches and some fresh fruit salad. You think you can manage today? I can stay longer, if you like," she said.

"Oh, sure. I'll be alright. Thanks for the food. You be on your way," he said.

Barbara patted his shoulder and saw herself out. She turned to glance once more, frowning. *He's a stubborn old mule.*

Dan decided to freshen up with a shower and ate some of the food Barbara brought. Feeling refreshed, he stepped out onto the back patio. Sitting in a weathered rocking chair, Dan listened to the birds singing in his small backyard oasis. With a slight breeze blowing, Dan's mind began to wander.

***

Dan found himself reclining into an enormous mound of hay as he heard the snickering of a nearby horse.

"Butterbean? Is that you?" Dan asked as a golden

palomino horse ambled up to munch on some of the hay. He stood up and instinctively grabbed the loose reins. *How did I know this?*

Dan looked around to survey his surroundings. *Dry Gulch. I'm not too far from Sarah's place.* He hopped on the horse and rode toward the teacher's homestead.

Sarah was hanging out her laundry as her son Jed plowed up a small patch nearby. Seeing Dan in the distance, she waved and smiled.

Dan waved back and gently spurred the horse. "Come on, Butterbean!"

"I see you've finally made it back from the last cattle run. I've missed you so," Sarah said to Dan.

"How long have I been gone?" he asked.

"Over two months, I reckon. I was afraid you found another to charm your heart." She smiled and tilted her head.

Feeling a bit dizzy, Dan stumbled over to the rickety chair on the front porch and sat down. He pulled Sarah down onto the chair next to him. "Sarah, I've not been myself lately. And I need to get this out."

She looked into his eyes, hers widening as he spoke. "I feel like I'm coming untethered and the only way to stay grounded is by setting my roots down…settling down."

Sarah's breath quickened but remained silent.

"I know I've been an old cowpoke, wandering from town to town. But since I met you, I've felt different… Whole."

He grabbed her hands and smiled. "What I'm trying to say is I want to share what is left of this dusty old life with you…and Jed. I know I won't feel right until I do."

She blinked slowly as a smile crept onto her face. "I thought you'd never ask, you silly fool." As she hugged him and whispered, "Yes," in his ear, Dan smiled, sliding out of

The Muskogee Kid

her arms and onto the ground.

It all went black.

***

Dan woke up with the beeping of hospital machines around him. Needles stuck in both arms. Wires running all over him.

"Wha...what is this? Where am I?" Dan asked as he tried to move his arms, but he couldn't, as they were tied down.

Barbara, looking haggard with dark circles under her eyes, bolted from the chair in the room and ran towards the nursing station. "Nurse! Nurse, he's awake!"

"Diane. Your father is awake! Go see him," she said.

"I don't need to see him. I'm finishing up on his paperwork. You can tell him what happened. He's not my responsibility anymore," Diane said.

Barbara frowned and went back to Dan's room. "Dan, do you know me?" she asked.

Dan blinked, and as his voice croaked, Barbara moved in closer.

"What happened?" he asked.

"You had some sort of 'neurological' event. You were completely catatonic for weeks. The doctor said your Alzheimer's is rapidly getting worse. They won't let you live alone anymore. Diane's here...but she's...she's signing custody over to the state," Barbara said, choking on her words.

Dan tried to speak. He knew he needed to tell her what was happening. How could he possibly explain this?

"I'm ok. I am...not losing...my mind," his voice creaked. "I've been at Dry Gulch."

Barbara tilted her head as her frown lines deepened. She patted his arm to soothe him. "It's ok, Dan...I'll come

Lisa Mildon

see you every day."

"No! I'm not hallucinating…please…believe me…" he said.

***

Dan led Butterbean to the coral and cinched up the gate. Wiping the sweat off his brow, he sidled up to the shade tree and gulped down a cup of water. Smiling, he waved as he saw his sweet wife, Sarah, feeding the chickens as Jed harvested some of the summer corn.

***

Barbara walked down the sterile hall lined with residents' doors decorated with various pictures or colorful summer cutouts of watermelons, flip-flops, and fireworks. She saw the familiar number 224 and slowly pushed the door open. Sitting there, staring out the window, Dan smiled blankly as the birds sang in the tree outside.

"Hiya Dan, I see you're looking handsome as ever," as she patted his arms. He rarely moved or acknowledged her anymore, but he was always smiling. *I guess he's happy, wherever he is,* as she started rubbing lotion on his dry skin.

***

Dan and Sarah were sitting on the front porch, both rocking in matching rocking chairs. They looked at each other as Jed strode up with his bride-to-be. Smiling at Sarah, Dan said, "Life is good." Then, he squeezed her hand.

Blood for Blood
by Clayton Barnett

Joseph paused in digging the next shallow grave. There were already three bodies buried, one above the other, with only a layer of dirt between them. He'd heard that one of the neighboring parishes was simply stacking the bodies outside the walls around the church grounds.

"Freak! Ghoul!" some boys from the village yelled from behind him.

Joseph stopped and looked over his shoulder, taking a rock in the back for it. They laughed and walked away, in no fear that he would fight back. He never did.

He had learned from Father Magnier that it was the middle of the fourteenth century after Christ, but not the exact year. Just as he didn't know exactly how old he was. He guessed mid or late teens. *My parents, maybe because Dad worked as a mason in the next town over, were among the first two to die. A sickness that caused a terrible fever, black swellings, and killed in a day. Just as a temporary measure, Father took me in and had me help around the church. But more and more died, including him, so all I do is bury them.*

Digging over, he dragged the body of a young girl and

carefully laid her down. More shoveling left a small mound. Looking about the courtyard, Joseph realized that if more died, there would be no place to put them.

"Just like that parish over."

He brushed dirt from his worn tunic and frayed pants, the latter held up with a rope around his waist, and walked to the small, one-room hut behind the church. The priest had found a too-small bed frame and filled it with straw for him. A small table with a wooden plate and earthenware cup were his only possessions.

Joseph walked past the church's front door – no one came any more, fearing the sickness as God's wrath – with Fido trotting along behind him. One of the apples from a nearby tree looked about ripe, so he pulled it down to go with the little bit of hard cheese, left over from his last, rare visit to the village market.

"They hate me," he muttered around the bite of apple. Fido made a curious sound as his master rarely talked. "No, not you, good boy. Maybe because Mom and Dad died first? Me alone at the church? If they blamed me, I know I'd be dead. They just don't like me.

"And that's why I try to not go to the market. I know it's a sin, but I did find Father's stash of coins and use them to buy just enough to get by, but the silence and stares from those few still alive are almost worse than the taunts and rocks."

Opening his door, Joseph was not happy to see some animal had knocked over the small wooden bucket he used to draw water from the creek, a bit down the hill. He picked it up with a sigh, wondering if he would cut his feet again on the rocks along the path. Joseph didn't bother to tell Fido to stay, as he never left his master.

"At least you eat well, on all those rats," he said,

Blood for Blood

provoking a wagging tail. He wanted to smile and laugh but had forgotten how. Walking through the trees down the soft slope, he kept an eye on the ground and the rocks.

Moments later, at the stream, Joseph could see some small fish in a pool on the other side but didn't know how to catch them. He knelt, filled his bucket, and stood. They turned back to the only home they had left.

He froze, hearing the groan from the opposite bank.

After so much death, nothing startled him anymore. Setting the bucket down, he and Fido splashed through the stream and looked about, wondering where the sound came from.

Another groan, to their right.

Around a large tree, Joseph saw what he first thought was a dead man: impossibly thin, skin like wrinkled parchment, and a color somewhere between brown and gray. Hairless. "He can't be aliv – "

The man groaned once more. *For once, can I help someone rather than just bury them?*

Not a particularly large boy, Joseph had gotten strong from digging so many graves. The stranger could not have weighed much more than Fido, empty bones held together by a wrap of skin. With him in his arms, they crossed back, pausing to collect the bucket, before going back up the hill to the church.

Joseph laid him down on the straw that was his bedding. Dipping the cup into the water, he tried to get the stranger to drink. A little went down, the rest over his drawn face.

I won't let him die.

"I...I'll run to the village to get some food! I'll be right back. I promise!"

The sun was near to the western horizon as Joseph ran to where he had hidden the coins. The market would be closing soon.

A handful of coppers had him running down the path. Coming into the village in such a rush, and recognized for who he was, the locals' reactions were from frowns to scowls. He didn't care.

Not knowing how much time the stranger had left, he ran to the tavern. There, Joseph asked for pease pottage, and could he please borrow the bowl?

The man behind the counter was as pleased to see the lad as anyone else and demanded twice the normal amount. He paid and grabbed a spoon on the way out, trotting back, trying not to spill too much.

"Mister! Mister!" he called, opening the door. "I have food for you!"

First propping him up, Joseph tried slowly to get one spoonful after another down the other's throat, and not just down the front of his chest. About half made it. The stranger closed his eyes, and the boy split the remainder with Fido. He stood and smiled for the first time in over a year.

"It's going to be all right, Mister. I'll take care of you."

***

Going to the tavern every day would be an impossible expense. Joseph spent more time at the market, getting some old soup bones and a mix of vegetables from the few stalls still open. The stranger ate and drank more but never seemed to get any better.

"Why is that?" he asked to the wind as he and Fido walked back to the church. "He is eating better than you and I do but still – ouch!"

A rock hit him on the back of his head. Turning, it was the usual two tormentors, with two more this time. All four threw another barrage of rocks. Joseph hunched down with

Blood for Blood

his back to them, to shield himself. *It hurts, but I won't die...*

Fido let a cry, then began to run in small circles. Blood ran from the side of his head and his mouth was beginning to foam. He fell over and was still.

The boys behind them were laughing.

"Fido? Fido!" Joseph dropped the food he had bought and pulled his only friend into his lap.

Fido was gone.

The four walked away. Laughing again.

I'll kill them. I'll kill all of them.

No way to carry both Fido and the food, he left the food. Night was falling when he tamped the dirt on his friend's small grave in the corner of the churchyard. Joseph plodded around to his hut. The stranger was able to tilt his head and look at the broken boy in the doorway.

"Why?" Joseph cried. "Why won't you get better? I've done everything I can, and you don't get better. Is it you? Is it me? Mom and Dad are dead. Fido's dead. You're going to die."

He took a few steps and fell to his knees at the bedside. "I wish I were dead. Mister? I don't want to live anymore. If you want my life, it's yours."

It grew darker and darker. He did not know how much time passed before he felt a hand on his head.

"I will," the stranger whispered.

***

For thirteen centuries, I have been lost on this world. In my arrogance, serving the Roman prefect, I cursed and struck an uppity Galilean who had been condemned to death. With a glance from him, I somehow heard, "You shall await my return."

As the decades passed, many about me aged

and died.

I did not.

I grew older and more feeble, but never died. Leaving the Roman province of Syria, I traveled first to the priests of Cybele in Galatia, there to learn. From there, across the desert and two rivers to where the Chaldeans have their schools of mysticism. It was they who told me of my affliction, and what I must learn to do. They gave me terrible knowledge; I gave them all the gold and silver I had stolen from the Romans.

Returning to the empire, I lived a while around the Aegean Sea. I learned a Greek word, νεκρομαντεία, which later, moving further west, was called necromancy in Latin.

An arm worn out? Take a new one. Gut hurting? Take his. One thousand three hundred years, harvesting humans like cattle.

That's not very nice, Cartaphilus.

I know, Joseph. I am not a nice person.

Why didn't you just do that to me at the stream, where I found you?

I was hoping, finally, to die. You, instead, did everything you could to help me. Even offering yourself as a living sacrifice, like Him I struck and cursed.

I don't understand.

In my boundless selfishness, there was a faint ember of gratitude. So, I am no longer just Cartaphilus; you are here, too.

Will I have to live forever? Will I be a bad person?

Forever? No. Bad? I...am sorry...

They stood from the straw bed. They marveled at the health and strength of their body. The tunic and pants were on the floor, empty. Those were put back on. Dawn was just breaking, and they were out the door and down the path to the village.

Blood for Blood

There was a laugh from the left and a rock came sailing out of the trees.

They caught it.

Cartaphilus? How did I... we...?

Quiet. I grant your wish.

Looking forward to a scuffle, the four boys were now athwart the path.

They fell over. All dead.

We go.

SPACE JUNK
BY GRATHEW

The derelict space station loomed over the table. Rust so intense it showed up though the blue tint of the hologram. "Adam, you sure this thing ain't a death trap?" Michale said, gesturing towards a ragged edge where something was once attached.

"It's an abandoned pirate base, of course it's a death trap. What would you expect from an under-the-table salvage job?" Adam retorted. "Lucy do you know what it is exactly that caused this station to, and I quote, 'suddenly become unguarded?'"

"Honestly, I don't have the foggiest. The Broker said it was a stable free-port not too long ago. Now he's paying to recover, 'The Specimen,' which is equally unhelpful. Best I have is that someone finally raided the place, thus abandoned. Would explain the damage and amount of debris," Lucy said, focusing on her scanner. "I just hope it's as empty as everyone says it is. I know Michael, you want those ghost stories to be true."

"Like hell I would. They said the station was haunted before. Now, it's been blasted by just about everything. No way we aren't gettin' sent to hunt a ghost. You know how much The Broker would pay for a ghost," Michael said, pacing the bridge.

"Can it, Michael, you know ghosts aren't real. Stop believing everything you see online. Now a killer robot or some kind of freaky creature, sure. Maybe…. Then again, it could be a plague for all we know. Steven, you got any input? It's not like you to be so quiet before a job," Adam said, turning to the pilot.

"Dunno, Boss. It's a mess out there with the debris. I agree with Lucy though, looks like there was one hell of a fight out there. If we have time, we could strip some of those hulls for parts. Hell, we could come back with Nick's crew and probably make more than what The Broker is paying us in salvage alone. Assuming we don't get clipped by debris, and end up staying in this graveyard," Steven replied, concentration showing in his voice.

"Well, we know it has power and can assume it's trapped. Think you can dock it, Steven? Or are we going to have to walk it?" Adam said, zooming out from the station and looking over the debris field.

"Depends, Boss, you want to come back to a ship in one piece or many?" Steven said as the ship lurched. "Because we're changing the delicate balance that got established; I don't think even Kay could predict what is going to end up where."

"That is correct," Kay chimed in, unhelpful as ever.

"Alright, so we are walking it. Suits will protect us if it is a damn plague. Might as well arm up too. Who knows what will be waiting for us over there? It's not like a personnel list is going to be up to date. If there are people over there, I doubt they will be friendly, it's been what? Six weeks of isolation?" Adam said, turning to Lucy for confirmation.

Space Junk

Lucy nodded, "About that, although there is enough power to maintain comms jamming, Kay, are you connected to their systems?"

"Affirmative, however, multiple main systems are offline. Would you like me to try and initialize them?" Kay replied.

"No, you'd probably just end up triggering a trap. Let me do it," Lucy said, trying to kill the AI with her voice.

For a moment, everything was as silent as their old ship could be.

"Communications with Red Owl's Free-Port established," Kay stated. "Sensor connection with Red Owl's Free-Port Established. Threats detected from Red Owl's Free-Port. Should I take action?"

"No, Kay. That's just their IFF making sure we are who we say we are. Adam, why can't we get rid of that thing?" Lucy said, glaring daggers at Adam.

"Because we'd need to replace the *Corvus'* computer core, which we can't afford. Once we finish this job, we will be able to. I know; I hate her too. One last job, then we will get everything sorted. No more of The Broker, no more Kay, and hopefully enough left over to get the rest of this rust bucket sorted," Adam said ignoring her glare. "Between what The Broker is paying us and what his client is paying us, we just might have enough to abandon this and get a *Corvus II*. Hence, we do this by the book. Play it safe and get everything squared away."

"That's why it's got to be haunted. They wouldn't pay so much if it weren't a ghost we were hunting," Michael complained.

"Mich," Steven said as he avoided some debris, jostling the ship, "shut up. Unless you want a thruster through your bedroom window." Lucy and Adam laughed as the color drained from Michael's face. "Boss, we are about to be as close as we can get. Go suit up and I'll pull us around to what says is a working airlock. Should be a straight shot. If you don't come out of it, make sure you make yourself obvious. Kay won't see you otherwise."

The three left the bridge and made their way down to the airlock. "Adam, you think we will need anything else? I figure cuttin' tools, and a med-bag. Salt probably wouldn't go a miss either," Michael schemed.

"Cutting torch is a good idea, same with the aid kit. What would the salt do to a ghost? I'm assuming you're going to stop the ghost with it?" Adam replied with an eyeroll.

"Ghosts get stuck in salt. See, ya throw it at them and the salt sucks up the ghost like little crystalline sponges. Keeps them from possessin' and shit. Good news, they can't phase through rust, so we should stick near it. If there's enough dust in there the ghosts won't be able to go invisible," Michael said, slowly turning into a crazed theorist.

"Michael, the station seems to be coated in rust inside and out. I doubt we will be able to get away from it in there. Dust-wise, the life support has been off for weeks, bet everything is covered in it. I doubt you'll have anything to worry about. Besides, if we're trying to capture the ghost, wouldn't salt spungin' it up be a bad idea?" Lucy said, stifling a laugh.

"Luce, this ain't a laughin' matter. Ghost possess you and steal your soul. It's how they create more ghosts and keep on unlivin'. I for one donn' want to be a ghost baby. Mama said I was a difficult enough pregnancy as was," Michael said, opening the door to the cargo bay.

"I didn't need to know that. I always thought you were one of those tube kids," Lucy said grimly. The cargo bay was

Space Junk

the picture of organized chaos. Boxes haphazardly stacked one on another. Different supplies clearly mislabeled. As if routine by now, the three split up and started to gather the required supplies. "Adam, long or short guns? Lucy held up one of each option.

"Short, old Red Owl loved his maze-like hallways. Besides, do you really want rifles in there? Before it got shot up it was held together duct-tape and dreams, now there might not be either," Adam said, shifting through different backpacks. "The Broker said the specimen was 'approximately man-sized.' I assume we will have to keep it pressurized, and it won't fit in a suit." He then moved to a different crate. "Michael, do you know where the lifebags went?"

"Oh yah. Remember when we were loadin' from Juniper Point? That blonde decided she knew where we wanted stuff better than we did. I'd guess they are over where you wanted them to put the reactor bits. Was the most logical place to put them," Michael said, refilling gas canisters for the torch. "Boss, we're runnin' out of torch juice. Got enough for one set of bottles, we ain't gunna be cuttin' our way out of there."

"Do you remember where Juniper Blonde put the medical supplies, Michael?" Lucy said, clambering over a stack of crates.

"Yah, she said they should be somewhere easy to reach, Luce, you're prolly standin' on them. She wasn't the tallest, you know how dock leaders are with 'easy access items.' I just wish she hadn't kept runnin' hee mouth every time I suggest where to put somthin'," Michael scoffed. "She got right mad, cutest thing in this bay in a good ling time."

Lucy opened the crate she had been standing on and found the medical kits. "I know you think I'm the opposite of cute. However, those hamelet-parrots were pretty cute. How did she even get up here to place this crate?"

She had a few helpers. Dunno what they were, other than the one's placin' stuff. As for the parrots, sure they were, but they didn't have bouncin' boobies when they got mad. Just claws, beaks, feathers, n' stuff," Michael said, reflexively dodging both the glare and box lid Lucy threw at him.

"Alright, calm down. Let's not kill each other, at least not in here. I don't need corpses to be added to the smells," Adam said, as he reordered some of the chaos. "If you tow have the stuff we need in here, let's get to the airlock. I'm sure Steven wants to make this a quick in-and-out before we make things worse out there."

Grumbles of agreement were the only reply. The three of them carried the gathered supplies down the hall and got suited up. The occasional burst from the thrusters highlighted the danger they were in. "I'm ready to do final approach if you guys are suited," Steven's voice came though the tinny intercom.

"Not quite Steve, we just got to the suitin' part," Michael said though the wall panel. "Can you give us like, five minutes? Maybe six."

"Alright, I'll start in, nice and slow. Should keep Kay from freaking out. Hey Lucy, she keeps saying unauthorized signal. Highlighting the center of the station. Is this something I should be worried about?"

Lucy pushed her head through the helmet seal. "I doubt it. It's likely a phone home, or something similar for when the station gets into this kind of state. Unless it starts trying to get to her or the *Corvus*, I wouldn't be that worried. How far out are you planning on parking?"

"Far enough. Probably where we scoped the debris field from. I'm dropping a probe before orbiting around

Space Junk

so I can see both sides of the station. That way if you find another exit, I'll be able to... Kay says there's now multiple signals? Looks like comms traffic that didn't get through the buffer before power got cut. Should I play it?" Steven said, fighting with Kay.

"Yah, play them. Pipe them down here too." Adam said, helmet in hand. "Hopefully it will give us an idea of what happened over there."

"Sure, Boss. One sec," Steven said, before a screech came though the intercom.

"Mayday! Mayday! This is Free-Port Seven of the Red Owls Gang. To any ships, we need Immediate assistance. All systems are failing and personnel are disappearing. If you can assist our coordinates are linked in this message," an exhausted frantic man came though the intercom. The message looped twice before Steven silenced it.

"I told Kay we didn't need to log it as a distress call, because we are already here. Are you guys ready? We're just about to the door." Steven couldn't hide the worry in his voice.

"As ready as we can be. Let us know when to jump," Adam said, cycling the airlock. Lucy and Michael nodded as the air was pulled from the room. The outer doors opened, revealing the debris-filled void they were cruising through as the ship glided to a stop. Opposite, and slightly above the boarding team, was the station's airlock. Together, the three jumped across. They landed inside the station's airlock, Lucy hit the cycle button, and the outer doors closed. With a roar, air filled the room. "Comms check. Steven, you hear us?" Adam said as the airlock cycle showed "complete."

"Loud but not clear, more than a bit of static, Boss. Kay says she can clean it up. How do I sound?" Steven's reply came through, if a bit garbled.

Grathew

"Same, it was better at the end. Every fifteen minutes, if we don't call you," Adam said.

"I got it, Boss. It's been the same playbook every time. Don't worry, I'll check in," Steven said, mostly clear.

While Adam couldn't hear Lucy and Michael's laughter through their EV suits, he could see it. He simply waved them into the station. They had work to do. The dark void of the hallways weren't going to search themselves, after all. The three floated out of the airlock, using their gloves and boots to shimmy though the microgravity. Using both walls and the ceiling, in addition to the floor. The only light came from their suits.

"See, this is ghost territory. I knew I should have brought more salt," Michael said as they entered the main promenade. It was a chasm of a space. Many balconies ringed the central space. "There's almost no power, and no gravity; ghosts probably ate the gravity generator. If we get it runnin' I bet we'll flush it out."

"We are looking for a 'specimen.' Supposedly it's in one of the labs. I'm keeping my money on plague. Look how clean it is in here. Not a murder bot," Lucy said, stopping to look at the station map. "We are pretty close to everything here. Adam, are we looking for tech or bio lab?"

"The Broker didn't say," Adam said, drifting across the open space. "He did say that we'd know it when we saw it."

"Guys you alright over there?" Steven's voice came across the radio. "Kay says there's something moving over there. She can't make heads or tails of it."

Lucy started digging though her pack. Michael started looking around frantically.

"We are fine. Does Kay know where it is?" Adam said as the group landed on a wall. "Is there one thing or many?"

"Kay doesn't seem to know what exactly it is, or where

Space Junk

it is. A few solo signals, and thus I assume not you guys. Mostly on motion trackers. You seem to be heading towards them? The data we're getting is bad at best."

"I sure hope not," Adam said as they entered the labs. "We will call you back, probably soon."

"Copy," Steve said before the line cut.

The three crept forward, weapons raised, through the labs. The first two were empty, implying disuse. The third had a robot disassembled, sparks jumping from power cables spilling from the walls. "Think that's what we're looking for?" Lucy said, looking over the disassembled robot.

"That don't seem very 'specimeny' to me Luce. Seems more like a sample." Michael said, looking over the robot. "Plus shouldn't it be less, broke?" Lucy rolled her head, making up for the helmet's deficiencies.

"Who knows. Wish we had something more to go off of than, 'you'll know it when you see it,'" Lucy said, shifting though the debris. "Honestly nothing super interesting. Circle back?" Adam nodded and the group continued on. As they worked their way through the halls, they started passing bodies. Most didn't show obvious signs of death. This changed to dismemberment as they approached the final lab, blood and limbs littered the hallway. Unlike the previous lab, the doors were broken out. Clearly it had been sealed once.

"This lookin' like somethin' else. Ghosts are cleaner than this. Maybe it is a monster. I didn't bring a net though," Michael said, looking at the twisted bloody bulkhead. "I got five on giant space cat."

"I'm just glad I can't smell this mess," Lucy said as she stepped over half a body into the lab. "Steven, life support is still off?"

"Yes, Kay is talking about systems attempting to auto

restart. Do you want her to give restarting it a try?" Their radio connection was straining against something. "Also, Lucy, you didn't come through all that clearly."

"Same for you, Steven. I think these labs were shielded. Don't. Let. Kay. Touch their communications system. Remember what happened on Tripal II?" Lucy said, moving back towards the door, attempting to find better signal.

"Copy. Hey Boss, maybe instead of replacing her, we can revert Kay to factory. She was good fun before Tripal. Also, I'm seeing a strange gravity reading. Is there gravity over there? The sensors are saying both yes and no," Steven replied, seemingly distracted with something.

"No. Everything is trying to decide if it is or isn't working. Are you seeing what we are seeing?" Adam panned his head around the room, attempting to give Steven a view of it.

"I wish I wasn't. That's a lot of mess. I'm guessing that's going to be our 'specimen' once you catch it." Nausea percolated through Steven's voice.

"I told ya. I told ya all!" Michael said. "We are hunting a ghost. And it's one that eats people."

"I don't think it's a ghost. Ghosts possess people. You said so yourself," Lucy said, finding confidence.

"True enough, Luce, true enough. Yet look at these people. This guy looks like he was stitched together by Doc Frankfurter. I'm surprised there isn't a bolt sticking though his nose." Michael prodded a body with his foot.

"It's Frankenstein," Lucy sighed. "You can read?" She attempted to glare through her helmet at Michael. Adam looked over the corpse Michael was spooked by. It was a patchwork of pieces. Strangely proportioned. One arm was larger than the other, skin was mismatched. There weren't the scarred seams one would expect if seemingly random

Space Junk

body parts were fused together into a person.

"I donn' think that's our specialist," Michael said, studying the corpse. "Its eyes are too far apart, and the arms are too long. No ghost would want to go in there." Adam and Lucy cocked their heads in confusion. "Adam this is probably where the ghost started, though. You could defiantly bring in a ghost with a body like this one."

"Right… I think we work our way up to the command deck and see what we can see up there. Maybe get something out of the computer systems. If we don't find anything we bag up what we can here and bounce. It's not like anything else fits the description." Adam said, waving the others out the door. "Command deck and then payday. This place is giving me the creeps."

"With the state of the station, I would be surprised if the computers give us anything useful," Lucy said, leading the group back to the forum. "I got a feeling that we are looking for whatever dismembered those people rather than the fused guy."

"You're prolly right, Luce," Michael said. "I just hope it's more ghost than wraith. Wraith would be the rippin' people apart kind of ghost."

"Michael, you are rather caught up on the supernatural. You sure it isn't going to be something like a virus or fungus?" Adam said as they floated towards the center of the station and the elevators.

"The Broker ain't interested in gettin' sick. He's interested in two things: Power and Women. How many women you getting with mushrooms and a bad cough? Maybe Luce, she seems to be into weird stuff like that," Michael mused as they approached the elevators.

"Rude!" Lucy said, not looking up from her tablet as she worked to bypass the elevator security. "A lot of this is fried; no I can't fix it." Lucy gestured with her helmet, replacing the annoyed look she would have usually shot Adam. "I can't get them to stop here, can send them to opposite ends and lock them there. We'd have to cut the doors open. Michael, we got enough for that?"

"Yah Luce, although I'd rather use less than more. Unless you got a spare tank of gas?" Michael said, starting to set up the torch. "Adam, can we hit the engineering section as well? More tools is more tools after all."

"Command end first, see if it's open. Besides, who knows what state the engineering section is in?" Adam then thumbed his radio. "Steven, you still out there?"

"Right on time, Boss," Steven's voice came back across the radio. "What's the plan over there?"

"We're headed to the command deck, seeing if we can't get a better read of what's what over here. If we can't walk in, we are headed to engineering to see if we can't get more cutting gear. I have a feeling we may need to cut open and weld shut more than a few doors." Adam was scanning the room, "Honestly, we are all on edge over here. Lot of creepy things over here."

"I hear that. Boss, let me know if you want to come back for a bit. I'd rather not burn you all out over there," Steven said, concern in his voice.

"Copy, we are at least attempting to get to the command station first," Adam said, as Michael cut open the doors. "Call you when we find something."

"Stay safe in there," Steven said, signing off.

The doors to the elevator opened once Michael finished cutting though them. Before he could say anything, a voice spoke, "Hello visitors! Hmm, perhaps you are salvagers or bandits. I would prefer visitors. I've been quite lonely." The suave voice was male. "Regardless of what you are, I'd like

Space Junk

to make a deal. It may cost you an arm or a leg, but I'm sure it's better than the alternatives."

Michael froze. "Th-that didn't come though the communications, or the intercom. I-eh-it must be a ghost."

"There's no such thing as ghosts. Must be some kind of prank message. You know the kind of speaker pranks kids like to leave," Lucy said, not quite as rattled.

"It doesn't matter what it is, plan stays the same," Adam said, attempting to take charge. "We hit engineering, then command. Strange voices or not. Job's a job and plan's a plan." Lucy nodded in agreement. Michael was still quivering with fear. Regardless, they entered the elevator shaft and began making their way down towards engineering.

"It's a ghost. What else would it be? Probably a wraith, it's gunna try and eat us," Michael said, whispering a bit too loudly into his microphone. "We should jump off the job, and go home before things get worse."

"Let's call Steven and let him know what's up. We can make a call with the ship's sensors." Adam attempted to calm him down.

"Ship would be able to tell us if there's anyone else alive here. Cryo would have hidden them from sensors," Lucy offered, clearly trying to find any other solution than Michael's. "Hey Steven, you there?"

The radio was silent.

"Steven, can you hear us?" Adam said, hoping his longer-range radio could reach the *Corvus*. There was no reply. "We should go back up. See if we can get a hold of Steven." Michael and Lucy mumbled in agreement.

A rumbling noise made all of them look up. An elevator car was falling towards them. "Above!" The group scattered as the elevator car fell off its track and collided with the neighboring one, blocking the path down. "Sound

Grathew

off, who's alive?" Adam said, checking his suit for leaks.

"I'm good," Lucy said, giving Adam a wave.

"I think I may have zigged when I should have zagged." Michael's voice had just enough static to show something was wrong. "I'm in one piece, but I'm on the bottom side of these cars. Think y'all are on the top side."

"We are," Adam looked over wreckage. "Do you think we can shift this stuff around to link up?"

"I wouldn't do that, looks like it caught a live wire. If it don't fry us when you touch it, it's gunna weld itself together in a bit." Michael's voice was still distorted. "Think it's messin' with the radio too. I can probably get down and power it off from the engineering bay. I'll keep the comms open so you can hear me talk to my tools."

"Lucy and I will find another way around. I don't want to split up any more than needed," Adam said, pulling open the door on the floor above the jammed elevator cars. "Don't do anything too reckless, Michael."

"I'll do what I can, but I ain't sittin' around with a ghost huntin' us. You keep our princess safe up there. Worst to worst, tell my mama I died gloriously," Michael forced a laugh.

"Gallows humor isn't your style. Stay safe down there," Adam said as the lever finally budged and the door opened. "We got a door open here. Plan is go up, call Steven, and then back down to you. Clear, Michael?"

"I got it. Torchy and I will make our way to the reactor and start pushing buttons," Michael said. "Just make sure you watch out for that ghost."

Adam and Lucy found gravity on this deck. "What do you think that voice really was?" Lucy said on a direct line to Adam. "I doubt it was a ghost, but Michael was right, it didn't come though the radio. I don't want to give him ideas,

Space Junk

but he might be right." Michael's ramblings about spooky corners underlined her point rather well.

"I honestly don't know. I assumed it came though the intercom," Adam said, trying not to validate Michael's theories.

"The system that shouldn't be working under these conditions? Let alone the lack of life signs on the station," Lucy said, nervously looking over her shoulder. "I think we just get the bumpkin, and get out of here. Tell The Broker that we couldn't find it, because we can't, and take the hit to our reputation. That or call him up and tell him we need more bodies."

"I could use some more bodies, living ones preferably," the voice returned. Lucy and Adam reflexively went back to back, weapons raising. "You don't need to be so hostile. I just want to borrow a limb or two. Maybe an eye, I could use better eyes. This set needs glasses."

"Who and what are you?" Lucy shouted into the ruined hallways.

"Hmm, that is a good question. According to this tag, I'm SH-138, but I've never liked name tags. I do presume that I am your specimen. Thus, we should be working together to get off this station," the voice seemingly coming from within their heads. "Thus, we should make a deal. I get put back together, you all get paid."

"Luce how you get round firewalls again? I'm getting computer issues." Michael's voice came through the radio.

"Thinking about it, he may be a better person to talk to, his mind isn't as closed to things beyond him," the voice said, followed by the sound of wind, and proximity alarms going off in their suits.

"Michael, something's headed your way!" Adam shouted into his radio. The line was quiet. "We need to work our way down there." Adam started moving, "Steven, you hear me?"

"Loud and clear, Boss, you're early, what's up?" Steven's voice was perfectly clear.

"Michael may have been right with the ghost theory," Adam said, stepping over bodies. "I don't know how, but he may have been right."

"Right. What's the plan?" Steven paused. "Kay says there's a weird energy signature over there, and a lot of movement."

"Lucy and I are split off from Michael, elevator car came down the shaft as we were headed to engineering. Plan is: get Michael and get out. Ideally, everyone in one piece. I don't know where we are going to come out of here. I don't want to work our way back to our entry point." Adam found an open maintenance ladder, "I think we found a way down. Might run into interference again."

"I copy all, Boss. Stay safe out there. Fill me in when we all get back here," Steven said, signing off.

"I'll go first," Adam said to Lucy. "I'm liking this less and less."

"Michael has stopped broadcasting. Think he's still alive?" Lucy said. "I know it could be interference, but that wasn't normal."

"Even if he's dead, he wouldn't want to be left here. 'Gotta take me back to Mama,' or something like that," Adam said, trying not to think of the worst of the worst options. Lucy nodded, and the two of them made their way down the maintenance shaft. As they went down deck by deck, the station was more ruined. "Michael, you out there? Can you hear me?" Adam called after the third deck.

There was no reply.

"This should be the engineering deck," Lucy said,

Space Junk

looking up from her tablet. "Does the door open?" Adam tried it, and it opened into a ruined hallway. Panels were twisted, soot coated everything, and dismembered bodies floated. "That's bad," Lucy gasped.

"Yep, Michael should be out there, though. How far to main engineering?" Adam said, starting down the hallway. "Michael you out here?"

"Hey, I figured out what's wrong with the power. The reactor wasn't shut down, so the batteries blew. That's what did in the station. You guys down here yet? It's getting spooky," Michael said through a new wave of radio interference.

"Yah, we are on your deck, the ghost is coming for you." Adam said, hoping Michael heard him.

"Next left, then it should be straight shot into main engineering," Lucy said. "Michael, we are probably five minutes, then we should get out of here."

"Got all of that. Ghost seems not to be bothering me too much. Strange bugs down here. I think we grab one and offer that up as the specimen. I don't want to catch a ghost," Michael said, clearly focusing on something else. "I shot a big one. Maybe there's little ones we can shove in a box or something?"

"Let's figure it out once we meet up. Stay there, don't worry about getting power online. Just stay safe," Adam ordered.

"Right, I'll button this up and see y'all soon," Micheal responded.

"Oh yes, those pesky insects. I could use some help dealing with them, I can't do anything with them. You all, on the other hand, are full of good parts. I'd rather you not feed them to the insects." The voice was clearly annoyed. "The last group just couldn't help themselves. Now I'm

Grathew

stuck suffering for their stupidity." Adam and Lucy ignored the voice, working their way through the hallway. Egg sacs and strange growths of organic paste appeared. "I'd be careful, those insects are technically crabs."

"I got life signs closing in, could be the bugs. Could be the voice," Lucy said, silencing her tablet. "Michael, we're a few doors down."

"I hear ya, the creepy crawlies on their way?" Michael said, clearly struggling with something. "I think I can get enough power to fix the interference to the *Corvus*."

A clicking noise came from around a corner, Adam gestured to Lucy, signaling "Let me go first." He rounded the corner to see a cream and blue-colored alien picking apart one of its brothers. Adam signaled, "Let's keep quiet." The two snuck past the strange creature. More of the packed biomass. "I think they are building a nest," Adam mumbled into the radio.

"Yah, they donn' hear too well. So you don't need to whisper. They seem to be able to smell fear though," Michael responded. "I think they workin' with the ghost."

"I assure you, I refuse to work with such lower lifeforms. You humans are bad enough," the voice said, its tone dripping with annoyance. "If you all are done with whatever it is you're doing, I do have a deal I'd like to purpose."

"Nope, I ain't makin' any deals with ghosts," Michael said, shutting the voice down. "Hey Flyboy, you hear us?"

"Hey Mikey, yah, I hear you. How's ghost hunting?" Steven said.

"Well, we found one, damn spooky too." Michael said. "I'm more worried 'bout these bugs. They seem to be eatin' this place."

"Boss, what's the play?" Steven said.

Space Junk

"Grab Michael, stuff a bug in a container, and get back to The Broker," Adam said, sneaking past a larger bug that was consuming a corpse, "Ideally with everyone in one piece." The bug stopped and twitched, as if it was smelling the air. It turned and stared at Adam. Adam shot it.

The gunshot echoed through the ruined station. The bug dropped dead. Clicking soon filled the air as bugs reacted to the noise. "You may want to run," the voice sighed.

Adam and Lucy ran down the hall into engineering, gunning down a couple of the smaller bugs along the way. "Michael, hit the door!" Adam called, sliding around the corner, gunning down another charging bug. The engineering doors slammed shut behind Lucy. "How do we get out of here? Preferably without going through those things. Ideas."

"We could take torchy here, burn though the hull near the edge, and let the atmosphere toss us out into space," Michael said.

"According to the computers, there's an airlock up a deck, should be able to get out there. Nice wide hallways should let us fight our way past them. Doors are even sealed off from the bug hive, assuming that's what this big biomass is on the sensors," Lucy said, reading from her tablet. "I think it's better than trying to burn our way out."

"Might I offer a deal?" the voice said. "If I could borrow some parts, an arm, leg, and eyes, I will be able to get you all out safely. Which is a win-win."

"We ain't dealin' with any ghost. You can go, haunt the bugs or the station, or whatever!" Michael shouted. The bugs banged on the door. "Whatever we're doing, we should do it now."

"Airlock! Lucy, point us in a direction," Adam said. Lucy opened a door from her tablet. No bugs in sight, the trio ran for it. A few of the smaller bugs crawled out of vents but didn't seem to notice them. "I'd like to grab one."

"You know it's too risky. The creepy-crawlies only like us with a side of fries," Michael said as they entered another elevator shaft. "Two decks up?"

"Two decks up," Lucy said, checking her tablet. "We may want to go three, there seems to be a bug nest between this shaft and us."

"My deal still stands. I can clear the way." The voice was clearly attempting to be persuasive.

"Ghost, if I sees you, and you stop bein' a voice in my head. Ma don't like it when I listen to the voices in my head!" Michael shouted.

"I can meet you four, well, three decks up now. Present my case in person," the voice said. "I'm aware that this isn't the most professional of communications."

The group stoppe and looked at each other. "I don't trust a ghost. Ma don't like 'em; I don't like 'em. Rather gun though the bugs than deal with a damn ghost," Michael started the conversation.

"For once I agree," Lucy said.

"Aww, Thanks Luce," Michael said. Lucy shot him a murderous look.

"We should keep moving. I'd rather not run into the ghost, But on that floor, there's some damage. Could cut through the floor and drop back down. Would keep us farther from the bugs," Lucy said, highlighting the route on her tablet. "It is safer. Well, outside of the ghost."

The sound of bending metal and insect clicking came from down the shaft. "I doubt the ghost would hurt us. Safer is safer," Adam said, deciding. A few of the larger warrior bugs started climbing their way up the elevator shaft. "Quickly. Lucy, can you get the door open?"

Space Junk

"I'll need more time," Lucy said, starting to bypass the door. Adam acknowledged her by opening fire on the bugs. Michael followed suit. The bullets pushed the bugs back down the shaft. "Got it!"

The door slid open. The three jumped through it. The door slammed shut behind them.

"I may have triggered the lock down on the elevator shaft accidentally. We will have to cut down to the airlock," Lucy said, rather exasperated.

"You did good. We are on our way out of here," Adam said.

"Stay back, you ghost!" Michael shouted, raising his rifle. A man came around a corner, hands raised. His clothes were ill-fitting, and his skin was a mixture of hues. His eyes were silvery, behind rather feminine glasses. His left leg was a stump, his right arm coated in a chitinous growth.

"As I said before, I'm not a ghost," he said. "My name is Cartaphilus. I want to go home, as do you. If I can borrow an arm, and a leg, I can work some magic and get us all back to your ship safely." Cartaphilus floated towards the group, somehow not held down by the artificial gravity. "I assure you, it won't hurt. Well, the leg might feel a bit strange. The bug growths are a bit unpleasant, but they aren't going to be a bother for too long."

Michael took off running. "I donn' wanna get possessed! Leave me alone!" Adam and Lucy took off after him. However, Michael was fast, and dropping things left and right. They lost him round a corner, the cutting torch left on the floor.

"Michael, where are you?" Adam said.

There was no response.

"Hey Boss, what's going on over there? Where do you need me?" Steven called in. "You've been quiet."

Grathew

"Found the ghost, it's a dude. Creepy dude, but a dude. Still don't know how he talked to us. Michael is freaking out and gone. These bugs are a problem, I think they are coming. I don't know if we have time to get to him." The clicking of the bugs started to get closer. "We have the cutting tools, will cut our way out. See if you can raise Michael and get him to…" Adam shot Lucy a look.

"Section A9 deck 12," Lucy said, finishing the statement.

"Got it," Steven said. "I'll work my way around the station to that side. Stay safe over there."

"I don't want to abandon Michael," Lucy said. "I can't stay here." She was pleading.

"We get out, I'll pick up more gear and come back. Assuming we can't find him before we get out," Adam said, picking up the cutting torch. "He's tough, he can hold on till I come back." Lucy didn't seem convinced. "Where are we going to cut through?"

"This way," Lucy said, leading Adam down the hallway. "You know I didn't mind the nickname."

Adam cut her off. "He'll be back. Michael is a tough bastard," We will see him again." Then they walked in silence for a bit. Only the sounds of the bugs crawling around the station.

"Here, between these bulkheads. Should put us right outside the airlock." Lucy was starting to come undone.

"Lucy, we will get out of here," Adam said, starting to cut through the floor.

"I can bring him back to you," Cartaphilus said in his ghostly way. "Back and in one piece. I won't need bits for very long."

"Go away, I don't want to hear you. If it weren't for you, Michael wouldn't have run off." Adam didn't stop burning his way through the floor. "Can you just leave us

Space Junk

alone? You've done quite enough."

"Fine, I'll be charitable. Don't do anything too stupid," Cartaphilus said. "I will expect you to realize I'm not objectively evil after this."

"Yes, because subjectively evil is much better," Lucy spat. Cartaphilus remained silent. Lucy's tablet beeped. "Adam, the bugs are coming this way."

Adam nodded, focusing on cutting. The clicking started closing in. Lucy opened up on the bugs as Adam kept working on cutting the floor.

"I'm through!" Adam said as the panel fell to the floor below. "Lucy! Go!" Adam called as he opened up on the horde that was now spilling into the hallway. Lucy jumped down the hole, Adam following quickly behind.

Lucy then led Adam at a run through the station. The sounds of bugs closing in all around them. Arriving at the airlock, Lucy went to work opening the door.

A man stumbled around a corner, seemingly confused, covered in the bluish ichor of the bugs. "Michael?" Adam called out to the man, who stumbled his way, nodding.

"My radio isn't..." he started before Adam opened fire on another wave of bugs closing in. Lucy got the airlock open.

"Steven, we're in the airlock, come get us!" Adam said, ushering everyone into the airlock, which started cycling as they entered.

"Copy, Boss. On my way," Steven replied, as the external doors opened. The *Corvus* drifted into view. "Door's open, get on board." The trio jumped across, landing in the *Corvus*' airlock, which started cycling. "Getting us to a safe distance," Steven said as the *Corvus* lurched, knocking everyone to the ground.

"Michael, are you okay?" Adam said, picking himself

Grathew

up from the ground. He then took a closer look at the man they'd pulled off of the station. It wasn't quite Michael. He seemed distracted, his eyes were glassed over.

"Yah, I'm fine. I think I've conquered my fear of ghosts," he said.

The Spider in the House of Chosroes
by Joseph M. Isenberg

Time: 31 October, 8032 AD
Place: The Residence of Tim and Clarissa Perkins, Residency District, Old City, Planet Halcon V

I looked around at the downstairs spaceport terminal on Halcon V. It was quiet, and old; even though the Comrades had been out of power on Halcon for decades, the place was still a little rough and dingy. I hoped to meet my ride into town. I wasn't long disappointed.

"Mr. Kirkwell? I'm Tim Perkins." The newcomer held out a hand, which I grasped eagerly. Despite being youngish, and very much out of place with a ruddy complexion and reddish hair, he otherwise looked like something from a picture of the old, pre-revolutionary Kingdom of Halcon, elegantly attired in a light summer suit.

"Pleased to meet you, Mr. Perkins, after corresponding for so long," I said. "I'm afraid the shuttle ran late, and to make matters worse, I just had a message from my hotel. They canceled my reservation, saying they've started 'renovations.' I have no idea where to go now. Do you have any ideas?"

"Common enough, Mr. Kirkwell. 'Renovations,' on Halcon V, really means, 'We don't feel like opening up a room for you, so beat it.' Welcome to Halcon, in other words. Everything happens, but nothing happens very urgently, and customer service is just something that happens on other planets. You can stay with us for a day or two, while we conduct business. We have lots of room. My wife and I laid on a little dinner party this evening. You're welcome to join us for that as well."

"I wouldn't want to intrude."

"Not at all. You'll have a chance to meet the owner of the company. He's one of the guests. Tomorrow will be plenty of time to negotiate business deals. We're very eager to earn a contract from the largest mining company on New Cornwall, at certainty. But tonight, we'll all be friends together. That's part of life on Halcon, too."

"Then, friend, I say, lead on!" Perkins took my luggage, and we went out to his waiting grav-car.

We flew at low altitude through the streets of the city, along dusty, tree-lined streets, past an enormous park, and past the massive Viceroy's palace. By then, we were in the old part of town.

"My wife and I were lucky enough to find a dilapidated villa here, just next to the palace compound. We've been fixing it up as we can ever since. It's not convenient to the office, but it has space for a growing family, a nice yard, and a wall so the children can play without wandering too far. Very secure, and close to a good school."

"You have children, then, Mr. Perkins."

"Call me, Tim. Clarissa and I have three so far," he said. "Because of the party, we've sent them off visiting my

The Spider in the House of Chosroes

wife's parents for the evening. We won't be disturbed."

The Perkins house may have started as a dilapidated villa, but it wasn't dilapidated any longer.. The repair had progressed a long way, and perhaps only a few cosmetic touches remained. Tim, Clarissa, or both, had a good eye, and the furniture was substantial, elegant, and old. The collection was fairly eclectic as well. The sort of thing a young man who affected an old soul might seek out, buy, and treasure.

There were antique desks and chairs from Stratford, for example, and a collection of rare, old Halconic religious paintings on glass, hanging on one wall. There were icons of St. Timothy and St. Clare, a very old rendition of St. Brendan the Space-Farer, suitable for a Space Fleet family, together with one of St. Michael, and another of St. George, with his obligatory dragon. The whole was surmounted by a beautiful image of Christ, Mary, and St. John the Baptist. Those must have cost a fortune to assemble, for little religious art survived the Revolution on Halcon.

Perkins must have sensed my curiosity, if not my reasoning. "I wasn't born on Halcon," he said. "I come off Planet Stratford, originally. My wife's from here, so we settled. Some of the things remind me of home, though, and of friends, so I keep them by me. The others are fairly typical of every home on Halcon V."

The rest of the guests had already assembled. Everyone was waiting in the parlor for my arrival before the start of dinner. I reddened slightly at the thought of holding up the parade.

"Clarissa and I just asked the neighbors around. We do this every year on the day, as something of a Stratford tradition," Perkins began. "We make it an excuse for a party."

He paused with me at the entrance to the parlor.

Joseph M. Isenberg

"Everyone, this is Henry Kirkwell from New Cornwall Mining and Metals. He's visiting us on business for a few days. Mr. Kirkwell, this is my wife, Clarissa."

Somehow, I remembered the correct Halconic response, though not the exact words. "I kiss your fingers, madame."

She smiled, graciously.

"You've corresponded with my boss at Clevermann Gravitic Tractors, I think," Perkins continued. "Here he is in the flesh, Ed Clevermann, with his wife, Iva. They have a vacation cottage on the east side of my house."

I saw the place as we drove up. Perkins' idea of a "cottage" was very different from my own. The Clevermann's were at the far end of the room, and so we simply smiled and nodded at one another. Neither seemed much older than Perkins or his wife.

Perkins wasn't done. "Iva's parents, Admiral and Lady Watson-ffyre, live in the cottage on the west side of the house and are visiting as well."

Admiral Watson-ffyre commanded the Imperial Space Fleet. His wife was a fairly popular entertainer and occasional meddler in politics. Perkins, it seemed, travelled in exalted circles.

"Finally, though by no means least, Admiral James Hargreaves, who retired to Halcon V. Perhaps he'll tell us something of his adventures."

I smiled at the notion. Not all the Fleet people I knew were exactly forthcoming about their adventures.

We went in for dinner. It was served in a formal dining room, of a sort not often seen in many modern houses. There were heavy chairs and a long dining table. The table was flanked on either end by ornate, carved sideboard cabinets, covered with cloth. Tim and Clarissa busied themselves for

The Spider in the House of Chosroes

a few minutes, ferrying covered trays and plates and pans of food out to the sideboards.

"We'll serve the meal Stratford-style, I think," Perkins said. "Treat it like a buffet and graze as you like."

Although the service was Stratford-style, the food was utterly unfamiliar, with the odd, spiced dishes of Halcon. It was novel, but it was wonderfully unforgettable.

As we ate, far too much, if I'm honest, we lingered at the table, chatting of this and that, until dinner was over.

"Shall we have," Clarissa asked Tim, "that other Stratford custom, of ghost stories?"

I tried to avoid scoffing a little, but I wasn't totally surprised when Perkins said, "Yes, I think so, *carissima maxima*. Let's adjourn to the office." He rose, and led us to a heavily paneled room, where he kept his work desk, and a small cabinet and bar for business visitors. The seats were vastly more comfortable, and there were plenty of places for all, even if we were a bit cramped. Perkins dimmed the lights a little bit as he went in.

Iva's mother said, "I seem to recall, Jim, you said something once about encountering a ghost, but you never have told the story."

"Nor do I want to now, Emm. There are worse things than mere ghosts, and things man was not meant to meet."

"Surely that's a bit extreme, Admiral."

"You are blessed, Mr. Kirkwell, to live in peaceful times," Hargreaves said. "But civilization always hangs by a thread, and I have spent my career keeping the thread safe. Still, since Emm insists, I will start off.

"It began—perhaps, what, sixty, no sixty-five years ago now. I was a Senior Lieutenant, newly promoted as such. I served in the Navigation Bureau of the Imperial Space Fleet. You may not fully understand, Mr. Kirkwell, what that means, as you are the only one here who is not a space bum, or married to one. As a practical matter, navigators have constant work driving ships into and through hyperspace. There are not many of us. The work is mentally challenging. Some would even say 'deranging.'"

I nodded.

"I aspired to higher command, so instead of taking a navigator's billet on a larger ship, I took a post as the executive officer on a patrol cruiser, the *Shackleton*. We were to spend a year in and out of your stomping ground, based at the spaceport of New Cornwall. But instead of staying there, we were to patrol the five or six star systems near it. There is nothing in any of them but asteroids. Our job was to bring such law and order as we could to the miners."

"A forlorn hope," I said.

"Quite so, and it should have been simple. Life droned on during that time, as life does. A few months into the posting, we had just precipitated into the star system 125 Epilox-beta. There are only a handful of asteroids there, and only one or two mining rocks."

I nodded. I said, "Anyone going there wanted to be well out in the sticks, desperate, or both."

"We expected to jump in, look briefly, refuel the vessel from the gas giant there, and evaporate back out. But, we heard a distress call. Well, an *Explorer*-class patrol cruiser can put on a good turn of speed when it has to, if it is well-maintained."

"I've seen you putting a boot up a maintenance crews' behinds a time or two before, Jim," said Admiral Watson-ffyre. "I shouldn't have liked to be your engine master."

"Exactly, Reg. Take care of the ship and all that. We were ready for everything, or so we thought. But we weren't ready for what we found.

The Spider in the House of Chosroes

"We discovered the signal came from a prospecting ship, in outstanding condition. It was drifting in space, with not a mark on it."

"Were the airlocks blown?" Clevermann asked.

"No, no sign of a boarding action or hull breach, either. We had to blow the airlocks ourselves when we sent a boarding party over. Oddest bedamned thing you ever saw in your life. Ed, Tim, I know both of you have fought a boarding action or two. Do you know much about the Fleet, Mr. Kirkwell?"

"No, I avoid going into space if I can help it. I don't much care for the sensations." But I understood now the ties that brought the rest of the dinner guests together.

"Wise man," Hargreaves agreed. "Ships are easily damaged in any kind of fighting. Even mag rifle shots can puncture the hull if you are not careful. That is what made it odd. The ship, Mr. Kirkwell, was utterly unscathed. Everything was functional, but the crew.

"The crew, that was horrible. There were bodies everywhere, in the most appalling, gruesome, contorted positions. Some few had missing limbs, though it was almost as though a surgeon removed them medically. They all had one thing in common, a look of pure, undisguised horror, though of what or whom, neither I nor any of the crew could fathom a guess. It was the oddest crime scene one could ever expect to find, for crime scene it was, and we were the law, with neither Imperial constables nor Fleet investigative officers to give us a steer on the right path."

"Were all the bodies like that?" Tim asked.

"No, not all, Perkins. We found one survivor. He was a battered, bruised man, more carcass than body, and so imponderably old we originally mistook him for a husk. He breathed a tiny bit, and the Doctorbotix machine confirmed he lived a while yet, though neither it nor the *Shackleton's* medic held out much hope."

Hargreaves paused a moment. "Do you suppose I could have something, Perkins?"

Tim nodded, and went wordlessly to his bar. A moment later, he passed a Halcon Eliberada over to Hargreaves. He made one for everyone else as well, then took a red berry juice and soda for himself. He sat back down next to his desk. Hargreaves resumed his tale.

"Well, we did not dare even move the old man to the cruiser. Instead, we thrust him in a cryogenic chamber, right there in the medical bay of the mining vessel. The skipper and I had a conference.

"Neither of us could quite believe the old man was the perpetrator. He looked scarcely able to move, for he had almost no muscles to speak of. On the other hand, he had an astonishing number of forged identi-discs when we looked through his cabin."

"Nothing odd about that," I said, "not out in the mining region."

"Indeed not, Mr. Kirkwell. Many crave anonymity. I crave it myself. But, think of the most furtive, devious miner you know. He might have, perhaps, two identities? Three? So many as half-a-dozen?"

"Doubtful that many," I said. "They're expensive to make, I hear."

"Then what would you say, Mr. Kirkwell, to fifty such. The oldest stretched back nearly a hundred years from the time we found the ship, and was for one 'J. Cartaphilus Ahasver.'"

"That was his name?" I asked.

"Perhaps," Hargreaves agreed. "Even that was for an adult, full-grown, and middle-aged."

The Spider in the House of Chosroes

"What did the genetic data say?" Clarissa wondered.

"Another perplexity. No two identi-discs matched. Some matched the old man, and some did not, even though they had his picture."

"That's not possible," Tim said. "Either only one should, or all the data should be the same."

"No, Perkins, be precise in your language. It should not be possible, yet there it was. It was pretty clear to the commander and me that some bigger crime occurred here, and that the old man had something to do with it. We hoped to keep him alive long enough to get to the bottom of it. We also hoped to collect the salvage money, if the prospecting vessel was a wreck, or the bounty money, if it was a criminal ship. The holds were filled with minerals, and the ship itself would fetch a tidy sum when it went for auction, if we could just wrestle her back to New Cornwall. The Imperial Legate's court and the lawyers could sort out the details.

"The skipper and I agreed that I should command the salvage crew, since I could also navigate. He also assigned me the medic, a pretty good assistant engine master, and two or three able spacemen. None of the ship's troops went, since neither the skipper nor I thought there was any danger."

Hargreaves took a long pull on his drink. "We made the crew transfers, and started. The prospecting ship needed to refuel. That would take some time, so I began work with that task. The *Shackleton* finished its refueling quickly, and evaporated out, bound for New Cornwall to start the legal proceedings.

"A week passed. We fueled fully, and properly. I laid in a course, and the medic approached me.

" 'Odd thing, sir,' he began, 'is the patient seems to be recovering in the cryogenic tube. In a day or two, we might be able to have him out and in a normal bed.'

"That completed the book of the good news. Twelve hours after we finished fueling and started for the transit point, the drive plates on the main intra-luminary engines overheated and gave way. We spent a couple of weeks creeping out to the hyperspace distance using just the fine maneuver plates."

The Fleet folks present all winced in unison. Even I realized it sounded awful.

"By the time we reached transit point, the old man was out of the tube and into a bed. He could even talk a little bit. On my insistence, he confirmed that the oldest of the identi-discs was his. He was Cartaphilus Ahasver."

"Was he really that old?" Clarissa asked.

"Older, he claimed. He told me that the ancients had a theory about the soul. They argued that a physical human body could live and exist only if it was kept animated by the soul. He told me, though I laughed, that he alone of all souls was fated to continue inhabiting a body, and that he had done so for nearly eight millennia."

"The ravings of a madman," Admiral Watson-ffyre said.

"Perhaps, Reg. I thought that, too. But the old duffer went on. He claimed that he learned methods to extend his body, to regenerate it, if you will. Well, I thought, that was part of his ranting.

"But on the other hand, there were certain details that gave some credence to his tale, besides the fact that he was undoubtedly old, if not that old. He had extraordinary history of the ancients. He was able to tell me of events, and of places, on Planet Home, where he had travelled, where he had been. He was either the most advanced savant, and scholar, and archaeologist, and historian of my generation, Reg, or he was a participant. That was his level of detailed

The Spider in the House of Chosroes

knowledge."

"You must have been in your absolute heaven, Jim," Admiral Watson-ffyre said.

"At that moment, Reg, yes. I was fascinated with everything he said, took notes, and determined to check, as I could, his information.

"His problem, he claimed, was that the longer time went on, the harder it became for him to regenerate or replace his injured, withering body. A soul can only animate so much, for so long, and while his knowledge was immense, his soul was, by now, sub-par for the simple problem of keeping on.

"I asked him precisely what he meant by that. He asked me to take him into the navigation suite of the *Shackleton*, to put a navigation headset on him, and to put on one myself. He proposed to show me, through the navigational neural link on the ship's computer."

Iva Clevermann seemed stunned by the notion. "Is that even possible, Admiral Hargreaves? I've heard of the old dual navigator experiments, back in the day, but, c'mon, those never worked. I think we've given the idea up in the Bureau of Navigation. It would be dangerous, in any event."

"I agree, Iva. You know more about the current state of the research. In my day, the Navigation Bureau never talked about the early experiments, for good reason. I was doubtful, too."

The pair chattered on for some while about the finer points of navigational work, with Admiral Watson-ffyre, Perkins, and Ed Clevermann adding an opinion or two along the way. I followed absolutely none of it. I finally gave in to curiosity, and asked, "So, did you try the experiment or not, Admiral?"

"I was skeptical it would even work, but decided to humor the old man. I told the medic to find him a wheelchair, and I would wheel him in. We went to the navigation console. I hooked him up, then hooked up myself."

We all shifted a bit nervously in our seats. Hargreaves grew a bit grim, and paused a long time before he went on. We all looked at him.

"I found myself almost in a trance. I do not know how else to describe it, and it was like no feeling I have ever had at the navigation console. We were not on the ship, either. It was perhaps some private corner of the old man's mind, or perhaps someplace else, a corner of hyperspace. It seemed like Planet Home. The air was filled with smoke, and though it was daylight, and sunny, there was a steady gray haze. There was, everywhere, the stench of death. Bodies lay strewn, unburied, and carrion crows flocked everyplace.

"'What is this place?' I asked.

"'This, James Hargreaves, is my doing, my handiwork,' the old man said. Somehow, he seemed fit, mobile.

"'You know it, if you know it at all, as Stamboul. A ruin now on your planet, with scarcely one stone standing on another. But in my day, it was at the center, the City of the World's Desire, as one fellow put it. It was occasionally taken by treachery, but only once by fair conquest. That, too, James Hargreaves, was my doing. I made the guns for the Conqueror.'

"I looked around. I could see, a few streets away, a massive, domed church. There were many fine buildings nearby, but no people moved.

"'Why?' I asked. 'Why destroy all this?'

"'Vengeance. Spite. My will was thwarted, and that, James Hargreaves, is ever a mistake. You see the aftermath. The date, if you wish to know, is the first of June, 1453. Only four days ago, the Conqueror stood here and recited poetry over my handiwork:'

The Spider in the House of Chosroes

"'The spider is the curtain-keeper in the Hall of Chosroes.'
"'The owl sounds the hours in the castle of Afrasiyab.'

"At that moment," Hargreaves dropped his voice to barely a whisper, "I believed him. Oh Merciful Great Author, I believed every bit of him. So, I could barely bring myself to ask, 'Why are you showing me this?'

"'I need you, James Hargreaves. Millennia ago, I was cursed. I could not die, but I continued to age. I was able to regenerate my body, not by taking parts, as I must now, but by taking a willing soul, by entering into a partnership with him. I cannot die, but I age nevertheless.'

"'Why should I do that?' I asked.

"'I sense that you are like me. You yearn for knowledge. You know that gives you the ultimate power over your fellow man. You are a kindred spirit.'"

"You're nothing of the sort," Lady Watson-ffyre said.

"Oh, Emm, you of all people know me better than that. I am very much like that, with only one exception, which is a limit. But in that moment, I recognized the old man for what he was. He had two attributes that I did not, besides his age. He was dying, even though he was not yet dead. That made him desperate. And he was dedicated only to his own ends. Whether that made him evil, or just amoral, is a nice question which we could debate all night. But the two factors together made him extremely dangerous. And there, wherever there was, was a place where he still had some vitality. I was fascinated, but I also realized I had to do something."

"Why couldn't you just rip off the headset?" I asked.

"Navigation computers on spaceships do not work that way, Mr. Kirkwell. They are easy to plug into, but to take off the headset, you must shut them down properly. Otherwise, it is very dangerous to the synapses."

Joseph M. Isenberg

Hargreaves sipped from his drink, finished it, and held it out to Tim. He nodded, took the glass, and started work on a refill.

Hargreaves started work on his tale, again. "The old man offered me something flat out. 'I know,' he said, 'that you will have to turn me over for an investigation when we reach New Cornwall. Answering those questions will be very unwelcome. Instead, why don't you help me? Work with me, and let me use your body as a vessel. All my knowledge and all my power, James Hargreaves, can be yours.'

"He reached for me at that moment, in that strange little vision we shared. I shied away. I doubted he would share anything; even in my youth I was not so big a fool as all that.

"I also guessed that I could shut down the navigation console eventually. I just needed to time to bring myself away from this shared…delusion? So, I reached down, and found a handy brick; the streets were littered with debris. I smacked the old man in the head with it, hard as I could, and sprinted off towards that domed church, fast as I could, as though the fear of the Infernal Ditch itself was upon me.

"I think that surprised him. He fell back for a moment, staggered. I had just enough of a head start to reach the plaza in front of the main entrance before he caught me up.

"But he did catch me up, as I was tearing up the steps and into the nave of that church, yelling like a banshee. The whole place was a ruin, looted, damaged beyond belief. All the hangings, the tapestries, the gold and silver were gone; many of the images had been destroyed or pried out, though the ones higher up were still intact. There were still bodies, though not so many as elsewhere.

"Yet in that church, somehow, there were a little party of monks, performing a service at what was left of the altar.

The Spider in the House of Chosroes

I bolted up to them, yelling, 'Help! For the love of all that's holy, help me!'

"What happened next was surreal. Some of the monks kept on with the service. From somewhere, others appeared, to join them. They wrestled with Cartaphilus Ahasver, and held him up. The last things that I remember were that one of the celebrants took me by the hand and walked over to one of the pendentive pillars supporting the dome. He said nothing, but just pulled me into it, as though there was a secret passage; there must have been, though I did not see it. As we entered, there was a brilliant flash of white light, and I remember nothing of the vision after that.

"The medic found both of us, slumped in our seats. The wiring of the navigation console, he told me, was smoking, and some circuits burned out. That was why the crew burst into the room in the first place. The old man slid completely out of his chair, and that ripped the headset away from him. That should have been fatal to one of his frail state, but his vital signs still barely registered. Some part of his brain, or something, kept him barely alive."

"I would have put him right out the nearest airlock."

"Yes, I daresay you would have, Perkins, and mayhaps you would have been right to do so. The investigation showed he killed every single other member of the crew on that prospecting ship, in his quest to keep his body functional. For his undoubted crimes and mayhem, going out an airlock would have been no better than Cartaphilus Ahasver deserved, and the galaxy would have been a better place for it.

"The idea crossed my mind. But I felt a certain awe, perhaps even reverence, and a sense that whatever I did, I must not do something like that.

"Well, I recovered enough to function again. The medic

told me the old man was bundled back into his cryogenic tube, his signs were stable, and bedamned but he was starting to recover slowly once more.

"I ordered the assistant engineer to load the cryogenic tube onto the prospecting ship's survey shuttle. Under the circumstances, I was willing to part with a few thousand Impers of salvage money in my account, and I would have thought it cheap at any number of times the price.

"The engineer readied that shuttle, and we saw to it that it had as much battery power as we could possibly contrive to give it, and as much fuel. The fusion reactor could go damned near indefinitely on low power, he assured me. I made a narrative record of what the old man told me, and loaded it, not only into the ship log, but into the shuttle data base.

"You know the astrography of the region as well as I do, Mr. Kirkwell. The New Cornwall district lies right on the edge of the Abyss Rift, with only a tiny number of systems beyond it until you reach the next galactic arm. And 125 Epilox-beta is the furthest point in the district. So, we just laid in a course and bundled the shuttle off across the Rift, on auto-pilot, at ordinary intra-luminary velocity. I took great care the course would not intersect any of the few systems within the Rift itself. The craft should not meet anyone until it is on the other side of the Rift. That will not happen for tens of thousands of years, at least. By that time, perhaps we will ourselves have colonized that area, but probably not. It will be a long time before J. Cartaphilus Ahasver is someone else's problem."

Hargreaves finished his tale and took another pull on his drink. He was visibly exhausted, but so were we all. The time was well past two in the morning. I knew I didn't want another ghost story, and I didn't think that anyone else did.

The Spider in the House of Chosroes

It was time to go. Tim Perkins rose. We all followed suit.

"You'll stay here tonight with us, Mr. Kirkwell. If you prefer to book into your hotel in the morning, we'll organize that. But you're equally welcome here for your entire visit."

"That's quite kind, Tim. Thanks." I went to the door of the office, but I couldn't resist one last question.

"Hargreaves," I said, "let me ask this. You say you escaped. But how do we know that this Cartaphilus Ahasver didn't win?"

"Well, Mr. Kirkwell, that is the root of the issue that got Cartaphilus Ahasver into trouble in the first place, is it not? Some things simply have to be believed, without being seen, as a matter of faith." He smiled and nodded. "Good night, Tim. Wonderful meal as always, Clarissa. I will see my own way home."

Hargreaves strode to the door, barely glancing at the house or the people around him. But I noticed he did give a very slight nod to those icons hanging on the parlor wall on the way out the door, as the guests all went out.

The Kotaran Mission: A Weapons of Legend Tale
by S. D. Croft

Non-Charter Space; Planet Monticari; Henu Mor Province in the Shan Mountains; Palace of the Great Lady Tempest (Formerly Queen Sha's Summer Palace); 18 July 2429 (Earth Reckoning).

The most feared order of mercenaries and assassins in the galaxy, only the Agnashi's ferocity and skill surpassed their advanced weaponry. Encased in form-fitting, custom armor, their helmet visors concealed their identities, adding to the order's mystique. Their skills with wrist-lasers comparable to the finest marksmen; an Agnashi could defeat multiple swordsmen with the *ruka'xac*, the two-bladed weapon synonymous with their order.

After the disastrous war with the Galactic Alliance and Independent Worlds, the surviving Agnashi numbered just two hundred, with five Agnashi Lords among them. Two centuries later, there were over two thousand Agnashi, not including two hundred fifty Agnashi Lords. The Agnashi-trained mercenaries under the Agnashi Lords' command numbered over three hundred thousand. Many of these men and women fled their home worlds as criminals. Selected and trained by the Agnashi, they served as soldiers or crew members on starships.

The Agnashi were commandos, capable of serving as small unit leaders or company commanders for Indigenous armies. Based on the mission, they operated alone, or in small groups of two to a dozen. Whether performing as mercenaries, assassins, or occasional bounty hunters, they charged exorbitant amounts. A single Agnashi could cost a client five hundred thousand per operation.

Like their subordinates, the Agnashi Lords operated alone or in small groups. An Indigenous army would hire an Agnashi Lord for millions, even billions, per operation. They would appoint the Agnashi Lord to command a brigade, division, corps, or even as a Field Marshal for that amount of money. The commando training of Agnashi Lords made them far deadlier than most field grade or flag officers from a standard military element.

Lord Farix was second in command of the entire Agnashi Order, outranked only by High Lord Blackhart himself. Respected by his peers, and feared by subordinates, many believed Lord Farix was the most dangerous in the order— perhaps the most dangerous man alive. They said Lord Farix was a sorcerer as powerful as any wizard. Other accounts said he was a wizard who left the Order of Light after a falling out. This is a fact: Lord Farix was among the five Agnashi Lords who began rebuilding the order two hundred years ago. At over two centuries old, Farix possessed a wizard's power, a field marshal's strategic mind, and an Agnashi's fighting prowess. Lord Farix was the most dangerous man alive.

The Kotaran Mission: A Weapons of Legend Tale

Then why the frick am I planning a wedding? Farix thought as he stood by Lady Tempest's chair at the head of the long table in the East Room, the site of many state dinners and diplomatic conferences. Ambassador Iren from Monticari and Ambassador Guang of Kor Prime were negotiating Tempest's marriage agreement with King Karsol of Kor Prime.

"The Great Lady's ability to bear children is, naturally, a concern of His Majesty's," Guang said.

"It would behoove you not to bring up the Great Lady's age," Farix said through his helmet's vocoder. At over eighty years old, the powerful sorceress's ageless beauty and litheness gave her the appearance of a twenty-five-year-old.

"As I look at the Great Lady, her beauty has no equal," Guang replied. "I assure you, Lord Farix, the Great Lady's age is the furthest thing from my mind."

"Then what is the issue, Ambassador?" Tempest asked, her greenish-blue eyes icy agates.

"Y-your knowledge of the Dark Arts, My Lady—"

"What of it?"

"A-as one who dabbles in sorcery from time to time, I'm aware—"

"We're not on a Charter World, Ambassador," Farix said. He pointed at the Tari/Zik'ral binary clone standing off the side with a drawn black hood, concealing his sharp-featured, Elf-like face covered by a sand-colored chitin. "There are methods available if they cannot have children conventionally."

"While on the subject," Lady Tempest said, "the king has a reputation for forcing himself on female servants." She smiled. "Once we're married, His Majesty's dalliances end."

"I-I...Yes, Great Lady—I assure you, we have no

knowledge of—"

"The king is not yet old enough to marry, but likely sired children. I trust you will deal with those women and children prior to our arrival on Kor Prime.

"O-of course, Great Lady."

"And let King Karsol know that I will not tolerate being groped and manhandled like one of his serving girls—"

"Lord Farix," General Goars said through commlink.

Skat! Right when this was getting interesting, Farix thought. "What is it?"

"Lord Khoeng wishes to speak with you—he says it's urgent."

He reached out telepathically to Lady Tempest. *There is something I must attend to. Lord Nyblis and Lord Scorpious will remain.*

I've got this well in hand, her voice echoed in the Agnashi's mind.

Guang is a sorcerer—

Of little consequence—he can barely light a candle—

Just be wary.

He reached out to Tempest's disciple, Lord Nyblis. Nyblis was a disgraced Na'dari known as Clive Dorgan from the Charter World Dirane, now part of the Carathian Empire.

Keep an eye on them—I don't trust these frickers.

Yes, My Lord, Nyblis replied, moving to replace Farix at Tempest's side.

As Farix approached the doorway, he stopped to speak with Lord Scorpious, their other disciple. "Monitor these ambassadors—I don't trust them."

The binary clone nodded, then grinned, bearing sharp, jagged Zik'ral teeth. "Yes, my Lord."

Farix took the mag-lift down four levels. A few minutes later, he arrived at the palace communications center. The

The Kotaran Mission: A Weapons of Legend Tale

door slid open, and General Goars and the other gray, armor-clad Reptilon clones rose from their chairs, snapping to attention.

"At ease," Farix said. He looked at the image of his longtime friend, Lord Kroeng, the Agnashi Order's third in command. A veteran of dozens of campaigns, Kroeng's face was a map of scars. His close-cropped gray hair was half-shaved in tradition on his home planet, Kor Prime. At sixty-five, Kroeng was fit as any twenty-year-old. Trained by Farix over forty-five years ago, Kroeng's fighting prowess was matched by few— all Agnashi.

"Kangol gi Azina," Kroeng said, reciting the Agnashi motto, Tarin for "Blood and Treasure."

"Kangol gi Azina," Farix replied. "Is something wrong?" he asked, still speaking in Tarin. Farix chuckled. "I told you, as long as High Lord Blackhart's on Bongoria and I'm here, you're in charge."

"This message is for you alone, my Lord." He smiled. "It seems Jornand Mensarius, the billionaire from Tytan—"

Skat! Farix scoffed. "I know who he is." *Billionaire, who's also the demon Sagikol disguised as a mortal. I can't stand the little skat-heel!*

"Well, he wants to hire you—and only you—for a job. He says it requires your specific skill set."

Yeah, a "Demi" with an Agnashi's fighting skill—what else is new?

"He's on the other channel—should I forward him to you?"

For frick's sake! "Fine, patch him through." Farix set his jaw. *Fricking Sagikol!*

Kroeng's image vanished, replaced by Sagikol in Jornand Mensarius' guise. The human/Tari hybrid's image brushed a hand along the sleeve of his blue, closed-collar velvet tunic, then buffed his fingernails on the breast.

"Clear the room," Farix told Goars and the other merc-troopers.

Once the troopers left, Farix glared through his visor at the demon. "What do you want, Sagikol? I'm busy here—I don't have time for your bollocks."

The human/Tarin hybrid scoffed, pushing a long lock of brown hair over a pointed ear. "Playing 'wedding planner' occupies the mighty Lord Farix?"

"Why aren't you with the other Deceptions?" Farix asked, already knowing the answer. "Did your brothers and sister kick you out—or was it just Lady Xhelobis?" He chuckled. "That must suck being bossed around by your younger sister."

"I left because of creative differences, or something like that," Sagikol replied. "If you would cease your juvenile attempts at baiting me, perhaps we could tend to the business at hand."

"You've wasted enough of my time—I'm deactivating the monitor."

"How does five billion *aonas* sound?"

Five billion? Holy skat! Farix scoffed. *It's fricking Sagikol—this must be a trap. But five billion* aonas… "Fine, you've got five minutes." *I'm gonna regret this!*

The demon narrowed his eyes. "I need you to go to Kuraz to capture a sorcerer—a necromancer who's crossed me!"

"I'm a merc and assassin—the best in the galaxy on both counts. Go hire a bounty hunter."

Sagikol scoffed. "Best assassin in the galaxy? There's an assassin on Kor Prime who may say differently."

Farix clenched his jaw. *Not if we met face to face.*

"No clever response?" Sagikol laughed. "Hit a nerve,

The Kotaran Mission: A Weapons of Legend Tale

have I?"

"Conversation's done."

"Hold on!" Sagikol said, tapping a finger on his pointy chin. "I tell you what—you do this errand for me, and I'll kill your rival top assassin—on top of the five billion."

Sounds good—wait! Farix scoffed. "Bollocks! It's forbidden for immortals to kill mortals." He chuckled. "That's why I'm in such high demand."

"I'm a billionaire! I'll hire assassins, including Agnashi, to do the job—now, what do you say?"

Skat! "Fine!" *I will so fricking regret this.* "Send me the location and any intel you have on this necromancer," he smiled beneath his faceplate. "Then I'll smoke him!"

"He's in the city of Kotaran, and he's to remain alive. You're now on the clock, Lord Farix." He clapped his hands and laughed. "Chop-chop!" The image vanished from the screen.

Well, it's obviously a trap. Farix shrugged. *Might as well go spring it and see what this arsehole's up to.*

He formed a portal and walked through the shimmering, quicksilver-like doorway. "Let's get this over with," he said, stepping through the portal.

***

Non-Charter Space; Planet Kuraz; City of Kotaran; 18 July 2429 (Earth Reckoning).

Farix stepped through a portal into the dilapidated city of Kotaran, which consisted of stacked modular structures forming buildings no higher than five stories. A rusted, old Kor-designed robot rolled past him on the dirt-covered street, one of its treads missing a track.

This place is a skat-hole—a perfect place for a necromancer. He looked up at the overcast sky, where Kuraz's sun struggled to break through the clouds. *Mid-morning—early afternoon, perhaps.* He chuckled. *Like it matters here!*

A sudden movement behind an abandoned hovercar prompted Farix to activate his HUD. Numerous yellow dots surrounded his position on the digital map. "Come on out! Show yourselves!" he said in Tarin.

A few human children with dirt-smeared faces and soiled clothing emerged from hiding. *The adults sent them out, assuming I'll show mercy.* He smiled. *These frickers don't know me at all.*

"Why do you hide from me?" Farix asked through his vocoder.

"We hide from the sisters and their golems," a small girl with long, matted blonde hair said, referring to an order of sorceresses known as *Arrellis ga Atar*, which is Tarin for "Sisters of Night." She wiped a grimy hand on her dirt-smeared gray smock. "Are you here to help us?"

Sorcerers and sorceresses never concerned Farix, and *Arrellis ga Atar* were weaker than most orders. The Agnashi Lord narrowed his eyes. *Golems? She spoke in Tarin but said the* actual *word from Earth.* "I'm here to find a necromancer," Farix replied.

A blonde boy wearing a soiled brown smock and blue trousers approached, stopping beside the girl. "The necromancer's with them—he taught them to make the golems!"

Well, this is an interesting development—consider my curiosity piqued!

A buzzing sensation in the back of Farix's mind brought him from his reverie. Like other demis, wizards in particular, Farix could sense sorcery's taint. He smiled beneath his helmet's visor. Well, that didn't take them long.

The Kotaran Mission: A Weapons of Legend Tale

Farix looked at the girl and boy, who he presumed were siblings. "The sisters are coming—you should go hide."

"Will you protect us?" the girl asked.

"Are you paying me?" Farix replied.

"We're poor," the boy said. "We have no mon—"

"Then the answer's no—now, go kick rocks."

The boy narrowed his eyes. "You won't fight them?"

Farix placed his hands on his hips and chuckled. "Come on, Kid! Who will bring me to the necromancer if I kill all the sisters?" The Agnashi Lord hung his head and sighed when the children remained. *How do I get rid of these fricking kids? They're distracting and annoying!* He smiled and raised his head. "I read somewhere that sorceresses bake children in pies—" He shrugged. "Or cakes or something."

"Where did you read that?" the girl asked.

"Some book about a sorceress who lived in a cake house." He pointed at the children. "A brother and sister like you two, except not as filthy, shoved her in an oven—"

A dusty cackle from behind interrupted Farix's retelling of *Hansel and Gretel*. Agnashi gazed at the source - a woman in a brown robe, leaning on a wooden cane. Six other sisters in brown robes stood behind her. Like their leader, their hoods were pulled over their heads, concealing their faces. Farix narrowed his eyes as the buzzing in the back of his mind intensified. *Something's not right; this sorceress order has imps for totems; they're a joke—they can barely master aeromancy!*

Farix glanced over his shoulder at the two children. "Don't say I didn't warn you."

The sorceress in front snickered. "A job well done, Children."

The girl and boy walked past Farix and stood before the sister, who tossed a small sack between them. "Five *aonas* for each of you," she said.

"Thank you, Mistress Kadis," the boy said, picking up the sack. He and his sister turned and faced Farix. The girl tapped her forearm with two fingers—a gesture equivalent to the Galactic Alliance's middle finger. The pair laughed and ran to their hiding places with the other children.

Farix smiled beneath his visor. As a mercenary, he appreciated the children's cunningness, while his demon half approved of their treachery. *A job well done, indeed!*

The Demi nodded to the sorceress in front. "Greetings…Kadis, is it?"

"Where are the other Agnashi?" she replied.

"I operate alone."

Kadis chuckled. "Do you expect us to believe that? Agnashi never operate alone—especially when facing the Dark Arts."

"I have no hostility toward you or the Dark Arts." *In truth, you're no threat to me.* He smiled. *You face your better— someone who could incinerate you with barely a thought. But alas, we must maintain this charade until I find this necromancer.*

"What is your business here in Kuraz, Agnashi?" another asked from behind.

We're getting nowhere— time to escalate this. "My business is my own, *Sorgi*," he replied, using a Tarin slur loosely translated to "witch."

"Watch your tongue!" another sorceress behind Kadis said in a reedy voice. "Or we'll pry you from your precious armor."

Farix chuckled. "Shouldn't you take me to dinner first?"

An invisible force struck Farix's chest, the impact taking him from his feet. Air escaped his lungs despite his armor catching the brunt of the *Air-Hammer*. He climbed to his feet, the air burning his lungs as he inhaled.

Something unseen wrapped around Farix, pressing

The Kotaran Mission: A Weapons of Legend Tale

his arms against his body. *Air-Binding,* he thought, feigning struggle. *I need to play along so as not to arouse suspicion.* He grunted. *This is humiliating! If Tempest saw me now, I'd never hear the end of it!*

"Not so clever now, are you?" Kadis said. She chuckled as an eldritch green flame danced in her hand. "Perhaps I'll finish you in a blaze of *Sorcerer's Fire*—your last moments alive will be the most excruciating."

Sorcerer's Fire is a horrible way to go, and surviving it's not much better. "No more—please! I surrender!" *Plus, all the trouble of getting a new set of armor—*

"We'll let the necromancer decide," Kadis said. She dismissed the Sorcerer's Fire and nodded to the six figures behind her. A hideous, rotten-toothed grin crept across her face. "He'll put you to good use, I'm sure."

A portal formed to Farix's left. Kadis pointed a bony finger at the quicksilver-like doorway. "In you go, and be quick about it—we mustn't keep him waiting!"

"W-what is that?" Farix asked, feigning ignorance.

"Aw! Is the mighty Agnashi afraid?"

I've traveled portals centuries before you were born, toothless Hag! "No—I've never seen one, is all."

"You're no good to the necromancer dead—at least for now," Kadis replied. Something invisible shoved Farix through the portal.

"Wait! Hold on!" the Agnashi said, crossing the threshold as the sorceresses cackled behind.

***

Farix stepped from the portal onto a dilapidated cobblestone courtyard. He looked at the grid coordinates on his visor's HUD. *Ten kilometers from the city entrance? Fricking amateurs!* The Agnashi Lord glanced up and around, assessing the overcast sky and the surrounding *permacrete* block walls. *No exit—good thing I have my jet pack. Worst case, I'll form an* Air-Hammer *and make my own exit.* Farix closed his eyes, reaching across light-years with his mind.

Tempest!

Why are you shouting? the Great Lady's voice echoed in his mind.

I'm at a castle or fortress of some sort in Kotaran, Farix replied as the sisters exited the portal behind him. The *Air-Binding* pushed him forward.

That's the Arrelis ga Atar's *temple,* Tempest replied suspiciously. *Why are you there?*

Kadis caught me in an Air-Binding, *and they're bringing me to meet this Necromancer—I'm in complete control.*

Sounds like it, she replied, her voice dripping with sarcasm.

The hard part's not killing them.

Don't kill them—I may need the sisters later.

Farix scoffed. *Why? They're useless!*

They swore fealty to Bezrath during the war—as his surviving disciple, they serve me now.

The Agnashi's mouth formed into a smirk. *The necromancer may say differently.*

We'll see about that!

Skat! What's that supposed to mean?

Apparently, I'm neglecting my servants. Once I'm through with this ridiculous wedding nonsense, I'll pay the Arrelis ga Atar *a visit.*

Don't let me keep you.

I'll see you soon—and don't kill those sisters!

For Frick's sake! Farix thought. *Between Sagikol telling me not to kill the necromancer and Tempest telling me to spare these* Arrelis gi Atar *hags, they're ruining my fun. This is Turtle Bay all over again—*

The Kotaran Mission: A Weapons of Legend Tale

A gong sounded, bringing Farix from his reverie. The buzzing in the back of his mind increased tenfold as scores of portals appeared atop the wall. Hundreds of sisters exited the shimmering doorways and stood along the wall, looking down at Farix like a murder of crows.

The gong sounded again, and the buzzing increased—now a familiar "sweet vileness" pervaded the back of Farix's mind. *I can almost smell it!* The *Demi* had not sensed it since the Third Roman Empire days of the twenty-second century—and before that, the fifteenth century during the crusades.

When the Dark Brotherhood trained me to master the Dark Arts at my father's behest. The Agnashi clenched his jaw. *I killed them all, save for Basurak, the only one among them who acknowledged me as his better. The others, all mortals, treated me, a Demi, as a worthless slave! And this one, I now sense, was among the worst offenders. I burned him with* Demon's Fire. *He was a burning corpse—how is he alive?*

"The necromancer has arrived!" a sister cried.

Farix glared at the remaining portal atop the wall before the temple proper. A thin figure of average height garbed in a black robe with his hood drawn emerged from the quicksilver-like doorway, joining four sorceresses.

Despite the necromancer's presence, Farix focused on the four tall figures in black robes behind the sorceresses. Each wore a matte-black helmet with large, twisted horns and chainmail covering their faces. *Those must be the golems.* The one in the center had a two-handed sword sheathed across his back, while the one on the right hefted a large war hammer at his side with apparent ease. *The head itself's got to be twenty kilos—too heavy for combat, even for a guy his size.* Despite the circumstances, Farix chuckled at the third's weapon— a flail with a crescent blade at the end of a long chain, wrapped around his arm. *It looks like an anchor! Even if this guy was strong enough to use it, he'd kill everyone around him!* The one furthest left also had a flail, the steelhead at the chain's end half-again the size of that of the war hammer.

The necromancer drew back his hood, revealing a gaunt face with a patchwork of silver, blue, and green synthetic skin the Tari designed for their cyborg soldiers. He outstretched his arms, and eldritch green flames danced in his hands. Farix scoffed. *He altered his appearance, but I'd recognize that arrogant piece of skat anywhere—and besides, his taint's unique, and my senses don't lie.* Farix clenched his jaw and squeezed his eyes shut to keep his temper in check. *I killed him almost a thousand years ago! How does he still live?*

The necromancer dismissed the flames and looked down at Farix like Ceasar would in the ancient Roman Coliseum. His lipless mouth stretched to a grin, exposing silver-colored synthetic teeth. Farix summoned flows of air as he looked at the necromancer's eyes—his right eye was a colorless, cloned implant, and his left one was robotic, with an ominous yellow glow. *Those eyes might be unnatural, but that glare shows nothing but pure hatred—which is fine, because the feeling's mutual.* "There's no use pretending, Iyum," the necromancer said, using Farix's old name. "I know who you are!"

Farix laughed, releasing the Air-Binding. The invisible bonds squeezing the Agnashi vanished as the six sisters behind him fell, screaming as they struggled against their bonds. He looked over his shoulder. "Shut your toothless mouths, or I'll forget my promise to the Great Lady and squeeze you 'til your brittle bones are dust."

Dismissing the *Air-Binding,* he looked up at the necromancer as the six sisters fled. "Cartiphilus? By Tevaljan's beard, it really is you!" Farix shook his arms to regain circulation as he walked towards the necromancer. "What's it been, a thousand years?"

The Kotaran Mission: A Weapons of Legend Tale

Cartiphilus' eyes narrowed. "Something like that."

Farix slapped the top of his helmet. "Yeah, that's right! The last time I saw you, you were 'extra crispy!'"

Cartiphilus clenched his jaw and huffed, glaring at Farix.

He looks angry; maybe I should stop, Farix thought. *Nah!* "All things considered, you look good for your age—what are you, a thousand and some change?"

The necromancer sneered at Farix. "I'm two thousand, four hundred and fifty-one."

You'd think the guy would find a sense of humor after twenty-four hundred years, right? Farix chuckled. "Well, for the record, you don't look a day over fourteen hundred!"

"Very droll, Iyum," Cartiphilus replied. "Unfortunately for you, you won't be laughing for long."

Farix glared at the sorcerer. "That's not my name!"

Cartiphilus chuckled. "It's the same meaning as Farix in Hebrew." The Earthite narrowed his mismatched eyes. "Even if they weren't, what do you propose to do about it?"

Farix smiled beneath his visor. "Finish what I started with you a thousand years ago."

The necromancer raised a hand, and the tall, broad-shouldered figure on the left stepped forward, his flail's anvil-like head hanging by its thick chain. "Well, Iyum, unless you can defeat my golem, you won't get the chance."

"It doesn't appear to be made of clay—and stop calling me Iyum!"

"It's a reanimated corpse—"

"Walking dead?" Farix guffawed. "Seriously, you're puppeteering a corpse?" He shrugged. "Well, you're a necromancer; that's what you do, I suppose."

"No, Iyum, this is necromancy beyond your reckoning!"

Keep him talking. Something odd's going on here. Otherwise,

Sagikol wouldn't have hired you or set you up—yeah, that's another matter to sort out later. Farix chuckled. "Beyond my reckoning? I'm over a thousand years old—I've literally seen reanimated corpses thousands of times." The Agnashi shook his head. "Face it, Cart, necromancy's a joke—"

"No, Iyum—you're the joke!" He pointed at Farix. "You're the ingrate who avoided his destiny by betraying his masters!"

Farix glared at the sorcerer. "None of you were my master. You refused to acknowledge the truth—that as a *Demi*, I was your better!" He shrugged. "And you all paid for your insolence."

Cartiphilus gestured to the towering figure next to him. "Perhaps when you face my golem, you'll learn something you never experienced from our lessons or the centuries-spanning life after your treachery." A silver-toothed grin creased the necromancer's face. "Consequences and humility."

Farix shook his head. *I'm the deadliest assassin and mercenary in the galaxy, with the body count to prove it. As a Demi, my knowledge of the Dark Arts surpasses all sorcerers while rivaling the wizards—even Merlin.* He smiled. *And at over a thousand years old, I possess the perpetual youth of a twenty-five-year-old with movie star good looks and washboard abs—for me, humility is an alien concept.* "I'm done talking, Cart—send down your meat-puppet so we can get this over with." *And as far as consequences go—I AM CONSEQUENCES! You'll find that out soon enough.*

The reanimated corpse next to Cartiphilus glanced at the necromancer, who returned his gaze and nodded. Farix squeezed his thumbs against his forefingers, activating his *ruka xac*, the bladed weapon synonymous with the Agnashi Order. As the five-decimeter blades unfolded from Farix's vambraces and locked into place with a *snap*, the Agnashi

The Kotaran Mission: A Weapons of Legend Tale

Lord watched the golem leap from the wall.

The golem landed lightly on its feet as his flail's anvil-like head shattered cobblestones a few meters away. With smooth movements contrary to the jerking gait common among reanimated corpses, the golem shrugged off his black robe, revealing gray armor beneath. He pointed at Farix with his free hand and waved his fingers, beckoning the Agnashi to fight.

Farix chuckled. *Well, well—it looks like the meat-puppet is self-aware. Probably shouldn't keep "Lurch" waiting.* With his *ruka xac* blades at his sides, the Agnashi dashed toward the golem at a dead sprint. As the reanimated corpse swung the flail above his head, Farix powered on his ion jet-pack.

When Farix was ten meters from his adversary, the golem hurled the flail's head at the Agnashi, who activated his jet-pack.

Farix leaped in the air, avoiding the flail. The hovering Agnashi fired bursts from his wrist-lasers, staggering the golem with scores of hits. *Skat! Hardly put a dent in him!*

The golem spun, swinging the flail upward. The steelhead struck Farix's back, sending him careening to the cobblestones. A prone Farix pushed himself up, his back throbbing despite his armor absorbing the blow. He staggered to his feet, groaning. "That was a bad idea!"

The golem charged, swinging the flail. Farix activated his jet-pack, which failed. He ducked the flail, firing wrist-lasers to gain separation. "That ion pack cost me five million *aonas,* Lurch—I'm taking it from your hide!"

The golem hurled the flail's steelhead.

"Skat!" Farix rolled, avoiding the blunt object. Back to his feet, he ducked the thick chain, backslashing his left *ruka xac* above the golem's knee. *Frick! Didn't even flinch!* He thought, slashing the right blade above the golem's beltline.

No effect! He doesn't feel pai—

The steelhead blindsided Farix, and everything went black. Sprawled on the cobblestones, Farix opened his eyes to the coppery taste of blood in his mouth and his left ear ringing. His eyes focused on the permacrete wall just a couple of meters away.

He straightened his head, glaring at dozens of sisters cackling from atop the wall, pointing down at him. Farix ran a gauntleted hand along the dent in his helmet's crown as he struggled to his feet. He regained his bearings, realizing the golem stood twenty meters away. *Skat! If I wasn't a Demi, that would've killed me!*

"Had enough, Iyum?" Cartiphilus asked.

Farix staggered, regaining his balance. "Nah, just feeling him out," he replied, drawing more laughter and jeers from the sisters. He summoned flows of air. *Laugh at this, Hags!* he thought, as the torrent's power increased, until even *he* struggled to contain it.

The golem faced Farix and swung his flail, shattering cobblestones with its anvil-like head. He waved his free hand, gesturing for Farix to fight.

Farix smiled beneath his visor, releasing a powerful *Air-Hammer*. The invisible, bludgeoning weapon of "solid air" struck the golem with the force of a speeding hovertruck, sending him tumbling and rolling to his feet twenty meters from where he stood.

Cartiphilus guffawed from above. "Nothing can hurt them—not even you, Iyum!"

Frick! Again, Farix summoned flows of air. *We'll see, Arsehole!*

The Demi released an *Air-Binding* on the advancing golem, who stopped short, struggling with his invisible bond. Farix tightened the binding. *Time to crush Lurch!*

The Kotaran Mission: A Weapons of Legend Tale

As Farix increased the binding, the golem struggled but did not appear distressed.

"Fool!" the golem said, his hollow voice echoing within the permacrete walls. "You cannot hope to suffocate me when I'm not alive."

"True," Farix replied, summoning an additional airflow. The cushions of air propelled the bound golem fifty meters above the courtyard. *Let's see how you hold up against gravity.* The Agnashi smirked, sending the golem up another fifty meters. *Just to stay on the safe side.*

Farix dismissed the airflows, and the golem dropped to the courtyard below with a resounding crash, shattering cobblestones in a cobweb pattern around the point of impact. As the Agnashi approached the golem struggling to his feet, he summoned *Demon's Fire.* Cries of shock and dismay reverberated throughout the gathered sisters as Farix raised a glowing red palm toward the golem. *Now, to end this!*

Farix launched a stream of crimson fire from his hand, which struck a barrier of the same color surrounding the golem. *What the frick! Who's shielding him with* Demon's Fire? Enraged, the Agnashi scanned the upper wall for the shield's source. A slight figure wearing a familiar blue jacket waved from a chair next to Cartiphilus.

Sagikol! That little pri— The flail's head struck Farix's shoulder. The Agnashi grunted, spinning to the ground. *Frick—that hurt!*

Farix struggled to sit up as his right arm dangled from the shoulder. He clutched his upper arm, and piercing pain traveled throughout his body. *It'll heal, but not fast enough. I could fight one-armed 'til I recover—but this thing's relentless!*

His pained grimace changed to a smirk. *Use his strength as a weakness.* The seated Agnashi collapsed on his side, his good hand opening a case on his belt.

"Finish him!" Cartiphilus yelled.

Farix smiled as the golem strode toward him with purpose, flail in hand. *I plan on it!* the Agnashi thought, removing button-sized *glotava* tablets from the belt case as he summoned air flows.

The golem stopped a couple of meters from the sprawled Agnashi, swinging the flail above his head.

Farix threw the *glotava* at the golem, the explosive gel tablets attaching to his armor. He released an *Air-Hammer*, striking the golem to gain a few meters of separation. The Agnashi lay prone on the cobblestone surface. He winced in pain as he moved his now-healing arm and pressed the detonator on his gauntlet.

The ground shook beneath Farix as the powerful explosion sent golem pieces all over the courtyard.

The Agnashi struggled to his knees as a movement to the right caught his attention. The golem's head and torso crawled toward him, his remaining arm dragging his upper body ponderously toward Farix.

"You just don't know how to quit, do you?" Farix asked, summoning *Demon's Fire*. He stood and walked toward the reanimated corpse. He stopped a few meters from the struggling golem, his hand glowing crimson. "You have any last words, Lurch?" A stream of red fire from Farix's hand enveloped the golem. "Yeah, don't care."

The Agnashi watched as the golem's still form burned to ash. He dismissed the fire and studied the smoking pile of ash and bones. *It's kind of disappointing; he didn't scream like my live victims do.*

Farix looked toward Cartiphilus with Sagikol beside him. The necromancer nodded to the sisters standing before the remaining three golems.

He looked down at Farix with a silver grin as the trio

The Kotaran Mission: A Weapons of Legend Tale

of golems jumped off the wall into the courtyard. "This isn't over yet, Iyum."

Farix summoned air flows as the golems charged across the courtyard with reckless abandon. "I disagree, Cart," the Agnashi replied.

Cushions of air propelled him over the golems, the circulating whirlwind carrying the *Demi* toward Cartiphilus and Sagikol. Both the necromancer and demon remained at their chairs—the enraged sorcerer standing as the smug demon sat.

Farix reached the wall's edge in front of Cartiphilus. Once the Agnashi's left foot touched, his right struck Cartiphilus' chest, sending the necromancer into his chair.

Before Cartiphilus could move, Farix pressed the *ruka xac's* point against his throat. The Agnashi glanced at the four sisters. "Whoever controls those things better stand down, or I take this arsehole's head."

"It is done, Agnashi," the nearest sister replied. "The golems will remain in the courtyard."

Farix looked at Sagikol. "Here's your fricking sorcerer—you owe me five billion *aonas*, plus ten million for my ion pack and damaged armor."

The demon, posing as a human/Tari hybrid, nodded. "Of course—a job well done, Lord Farix."

Farix nodded at Cartiphilus. "I'll knock off half to kill this fricker here and now."

Sagikol chuckled. "That's not possible."

Farix narrowed his eyes. "Why?"

"I'm immortal, Iyum," the necromancer said.

Farix scoffed. "Bollocks! You're wearing cyborg skin, for frick's sake!" He increased pressure on the *ruka xac's* point. "Call me 'Iyum' again and see what happens!"

"Fine! 'Farix' it is." The necromancer sighed. "It's

true—I'm no Demi, but I'm immortal, nonetheless."

Sagikol laughed. "Being a 'Demi,' you may not sense Cartiphilus' unique imprint within sorcery's taint."

Farix scoffed. "Don't be insulting, I can sense it—I just didn't know what it meant."

"It's a curse," Cartiphilus replied. "I'm doomed to live until the end of days—immortal but without a *Demi's* healing ability."

Alarmed cries from the walls drew Farix's attention.

"Portals!" the nearest sister said.

Farix! Lady Tempest's voice echoed in his mind. *We have arrived!*

Watch out for the golems.

Golems?

You'll know when you see them—there's three on the courtyard.

Sagikol's green eyes widened as he looked past Farix to the courtyard below. A black, mirror-like portal formed behind the demon as he stood and bowed. "Alas, it's time to take my leave." He walked to the swirling, ink-like portal and stopped, facing Farix with an impish grin. "Until next time, Lord Farix."

Which will be far too soon, Farix thought as Sagikol stepped through the portal. He glanced at the nearest sister, a tall, cadaverous, thin woman with pale, wrinkled skin and long, wispy white hair. With the *ruka xac* point still pressed against Cartiphilus' throat, Farix looked at the necromancer and tilted his head toward the sister. "What's her name?"

"I am Mother Jhadis, head of *Arrelis ga Atar*," the sorceress said in a reedy voice.

"Well met, Jhadis—now stand down your golems, or I take Cartiphilus' head."

"There's no need, Agnashi," Jhadis replied, nodding toward the courtyard behind him. "We serve the Great

The Kotaran Mission: A Weapons of Legend Tale

Lady."

Farix summoned flows of air as he looked over his shoulder.

The Great Lady Tempest looked every bit like the queen she would become in a black gown with silver trim. The silver circlet adorned with a black rose rested on her forehead as cascades of spiraling brown curls fell past her bare shoulders. As deadly as she was beautiful, crimson flames of *Demon's Fire* danced in her hands as Lords Nyblis and Scorpious flanked her, their sword blades alight with *Sorcerer's Fire*. Two platoons of gray-armor-clad Reptilon clones from the Agnashi-trained Black Rose Regiment marched behind, four abreast, from the large, quicksilver-like portal with laser rifles at low ready.

Tempest narrowed her greenish-blue eyes at the towering golems, who took knees as one before her. She looked along the walls at the gathering sisters, the crimson flames vanishing as she spread her arms. "*Arrelis ga Atar*, I have returned!" she said in perfect Tarin. Hundreds of sisters bowed their heads to their returning mistress. "Mother Jhadis and Lord Farix, please come forward."

Bring this necromancer with you, Tempest's voice echoed in his head.

Trust me, I wasn't leaving him alone. Farix lowered his *ruka xac* and released the *Air-Binding*.

Cartiphilus struggled against the bindings. "What is the meaning of this?"

"The Great Lady wishes to meet you," Farix replied as Jhadis glided on air cushions to the courtyard. Farix tightened the Air-Binding, making the necromancer wince. "Don't embarrass me."

Cartiphilus grimaced. "Wouldn't think of it."

Farix scoffed as he loosened the binding. "Bollocks!"

He summoned additional airflows and glided down on an air cushion with the bound necromancer at his side.

When they touched down on the cobblestone surface, Farix shoved Cartiphilus at Tempest's feet next to the prostrating Jhadis. "Kneel before the Great Lady!" the Agnashi said. He looked at Tempest. "I trust everything went well?"

"The wedding takes place in three months—the day after His Majesty's eighteenth birthday."

"A short betrothal."

Tempest scoffed. "Indeed!" She tilted her head towards the prostrating Cartiphilus. "And who is this?"

Farix grabbed the back of Cartiphilus' robe and hoisted him to his feet. "This is Cartiphilus from Earth—an original member of *our order*."

"Didn't you destroy the original—?"

"I did—apparently, this skat-heel's immortal."

Tempest narrowed her eyes, studying the patchwork synthetic skin stretched across Cartiphilus' gaunt face. "How—?"

"He's not a *Demi*—"

"I am cursed, Great Lady—" Farix cuffed the back of Cartiphilus' head. "Ow!"

"Speak when you're spoken to," Farix said. He looked at Tempest. "He's cursed to live until the End of Days." The Agnashi shrugged. "Since he's not a *Demi*, I plan to separate his head and body and bury them in permacrete slabs on different worlds."

Tempest looked at the Earthite. "How does this discipline of Necromancy work?"

Cartiphilus sighed. "In simplest terms, when the being dies, the necromancer casts spells in a ceremony to keep the spirit between the realms of the living and the dead.

The Kotaran Mission: A Weapons of Legend Tale

After five days, the spirit returns to reanimate its corpse. During that time, a sorcerer tethers the corpse with power to sustain it."

Wait! "Spirits possess the corpse, like a vampire?" Farix asked.

"No, a vampire is a corpse possessed by a demon—these golems are corpses possessed by their own spirits."

Farix scoffed. "So, all I had to do to beat Lurch was kill the sister tethering him."

"Easier said than done, but you are correct, Lord Farix."

We could put this form of necromancy to good use—we will need him, Tempest's voice echoed in Farix's mind. She tapped her chin with her forefinger.

Farix clenched his jaw. *She's right. If used correctly, these so-called golems will be a combat multiplier against the Na'dari and wizards, not to mention conventional forces.*

I agree—but we cannot trust him!

Tempest tapped her chin with her forefinger, staring at the kneeling golems. "That is remarkable; it would be a shame to waste a useful asset."

"And permacrete," Farix replied.

"Against our better judgment, I'll allow you to remain here to train the sisters in this discipline of Necromancy," Tempest told Cartiphilus.

"Thank you, Great Lady!"

"Heed this warning, Cartiphilus—should you stray, Lord Farix will ensure you await the End of Days from many places." She narrowed her greenish-blue eyes. "In many pieces."

"Y-yes, Great Lady."

Tempest looked at the prostrating sorceress. "Rise, Mother Jhadis."

The sorceress stood. "Yes, Great Lady?"

"As my disciples, your order will undergo many changes to serve my needs, but to your benefit in power and appearance." She placed a hand on the older sorceress' shoulder. "Do you know of Lady Xhelobis, my former familiar, and her brothers, Lord Arvertis and Lord Tuzakis?"

"They are the Deceptions, Great Lady."

Tempest smiled at the sorceress. "Lady Xhelobis has seen the same potential with your order as I have—the Deceptions have agreed to become familiars for the *Arrelis ga Atar.*" Tempest gestured to herself. "As a condition, she will insist on making you more presentable, as she had with me."

Jhadis cried out and fell to the ground in prostration. "Thank you, Great Lady!"

She could've broken her hip! Farix thought.

I don't understand what happened, Farix said to Tempest through telepathy.

Lady Xhelobis will change their current appearance to that of beautiful young women, as she did with me.

Farix looked around the courtyard. *That's a lot of beautiful young women,* he chuckled. *Are you sure you can handle the competition?*

The palace in Su Cron is a nasty place with scores of sorcerers among my future husband's servants. If we're to survive as an order, we'll have to take over—and we'll need powerful sorcerers and sorceresses to achieve those ends. No, my Lord, not competition—what you see around you is my pool of Ladies in Waiting and future queens—and not of Kor Prime alone.

This is a brilliant power move! This, right here, is where the Order of Darkness begins its takeover of the galaxy—planet by planet, Farix thought. "I must say, My Lady, King Karsol is a lucky man to have a woman with such unmatched beauty,

The Kotaran Mission: A Weapons of Legend Tale

intellect, power, and foresight as his future queen."

"Thank you, my Lord," Tempest replied. "That means a lot coming from you." She narrowed her eyes. *Of course, you're being facetious.*

I'm telling you the truth—except for one thing, Farix replied. *Karsol better learn his place, or he may become a golem by age twenty."* Farix nodded. "That's the honest truth, my Lady."

A Tale of Tails
by R.N. Warren

Ogden's lungs were on fire, and his muscles screamed at him to stop running, but he had a job to do. The mischief was safe because of his daily duty— at least, that's what he had been told.

He paused by every crack and crevice along his route to peer out at what he had been taught were "danger zones." If the zones were clear of obstruction, and nothing had noticeably changed within them, then he had nothing to report to his superiors.

The day started like any other. He had scurried out from the warm hideaway at the top of the unnaturally smooth structure he called home to begin his descent into Rafter, the mischief's main village. Rafter was a cozy place, nestled in the highest point of the strange cave they shared with the humans who occupied the lower levels. As a thrifty and frugal population, many items forgotten by the humans were repurposed to expand Rafter. Ogden admired the newest edition on his way out. Some lucky rat was adding bedding to the Christmas cookie tin.

He remained inside the walls, knowing the danger

lurking in the open on the lower levels. If the humans ever spotted one of the Runners, it would spell doom for them all. Only the quickest rats were ever chosen to join their ranks, Ogden was prouder than anyone when he was selected. The Runners were well respected in the mischief, but much had changed since he began serving.

Ogden followed his set path, the same one he took daily, only this time, a crumpled figure lay dangerously close to a newly formed hole in the wall. Pieces of plaster still fluttered from it, raining down like flakes of snow onto the figure, twitching in pain. His claws dug into the wood without hesitation as his four legs carried him swiftly to the rat's side.

"Are you alright? What happened?" Odgen caught his breath as the beautiful, silver-furred rat turned to meet his gaze. The ruby eyes that met his were clouded with fear and pain, but when she spoke, her melodic voice removed the veil of monotony that had cloaked his days.

"I was on food collection duty," she winced as she sucked in the air to speak. "The humans had been shouting, but it happened so suddenly. I was moving as quietly as possible, then a bald fist—" She squeezed her eyes shut. Ogden waited until it became clear she wasn't going to continue.

"What's your name?"

"Melanie."

"Can you move, Melanie?"

Melanie nodded in response. When she saw his mouth open once more, she jumped to speak, as if she were scared he might ask something that she didn't want to answer.

"I don't know."

"You... don't know?" he repeated, slightly befuddled.

"I don't know if I was seen." When Ogden looked in

A Tale of Tails

her ruby eyes, his own anxiety and fear reflected at him. He swallowed hard, struggling to assume a neutral expression while inwardly beating back the terror that constantly surrounded him. He lifted the injured rat onto his back without another word and began to climb. The physical climb was effortless, despite the extra weight. The decision of what to do next weighed on them both.

Neither of them spoke until they reached the next stop on Ogden's route. It was a strange, round barrier, much like the walls that protected their mischief. He had overheard the humans calling them "win-dows." The window was invisible; it could be seen through, but not passed through.

"Why aren't you bringing us straight back?" Melanie glanced at her new grizzled friend, curious as to why he hadn't immediately dragged her before Chief Red Berry Crunch. She was fully aware protocol dictated that Runners bring information on any suspected sightings to their superiors immediately.

"It just... seemed like we could both use a minute to process. This will be the first time I've ever had to report an incident occurring in a danger zone." Ogden laid her down gently, so she could gaze out the window. He folded his paws into his fur to hide their trembling, barely keeping his breathing under control. It wasn't just reporting the incident that had him panicking; it was the rat responsible.

He had heard the name Melanie before, there wasn't a rat in the mischief who hadn't. He had also seen this rat's quick silver fur streaking by the corner of his eye while he was on duty before. He had never imagined that slippery silver rat would shine with such a rich beauty up close. He had also never imagined *Melanie* would be so vibrant. The image of her mother, the Chief of Rafter, and her domineering form swam before his eyes. The rat before him bore no resemblance to her mother, but her status as the next Chief was undeniable. It pained him slightly; beholding such beauty meant coming to terms with his lack of it.

"I gave you my name, but didn't ask for yours. I want to know, now," Melanie whispered softly. Despite his efforts, she hadn't missed his shaking paws. When their eyes met again, the fear had not disappeared, but a measure of curiosity began to peek out from behind its clouds.

"It's Ogden." He looked away, rummaging around the old fluff that lined some of the walls. He thought briefly about lying to Melanie, telling her his name was Bouillon instead. Her status gave her certain privileges he wasn't afforded when it came to breaking the mischief's rules. He had heard more than a few stories about innocent rats being thrown under the proverbial shoe when any of the Chief's kids were involved in mishaps. Knowing Bouillon, giving her his name would backfire the moment they stepped paw in Rafter. He might be a loyal friend, but that didn't make him quick to catch on. They had gotten *into* sticky situations because of his mouth, Ogden doubted it would get him *out* of one now.

He pulled out a large length of strong, sticky, silver "uck Tap" the Runners used to bind wounds in a pinch on duty. His next idea was a terrible one. He decided to attempt to win her favor, thinking she could negotiate on his behalf. He restrained the urge to roll his eyes. If it had been any other rat, *he* would be the one negotiating for *them*. He was a top Runner, he could sway his superiors, but he'd never even spoken to the Chief. The Chief always made the final call; if he was blamed for hurting one of her pups, he was toast.

He examined and dressed Melanie's wounds enough for her to move about on her own. He worked quietly and

A Tale of Tails

quickly, so he could hide his face. There was no way he could meet her eyes. He was about to suggest that they finish the trek back to their mischief when a tear in the corner of her eye caught his attention.

"Is the uck Tap too tight? I can loosen it! If we can make it back, we can get you some aged berries to dull the pain." Ogden was immediately sweating, was he already messing up?

"I may have just doomed us all! Why are you being so kind to me?" The fear and guilt Melanie had been drowning in were apparent in her voice. Ogden recognized the look in her eyes. He had seen it a thousand times in his own reflection.

"You had a good reason! Food collection is one of the hardest and most dangerous jobs in the mischief. No one will blame *you*."

"Except I wasn't assigned that job!" Melanie gasped and thrust her paw over her mouth, wishing words were a cheddar she could swallow. She hadn't missed the way his tone soured when he spoke of blame, but she had to make him understand.

That revelation took Ogden aback. Now that he thought about it, she hadn't been carrying a standard food collection satchel. The Chief would never approve of assigning her to such a dangerous task! He had never seen her on a food collection route before, either. He had simply assumed, because she was on the route, but her paws weren't as worn as other food collectors. Why would they be? *She wasn't out risking her life for the good of the mischief, she was just out causing trouble.* Ogden barely kept his expression under control, he couldn't believe he might be exiled from Rafter because of the whims of a spoiled rat like her.

"Then what were you doing there?" Ogden could hear

the hostility in his own voice and winced inwardly. He still had to win her over if he wanted the slimmest chance at remaining in Rafter. He was already resigning himself to losing his position as a Runner, maybe they would assign him to Waste Detail instead...

"My little sister, Popcorn... She's sick. The healer said she only had a few days— she wanted a blackberry! I hadn't been outside in ages, but I thought I could use the route we used to sneak out of. I was going to be back before anyone even noticed... But, the old route was sealed off. I was searching for another way when the shouting started." Seeing the distrust forming in Ogden's eyes, Melanie poured as much truth and desperation into her voice as she could.

He had been so sure nothing she said would sway him. He had his occupation to protect and principles to uphold. He didn't account for the memories of a small pup resurfacing, the simultaneously shriveled and puffy body, still transitioning from pink to grey. The brother he never got the chance to know, the eyes that never opened. The weeks of watching him struggle to cling to life still haunted him. No amount of jealousy or bitterness could be greater than that pain. He knew if he had been given the choice, he would have traded anything for his brother's recovery.

"Your sister, how old is she?" Melanie knew when he asked this, she had him. A sadness had entered his eyes she didn't expect, with a depth she feared she had merely been introduced to. When Popcorn's face swam to the front of her mind, everything else faded away, including her concern for Ogden's demons.

All she could think of was her tiny sister, fighting for her life back home, waiting for her to come home. She had her own demons to fight, like the risk she was taking by leaving Popcorn's side. The guilt of not being there to hold

A Tale of Tails

her paw if she had to say goodbye would destroy Melanie.

"She just saw her first winter." The pain and sadness eclipsed her eyes so totally that they swallowed whatever fear or regret remained. Ogden quietly observed the changes in Melanie; there was no choice for him to make in this moment. He couldn't do anything for his brother, but he *would* help Melanie ease her sister's journey.

"How much do those injuries of yours hurt?" Ogden's countenance shifted into one of shenanigans, a childish emotion he didn't have much experience with. There was no more obligation to his kindness.

"What are you asking me?" Melanie was shocked by the shift, curious as to what spurred it on.

"Are you up for finishing that blackberry hunt?"

Melanie looked up into the rat's face. He portrayed confidence on the surface, but she saw through him. The way he avoided eye contact reminded her of Popcorn.

Melanie's life had flashed before her eyes when the human's hairless fist flew through the wall. Her thoughts had reached out to her sister, her small, thin body curled up and shaking, racked with coughs. Despite the weak state she was currently in, Popcorn had always been Melanie's strength.

"Blackberries have always been Popcorn's favorite treat. They are in season but incredibly difficult to come by. There are only two routes I know of that a rat could take to bring back blackberries. The Chief stopped sending Collectors out for the berries because the risk wasn't worth the reward. One route was through the yard, two hounds could come out snarling at any time, so that route isn't great. The other route was past the great metal beasts, which is twice as dangerous, because it involves crossing an open portion of the lower levels. You can't usually guarantee that you'll even find a berry, but thanks to you, we can." She gestured out the window Ogden had patched her up in front of.

He didn't miss the way she referred to her own mother as Chief, or the bitterness in her voice when she mentioned the canceled berry collection duties. Ogden squinted in the direction she indicated and gasped. The bush was barely visible, but it was there, and it was full of ripe, glistening berries.

***

Melanie had always been an excellent climber, and that giant, bald paw had put her skills through a true test. She had gotten away with her life, and a strange, stoic rat had offered a helping paw. Part of her knew she was overconfident, but something about the quiet strength she saw in the nervous rat beside her inspired her to finish her mission. Despite her injuries, she trusted her adrenaline, and this Runner, to see her through. The image of Popcorn with purple juices dying the fur around her nose, smiling with berry-dyed magenta teeth, leaving a trail of purple in her wake, echoed like her laughter through Melanie's soul.

Melanie had explained to Ogden that she had attempted and failed both routes she knew of. When she turned her desperate eyes on him, he froze. Instinct took over, he sniffed the air and began walking down a path he knew led in the general direction of the bush. Once they arrived at the crack, the path would split off in several directions that weren't on the Runner's routes.

Ogden had *no idea* where those paths led. Why did the prettiest rat the in the mischief have to be the Chief's daughter? Why did the knowledge that she was following him send his anxiety was through the roof?

A Tale of Tails

How was he going to explain why he didn't report the hole in the wall immediately? What was he going to tell his boss about why he took a detour, on work hours? Even if he got Melanie to her blackberries, they could still be caught by food collectors on their way back. If they were caught, would she pin it on him? He felt true self-hatred for even considering it, but what if she was lying about her sister and just wanted some berries? Despite the self-hatred, he knew that even if that was the case, she wouldn't be punished; not like he would be, if he took the fall.

A shift in the air froze Ogden in his tracks. His nose twitched as he raised his head to take in more of the faint scent.

"What do you smell, Ogden? Do you know what to look out for on this route?" Melanie took a sniff of her own and identified several obstacles; but at the end of the path, the smallest whiff of blackberries.

Ogden marked the challenges they would face and mentally traced their path. He drew the route in the dirt with a single claw to walk Melanie through what was to come. Ogden's brothers had dared him to spend a night in the yard once, and he had done so successfully. However, he had also lost one of his back toes in the process. He had never been back down this path since that night, and he never expected to be again.

Melanie watched as a shadow crossed Ogden's face. She didn't know what he was remembering, but when she saw him wince, she nudged his shoulder with her nose. Her gesture of comfort knocked him out of the dark. Ogden took a deep breath before heading down the dark tunnel ahead of him. They moved through the walls silently but for the occasional scritch of claws.

"Stay close behind me, we're going to crawl over some

nails up ahead, then it'll get tight. When the walls start closing in, try pushing that cloth scrap you brought ahead of you, you'll lose it if you drag it behind you."

Melanie's eyes adjusted quickly in the dark, but the crawling felt endless. The scrap threatened to tangle in her legs and around her tail at every turn, but when she followed Ogden's suggestion, it was suffocating. If she moved too quickly, it would catch onto wooden splinters and begin tearing and unraveling. Ogden heard grunting the third time the scrap stuck itself to the walls.

"We're going to have to think of something else, or we'll never make it."

"Could you help me tie it? I have an idea."

Two minutes later they were back on the road, Melanie grinning with satisfaction. A scrap-turned-knapsack folded smartly and tied functionally over her back.

The progress was steady until they reached their first obstacle.

Usually, heights don't bother rats that spend as much time climbing as they do running. That fact changes once you leave the walls. Out in the open there are many surfaces that claws can't get a good grip on.

One such surface currently barred their way forward. It was cold, slick, and unyielding. They had been running at full pace through the walls, leaping across and balancing on beams. They used their tails to swing across gaps that were too far to jump and pushed the air from their lungs to squeeze through cracks. When the two rats hit their stride, they were a blur of brown and silver.

The scent had led them to turn down a corridor that neither rat had explored before. A cacophony of unfamiliar scents almost convinced them to turn tail. The whiff of blackberry was tangled up with the rest, but it remained

A Tale of Tails

traceable. Ogden swallowed hard, rubbing his nose with his paw to clear the web of scents before leading the way. He had taken ten steps into the dark before colliding with what was referred to as a "grille."

When Bouillon and Ogden started training as Runners, their supervisor, Taffy, showed them their routes and shared the stories of the Runners who came before. Those stories included the names humans used for some of the strange objects found in the lower floors. Ogden's favorite story involved the blinds humans used on the windows to block the sunlight. Later on, they had passed a rectangular metal square with a smaller version of those blinds, but they instead blocked the cold or warm air that seeped from the tunnel beyond.

Bouillon had peeked through the metal and Laffy had snapped, "*Never* venture into the ducts beyond these grilles! There are some stories so gruesome... please, don't make me retell them."

Laffy's haunted face was staring at Ogden now. He had to choose between dooming a girl to a fate he had lived through, or stepping into something that traumatized his friend, but was unknown to him. If he had been alone, he knew what choice he would've made.

Ogden glanced at Melanie. She was already shoving her pack through the metal folds, into the tunnel beyond.

"Wait!" The squeak Ogden let out was feminine in pitch; his ears reddened when Melanie cracked a smile, but she didn't stop.

"I have to at least warn you of the danger before we go any further!" That stilled her for a moment. She thought of the stories of rats getting sliced by fans in the airducts, but then she wheeled on him.

"Do you really think I'd be here without knowing the

risks? I have heard *every story*. I know of a hundred different ways I could die or be killed attempting this. But there is *nothing* that will stop me from getting these *stupid* berries to my *beautiful* sister. Because she needs me, and there is nothing I wouldn't do for her."

The authority she threw into her voice as she spoke those words was identical to her mother's. Melanie sighed as she squeezed through the grille into the airduct. If he hadn't known who she was before, he certainly did now. As she wrapped the pack back around herself, she began to steel herself mentally for the confrontation. If he tried to drag her back, for her "protection," she would make a run for it.

Ogden felt every word Melanie threw at him. He took a moment on the other side of the grille to examine what she had said. Then, when he could set his expression to neutral, he slipped through the grille. They traveled in silence; it was no longer a jovial sprint. The tension was at a breaking point when the airduct took a sharp turn up. They could see where it continued forward. It was only a short trip up, but the ledge was just out of reach.

Ogden watched stoically as Melanie attempted several dramatic leaps, she got one claw over the edge once, but eventually sat down. Ogden finally broke the silence, dousing the tension with his words, "I had a brother." It all fizzled away as Melanie registered his use of the past tense.

It made sense to her now, relief washed over her, he wasn't doing this for her. He wasn't doing this to impress her mother either. They were *both* doing this for themselves, they were *both* doing this for Popcorn.

***

Ogden stood on his back paws, bracing himself against the slick metal wall with his head tucked down. The path of the

A Tale of Tails

airduct continued above his head. Melanie began to run. She dug her claws into his back when she reached him. The airduct swallowed her in one gulp as she flung herself into its mouth.

Silence stretched for several moments. Ogden stretched his back, hoping Melanie didn't puncture his skin, while he waited for Melanie to try to pull him up. Honestly, he was doubtful it would work. He knew he shouldn't make assumptions, but he had also never seen smoother paws.

An hour later, Ogden was sweating and pacing, imagining all kinds of terrible conversations he would have to have if she didn't return, when he finally heard her voice again.

"Sorry, there is some neat stuff up here! It gave me an idea!" Ogden nearly sobbed in relief at the sound, but his stomach flipped when he thought about what 'neat stuff' could entail. Images of the horrible traps humans laid out for them flashed through his mind.

"Uhm, hey! Why don't you help me up before you mess with anything else?"

"There is no way I'm pulling you up alone, but I think you can pull yourself up with this!" Two thick, knotted ropes flopped down the bend in the airduct, almost smacking Ogden in the face.

"A little warning next time!" His words were harsh, but he was genuinely impressed. Melanie had meticulously knotted the rope so it was thick enough for him to climb if she could hold his weight. Melanie gave him the go-ahead, and he climbed up with ease. She had threaded the rope through one of the slots in a grille not far from where she must've landed. She had tossed both ends of the rope down after lacing it through.

"So, you didn't have to pull my weight after all…" It

dawned on Ogden that the one who got the elevator pulley system working in the Crunch doll house mansion was not the Chief but her daughter.

Progress was slower than before. Running on such a slick surface was tricky to get used to. Their claws clacked against the metal surface; their usually quiet steps were hard to muffle. Their stomachs were beginning to ache by the time they reached the grille that would take them outside the safety of the walls.

When they peeked through the slits, and the entire layout of the lower level was visible. Ogden could see the similarity between this space and the few doll house homes he had seen.

Melanie peered out the blinds in awe, everything was *massive*. She grew up in the biggest, most elaborate doll mansion in Rafter; the dolls it was built for were larger than the Chief. Melanie recognized almost everything she saw, though she had no clue what their functions were. Her curiosity spun out of control, as she realized that if she had the chance to observe the humans from here, she could figure out what everything in their house was meant to do. Fixing the elevator when she was little was a fluke, but what if she could get other items functioning? The scent of blackberries snapped her back, and it was much stronger now.

They were getting closer; they just needed a quiet moment to leap.

It felt like hours before they both felt comfortable enough with the stillness of the house to make the jump. The scent of food wafting from somewhere below them was intoxicating, and their stomachs would not stop singing in response. The adrenaline cut through the hunger when they leapt from the airducts to the shelves below.

A Tale of Tails

For the first time in his life, Ogden was outside the walls. He had spent most of his days running the perimeter, glancing at what lay beyond. He never imagined he would cross that line, but now that it had been crossed, he looked out at what lay beneath him. Right now, they were above it all, but when they reached the floor of the lower levels, the perspective would shift.

"We might already be responsible for one sighting, should we really be doing this?"

Ogden was shocked by her question. *How could she be second guessing herself now?* It was far too late for doubts. Hadn't she already taken that into consideration?

"If you've been spotted once, does a second time change the outcome?" His question was cold, but he wanted to know how she would respond.

"If I haven't been spotted, risking it a second time is beyond foolish." The guilt written on Melanie's face as she spoke told Ogden much more than her words.

"We're too close to turn back empty-pawed."

They bolted across the top of the shelves, close enough to the wall to be hidden from view. The struggle began when they had to concoct a way down. The difficulty level increased when Melanie suggested they stop halfway to grab the baby tomatoes off the counter to "refuel." Ogden's stomach was rumbling with a force that shook his entire body, so he didn't argue.

They plotted every step of their route from their vantage point, picking out places to hide along the way to catch their breath. Melanie made sure they agreed on everything, because once they started the sprint, there would be no turning back. Ogden counted them down when the coast was clear, and they began.

R.N. Warren

***

Melanie leapt off the top of the shelf. Catching the edge with her tail, she swung herself onto a pile of platters that rattled and clanked under her weight. She softly rolled off the plates towards the shadows lurking in the depths of the top shelf.
She didn't wait to see if Ogden was keeping up with her; maneuvering in the lower levels left no time for hesitation.

Ogden was acting on instinct rather than leaning on logic the instant he jumped after Melanie. She was easily one of the most agile rats he had ever seen. She glided between cups and saucers, vaulted over piles of plates, and slipped through the spice rack without a sound. Ogden had just reached the spice racks when his ears caught a sound that stopped his heart.

Thunderous footsteps shook the world as they approached. Melanie could feel each boom vibrating throughout her body, and locked eyes with Ogden. His eyes as wide as the saucers they just passed, he was still in the spice rack.

***

Melanie squeaked, startled by how badly he had hidden. Was stealth not a part of Runner training? She was going to speak with her mother about that if they made it back to Rafter. Knots of worry were twisting her stomach; he was going to get them caught. She almost hissed at him to hide, but the human was too close now to risk moving at all.

A breath later, the human boomed through the room like a storm. Wind kicked up in its wake, thunder followed every footstep. It interacted with the objects scattered around with a reckless disregard for their preservation.

A Tale of Tails

Everything the human touched or moved was accompanied by a dissonant crescendo of clangs as the flurry of motion slowly approached where the two lay waiting.

Their breathing was shaky, their paws sweaty. This was the second time Melanie wrestled with the fear of discovery, and they hadn't reached the blackberries yet. At this rate, they were due for two more encounters on their way back to Rafter, and she prayed that was not the case.

***

Ogden was paralyzed, his brain had short-circuited from the fear and adrenaline pumping through him. He squeezed his eyes shut when the human began to approach the spice rack. As the steps became almost deafening, some survival instinct kicked in.

Ogden's eyes flew open in time to see a colossal form, its presence was overwhelming. He watched in frozen terror as the vast torso slowly bent to reveal a flat, bald face. It was the size of the plates Melanie had landed on. Just the face of the human was twice the size of their entire bodies.

The human had no whiskers, its face was pink, but its eyes hadn't spotted him yet. He prayed to the Great Cheese above that it wasn't searching for the Star Anise or Grains of Paradise. He had chosen to hide behind them because they had the faintest scents around the room. He hoped that meant they were rarely used.

Melanie could not watch. When the human hand started to descend in Ogden's direction, she bit back a squeak and covered her eyes with her paw. Glass bottles began to clink, and Melanie's heart raced. She peered out between her claws and almost vomited in fear.

The human's front paw was five inches away from Ogden's body.

Ogden watched as the human's hairless paw descended to grab the cinnamon. Only three spices separated him and the strange, lanky, clawless paws. Despite the closeness of the hand, Ogden never took his eyes off the human's. The human's eyes never clocked him, but he knew he had barely passed that stealth check.

When the footsteps were a safe distance, Ogden bolted for Melanie's hiding spot. After a quick discussion, they moved again. When the human had left the room, the rats swung down to the counter and ran toward the tambour door.

Ogden lifted the door from the bottom, like Melanie had instructed. It slid upward like she told him it would, but it was heavy. He barely kept it aloft long enough for Melanie to slip under. Once she was inside, she immediately spotted a strange, solid piece of plastic and wedged it under the tambour door. Ogden sighed in relief as he let the weight of the door fall on the plastic. It held, and he slid under after Melanie.

It was dark inside the cabinet, plastic boxes, sheets, and spears were crammed inside with no obvious pattern. Some of them appeared like they could be fitted together, others appeared to fit with nothing at all. They carefully picked their way to the back, bottom corner to settle in until the sun set. After that close call, they weren't risking another move until they knew everyone was asleep.

Ogden's stomach rumbled in protest as he curled up for a rest, he had forgotten all about the cherry tomatoes. The sound of smacking came from the corner next to him. Ogden bolted back to his feet; Melanie was biting into a tomato!

"When did you get that!?"

"We passed by the bowl on our way here. I snagged

A Tale of Tails

it while you were focused on the door." After stuffing herself on half the tomato, she glanced at Ogden, who was unabashedly drooling while his stomach rumbled. She passed him the rest and then curled up for a nap.

A few hours later, she was shaking Ogden awake, who had fallen asleep after finishing the tomato. She had peeked out of the tambour door and confirmed that everything was cloaked in darkness. The timing was perfect.

They made their way outside without incident. The dog door provided a perfect route to the backyard, but it also meant there was something other than humans to watch out for.

Once they made it outside, their senses turned upward. Some of the last threats standing between them and the blackberry bush would be coming from the sky. They stuck to the wall and scuttled under objects as much as possible, swiftly skirting the side of the pool before plunging headlong into the blackberry bush at last.

Melanie's heart soared as she burst through the leafy curtains that veiled her juicy treasures from sight. The berries were hard to spot in the dark, Ogden sniffed the air to track their scent. It didn't help much, they were too close to the source.

Melanie began climbing the spike-covered branches and spotted a bundle at last. It didn't take long to pick a few blackberries and stuff them into the cloth she had dragged along. The climb down was slow, she had to brace herself more carefully with extra weight throwing her balance off.

By the time she hit the dirt with a soft thud, Ogden was looking frantic.

"What's wrong?"

"Oh, thank Cheese! I thought it had gotten you!" He was hissing the words through his teeth and flapping his paws wildly in the universal sign to get down and quiet. When she obliged and crouched next to him, he pointed to a dark figure perched on the roof.

"Have you figured out what kind it is?" Melanie squeaked the question softly, but what she was really asking was, *Can it eat us?*

"It's an owl." The way Ogden spat out the word *owl*, the venom that dripped from his tone, Melanie knew there was history there. They had grown closer as they ran together, but she didn't think it was enough to go prying into his past. Especially with a memory that clearly still tortured him.

"What do we do? Should we wait it out?"

"It won't leave till the sun rises. By the time that happens, the humans and their hounds will be out. I'd rather deal with the owl."

"Alright, I might have a plan."

A few minutes later, they were slowly walking through the grass, clutching flowers they were using as umbrellas and covered in hound feces.

"This was a horrible plan."

"I know you've said several times that you "hate everything about it," but that owl hasn't glanced our way once!"

"Uhm," Ogden's gulp was cartoonishly loud as his body seized in terror, "I think you spoke too soon." Melanie's eyes flew to where the owl was perched moments before, but the ledge was vacant. The utility of the flower umbrella withered on the spot as it blocked a portion of the sky from their view.

"Did you see where it went?" Melanie was frantic but was reluctant to move too much if they hadn't yet been seen. She looked back at Ogden, and he was gone. His daisy umbrella lay in the grass a foot away, rocking gently in the

A Tale of Tails

breeze.

Her heart started to sprint in her chest when a strong breeze rolled it over, revealing a splatter of red that coated some petals. She caught the coppery scent on the breeze, dropped her own flower, and sprinted for the closest bush.

***

Ogden was squeaking and squirming for his life. He was clutched in the claws of a massive bird. Its sharp beak shone in the starlight, and its claws dug into him from all sides. He was keenly aware of the warm gush of blood that was pouring from a gash in his thigh.

Every time he flailed in a futile attempt to escape, the claws jabbed at him from a different angle. When he felt the owl begin to circle, as if it was preparing to land, he grew more frantic and sunk his teeth into the flesh of the owl's claw.

It let out a shocked hoot, released him, and Ogden began to fall.

***

Melanie couldn't think, the stress was scrambling her thoughts and shredding her reason to ribbons. The sky was slowly creeping away from its inky, black state; they were running out of time. Her mind moved a million miles a minute, in ten different directions. If she didn't make it back inside the walls before the sky became blue, the humans might spot her, which endangered the entire mischief. Her sister was waiting for her back home, and she finally had the blackberries.

There was nothing stopping her from returning to Rafter and slipping back home with no one the wiser.

R.N. Warren

Melanie took a deep breath in, attempting to slow her heart and thoughts. The rusty scent of blood clawed at her nostrils and conscience. She set her shoulders, shoved her emotions into a closet, locking them away, as she ran out of her hiding place.

***

Ogden landed with a crunch in a nest crafted from sticks and twigs, lined with feathers and leaves. A searing pain washed over his body; the waves originating from his back leg. He still had blood trickling from the gash on his thigh.

Closer to his paw, that same leg now throbbed with a sharp pain from within. He sighed with relief when he glanced down and saw that it was not bent at an odd angle. When he tried to put any weight on it, it bucked underneath him. He stood on three legs, holding the fourth up, preventing it from encountering the ground.

Surveying his surroundings had him looking for an escape route. The nest had no large remnants of former meals, but Ogden, with his face so close to the ground, saw hundreds of tiny white finger bones that speckled the nest. He threw up the tomato he had eaten with Melanie. As he heaved up the pink mush, he wondered what Melanie would do. He prayed she headed inside without him.

He froze as the weight of a massive bird landed beside him and hooted, "You haven't been here a minute, and my nest is already a mess! I just moved here you know!"

"P-p-please don't eat—"

"Oh goodness. Is that why you're shaking?" The owl shook its head from side to side but looked completely behind itself with every shake. "Listen, I'm a vegetarian."

Ogden's jaw slackened; he didn't believe this owl for a second. He knew it was lying. He could see the boney proof

A Tale of Tails

beneath his paws, but he didn't know why it wasn't eating him already. The longer they talked, the longer he lived, the longer he had to think of a plan.

"If you're a vegetarian, why did you pick me up?"

"The hounds are coming out now. You would've been spotted, I saved you. You're welcome!" The owl puffed out its feathery chest and Ogden scoffed in disbelief.

"SAVED ME? YOU CUT ME!" Ogden gestured wildly to the gash on his thigh. The owl winced at the splatter of red.

"Sorry... I sharpened my talons yesterday. Bad timing."

"The humans' hounds don't come out until the sky lightens, it's not time yet! Even if it was, you left behind my friend!" Ogden could feel his temper rising

"Okay first, I can only carry one at a time. Second, saving one life is better than saving none, isn't it? And finally, I do hate to break it to you, but today is the day they change their schedules."

The owl stretched out a fluffy brown and tan wing in the direction of the doggy doors through which Melanie and Ogden had passed. Ogden watched the flap skeptically; he didn't believe a hoot that came out of that beak. Ogden refrained from rolling his eyes, he steeled himself to keep the cavalier owl talking.

"What's your name, and why do you care about saving anyone?" Ogden asked. If he played his cards right, he might buy enough time to devise an escape.

"My name is Olive. Olive the owl. I fell out of my nest when I was young. I broke my wing and couldn't fly, I couldn't get food for myself or water, I was too small and slow. It wasn't till much later that I found out who it was, but every morning someone brought olives and an acorn cup of water to the burrow I hid myself in. I know it wasn't my family; I watched them flying above me every day, they never looked down. When my wing healed, I left to find a nest near an olive grove. I haven't wanted to eat anything else since. That's why everyone calls me Olive. The other owls think I'm odd, but none of them helped me, so I'm not bothered."

Ogden squinted at Olive. His head was telling him Olive's story was ridiculous, but when he looked into the owl's eyes, his heart faltered. He was about to ask who had helped when he heard the doggy door flap open.

***

Melanie was running at full speed, her breathing was steady, but she could feel the nervous energy eating away at her. The blackberries were still strapped securely to her back; she felt their weight with every bound. Her nose was in the air, the flower was long gone, she followed the bloody scent with a total disregard to her own safety.

She reached a brown fence she would have to climb straight up to reach the branch of tree the scent felt strongest. The fence was fifteen feet tall, and unforgivingly straight. The wood it was made of was rough enough for claw holds, but she had never scaled anything so tall without breaks. Melanie pulled the blackberries to her chest, wearing them in a frontpack instead of a backpack. If she fell, the berries would survive.

She began the climb with a fiery determination that was slowly replaced by the fiery burning in her forearms as she put one paw in front of the other.

Melanie was halfway up the fence when she heard the flap of the doggy door. The shock caused her grip to slip. She dropped down two feet before her claws dug into the wood deep enough to catch herself.

A Tale of Tails

For a split second, she thought on the bright side, maybe Ogden had gotten free and reached the flap? Then the jangle of metal from the collars around the hounds' necks reached her ears and her palms began to sweat. If she hadn't decided to come for Ogden, would she have run into them on her way back inside? She couldn't think about it now, her arms were screaming at her. She had just lost progress because of distractions. If she slipped a second time, she wouldn't make it.

***

Ogden's heart stuttered as a chill spread through his veins. Melanie was certainly in danger, and he was uncertain about Olive's intentions. He didn't know what move to make. If Melanie had already gone inside, she was either hiding or in danger. The same could be said if Melanie had remained outside, but Ogden had no clue what she chose. Did she stay behind or go ahead?

"Didn't you say there were two of you?" Olive's searchlight eyes beamed across the lawn, catching everything despite the dark. One massive, muscle-bound hound was stalking around the yard's perimeter. Another smaller hound darted beneath short tables and under bushes before locating a bone the size of the Chief and beginning to gnaw.

Olive spotted the stirred bit of dirt left by her talons when Ogden experienced his first flight. She was going to have to get closer to follow the light tracks left behind by his companion.

"The hounds call the backyard their home. They prowl all hours of the day, guarding their territory from *pests*," Olive explained in a grave voice. "It is unusual for them to be out when the sun has not risen."

Ogden squinted his eyes, "The family dogs... they

sleep on the lower floors at night. Ack! That bone is twice my size. Can you tell where she went?"

"I'd have to get closer, but the *teeth* on those hounds…" Olive eyed a featherless patch on her wing.

"Hold me in your claws again, just focus on flight." Ogden's eyes were wild with fear and helplessness.

"I can fly low enough, but you'll only have a second to check."

***

Melanie squeaked through the effort of passing one paw over the other. It felt like forever, her arms had gone numb, and her body was ice cold. She was running through every horrible memory in her mind to fuel the fire that kept her climbing. Her determination was just beginning to sputter as exhaustion began sinking in, when a familiar voice reached her ears.

"A second is more than enough, I just need to be low enough to see it." Melanie was baffled by the panic she heard in Ogden's voice. She let out a squeaky huff of breath as she reached the top of the fence and crumpled exhausted against the tree branch that crept along its flat top.

Ogden and Olive both snapped their heads in the direction of a faint rustle of leaves a few branches away. They were both glaring intensely at the branch when a small, silver-furred head popped into view.

"Melanie?" Ogden and Olive exclaimed in unison, their mouths forming two Os.

"How do you know her name?" Ogden hadn't mentioned Melanie by name, *so how?*

"How *do* you know my name?" Melanie would've thought Ogden had told the owl, if not for his question. The excitement of the reunion of the rats was snuffed by

A Tale of Tails

their baffled squeaks and the tense nature of their situation.

Curiosity raged in Ogden's head. *How did Melanie get here? How did Olive know who she was?* She looked exhausted. Her fur was matted from sweat, her paws were red and raw. Her claws were bleeding where they connected to her paws, as if the weight of carrying her had begun to tear them loose. She was terrified and shaking, but she cradled the pristine blackberries as if they were Popcorn.

Melanie eyed the blood on Ogden's thigh, then clocked the blood in his whiskers and the bite on the owl's foot. She steeled herself for a fight. She whimpered internally at the thought of using her claws, they were throbbing painfully and every step hurt.

When Ogden skittered to her side, the owl made no move to stop him. Melanie leaned against him. He silently supported her as they quickly caught each other up on what happened during their solo adventures.

Olive waited patiently, watching the two rats with barely bridled glee. She had returned! Olive had always believed she would come back one day. If those flowers hadn't been covering their fur, she would have spotted the silver rat sooner! Olive held her tongue until the rats had finished exchanging greetings, before finally bursting.

"It is you! Melanie, the silver rat! You saved my life when I was an owlet!" Olive searched for any sign of recognition, but Melanie was overwhelmed.

"I'm sorry, but I— Wait, what was your name again?" She'd never seen a fully grown owl so close before. She was barely registering anything other than the glint of beak and talons.

"Olive! I was much smaller at the time, so maybe I look different—" The owl's words pulled forth a distant memory from Melanie's childhood. She remembered resting on a withered, silver rat's lap, listening utterly raptured by the tale the hunched rat spun out before her. It was an adventure of epic proportions, and as Melanie grew older, she believed less and less of it to be true.

"No, wait! My Nana Mel used to tell me stories about a flightless owl in the woods."

"Are you talking about Elder Melanie Marmalade?" Ogden remembered the outlandish tales she would tell the pups, her memory was notoriously shoddy, but her talent for spinning tales was legendary.

"Yes! She is my grandmother."

"But she lost her position as Tale Weaver for spreading the story about a vegetarian owl."

Both rats glanced guiltily in Olive's direction, the owl looked stricken.

"Let me make sure I understand." Olive's hoots took on a scolding tone. "You aren't the one who saved me, you're her granddaughter. The Melanie who saved me lost her job because she talked about me, and no one believed her?"

Ogden and Melanie looked at their paws, ashamed. The Elders had never believed Marmalade's tall tales; they only saw the risk in telling a young generation that *some* owls might not eat them.

"She left in search of an olive tree when I was very young and never came back. I'm so sorry, Olive. She left behind a note for my mother, but my mom almost burned it because it was written for you. We didn't think you existed at the time, and she wrote nothing for her daughter. But my mom couldn't bring herself to throw it away, either. So, she crammed it under the wobbly table leg in her study. The table has been stable ever since."

"Do you think there's a way I could read it?" Olive's hoots grew frantic, and her round, golden eyes were misting

A Tale of Tails

with emotion.

Melanie and Ogden exchanged glances. They had gotten good at reading each other over the course of their journey. It was apparent that their time apart hadn't hindered that ability. The hesitation and concern surrounding the decision to trust a predator superimposed what lay beneath. The trust that had grown between them, the kinship from shared horrors, and the team they had become. There was something more there too, something lurking in the depths that neither rat was ready to acknowledge.

Ogden knew the fastest route home would be hitching a ride on Olive and having her fly them to the Eastern Eave entrance. There was enough of a ledge there that Olive could have a runway. The trip to Rafter from there was only a four-minute scurry. Melanie could be home with Popcorn in ten minutes.

Melanie knew Ogden's career consisted of steering danger away from Rafter. She wouldn't jeopardize that by bringing a potential threat to their home. They would have to verify Olive's story somehow before they brought her anywhere on the roof.

"Can you read Scratch?"

"Yes, she taught me."

"Olive. I know how horrible I'm going to sound when I say this, but I'll give you the letter under a few conditions."

Olive agreed to the terms Melanie had laid out, but it was clear in the stiffness of her movements that she was offended. Melanie understood why she was upset, and she had every right to be. She had been abandoned by her own family when she failed to fly and broke her wing. The only creature who cared for her was a young silver rat who patched up her wing and brought her food. Melanie Marmalade had taught this owl how to read Scratch, introduced her to a vegetarian diet, and befriended a discarded owlet.

Olive hadn't stopped searching for her ever since, waiting for her friend to return. A rat's lifespan is much shorter than an owl's, Nana Mel probably ventured out one last time to say goodbye.

Olive brought them one at a time to the spot they agreed would serve as the best proof of the owl's vegetarianism. It was the largest pile of olive pits either rat had ever seen. The pile was scattered against two trunks in a mountainous pile that Ogden briefly considered skiing down. Melanie grabbed a pit, scarred with deep grooves and gashes that could only have been made by a beak. She added it to her pouch and nodded.

Thirty minutes later, Melanie was soaring through the skies towards the Eaves, praying to the Holy Cheese above that her mother would see reason.

***

Ogden was pacing on the ledge, waiting for Olive and Melanie to fly in. He was whispering under his breath, trying to hype himself up for the difficult conversations that lay ahead. The hardest one had to come first, before everything came crashing down around them. *As soon as she lands,* he kept saying to himself, *I'll tell her.*

When Olive came in for the landing, Melanie rolled gracefully to her feet without squashing a single berry. It was incredible. When she grinned back at him, all the words he so carefully selected slipped through his fingers. The exhilaration from the flight, the satisfaction of completing her mission, and the joy of the upcoming reunion with her sister filled Melanie with a wild glee and reckless confidence. When her eyes settled on Ogden, that feeling that had been simmering overwhelmed her. She couldn't help herself; she

A Tale of Tails

waltzed over and kissed the buck. Olive covered her eyes with her wing.

***

The next winter, Ogden and Melaine knew she had not been seen when the fist had punched its way through the wall. Amidst the fear, they had found each other, and neither one was willing to let go.

Melanie was expecting. Every time Ogden thought of this, his heart swelled with joy and anxiety gnawed at his gut. His job had too many close calls over the last few moons, and the food collection workers had more missing persons than ever.

"Are you heading out for your search?" Melaine called from the soapbox bed they had built together.

"Yes, Chief Red Berry is desperate for a new food route. You know James vanished on his shift yesterday?"

"You still insist on calling her Chief, you could start calling her Mother-in-Law one of these days."

"Uhm... Maybe if I find us the next food route," Ogden began, before muttering under his breath, *"any sooner and she might strangle me."*

"I heard that! She likes you more than you think, after all, you did bring her daughter back with a bushel of blackberries in tow."

"I brought her daughter back injured, she's never going to thank me for that."

Melanie grinned and tapped her nose to his before pushing him out the door with a homemade lunch sack between his teeth. They both knew it wasn't bringing her back injured that sent her spiraling (though that didn't help), it was bringing her back pregnant that stiffened her fur.

R.N. Warren

***

Ogden wandered through the walls, following his nose. He had been promoted when he married Melanie, though the kindness of the gesture on the Chief's part was debatable. His job was more perilous than ever, and the entire mischief's hopes were riding on his shoulders.

He followed his mental map until he reached unfamiliar surroundings, and then he kept going. His nose on high alert for anything that might resemble food. It wasn't long until he picked up a hint of what had been leading him down this path for the last few nights. It was faint and confusing, because the whiffs he got contained so many different scents. It was overwhelming: sugar, syrup, beans, dried meats, and fruits. But none of it smelled rotten.

It seemed like someone, or something, had been stockpiling food for many moons. As the scent grew stronger, the path grew more demanding. He was jumping over scorching pipes, scrambling down a ladder of nails, and squeezing through impossible cracks.

When he rounded the final corner, a massive, hairless, clawless foot crashed down inches from his whiskers. He almost couldn't stop himself from letting a frightened squeak escape from behind his long front teeth.

The stress of the moment had him gnawing on his tail, something he hadn't done since he was a pup. He stayed stock-still and silent as the ugly bald feet thudded against the floor. He was safe in the corner for now; as long as the human didn't look down.

Ogden used the moment to take stock of his surroundings. A moment later, he bit down hard on the tail he was still gnawing. He had to be dreaming.

This place couldn't be real. There was too much! Nothing could eat all this, not even the strange, bald two-leggers. They

A Tale of Tails

might be large, but surely, they couldn't consume this much food. The mixed smells made sense now, this room held boxes of differently shaped dried sticks, metallic packages full of crunchy, cheesy treats. There were peas, corn, peaches, and pears trapped inside metallic casings. Bags of potatoes, onions, and garlic were littered on the floor, just a few bounds away. Strange sacks containing sugar, flour, and other powders were on the shelf above him.

The sheer amount of food decorating the walls in this room was almost frightening. The entire mischief could be fed for hundreds of winters without ever having to step paw outside. The true challenge now would be deciding how to open these containers without the humans noticing or just figuring out how to open them at all, or even figuring out what these foods were. Some of the things he saw and smelled in that room were things he'd never experienced before.

As soon as the feet left the food-filled room and the lights went out, Odgen risked a trip to the sacks on the floor. There was a netted sack filled with tiny potatoes that caught Ogden's eye. He grabbed one of the potatoes, judging that it was about the size of the biggest toe on the hairless foot that almost crushed his nose.

After some maneuvering made harder by the addition of the baby potato, he finally made it back to the mischief with the best news. He headed straight to Chief Crunch with the starch offering and the mental map he had crafted over the last moon. He wasn't planning to stop for anyone, but a familiar golden-furred rat rounded the corner and crashed into him.

"Uncle Ogden!" The buttery squeak of Popcorn's voice spread a grin across Ogden's face and he bent down to rustle her fur.

"You should really watch where you're going. One of

these days you're going to crash into something that won't just dust you off." The small fluff of a rat stuck out her tongue before yanking on his fur in excitement.

"Olive's back with more berries! She told me to tell you she tried out the fermented berry recipe you gave her. How come I'm not allowed to try that one?"

"You're going to have to ask Melanie about that. I have to report to the Chief, I'll come hang out with you and Olive after." Ogden winked at the young rat, who popped with happiness at his words and scurried off.

***

"Well look who it is! Anything new to report?" The Chief's words sounded jovial, but Ogden didn't miss the hard look in her eyes. He stepped forward timidly, knowing the negative feelings the Chief held for him after bringing her daughter home injured hadn't vanished.

"I found something!" The pure joy and light that emanated from Ogden's eyes clearly took Red Berry aback, because in response she sat up straighter and scooted to the edge of her elegant doll's throne.

"I'm listening now, but I won't be for long. Speak!"

As a reply, Ogden thrust the small potato into the Chief's lap before announcing, "And there's more where that came from!"

Chief Crunch swallowed hard. "How much more?" she asked in a tremulous voice.

"More than we could ever possibly eat."

"More than the entire mischief could ever eat? You aren't pulling my paw, are you?"

"Follow me, you *must* see this for yourself. I would've taken Melanie right away, but in her condition... I would never ask her to risk it."

A Tale of Tails

"Glad to see my daughter's safety finally means something to you." The Chief's shadow dispelled light from the room as her massive form rose from her throne. Twin indentations were pressed into the fur on both of her thighs. The mighty throne ransacked from the American Doll Cemetery was plush, but ran a bit snug.

Finding the route back to the pantry was aided by the same scent that lured him there the first time. They were only two turns away from their destination when the Chief's ears twitched.

"Stop! They approach." Chief Red Berry Crunch furrowed her brow, Ogden understood why when the sound reached his ears. Something about it was off, the stampede of a swarm, instead of the steady thumping of a pack. They froze with ears high.

"Maybe we should try this again at nightfall," Ogden broached, his wife's round belly and the hairless foot flashing through his mind.

"We go on carefully, the mischief needs this." The Chief's shoulders were tensed in determination, she approached a small crack to examine the human's stomping ground. Brown boxes lined the floor in the hall, each one filled to the brim with items like their miniature counterparts in the Doll Cemetery.

Chief Crunch's eyes widened, involuntary squeaks of fear clawing up her throat. She remembered the stories passed down from Chief to Chief through generations. She was familiar with the pattern they were living through. The primary job of the Chief is to guard the tales of the human inhabitants in order to make informed decisions for the good of the mischief.

She knew they had been living in a period of "moving." A lot of activity, brown boxes and trucks had been recorded, followed by quiet. The silence was broken only by a few sporadic visits from two-leggers. Before a new wave of brown boxes came, followed by a new family of humans. No one knew what happened to the first family of humans, many assumed they lost some kind of turf war. Now the pantry was full to a degree that no one had seen in years. That meant the new family moving in would be larger than the last. They were in more danger of discovery than ever.

If they were ever found, she knew what patterns to watch for. The arrival of two-leggers dressed in white, invading the mischief's location. Remember the metallic beast they crawl within, for one day they will return, bearing contraptions that kill and maim.

The Chief gnawed her lower lip.

They continued on, the rhythm of their hearts beating at a faster tempo. Ogden hadn't missed the reaction the Chief had to the brown boxes, but his thoughts of food-covered walls kept him occupied.

He thought of the kind face he left at home and her swelling belly. He thought of Popcorn and the blackberries that started a relationship. Popcorn, who was young with a bright future, one that could be aided by the introduction of a large store of food. The ability to not worry about one's future is something he wanted for the whole mischief.

He remembered the days when the mischief's lettuce was wilted, the bread moldy, the tomatoes nothing but brown mush. His mother's smile as she gave him her own portion remained always at the front of his mind. He didn't want those memories for his child. He didn't want them for Popcorn.

He wanted them to have enough.

Redemption's Secrets
by Randi Perrin

My pencil scratches across the pages of my sketchbook as I twirl rainbow strands of hair that have escaped my ponytail around my finger. I'm supposed to be manning my dad's booth at the fall festival in our podunk town, but everyone is more interested in fried goods and trying to win a goldfish than they are picking up pamphlets about STDs, condoms, or an apple from this table.

All the better, because I don't want to be here. I hate everything about this place. Redemption, Kentucky—there's not a damn thing redeemable about this town or its stupid festival. More like Rejection, Kentucky.

I get lost in the sketch, which is an old tree raining leaves onto the tire swing that hangs from the thickest branch. Behind the tree is an ancient farmhouse with a wraparound porch that spans the entire front. The three steps that lead from the yard to the porch each feature a jack-o'-lantern.

A siren wails from the booth beside me, shattering my illusion of solitude, and I'm reminded that I'm in the middle of a festival pushing my dad's stuff because he's too busy to do it himself. Because who doesn't want to get a free condom from a seventeen-year-old who makes her disdain for this place known, wears combat boots, dyes her hair rainbow colors, and has perfected the resting bitch face? By all rights, I should have a line a mile long!

I glance up to see the quarterback of the football team, Diego Vasquez, mock-blowing at the muzzle of the pellet gun mounted at an awkward angle in front of a target. This game has probably been illegal for the past twenty years because of safety concerns, but it's the one where would-be hunters shoot pellets to win prizes. Hits closer to the bullseye bring bigger prizes. The drunker the shooter, the fewer prizes they must hand out. Carnies win. Again.

The carny sneers at him. "You can't do it again, *kid*." Guess he hit a bullseye while making it look easy, much to the delight of the little kid with him. Diego may be a world-class asshole, but it looks like he just made that kid's entire weekend.

Diego catches my gaze and winks before he pulls the trigger again so quickly, it's as if he didn't bother aiming this time. Once again, the siren screams in the evening air, making the middle-aged, beer-gutted jerk of a carny sputter his disbelief.

He crouches down to be eye to eye with his little friend. "What's it going to be, Teddy?"

The little kid jumps up and down and points at the snake. "La culebra! La culebra!"

"In English, dammit," the carny sneers from around a half-smoked Marlboro that dangles from his lips. "You're in America. Act like it."

I stomp out from behind the booth for the Appalachian Clinic and stand behind Diego. "He said 'the snake,' *pinche pendejo*." I plant my feet, cock my hip, and flip him off, a

Redemption's Secrets

silent dare to say something to me.

The carny gives me the evil eye as he tugs down the green snake and hands it to Teddy. "The second one?" He crushes the cigarette under the toe of his boot. It's painted all over his face that he hates his job, or maybe it's the fact Diego made his game look like child's play. Maybe both. Maybe he wasn't loved enough as a kid. Who the hell cares? It's no reason to be a jerk.

From his spot low on the ground, Diego turns toward my voice, eyes wide, mouth agape… and then he loses his balance. With a deft, blink-and-you'll-miss-it stumble, he stands, never once taking his eyes off me. "The purple panda."

Teddy shakes his head and pouts his bottom lip. "Yo quiero la culebra."

Diego's shoulders shake with laughter. "You don't need another snake, buddy. As it is, this one will keep you up at night, and I share a room with you."

The carny tosses the cheap stuffed animal at him and mutters some slur under his breath. I stare daggers at him, begging him to be dumb enough to say it again. He keeps his mouth shut. Maybe he's not as stupid as he looks, after all.

An hour later, I'm sitting at the booth with a still-full basket of apples and condoms, staring at the smiling face of someone on an STD pamphlet, which makes zero sense. If I'd just been told I had a disease that made my naughty bits burn, I don't know that I'd be smiling like a fool. At the game to my right, there's a new carny swindling money from people in the name of cheap stuffed animals. Jackass Carny is on the other side of the festival running a different game, where I can no longer hear him belittle people.

I stare at my sketch of the old tree and pull the pencil

from behind my ear to add some shading, and, finally, my initials to the tree itself. A.J.

A shadow moves over my drawing; dark storm clouds rolling over the idyllic scene.

"Thanks for your help back there, Jenkins. Where'd you learn to swear in Spanish?" Boots crunch the gravel as the figure moves a step closer to the table.

"Spent my summers on mission trips in Central America—Mexico and Costa Rica, mostly. Guatemala once. Church kids are hardly innocent." I look up to find Diego staring at me as if I'm some circus oddity he expects to perform just for him.

"Dope." The verbal skills of teenage boys are off the charts.

"Not going to jerk off in front of me, Vasquez?" My name is easy, Amelia Jenkins. But on my first day of school in this wretched place, the teacher introduced me as Amelia Jerkins, which is why all the jocks make jerking-off hand motions when they pass me in the halls.

He shakes his head. "Nah, today, you're my hero."

I roll my eyes. "I still won't piss on you if you're on fire."

He shakes his head and gives me a knowing smile. "You like me, you know it."

"Bzzzzt. Wrong answer. Thanks for playing." I toss an apple at him. "Here's your consolation prize."

He catches the apple and takes a bite, spraying bits all over the place. "Whaf?" he asks around the fruit before swallowing. "You couldn't even have the decency to give me the condom prize?"

I hold my index finger in the air. "One, since when is a condom a consolation prize?" I add my middle finger to make a peace sign. "And two, why would I want to

Redemption's Secrets

deny myself the pleasure of being sprayed in bits of half-masticated apple and your DNA?"

Diego laughs before grabbing a handful of condoms and shoving them into his pocket. "You know the condom is to keep DNA from being sprayed, right?"

"Lucky for you, Vasquez, we will never have to worry about that."

Expecting a smart-ass answer, I'm surprised when he reaches out and spins my sketchbook around, so it faces the right way to him. His chocolate eyes remain locked onto the tree I drew. "This is amazing," he whispers.

"Thanks." I drag my black combat boot-clad foot across the ground and look away. Compliments make me awkward, especially about my artwork that I've never shared with anyone before. Save for my dad, who bought me the sketchbook as a gift to soften the blow before we moved to this little slice of Appalachian hell.

A heaviness in the air hangs over us and dries up the conversation. I glance up at the hill that stands sentry watch over the entire town, complete with a skeleton tree near the ledge. I've never been up there, but it wouldn't surprise me if the tree had a face and guarded the hill like a barren version of the orchard of sentient trees that threw apples at Dorothy in *Wizard of Oz*.

Someone comes to my table—the first all evening, save Diego—so I turn my attention to the college-aged kid. He's just here for the free condoms. I fork over a handful, along with a pamphlet that screams "I've got gonorrhea, now what?" in large black letters, and it's accompanied by a smiling college kid who reeks of douchecanoe playboy. That's the only reason I can come up with for why he'd be happy about getting the clap.

Diego looks at me with a sheepish smile.

"What?"

He shrugs. "You clearly don't want to be here."

I cross my arms in front of my chest. "By here, do you mean at this table or in this town?"

"Yes," he says with a laugh.

"I should think the answer to both is obvious."

A tiny smile spreads across his face. "Wanna get out of here? We can go to the top of the hill and spy on the whole town."

"The whole town?"

He nods.

I have my doubts about the whole town, but there's only one way to find out. My eyes whirl between the table, the hill, then back at the table, and finally at Diego's face, home of a cheesy grin that is excited as the little kid when he won him a snake "I mean, the stuff is free, it's not like I have to be here, right?"

"Exactly," Diego says, holding out his hand. I brush it off and walk around the table on my own. "I should warn you, there will be a little fence-hopping involved."

"You've been up there before?" The question is stupid. Why would he offer to take me up there if he hadn't been before? Still, it's too late, and the ridiculous words are out there, taking an axe to my IQ.

"Well, duh," he says.

If this is the way the evening is going to go, I need to stop talking or I can kiss an acceptance to Northwestern goodbye.

"Everyone goes up the hill to make out." He chokes on a laugh. "Not that you'd know anything about that."

"Don't get any ideas while we're up there."

"I would never, Jerkins."

Redemption's Secrets

***

After scaling a fence, catching my hoodie on the chain link and practically strangling myself as I try to walk away, Diego and I trudge up the hill, me gasping for breath, him just talking about whatever random shit that pops in his head without the slightest bit of discomfort. He's rambling about how the University of Kentucky is recruiting him to play for them next year.

I cannot stress this enough—I don't care.

"Hey." Pause. Gasp for breath. "Vasquez." Gasp. "How… did… you… kill… that… carnival… game?"

He turns around and waits for me to catch up to him. "You won't believe me."

I choke out laughter as I navigate around some rocks, but trip and fall instead. I land in his outstretched arms as the words "Try me" fall off my tongue.

Diego closes his eyes and takes a deep breath before returning me to my upright and locked position. "Promise you won't make fun?"

"I'll always make fun of you, but not about whatever you're going to tell me." I make an X over my heart with my index finger. "Cross my heart, hope to die, stick a rusty needle in my eye."

"Okay, I don't need that much of a promise, but okay." He takes a deep breath. "We emigrated from Mexico when I was a toddler. My dad got a job doing maintenance for a traveling carnival. I ended up knowing all the carnies, and I was a cute kid, so they all taught me the secrets to their games."

"Aren't they all rigged?" I ask. My heart rate is less erratic, but nowhere near normal.

"Some of them," he says with a wink. "Anyway, he and

Mom got their citizenship, so they decided it was time to put down roots. I don't know why, but this is where they chose. Dad got a job in the mines, and then when he got sick, they bought the store."

I know the rest of the story. Everyone does. His dad died a few months later, leaving Diego, his mom, and his older sister on their own. They struggled for the first few years, but finally found their footing. It's a cross between a convenience store and a farmer's market—it's mostly snacks and drinks and just enough pantry staples you can pull together for a quick meal without having to drive forty-five minutes to Walmart. In the back is a wall of nothing but produce from local farmers during the summer months. In the winter months, Mama Vasquez sells homemade empanadas and tamales and the best birria taco kits. Given its proximity to my dad's clinic, and his inability to boil water, we eat a lot of her food. Not that I will ever tell Diego that his mom is the reason I haven't starved to death.

We top the hill, and I've never been more grateful to see flat land than I am right now. That hill is deceptively steep. I hate the mountains. I put my hands on my knees and take a moment to catch my breath.

When I look up, I'm staring at a farmhouse that used to be white but has yellowed with time, weather, and decay. The once-black shutters are gray and crooked. On each of the three steps sits a different jack-o'-lantern, just like the ones in my picture. I lean down to pick up a pumpkin and trace the jagged cuts that make up its face. It's not just any farmhouse, it's the one I drew this evening.

I turn back to Diego, who is still standing by a tree. "Think fast, football boy," I say before I pick up a pumpkin and heave it in his direction, lobbing the pumpkin at his head, which misses by a mile. Guess it's a good thing he

Redemption's Secrets

plays football and not me.

"Milly, for real, why are you throwing rocks at me?"

"It was a jack-o'-lantern. Oh, and my name is not Milly."

He rolls his eyes as he bends down and picks up a flat rock and closes my fingers around it. "That," he says, pointing to a rock about ten feet away from him, "is not a pumpkin. And would you rather me call you Jerkins?"

I put my rock-free hand on my hip. "Fine, Milly it is. But if another soul finds out I let you call me that, I will grab your balls and twist as I drag you down Main Street. Do you understand me?"

He grabs his crotch and gives me a meek nod before he runs his fingers across the bark of a hundred-or-so-year-old (I'm guessing) oak tree. "It's a shame they haven't done something with the land since the house burned down," he says.

I cock my head to the side and look at him as if he just sprouted a third arm. "What are you talking about? The house is right there. It's where I got the pumpkin." I turn and point at where I just picked up the jack-o'-lantern, seeing nothing but thistles and what happens when Mother Nature reaches middle age and lets herself go. "I swear there was a house here a minute ago."

Diego laughs at me. "If by a minute ago you mean a couple of decades ago, then yeah. Sure." The bark of the tree is littered with initials, teenagers from years gone by, leaving their marks behind. "It burned down and took most of the trees on the hill with it. Save for this one, this one somehow survived."

"What happened up here?" If curiosity killed the cat, I'm digging my grave, but he can't just tell me part of the story like that.

Randi Perrin

He drops to the ground, his butt crunching six inches of dead orange and brown and red leaves, before leaning against the tree to look out over the town. "It happened before we moved here. All I know is that everyone claims it's haunted." He looks around and shrugs. "But I've seen nothing to substantiate that."

Ignoring the fact the star football player just used a word like substantiate—and correctly—I drop to the ground beside him. From here, there's a perfect view of a silent Main Street. It's quiet most of the time, but now that the festival is going on, it's an absolute ghost town.

Sheriff Minton slides into the bar, checking over his shoulder before he closes the door behind him. I nudge Diego with my elbow. "Looks like the sheriff is going to be drinking on duty tonight."

He shakes his head. "Sheriff Minton doesn't drink, not a drop."

"You sure? Because I hear he's there all the time." The good ol' Redemption gossip mill is such a well-oiled machine that you can't sneeze without someone showing up on your front porch with chicken soup.

"He drinks nothing but that awful stuff Myrtle passes off for coffee over at the diner. He goes in every night for a shot of Manda, the bartender. Been doing it for years, and either his wife doesn't know or doesn't care. I'm not sure which."

I narrow my eyes. "How do you know that?"

He gives me a half-smile as he palms his floppy bangs up out of his face. "My sister is the other bartender."

A few minutes later, the sheriff slips back out of the bar and passes my dad, who is walking back to his clinic from the Vazquez family store. The sheriff lifts his hand in a one-finger salute behind my dad's back. Then Sheriff Minton

Redemption's Secrets

adjusts himself and slips into Myrtle's diner, probably for some coffee and her famous Derby pie.

"Did you see him just flip off your dad?" Diego asks.

"Dad can't stand him, but I didn't realize it was that frosty between them."

Leaning against the tree, I take a deep breath and close my eyes. Something brushes against my hand, and I jerk it away. No way am I giving Diego any ideas that maybe our initials belong on that tree, too. When I open them again, Diego is gone.

"Diego? You did not just leave me up here all alone to get busted, did you? You are such a jerk."

A male voice on the other side of the tree catches my attention, "Diego? Is that you?" Because who else would it be? Come on, Amelia.

There's no answer, just a giggle. I peek my head around the tree and find a girl about my age in the tire swing, and a tall, rail-thin guy pushes her. She's wearing a pair of overalls that seem to be a size or two too big for her, with a tiny crop-top underneath. Because it's late October, she's also got a black cardigan covering the whole thing. On her feet are ancient Converse All-Stars that might have been white at one time, but no amount of cleaning will ever get them there again.

The rope tied to the tree creaks its discomfort each time it moves backward. The lanky guy stands behind her, his right foot forward, holding the brunt of his weight, big toe poking through a hole in his shoe. If there's one thing my dad can't stand, it's people who do not have proper shoes—he would probably offer this kid the shoes on his own feet if he were here right now.

Pressing myself tight against the tree, I eavesdrop on their conversation.

Randi Perrin

"I can't join the Air Force now," she says, her face crumbling under the realization.

The young man catches the swing and places a soft kiss behind her ear and squeezes her arm. "Yes, you can. You'll just have to wait a bit."

She leans into him and places her head against his shoulder. "Dad won't see it that way."

"Once you're eighteen—in three months and three days, not that I've been counting—you don't need his permission anymore. We can do whatever we want." He shakes his head, burrowing his face in her thick, wavy hair that is just one shade darker than dirty blonde.

"I will always need his permission," she replies with a defeated sigh. "You know how he is." Her index finger traces the lines the knuckles form on his hand. It's more than a little gross how much these two must touch each other. What ever happened to autonomy, anyway?

He walks around to be in front of the swing and smiles down at her, placing his hand on her stomach, highlighting a bump I hadn't noticed before. He tucks a strand of hair behind her ear. "I'll get us a place and a job. We'll be okay."

She shakes her head. "What about your classes?"

"College can wait. You and this baby are more important than anything." He drops to one knee and holds up a dainty ring. "Let's get married in the spring, right before the baby comes. Then you can enlist with my last name. We'll go wherever they send you, and he'll never find us. We can take his power away, just say—"

The smile she gives him practically cracks her face in half. "Yes. Yesterday. Today. Tomorrow. Yes."

He stands and tries to slip the ring onto her finger, but his hands are shaking so much that he drops it into the leaves at his feet. With frantic motions, he kicks the dried

Redemption's Secrets

leaves away, flinging them in every direction, trying to find the tiny wisp of silver. She places her hand on his shoulder to stop him.

"It's okay. I don't need a ring. I just need you."

"What did I do to deserve you?" He rises to his feet, brushing the leaves off his jeans before helping her down from the swing. "I love you Ry," he whispers as he nuzzles his face into her hair.

"I love you more." He's wearing a shirt for the band Nickelback, and I shudder. She just said "yes" to a Nickelback fan. Gross. I think my dad may have listened to them when he was younger, and to this day, I'll never understand why. Some of his music I'm okay with, but I will never be okay with that shit.

From down the hill, the bells on the church rip through the quiet town to announce it's six o'clock. The girl's smile and shoulders fall. "Dad will be home soon; get out of here."

"Not much longer and you won't have to answer to him anymore," he says.

"Eight months and three days," they say in unison.

"And I can't wait," she says, placing a soft kiss on his cheek. She starts toward the house, refusing to let go of his hand until their arms stretch as far as they can go, and the sound of tires on gravel at the bottom of the hill destroys any sense of privacy they might have had. She walks into the house without turning back, and he takes off running in the opposite direction of the oncoming car.

A pickup truck with a shotgun mounted in the back window tops the hill and stops two inches shy of hitting the already-splintered corner post of the porch. He must not always be that lucky. He slams the door of the truck and stomps inside, hitching up the gray pants of his sheriff's uniform, grumbling about a beer.

Once he's out of sight, I sit with my thoughts. Who are those teenagers? Who the hell is he? And why is he clipping that poor girl's wings if she wants to fly? Why is marriage, of all institutions, the only way out for her? It sounds like another prison. It's none of my business. I rise to my feet and start walking down the hill, following the driveway.

I keep walking until an invisible vice squeezes me in the feels, reminding me that this girl's angry mountain of a father doesn't want this. The lovey dovey shit may nauseate me, but I loathe the patriarchy even more. Men, who the hell do they think they are?

I shrug. It's not my problem. What is my problem is finding Diego.

I take a few steps down the hill, but the vice squeezes harder, adding a twist and an ache in my chest cavity until I turn around. My problem or not, I do not want whatever the sheriff has in store for her if he finds that ring. Who knows what he might do to her, the poor kid with holes in his shoes and poor taste in music, or worse yet, her unborn baby?

My feels guide my feet back to the base of the tree, just under the tire that sways in the cool night breeze. Only a few minutes of daylight remain, but how far could it have gone? I will just come back to give it to her another day.

Crawling around on the ground, wetness seeping into the knee of my jeans, I toss leaves into the air and watch them flutter back to the ground like I did when I was a kid. With the third handful of leaves, something shiny catches my eye and defies gravity, flipping over and over, like the coin toss before a football game. The ring moves in slow motion, so I hold out my hand and the tiny, perfect circle lands in the middle of my palm. I slide it onto the ring finger of my right hand, a jolt of electricity sparking up my arm, stopping where the vice grip in my chest begins.

I don't have long to revel in my win before the front door opens and the old man barrels out of the house, open beer can in hand. His duty belt no longer weighs down his pants, and the gray shirt is untucked and unbuttoned, revealing a hairy chest that reminds me of a bear. "The hell is going on out here?" he bellows as he stumbles to his truck and jerks the shotgun off the back window. Lifting it to his shoulder, he loses his footing, tries again, and takes aim in my direction.

"Amelia," a voice calls to me on the breeze. "Amelia," comes the voice again, the sound snaking around me like satin across skin. It's distant, but close by, and it's disorienting. I wobble on my feet, struggling to stand upright. Something is pulling at me like a wave ebbing away from the shore, wanting to take me with it. I'm tempted to let it. That is, until it adds one word.

"Run."

It's as if I'm in a cartoon and my legs are moving as fast as they can go, a blur of motion below me, but I am not moving. From behind me comes a shove, and I can finally propel myself forward. I run down the hill, following the well-worn tire tracks that comprise the driveway, twigs and dead leaves crunching under my feet.

"Yeah, you better run," the old man grumbles just before a shot rings out, temporarily deafening me. My right arm stings and I think it's bleeding, but no time to check now.

I keep running, muttering, "He's going to kill me." True or not, the mantra keeps my momentum going as I draw ragged breaths with each step. Now is not the time for semantics.

Randi Perrin

I reach the bottom of the hill and take a second to catch my breath. A giant drop of blood falls from my right arm and splashes onto my combat boot. I waver on my feet. Not blood, come on, anything but blood.

Another drop lands on my shoe before I build up enough courage to look at my arm. My favorite hoodie has another battle wound and now I'm sporting a huge gash that oozes blood and plasma and whatever the hell else that should be inside my body instead of out.

One last glance at my poor hoodie and I collapse into a heap of Amelia. As soon as I hit the ground, I roll ass-over-head, until I finally come to a stop in the gnarled and knotted roots of a giant tree. My vision blurs around the edges, but I struggle to my feet. I make it one step before the roots, seemingly with a mind of their own, wrap around my ankles and tug me back to the ground. This time I fall face first into a rock, the craggy tree roots tearing into the tender flesh of my stomach.

My head throbs, pain everywhere—as if Thanos's giant hand is on top of my head and he is pushing down while making a fist around my skull.

Two figures rush toward me.

The first places my head in its lap, stroking my head with phalanges of ice, humming what sounds like "Hush Little Baby." I grasp the hand to move it to the part of my head that really hurts, but all my fingers feel are ninety-eight-point-six-degree cheeks and a couple smears of blood on my fingertips. The humming continues as a chill settles over my body and I relax into it, welcoming the numb that washes over me and dulls the pain in my head.

Feet thunder over to me, as if a herd of elephants come to a stop six inches from trampling me to death.

I close my eyes, and when I open them again, it's only

Redemption's Secrets

Diego; my head resting in his lap as he uses soft touches to tame the wild hair that broke free of its ponytail during the fall.

"Dios mío," he whispers. "Milly, can you hear me?" He holds up two fingers in front of my face. Or maybe it's just one. Who knows? Who cares? "How many fingers am I holding up?" The words are faint, as if I'm listening to them underwater.

I open my mouth to tell him two, but no sound comes out. The Thanos-grip on my skull tightens, weighing down my head to the point my neck no longer supports it. I make a peace sign with two fingers on my left hand before my head lolls to the side and a curtain of darkness falls over my world.

***

"Now, from where I sit," Sheriff Minton says, his fuzzy figure lighting a cigarette and then putting his feet up on the desk, "I saw you coming off the hill with a pocket full of condoms and a passed-out girl in your arms with defensive injuries. You do the math."

The sheriff is not talking to me. He is talking about me, a fact that hurts. Almost as much as my head. My game plan when we moved here was to avoid the law. Not that grappling with cops is a pastime of mine, but my entire purpose was to make this side quest to hell short and painless before returning to Chicago for college.

I moan and struggle to sit up, rubbing my eyes so the room comes into full focus.

Sheriff Minton puffs away at his desk. I'm lying on a very uncomfortable pleather couch, Diego sitting in a matching chair to my left, anxiety fueling his bouncing leg, his eyes darting between the sheriff and me.

Randi Perrin

My dad races into the office, doctor's case in hand. He rushes straight to me and goes full concussion protocol; he's done it to me many times over the years, though this is the first time I've failed it. Blood streams down my arm and stains my shirt. He wraps fresh gauze around my arm, which blooms with crimson as soon as he lets go. "Going to need stitches," he mutters. He lifts my shirt partway, just enough to reveal the zig-zag scratches across my belly. Dad glares at Diego and turns his attention to Sheriff Minton, motioning to him they need to go outside.

"I thought you just hit your head when you fell," Diego whispers.

I shake my head, my eyes refusing to break eye contact with him, as if I'm afraid he might disappear if I close them again. His eyes are at least a better focus than the look of disappointment Doctor Dad will have for me while Sheriff Minton fills in the details—even though I am sketchy on them myself.

Diego runs a thumb across my cheek. "You scared me—playing in the leaves without a care in the world."

"That scared you?" I ask.

"No, that part was actually adorable." I cringe at the adjective. I am many things, but adorable is not one of them. "When you took off running for no reason, then fell and rolled down the hill until a giant tree root caught you before I could."

"Good thing you're not a wide receiver then," I say with a laugh, which only makes my head hurt more, so I close my eyes. Everything hurts. Especially my right arm, which has already saturated the gauze that was just placed there. Each gash, each drop of blood, a tiny fire burning across my skin, as if I'm being sent a message to not think.

"Did you see the sheriff with a shotgun?" I whisper to

Redemption's Secrets

Diego.

Diego gives me a sad smile and shakes his head. "For your sake, I wish that were true. But there was no one else out there but us, and when Sheriff Minton showed up, he only had the nine-millimeter, not a shotgun. Maybe you hit your head harder than we thought."

Dad returns to the room, his mouth set in a grim line, and sits down next to me on the couch. He tosses my bloody arm over his shoulder and motions at Diego to do the same on the other side. Together, they stand and drag my limp body out of the sheriff's office and out to Dad's snow-white BMW. There are houses in this town that cost less than his car.

Diego mouths the words, *call me*, before my dad slams the door closed. Apparently, any conversations—with Diego or the sheriff—are over.

***

The following morning, my head feels as if I cracked it open and am just a slow leak away from my brains leaving my skull. My limbs move, but I have no control. It's as if a jellyfish's tentacles are being pushed around by the surrounding sea. Bandages ensconce my right arm, no doubt covering several stitches that I don't remember Doctor Dad putting in.

Dad throws his stethoscope back around his neck and sits down at the foot of my bed, but remains silent. It's a choose-your-own-adventure-style lecture, I guess. At least he didn't say he's disappointed.

After a few minutes of the silent treatment, he grasps my right hand and holds it to my face.

"What is this, Amelia Marie?"

I roll my eyes. "My hand." The duh isn't said out loud, but it might as well.

Randi Perrin

He shakes his head as his fingers tighten around my wrist, as if he is doing everything in his power to keep himself from thwapping my disrespectful mouth.

"Thanks for the lesson in basic anatomy," he grumbles. "What's on your hand?"

"Your teeny, tiny pinkie finger," I reply with a giggle. His finger has always been missing the top knuckle, which in my post-concussion haze, I find funny as hell. He never talks about it, so my guess is that he was born with it and mocked in school, so now it's taboo.

"Not that," he growls.

My jellyfish arm moves closer to my face in slow motion. A thin silver band with the tiniest shard of a green gemstone sitting on top comes into focus.

I quirk my lips into a half-smile. "A ring." Pieces of the night before slot into place in my mind. A hillbilly proposal. Playing in the leaves. A disembodied voice telling me to run. Pain.

He drops his head and scrubs his hands across his face. "Amelia." Those three tired syllables tell me the story of his exhaustion. It's much deeper than just a bloody, concussed daughter picked up by the law.

"It's just a ring, okay? I found it on the hill."

"You went onto the hill?" he asks, his eyes wide, as if his daughter morphed from seventeen-year-old menace to felon right before his very eyes. "I thought Junior was kidding about that."

"Yeah, I did. But it was Diego's idea," I spit out before he could say another word. "I swear I won't keep the ring. I will take it back up to the girl who lives up there when I can think straight again."

"No girl lives on the hill." His voice is devoid of emotion. "There's no house."

Redemption's Secrets

"If there's no house, no girl, how did I get the ring, and how did I get shot last night?" I motion to myself.

He holds out his hand and nods at the ring. That invisible hand deep down inside me squeezes my feels, tighter than it did last night, and I struggle to breathe.

His face pales. "Sheriff Minton shot you? That's a new low, even for that family."

I shake my head. "Not him. A different sheriff… the old drunkard on the hill. About crashed his pickup into the porch."

The color drains from my dad's face and he pulls his lips in a tight line, closing his eyes. I've had seventeen years to figure out my dad, but the only thing I can say for certain is whatever comes out of his mouth after he does that, I won't like it.

He pulls his lips in a tight line, as if he's debating what to say next. Instead, he tosses my sketchbook on the bed. "Diego had this on him last night. Said you might want it back."

"That was nice of him," I mutter, trying to figure out when he could have even grabbed it. Did he leave me on the hill? Is that why he didn't see the two teenagers or the crazed lawman with a gun chasing me?

I reach into my bedside table and pull out a pencil before flipping pages in search of a blank one. The girl in overalls with untamed hair on the tire swing is calling out to me, wanting to be drawn.

"Wait, go back," my dad says after I flip past the sketch of the house I did last night. I go back a page and hand it to him.

"What about it? It was just a house that came to me yesterday while I was at the booth. But then I saw it on the hill. It was a creepy coincidence, not going to lie."

Randi Perrin

He shakes his head. "There is no house on the hill." I wonder if he's as tired of saying that as I am of hearing it.

"Have you scaled the fence to go up the hill? How would you know?" I feel like the more I hear it, the more he and Diego are trying to gaslight me. What good does that do? I flip to a blank page and scratch my pencil across the paper in long, wispy lines, trying to capture that girl's hair in the wind.

"I know because I…" he trails off and I lift one eyebrow, my interest piqued. "It's nothing, never mind, forget I said anything."

He watches for a few minutes and then shakes his head. "I know you want to lie in bed and sketch," he says. "But you're going over to Mrs. Garcia's today."

I groan. The lady next door is ancient, and has an unexplainable rapport with my dad, though I can't for the life of me figure out why. She's nosy, has an annoying dog, ugly orthopedic shoes, and a car that is older than I am and has an exhaust leak that the entire neighborhood can smell as she passes by.

"Really, you can't just give me painkillers and allow me to stay home?"

He shakes his head. "You hallucinated a house and being shot before concussing yourself. So no, you cannot be alone."

I point to my arm that's all wrapped up. "I didn't imagine this; you wrapped it yourself."

He shakes his head. "It's just a gash. You fell down a hill. A million different things could have caused it." His words feel empty, as if he doesn't believe them either, but he's being forced to say them by some unseen force holding a weapon to his head. "You will hang out with Mrs. Garcia until this evening. Then she will take you to the festival,

Redemption's Secrets

where you will sit at the booth and hand out candy to the trick-or-treaters—I'll be up to join you as soon as I'm able. No leaving the booth. No playing games. And you will keep your distance from that football friend of yours."

I roll my eyes. "He is *not* my friend."

Is Doctor Dad even for real? A babysitter who is older than the dinosaurs, followed by my definition of hell, returning to the festival to hand out candy to a bunch of underage panhandlers the day before Halloween because this stupid town can't even trick-or-treat like normal people. He must hate me. That's the only explanation for punishment this severe.

***

I flop onto Mrs. Garcia's couch as her Chihuahua, Toby, yips his little head at me so hard his feet come off the ground. Dog yaps at everything. Mailman? Yap. Me or my dad walking by? Yap. A bird? Yap. A plane? Yap. He'd probably yap at Superman.

"Toby," Mrs. Garcia snaps as she enters the room, "be nice to our guest." The dog stops his incessant barking and sniffs me instead. She's the annoying as fuck dog whisperer. Who knew? He takes one final sniff and walks over to his owner, who scratches his head. "Good boy." She hands him a treat, and he trots out of the room to do whatever the hell it is annoying dogs do all day. It better not be yapping, because with this throbbing in my head, I'm liable to do something we'll all regret.

I open my sketchbook to the picture of the girl from last night, which is taking shape. The motion of her hair behind her as the swing slices the air is perfection. I have even added a rough sketch of her face, but I'm going to need color to get her features just right. I rarely use colors, but the graphite just does not do the light steel of her eyes justice. They are a shade lighter than my own, and I've never been able to get that color right either.

Mrs. Garcia smiles at me. "What are you drawing?"

I shrug. It's a valid answer—I do not know who this girl is. I just want to draw her. I want to create her features out of nothing and give life to her in the hopes I can find her again to give her back the pathetic excuse for an engagement ring that is currently wrapped around my right ring finger.

"Your mom loved to draw, too. She was quite good at it."

My eyes fly up from the sketchbook and lock onto hers. "You knew my mom?" I know very little about her. Whenever I would bring her up, Dad would lock up tighter than the gold vault at Fort Knox. I learned early to avoid the taboo subject. But I always wonder.

Mrs. Garcia nods.

"I didn't even know she was from here. Just Dad."

"Your dad became a different person after she died. Changed colleges, changed majors, changed states. I didn't think we'd ever see him again."

"My mom's dead?" The words feel stupid the moment they roll off my tongue, but my dad has never confirmed or denied her whereabouts. Just that she is gone.

The old woman pats my left arm in a move that screams "bless your heart" without saying the actual words. With a final pat on my arm, Mrs. Garcia clears her throat and stands. The subject is now dead, just like my mom. "I need you to help me with a few things," she says as she wipes the dust off a shelf before covering it with a dark cloth.

Sure, ask the poor concussed girl with battle wounds from a hill to do a few things. That sounds like a safe bet.

She points to a box teetering on the edge of her dining

Redemption's Secrets

table. "Grab that box and bring it over here so I can build my ofrenda."

I blink back in surprise. "Ofrenda? Halloween is tomorrow. Isn't it a bit early?"

Mrs. Garcia gives me a knowing smile. "You are correct, it is early, but not too early. Everyone I love has gone before me, so let an old woman feel close to her loved ones for a few days, okay?"

"I didn't know you observed *Dia de los Muertos*."

"You've never spoken more than two sentences to me. How would you know?" Oh, old lady has bite. Respect to the neighbor. "My husband was a very proud Mexican. We observed it every year. It seemed each year our ofrenda got larger and larger. I didn't do it after he passed, but then when my daughter went missing the following year, I hauled out the banners again because it was the only thing that allowed me the chance to feel close to them, even if just for a few days."

"Your daughter went missing?" I place the box onto the shelf she cleared and watch as she opens the lid. She pulls out a photo of two girls my age with their arms draped around each other. On the left is a short, Hispanic girl with long hair in a mess of curls, her mouth agape in mid-laugh. On the right is the girl I saw being proposed to last night. In the picture's background, the skinny kid with holes in his shoes watches the two girls. He's wearing a Coldplay shirt this time. Strike two.

Mrs. Garcia wipes a tear from the corner of her eye before skimming her fingers across the glass of the frame. "They never found her. I'd like to believe she ran away and built herself a good life, but I'd be fooling myself."

"That's horrible." I point to the boy with questionable taste in music. "Maybe he did it. He looks like a creeper."

Randi Perrin

The old woman lets out a sharp laugh that makes Toby growl from the bed he's curled up into, near the window. "Erick? No. They grew up together. Maria's best friend was his girlfriend, that's her," she says, pointing to the other girl. "Ryanne Minton."

I cock my head to the side? "Minton? As in …?"

She nods. "Yes, Junior, I mean Sheriff Minton, is her brother." I spin the ring on my finger. I risked my life to save the ring for a Minton? How on earth could the events of the past twenty-four hours get any worse? "He moved back here to take over as sheriff after the tragedy."

"What tragedy?" For the first time in, well, ever, this town might be a tad interesting. There are secrets and inquiring minds want to know.

Mrs. Garcia sighs before placing the photo back into the box and pulling out one of Maria by herself that she places on the ofrenda. "There was a fire, but I'm sure you know that. It was a long time ago, and there's no need to dig up those old ghosts. Just know there's more to this town than you think."

I roll my eyes. This town is everything it seems, which is boring with a heaping side of yawn.

Opening my sketchbook, I turn to the half-complete drawing of Ryanne Minton. "I drew her this morning. Not a clue who she is. I just saw her last night when the skinny kid proposed to her on a tire swing in front of the house and everything."

The old woman sits down and takes a deep breath. "That's not possible," she breathes on the exhale.

"Then how'd I draw a complete stranger who is in your photo?"

I flip back a page to my drawing of the house. "She was right here," I say, placing my finger on the tire swing, tapping at the spot, graphite staining the tip of my finger gray. "She was talking about joining the Air Force after she has the baby. All she wants is to break free from her father."

"Away from him and out of this town," Mrs. Garcia whispered. "She was obsessed with planes after a family tree project showed she had a distant relation to Chuck Yeager."

"Can't say I blame her for wanting out," I say, which earns me a growl from Toby and a glare from his owner.

Mrs. Garcia places her hands over mine, stilling my finger that was still tapping against the image, with a look as if I'm a lost puppy. Hell, maybe I am. "Oh, sweet child, you have so much to learn."

"Then teach me."

She shakes her head. "Not my place. Forget I said anything." She busies herself pulling pictures from the box as she arranges them just so. Every now and again Toby barks and she adjusts the picture again. That dog clearly runs the show over here.

With the ofrenda set up, she pulls the pencil from my hand and slides it behind my ear. "Come on, you need to keep your hands busy."

"My hands *were* busy," I say, reaching behind my ear for my pencil, but she catches it and pulls me off the couch.

"I need to make pan de muerto. It was Maria's favorite, so I need some for my ofrenda." She closes her hand into a fist, each knuckle cracking with the movement. "These hands aren't what they used to be."

***

I'm handing out toothbrushes and tiny tubes of toothpaste in little baggies with baby oranges to trick-or-treaters at the festival. The kids look about as thrilled with their gifts as I do handing them out. A match made in bumfuck hell. What kind of idiot doctor sends his concussed daughter to go hand out the worst trick-or-treating prize in the history of time by herself, anyway?

I'm staring at the bags as they drop into pillowcases and plastic pumpkin buckets without looking up. The last thing I want is any of them to recognize me so they can egg my house later for the lamest trick-or-treating "gift." I use that term as loosely as possible—across the way, there's a carny giving out full-sized candy bars to green-faced kids as they come off the Gravitron. His timing sucks, but at least he received the memo of what Halloween is all about.

The horde of small panhandlers moves toward the table set up for Myrtle's Diner, where she offers cups of warm apple cider to the kids and the black sludge passed off as coffee for the adults accompanying them. I swear I see her pour something from a flask into a few of them.

A kid comes up from behind me and screams, "Trick or treat!" The dull, constant throb in my head sharpens like an ice pick jammed into the back of my eye. I jump in my seat, balling my fist, ready to clock whomever it is. He's older, not in a costume, and this is probably his last year trick-or-treating before he becomes a hooligan who goes to the next town over on Halloween to steal candy from babies.

I suck in my lips, biting the top one hard. As if I wasn't in enough pain already. I throw the kid his toothbrush and orange and point him to the next booth because I sure as hell don't want him here. Instead of leaving, he inspects his bounty and throws it right back at me. I wince, preparing for impact, but a hand blocks my line of vision just in time to catch it and throw it back at the kid, chasing him off.

Once the kid is gone, Diego helps me back into my chair. "You okay, Jenkins?"

I nod. I'm not okay, I hurt and I cannot escape this

Redemption's Secrets

tightness in my chest—*am I too young to have a heart attack?*—but thanks to Diego's quick hands, at least I didn't get a fresh concussion.

He crouches down in front of me, worry in his eyes, as if I'm fragile and about to break. As if a stupid kid or a roll down a hill could break me. Just mess me up a bit.

He places a hand on my knee and gives it a light squeeze, which relaxes my fight-or-flight response, my lips quirking into a smile against my will. Damn my autonomic nervous system.

"Come on Teddy, let's go to the next booth."

Next to him, I don't see Teddy; I see Coco, complete with a red hoodie, makeup, and a kid-sized guitar dangling from a strap on his shoulder. It should be illegal for the kid to be this cute.

"No, you don't have to." I glance at my stash of Doctor Dad-approved goodies and shake my head. "But you deserve better than this."

At my feet is a tiny cooler Mrs. Garcia was kind enough to pack for me. This is the first chance I've had to peek inside, but I bet there's something good. The blue lid creaks as I open it. Inside I find a few bottles of water, some pan de Muerto that we made this morning, a bottle of ibuprofen (bless this woman), and a package of Reese's Cups.

"Would you like a Reese's Cup or a pan de Muerto?" I ask as I shake three pills out of the bottle, the maraca-like noise reverberating around my brain in an unpleasant staccato.

"Both," Diego replies as he twists the cap off a bottle of water and hands it to me.

Popping the pills into my mouth, I take a swig of water and swallow before closing my eyes, grateful for the slight reprieve in pain the darkness grants me. "Wasn't talking to you." My gaze settles back on Teddy, who is in a staring contest with the baked goods. Smart kid. I pick up one of the sweet treats and peel off the dough across the top and hand the rest to Diego.

He gives me a coy smile and pops the sugary dough into his mouth. Swallowing, he brushes his hand off on his jeans and gives me a concerned look. "Can I ask a question?" Diego asks softly, as if the next words out of his mouth are going to hurt. "Why are you even here?"

"Dad decided this was my punishment for last night's antics."

He shakes his head. "Not what I meant. You hate it here. Why did you even move here?"

It's a question I ask myself all the time. "I miss Chicago. I won't lie about that," I reply. "The grant that funded Dad's position doing research on epilepsy and seizures at the neurology clinic dried up. He could have found another job in the city, but his savior complex kicked in and he returned to his hometown to," I raise my fingers to create air quotes, "'be the doctor they so desperately need.'"

Teddy takes advantage of my conversation with his uncle and rips a dough bone off another pan de Muerto in the cooler. He shoves it into his mouth before I can stop him. As if I would. The kid's adorable.

Diego's sister comes running toward my booth, and Teddy takes off in her direction, arms outstretched as if he hasn't seen her in a week. "She's going to finish taking him around," he whispers. "It's just you and me now."

I roll my eyes—or I try to, but the headache makes me close them instead. "Vasquez, it will be a cold day in hell when I'm ever okay with it being just you and me."

"That's not what you said last night," he says, with a soft elbow nudge. He drops his lips close to my ear and whispers, "Milly." The warmth of his breath sends a tiny shock of electricity down my spine.

"I rescind the use of that name," I say, metaphorically stomping any ember of that jolt that might remain with my combat boot.

"Okay, Jerkins, whatever you say."

My gaze flits up to the top of the hill. That squeeze in my chest tightens, tugging at me like an invisible rope lassoed around my torso. My legs, acting on their own, move a step toward the hill, and then another one.

Diego catches my gaze and lets out a low rumble of a laugh. "You want to go back up the hill?"

"You got anything better to do, Vasquez?"

He gives me a long, languid look and scoffs. "I have a pocket full of condoms left from last night."

Teenage boys are the literal worst.

He releases a sigh and points to my head. "Remember what happened up there last night?"

As if I could forget.

"Yes." The reply is automatic—I hear the word but don't remember telling my body to form it. It's as if I'm an innocent bystander in my life. The squeeze around my heart steals my breath and the lasso tugs at me. If I don't move, it's likely to rip my body in half. I take another step toward the hill, then another one, before I'm running (and I cannot emphasize this enough, I *don't* run) and Diego has to jog to catch up to me.

I scale the fence as if it were an Olympic sport and I'm Michael Phelps. No uncoordinated falls or catching my hoodie today; nothing is going to slow me down, not even Diego, who is still struggling over the fence when I run up the hill.

As I reach the summit, the edges of my vision blur

even more and pain sparks in my head. Despite it all, my feet move of their own volition.

The house comes into view and my neighbor's car pulls up and parks next to the truck. *What is she doing here?* Mrs. Garcia gets out of the car and rushes to the door. "Mrs. Garcia, wait," I call out, but she doesn't hear me before she slips through the door.

In her haste, the door doesn't latch closed, so I slip in behind her. Maybe I can find Ryanne and return her ring. I press my thumb against the ring, which practically burns with heat, yet there's no pain. It's like I'm being reminded it's there.

Inside, the living room has two plush couches facing each other, no television. Above the mantle is a giant cross. On the long coffee table between the furniture sits four well-used Bibles. There is not a thing out of place or a speck of dust visible, not even floating in the light that streams in through the windows.

A cry of agony tears through the silence of the house, and that squeeze in my chest tightens enough to steal my breath. Mrs. Garcia doesn't seem to notice me as she runs up the stairs, taking them two at a time. Nimble for an old woman.

She rushes into a room, but I stay just outside the door and peek inside. The walls are a cheerful yellow color. In the corner is a vanity with photos of teenagers taped around the edges of the mirror. I recognize Maria and Erick in a few of them.

By the window is an easel with a partially finished canvas. I recognize the view; it's the town from the top of the hill.

Ryanne is lying on top of the fluffy, white comforter of the bed, her wrists pulled over her head, bound by handcuffs

Redemption's Secrets

wrapped around the metal bed frame. Her bottom half is drowning in a pool of pink-tinged fluid. There's not enough bleach in the world to make that white again.

"What have you done?" Mrs. Garcia screams at no one in particular. Ryanne winces at her voice.

Ryanne's dad, the other Sheriff Minton, Senior, I guess, lumbers out of another bedroom and steps into his daughter's room. He's wearing a wife-beater that is more gray than white and a pair of dirty jeans, an open beer bottle in his hand. With disheveled hair and a tattoo on his upper arm of a heart with the word *Mom* across it, could he be any more of a cliché?

He belches and holds out his beer, unwrapping his finger from the brown glass to point at Ryanne. "It's not what I done, it's what she's done. The child went and got herself pregnant out of wedlock with that useless boyfriend of hers. Been hiding it for months."

Mrs. Garcia nods. Based on her emotionless reaction, she probably knew this already.

"We need to get that demon baby out of her. I can't make her pure again, but I can get rid of it."

Another scream erupts from Ryanne, who closes her eyes and scrunches her face in pain. I don't know a thing about childbirth—nor do I ever want to—but I can feel that something isn't right. A heartbreaking combination of fear, loss, and longing wrap around her pained screams. It's not a pleasant combination.

Mrs. Garcia takes a deep breath. "Tell me what you did. I can't help if I don't know what you did."

He motions to the floor, five empty medication vials lying haphazard near the dust ruffle with embroidered daisies on it. She bends down and picks up a vial, which she throws at him in disgust. "All of them?"

He nods.

"At once? No IV?"

"Do you see an IV?" the old man replies.

Mrs. Garcia's face contorts as she weighs what comes out of her mouth next. "Why me? Why did you call me?"

The old man grins. "Because I know you won't go running to anyone. If you do, I might have to reopen the hospital's missing OxyContin investigation. New evidence and all."

She grasps her chest. "You wouldn't."

He motions at his daughter. "Don't. Try. Me."

On the bed, Ryanne lets loose a cry of pain much like that of a dying animal.

"Ryanne, baby," Mrs. Garcia pleads. "Stay with me." She glances down and notices a crochet hook at the end of the bed. "Did he break your water?"

Ryanne nods, a tear slipping past the corner of her eye. "Is my baby going to be okay?"

Mrs. Garcia glares at Ryanne's father, who has taken up residence on the stool at her vanity, his booted feet propped on the fluffy comforter.

"Ryanne, I'm going to do my best." She crosses herself and glances upward, as if pleading to God for a helping hand.

The old man in the corner scoffs. "Don't give the girl false hope. She knows the answer."

Ryanne's eyes grow wide.

"Don't listen to him, baby," Mrs. Garcia says, her voice soft as she strokes Ryanne's hair that is drenched in sweat and matted against her head—a far cry from the hair flying behind her in the tire swing last night. "Focus on me."

The girl is in misery, each contraction contorting her face into shapes and expressions no living creature should

Redemption's Secrets

ever have to experience.

And it's all her dad's fault.

What a monster. All in the name of what? The perception of his family in town?

With a deep breath, I lean my back against the wall separating me from this horror movie scene. I drop to my butt and stare at my hands. I can't watch what's happening in front of me. It's so inhumane. Why is this guy like this? And why is Mrs. Garcia just rolling with it as opposed to calling the paramedics, the cops, anyone?

For the next few minutes, the sounds coming from the room rival that of any over-the-top medical drama on television with a birth scene. The screaming, the yells of "push," followed by "breathe." I don't peek my head back in until it goes silent again.

Fearing Ryanne is dead, I take a quick look. Mrs. Garcia shoots a deadly glare across the room at Elder Sheriff Minton, but her face is angelic as she gives Ryanne a sweet smile. "It's a girl." She holds the baby close as she leans down so Ryanne can see her daughter. "Do you have a name?"

"Not that it matters," the old man bellows, standing up. "Give it to me."

"It?" Ryanne yells. "Her name is Amelia."

Mrs. Garcia's face falls before locking eyes with the man and shaking her head. "No need for any of that."

Her father tosses the empty beer bottle onto the floor, clanging it against the vials on the floor. "Good, now get rid of it. Bury it, throw it in the creek, I don't care. I just want it gone."

"No," Ryanne screams again. "No."

For a moment, I stop breathing. Is that…?

I don't start breathing again until the old man yells,

"Amelia is dead!" She lets loose a wail loud enough to wake the dead. "Oh, shut up child, you claim you can speak with the dead, go do that." His words slash through the silence and hit Ryanne in the heart, their impact exploding across her face in slow motion.

The man made the direct hit he was aiming for, and I just want to run in there and beat him with my fists and yell, "Don't you see me? I'm right here!"

Mrs. Garcia gathers soiled blankets and towels. "I'll take these home and wash them." Before the old man can say a word, she rushes out of the room, blankets and a baby wrapped in a ball in front of her.

I sneak inside the room as the old man leaves and pull the vanity stool over so I can sit next to Ryanne. "You know, I'm not dead," I whisper. "I don't know what just happened here, but I'm okay. A little confused." I pull the ring off my finger and try to put it on hers, where it belongs, but my fingers rake through her skin as if it's not there. The only thing I feel is ice cold. "A lot confused, actually, but I am okay". She never once looks in my direction; she doesn't know I'm here. It's fine. I will just put the ring back on and we will sit here in icy silence together.

***

Fifteen minutes later, Erick runs into her room and kisses her forehead. "Our daughter is beautiful. I'm so proud of you."

She shakes her head. "But I thought Mrs. Garcia… "

He wraps his hand around hers and squeezes. "That's what she wanted your dad to believe. She snuck her out of here in the dirty laundry before she could make a noise and ruin her cover."

Ryanne smiles at him and lays her head back against

the pillow. "Maybe it's all going to work out after all," she whispers.

"I told you it would," he says before placing his lips against hers in a chaste kiss. The handcuffs that bound Ryanne's hands rattle against the headboard. He takes a step back and Ryanne's entire body convulses, each movement faster than the previous one, the handcuffs rattling off an angry staccato response to his statement. The icy silence has turned into a frigid cacophony that assaults my senses.

"Oh my God, oh my God!" Erick exclaims. He paces for a second before trying to lay her on her side, but her body won't move into that position because of her restraints.

He pulls out a pocketknife and tries to pry open the lock on the handcuffs, but the only thing he accomplishes is cutting off the tip of his pinky finger. "Sonofabitch," he hisses as rivulets of blood snake every which way down his arm. He reaches down and tears off a strip of the daisy dust ruffle and wraps it around his hand and paces the room.

The fear in his eyes radiates through the air and washes over me and I start to shake, a tear or two slipping free from the corner of my eyes. What the hell is wrong with my feels up here on this hill?

The pain of his conflict knocks me to my knees.

What I don't understand is why he doesn't call for help—didn't they have cell phones seventeen years ago? Maybe not in this holler. Just one more reason this place sucks. What about a landline? Surely those existed in this backwards town then.

Maybe he knows, somehow, that help will never come and it's up to him to be the doctor she needs.

All because of me.

The weight of it lands hard on my chest, crushing my lungs and stealing my breath. The house falls silent.

Randi Perrin

Ryanne stops convulsing.

And breathing.

Erick drops the makeshift bandage from his hand and stands over her, clasping his hands together, putting his weight into her body. He does this once. Twice. Three times. Each exertion causes more blood to seep out of his hand, but he ignores it. Then he drops his ear next to her mouth for a second before starting chest compressions all over again. He repeats this process three times before he collapses onto the floor, sobs wracking his body.

My lungs finally sputter back to life, but I know no inhale and resulting exhale will ever be the same.

The squeeze that has been in my chest all day constricts again, piercing pain radiating throughout my torso. It's as if someone wrapped barbed wire around my heart and is tightening it, each barb slicing me in such a way I know it will never heal.

From somewhere in the house, a door slams. "Shit," Erick mutters as he struggles to his feet, hand still dripping blood. His face is white as snow and I'm not sure if it's because of the heartbreak or blood loss.

He leans down and gives Ryanne one last kiss on her forehead before he shuffles out the door, leaving a trail of blood behind him.

"The fuck are you doing here, boy?" The eldest Minton snarls as he steps out of his bedroom onto the landing. "Thought I told you what I'd do if I ever saw you on my property again." His hand rests on the weapon on his hip, finger toying with the release on the holster.

"Haven't you killed enough people today?" Erick asks, tears rolling down his cheeks.

The old man's lips quirk into a sinister smile. "The Lord giveth, and the Lord taketh away. You led her down a path of sin and now we must reap what we sow. I hope you can live with that."

Erick glances over his shoulder and takes a step down the stairs, away from the old man. Then another.

The old man takes a step in Erick's direction, and Erick takes another step down, never taking his eyes off the weapon. It's the slowest chase in history.

The old man seems to revel in the torture he is inflicting on the teenager, so he takes another step forward, only he doesn't realize how close he is to the steps, or the slickness of the blood Erick's wound seeped onto the floor. He loses his footing and falls backwards, his head cracking against the hardwood. Blood pools under his head and a moan gurgles up his throat. Erick puts two fingers on the old man's neck and smiles.

He disappears into Ryanne's room and returns with a half-empty book of matches. He strikes a match, the dancing flames reflecting in his eyes. "The Lord giveth, and the Lord taketh away, sir." He drops the match onto the man's chest, his dirty wife beater erupting into flames. "I hope you rot in hell." He goes down the stairs and out the door, lighting matches and tossing them to the ground—leaving a trail of flames and destruction behind him.

***

My eyes flutter open and I release a soft moan, but I can't move. I'm trapped. I struggle against the restraint, which releases its hold on me.

"Amelia." My name is soft, a whisper of a prayer. "You're okay."

It takes a couple of breaths before I realize the restraints are Diego's arms. I snuggle against him, my ear against his chest, rising and falling with each breath he takes. The metronome of his heartbeat is a soothing balm on some nerves that are frayed and dangerously close to catching fire.

"I'm okay," I agree, settling in against him, wrapping my arms around his body. "Can I just lay here for a few minutes?"

"Of course." His arms tighten around me, the squeeze stopping just shy of being unpleasant. "You want to talk about it?"

I shake my head, my hair flying from side to side.

His response is a soft kiss against my forehead. Visions of Erick and Ryanne dance through my head, putting a smile on my face.

Diego wraps his arm around me again. "I don't know what you were experiencing, but it was intense. So many tears from the girl I thought didn't have tear ducts."

"It was tragic," I whisper, as if I'm afraid the trees might hear. Or the ghosts on the hill. "But I learned a lot, too."

"Tell me later?"

I nod against his chest. "Promise."

He wraps his arms around me tighter, a reassuring hug that I hate to admit I could really get used to. "Hey Amelia… do you smell something burning?"

"Amelia," comes the disembodied feminine voice I only hear on the hill. "Run."

Why Can't You See
by Abigail Christine Cahoe

Why can you not see

The little girl that you are holding in your arms

That the doctor made a mistake

When he said, "Congratulations, it's a boy!"

That I am not a boy named Christopher Alan

But that I am a girl named Abigail Christine

That I am not your son

But that I am your daughter

Why can you not see…

Why can you not see

That I do not want to wear the vest and trousers

But would rather look like all the girls

Abigail Christine Cahoe

In their frilly dresses, tights, and Mary Jane's
That I want to look cute and pretty
Not handsome
That I want to twirl around and dance
Having my skirt flair out showing of my pink ruffled panties
And have people say how cute your daughter is
Why can you not see

Why can you not see
That I do not interact with boys
But would rather spend time with the girls
Doing girly things
That I am shy, and introverted
That I stay to myself because I do not feel like the others
That I seem to have more in common with the girls
That I do not like playing with other boys
Why can you not see

Why can you not see
How much I idolize you
How much I think of you as who I want to be when I grow up

Why Can't You See

How you are the only one
That I take pleasure from calling me by my male name
"Christer" your special nickname for me
How I want you, my teacher, to be proud me
Why can you not see

Why can you not see
How my life changed after her
How I learned just how cruel being a kid can be
How hard it was for me to go to school
How hard it was to know that the grown ups
Those supposed to protect me
Aided and encouraged the abuse
How much I needed love and support
How much I needed to know you had my back
How much I needed hugs… to know that you cared
Why can you not see

Why can you not see
The Sense of Hope you give me
That it might be possible to have this sense of wrongness

Abigail Christine Cahoe

But possibly live a "Normal" Life
With you as my girlfriend, my lover, my wife…
But who am I kidding
You do not even know I exist
You do not even see me
Why can you not see

Why can you not see
That I have the emotional state of a girl
I wear my emotions on my sleeve
That I cannot ignore them
That I am so lonely, isolated, alone
That I yearn for the closeness I see with girls and their girlfriends
That I wish for God to correct his mistake
And make me what I was meant to be
A Girl, A Woman, ME!!!
Why can you not see

Why can you not see
How much a role model you are
How much I respect you

Why Can't You See

How much I value your friendship
The issues that will ultimately lead to an end
The jealousy and betrayal I felt when you asked
One of the girls in class to babysit your kids
The look on my face when I saw your wife's clothes in the closet
Causing the wheels turning in my head to finally
Experience what I know is the truth
Why could you not see

Why could you not see
The pure joy I experienced
When I tried on that first dress
When I tried on that first bra
That first pair of panties
That first pair of high heels
That feeling of content rightness
That washed over me
That I was Home
Why could you not see

Why can you not see

Abigail Christine Cahoe

The turmoil that is brewing inside me
How cute some of you look to me
How I want to do more
But know that I cannot
How I want to be your girlfriend
To have you hold me, protect me, love me
Why can you not see

Why can you not see
That telling the truth might have been the way to go
That there was nothing to be embarrassed about
That years of denying only held you back
That if you were honest you could have been a whole lot happier
That being truthful, might make the transition a whole lot simpler
That you were only hurting your self
Denying what you knew was the truth
Why can you not see

Why can you not see
That I need support, love, understanding
Not your sarcasm, and denials

Why Can't You See

That your own mother sees the truth

And sort of accepts me as her third granddaughter

That everyone at work knows

And doesn't care

That I am not embarrassed about being me

Why can you not see

Why can you not see

That I am a girl

Why can you not see

That I am a granddaughter

Why can you not see

That I am a woman

Why can you not see

That I am your daughter

And that I love you

And need you

Thank you for being there for me when it REALLY mattered!

Carma Shoemaker

Following Jack
by Carma Haley Shoemaker

Chapter One

"Here you go, my love," Jack said. The heaviness of the food on the blue ceramic plate caused an audible clunk on the wooden table. Jade paused for a moment and inspected her dinner, noticing it was all her favorites.

"It's not my birthday," Jade said, smiling and leaning back in her chair. She folded her arms over her chest and stared at her grandfather. "So, why the special dinner?" Jack placed his own plate on the table and sat down.

"Can't a grandfather make a special dinner for his favorite girl for no reason?"

Jade giggled and took a bite of her corn casserole. "No," she said. "No, he can't." She took another bite. "So, you wanna tell me what's going on?"

"Eat first," Jack said. "Then we'll talk."

"So, there *is* something!" Jade snapped, tossing her fork on the plate.

"Jade, please," Jack snapped back. "Eat your dinner before it gets cold, then we'll talk." He took a bite and chewed. "I promise."

Jack had never raised his voice to Jade. Never yelled. Never snapped. She knew whatever he needed to discuss with her was serious – but it *could* wait until after they'd finished this wonderful meal he spent all day preparing.

"Of course, Grandfather," Jade replied, her voice much calmer. She picked up her fork and returned to eating. "This is delicious. Thank you for making it." Jack nodded and smiled. Other than the sound of clinking silverware, the remainder of the meal was relatively silent.

When they'd finished eating, Jade cleared the dining room table and Jack brought a pitcher of tea and two mugs to the living room. The pair settled in on the couch, and after adding cream and sugar to his tea, Jack turned slightly in his seat to face his granddaughter.

"Jade," Jack started talking in a low, calm voice, "the war between the Gianas and the Dragkanis is getting extremely violent and out of control."

"I know," Jade said. She brought the mug to her lips and blew on the hot tea before taking a sip. "After what happened a few days ago, everyone knows. But you don't need to concern yourself …"

"You're the only one who can stop it." Jack's words were direct and abrupt. "It's up to you, Jade. You must do this."

"Grandfather," Jade set her mug on the table and leaned in, "you've invested too much of your time and energy into this war lately. You need your rest. With all due respect, you're not a young man anymore."

Following Jack

"Young man or not," Jack's voice rang of slight irritation, "there are things our family legacy allows us to do that no one else can. And yes, because I'm not as young as I once was, I must rely on you to take up the mantle."

Angry, Jack stood up, walked to a bookshelf, and grabbed a box. Sitting next to his granddaughter, he opened the box and pulled out a small cloth pouch. He opened the pouch and poured its contents into her hand: six beans.

"Are those what I think they are, Grandfather?" Jade asked.

"Yes, my love," Jack replied. "Now you must listen very carefully to what I'm about to tell you."

***

Jack proceeded to explain to Jade that she needed to recruit at least five strong, brave people she could trust to go with her. He told her not to share the details of where they were going, until the morning their journey began.

"Why can't I tell them where we're going?"

"Because if you tell them, they will surely betray you. Trust me," Jack said. Jade nodded. "Do you have anyone in mind to ask to join you?"

"Perhaps Avery," Jade said. "She's strong as an ox and smart as a whip."

"And the daughter of the blacksmith," Jack added. "Her weapons will be of the best quality. Good choice. Who else?"

"Maddox," Jade replied with a small amount of trepidation. She waited for her grandfather's reaction. Nothing. "He's the best archer in the region," Jade added, "and he's a great tracker, with an animalistic sense of direction and ability to navigate." Jade paused again. Her grandfather remained stoic, offering no reaction either way to her choice. "I know you think he's—"

"He's arrogant," Jack interrupted, "and a bit of a womanizer, but your thoughts about him are spot on. Another great choice. That's two. Next?"

"Wayne and Dawson – the farmer brothers," Jade replied confidently and scooted to the edge of her chair. She knew her grandfather would favor this choice. "They're both big *and* fast." Jack smiled and nodded his head with approval. "And, of course, Effy." Her grandfather quickly leaned toward her, his mouth agape, ready to air his grievance. Jade held up her index finger to stop him from speaking. "I already know what you're going to say, Grandfather," Jade said. "She's my best friend – but that's not why I chose her. And yes. She may not be big, or strong, like the others. But Effy has, um, let's call them, *special* skills we may need."

Jack chuckled. "I know all about Effy's *special skills*," he said. "And it's not her wonderful baking expertise we're talking about. Remember, I've bailed her out a time or two myself for her special brand of thievery." Jack let out a long sigh, sat back in his chair, and crossed his arms over his chest. "But I must I agree, she is sly and sneaky, and those skills will definitely get you in places you need to go." He slapped his palms on his thighs, making a loud smack before standing. "Well done, Jade. Wonderful choices."

"Thank you, Grandfather." Jade stood as well. The two embraced.

"Now, if you don't mind," Jack said, "I think maybe I will rest until it's time for dinner." Jack kissed Jade on the cheek and slowly walked into the next room. Jade heard him groan and moan as he laid down on the couch for a nap.

She'd never thought of her grandfather as old. Now, as the years caught up to him, she knew he wasn't long for this world. She knew he would soon be going home to join their ancestors.

A single tear rolled down her left cheek imagining a world without her grandfather. Jade quickly reached up and smacked the tear away and moved to the kitchen to start cooking dinner.

Chapter Two

Jade went to the clearing her grandfather told her about, and planted five of the beans. She kept one last bean safe in the pouch, just in case. She covered them with soil and watered them, just as her grandfather instructed her to do.

She then made her way back to town and knew it was time to start asking the others to join her on the voyage.

"Shit," she said out loud. "What the hell do I say to them? Hey, wanna come with me on a journey up a beanstalk to rescue an ancient egg and stop the war between the dragons and the giants? They're not going to join me. They're going to jump me and lock me away."

***

Her grandfather had told her not to tell the others anything about what they were doing or where they were going, but she didn't feel right asking them to risk their lives or to go on a journey without telling them the truth.

So, instead of keeping them in the dark, she made each of them swear a traditional blood oath. Of course, Maddox was weird about it. The farm brothers told him to leave then.

One of the brothers said, "If you can't swear a blood

oath, then that tells me that you are someone who can't be trusted anyway. So, I'm not sure I want you on this journey. It's better to learn that about you now, Maddox."

"That's true," the other brother said. "Better to learn the truth about you now, than a few days into the journey, when I need to rely on you and discover I can't."

Maddox got tired of the ribbing and decided to take the blood oath. "Fine, I'll do it. And just for the record. It's not that I can't be trusted. It's just I like to know what I'm getting into before I swear an oath that will make me bleed out of my eyes if I betray it."

They all sliced their palms and joined hands as Jade recited the words of the blood oath:

From now until 10 moons from now,
We each freely invoke this vow,
Our journey's secrets we shall keep
king sight and sound to forever sleep

The group then repeated together three times:

To these friends my blood oath I keep
Risking sight and sound to forever sleep.

Once the group had bound their wounds, they built a fire and gathered around. Jade began to tell them the details of the journey to Cloud City, and what they were to retrieve.

Effy, her best friend, didn't even bat an eye. She said that she would go wherever Jade needed her to go. Even if she thought Jade was losing her mind.

The brothers agreed to go because it would get them off the farm for a while. And, it sounded like an adventure and a story they would love to be able to tell their grandchildren one day.

Following Jack

Aster agreed because she was tired of working in the heat. "Cloud City is probably a lot cooler than here. And I could use a vacation from this heat. I'm in."

Maddox took some convincing. He wanted to know what was in it for him.

"If, and not when, we return the egg to the dragons," Effy said, "we will be in their debt. And when we stop the war and save not only our town, but every town in the country, we'll be heroes!"

"Heroes?" Maddox's eyes widened. "Like real heroes?"

"Yes, Maddox. Real heroes! Everyone around here will know who you are. All the men will want to be you, and all the women will want to be with you. Effy glanced at Aster, who rolled her eyes. "You'll never have to pay for your own drinks again – like ever!"

"You're going to have to get an assistant," Dawson said.

"An assistant?" Maddox looked at Dawson, confused. "For what?"

"To keep a schedule for all the girls wanting to take a ride on the Maddox Machine," Dawson joked. Everyone laughed. Maddox smiled big enough to show all his teeth.

"You think so?" Maddox asked.

"I know so," Wayne replied, lightly punching his shoulder.

"Okay, Jade," Maddox, still smiling, grabbed the bottom of his bow and stood to Jade, "I'm in. When do we leave?"

Jade nodded at Maddox and grinned. "That's great, Maddox. She stood and turned to face the group. "We leave in three days," Jade said with confidence. "Meet me at the clearing on Stone Bridge Road at sunrise. Bring water, a bedroll, bread, dried fruit, and, of course, your weapons. Equip your pack as tight and light as you can. We'll be climbing." Jade grabbed her things and turned to walk home. "Oh, and Maddox…"

Maddox stopped what he was doing and locked eyes with Jade. "Yes?"

"Don't be late," Jade said. "We will leave without you."

"And then you'll be known as '*the one who was left behind*,'" Effy added. She walked to stand beside Jade.

"I won't be late!" Maddox shouted. "I'll be there. Don't you dare leave without me." Maddox walked away, his strides long and hard with confidence and determination. "Three days. Sunrise. Clearing on Stone Bridge Road. I'll be there!"

Once Maddox was out of sight and earshot, Jade and Effy turned and looked at each other and broke out in laughter.

"What the hell?" Jade asked.

"He has an ego," Effy said. "I know how to stroke it."

"Oh, *ew*!" Jade made a disgusted face and pushed Effy away. The pair began walking the trail back to town.

"What?" Effy shrugged. "It was only once. I was in a slump, and I'd been drinking. You can't blame a girl if she's in a slump." Effy hopped onto a short stone wall that ran parallel to the trail and continued walking with Jade.

"I can if it's *Maddox*," Jade laughed. "There's a lot better slump busters than Maddox."

"Oh, really? And you know this how?"

Warmth rushed up Jade's neck to her cheeks and forehead. "Um, well, I just assumed, uh … you know … there's other men here …"

"Jade Caulder," Effy's words sounded like a scolding mother. "You are so busted."

"Oh, shut up," Jade laughed. "We have work to do."

Effy jumped off the wall with a front flip and the pair continued walking down the trail. Jade bumped her hip into

Following Jack

Effy.

"Slut," Effy said. The pair laughed and joked until they reached the edge of town and went their separate ways.

Watching Effy as she walked away, Jade was reminded of how they used to laugh together when they were young girls. At that moment, she felt happier than she had in a long time.

***

Jade and Effy worked to get ready over the next three days, and Jack told them the things they would need to know.

"Once you're at the top, hide everything but what you need to retrieve the egg close to the beanstalk. Not next to it, but close enough that you can get it quickly."

He then got a tablet and began drawing a map, to show Jade exactly where to go, where the egg was hidden, and places to hide if necessary. "Do not lose this," Jack told her. "And do not give the map to anyone. You always keep the map. Under no circumstances is anyone else to have, hold, or take the map. Do you understand? Effy, you know I love you like family, but this means you, too. Unless something happens to my granddaughter, you do not let anyone take this map from her. You protect her – and this map – with all your skills. Can you promise me that?"

"Of course, Grandfather," Effy replied.

Jack continued to tell them of the things they would see. "Odd animals and items that do not exist in our world, and you will have a hard time believing your eyes when you first see them. But believe your eyes. For they are real. But trust me, leave them where they are. Do not take them. If you do, the giants will know, and they will come after you."

Carma Haley Shoemaker

***

After three days, Jade and Effy went to the clearing as planned. As they approached, they saw the others standing there, with all of their equipment, staring up into the sky.

"Well," Jade said, "it has grown. Just as Grandfather said it would."

"Good morning, everyone!" Effy shouted. "Are we ready to go on a great adventure?"

"That's our adventure?" Dawson asked. He pointed to the beanstalk.

"Where do you think we were going, Dawson?" Effy replied. She smiled at Dawson, hoping he'd be charmed by the dimple in her left cheek and not back out on her.

"I don't know," his voice raised an octave. "I always thought those stories were bullshit. You know. Drunk old men making shit up. I didn't think those stories about going to the giant's castle were real!"

"Well," Jade said, wrapping cloth around her hands to help her climb. "They were very real. And now, the giants and dragons are fighting, and their bullshit is literally raining down on our homes. And it's up to us to stop it. Are there any questions before we get moving?" Avery put her hand up. "You don't have to raise your hand, Avery," Jade said, chuckling. "What's your question?"

"So," Avery paused, "all we need to do is climb it, go to Cloud City, find the egg, and bring it back?" She made it sound so simple.

Jade turned to look at Effy. Effy shrugged. Jade looked at Avery and smiled. "Yep," Jade replied. "That's the gist of it. We do that and we stop the war and save everything and everyone. Pretty cool, huh?"

"Nice," Avery said. She walked to the base of the

Following Jack

beanstalk and looked upwards, using her hand to shade her eyes. She pulled the strap at her waist to tighten her pack and secured her weapon one last time. Avery looked petite standing next to the robust vegetation that reached vertically beyond their sight. "Can I go ahead and start climbing?" she asked.

"Um, yeah. Sure," Jade said. She motioned toward the beanstalk. "Go for it." Jade looked at Maddox, who had not yet joined the conversation. "Maddox," Jade attempted to get his attention. He didn't respond. "Maddox!" she shouted. Maddox snapped his head and looked at Jade but stayed silent. "You're quiet this morning. You okay?"

"Um, yeah, yes," Maddox said, stuttering his words. "I'm … I'm bean, I mean, I'm okay."

"What's going on with you?" Effy asked. "You're not *scared*, are you?"

"What?" Maddox scoffed. "Scared?" Maddox puffed out his chest. "Hell no. I was just thinking how much of a hero I'm going to be when everyone gets a look at how big this fucker is." Maddox took a big, deep breath and let it out in a huff. "Let's do this."

The brothers played rock, paper, scissors, to decide who'd be last up the beanstalk, and get the most action – should they be attacked from behind. Wayne lost. He sulked and climbed onto the beanstalk behind Maddox. Dawson's showed off his dimple in his left cheek with a full teeth smile at his win.

Jade and Effy secured their gear, checked each other's packs, hugged, and began their ascent, following Wayne. Before starting his climb, Dawson looked up from the ground.

"You comin'?" Jade asked, looking down.

"Just checking to make sure everyone's doing okay,"

Dawson replied.

"We'd be better if you got your ass up here," Effy said.

"I'm coming, bossy ass," Dawson said, gripping a vine and pulling himself onto the massive greenery, and joining the group on their long climb up the beanstalk to Cloud City.

***

The first few hours of the climb seemed effortless, almost easy. The group made good time, stopping for breaks every few hours to rehydrate and replenish their energy.

Spirits were high. The brothers told corny jokes, and the others groaned and chuckled. When Maddox complained about getting tired, Avery sang one of her rhythmic work songs to keep everyone motivated a while longer.

"When the fire's hot and the steel is running," Avery's voice rang out like an alto angel.

"Boom, clang, boom, clang." The others smiled and sang the response verse loud and with heart.

They continued smiling, singing and scaling the beanstalk with ease. Avery and Maddox remained at the top and led the way. Wayne and Effy kept their place in the middle of the group. Dawson and Jade brought up the rear and climbed nearly side-by-side, keeping each other company as they ascended.

Dawson reached upwards for a vine, but it moved. A large serpent-type creature popped its head out and clamped its teeth into the meat of Dawson's hand.

"Fuck!" Dawson yelled. He jerked backwards from the creature and lost his grip on the stalk and tumbled off.

Jade reached out in vain, watching Dawson fall, screaming on his way down.

Wayne heard the commotion and yelled after him. the

Following Jack

others joined in. Jade looked up. She looked up at Wayne and saw the look on his face. The look of disbelief, of shock, of horror.

"Jade," Wayne snapped. "Jade, what the fuck just happened?"

***

At long last, they found a place on the beanstalk to rest. Using the ropes Jade and Effy brought, they tied themselves to the beanstalk, so they wouldn't fall during the night. They made a plan that after they made their escape and got away with the egg, if they got separated, they would meet there.

Jade crawled over and sat next to Wayne. The pair sat in silence for a moment. Wayne let out a deep sigh and Jade slowly reached over and held his hand.

"I'm fine," he said, his voice quiet and timid.

"I know," Jade replied.

"I'm okay to keep going," Wayne said.

"I know," Jade said. She placed her other hand on top of his.

"Dawson would've wanted me to keep going," Wayne continued, "to get the egg and stop the war.

"I know," Jade said. She lightly brushed her thumb over the back of his hand. Wayne quivered slightly.

Effy hummed a familiar melody. Wayne hung his head, and his breath hitched. Avery sung along to Effy's humming – the Song of Mourning. It was the song that was sung at the funeral of a lost loved one. The others joined in.

Wayne leaned his head on Jade's shoulder and cried. Jade slid back until she was against the stalk and lowered Wayne's head onto her lap. She gently stroked his shoulders and his back as he sobbed at the continued singing

Wayne eventually cried himself to sleep. One by the

one, the others laid their heads down to rest as well. After everyone was asleep, being left alone with only her thoughts, Jade doubted herself.

What have I done? Tears welled up in her eyes. She turned her head away so no one could see her — even though they were all asleep. *I got him killed. Dawson is dead because of me. We need to turn back. Grandfather will understand. Won't he?*

Tears continued to fall as she leaned her head back, closed her eyes, and drifted to sleep.

Jade awoke to rustling noises and the firm grip of a hand on her shoulder. She rubbed her eyes before opening them to take in her surroundings. Wayne appeared agitated and frantic.

"We have to go," Wayne said. "Get up!" He shook his friends, one by one. "Get your things. We gotta go. We need to move. Now. Come on."

"What is it?" Effy rubbed her eyes. "What's wrong?"

"We have to get the hell out of here," Wayne said. "Now, like now. Come on. Hurry. Hurry the fuck up."

"Wayne, please," Jade grabbed his arm. "Calm down. Tell me what's going on? Just tell us what it is."

"Jade ... dammit," Wayne's voice became angry. "We're being hunted."

"Hunted?" Jade asked. She instinctively reached for her sword. "By what?"

"Teryractalys," Avery answered. "Large bird creatures. No one knows where they came from — thought to be pre-historic. Very territorital. I think we may be near or in their nesting ground."

"Whatever they are" Wayne spoke through gritted teeth, "we need to move — now!"

Following Jack

***

"Stay low," Wayne said. If you're too big of a target, they'll attack."

"Why are they attacking?" Effy asked.

"We must be in their nesting grounds," Avery said, doing her best to stay a small target. "This bird wouldn't attack unless they felt threatened."

"Then let's get the hell out of here," Maddox said.

"We need to move slowly," Wayne interjected. "Slowly!"

The group used slow movements as they packed up their equipment, keeping their eyes on the birds, which continued to circle. Once everyone had put on their packs and had their weapons in hand, they again ascended the beanstalk.

"What do we do if they attack us? Effy asked. "Ask them nicely to go away?"

"No!" Wayne scoffed. "You defend yourself. Kill one if you have to. Better them than us."

"Won't that just piss them off?" Avery yelled.

"I think we're about to find out!" Effy shouted. "Here come a few of them now!"

Three birds broke away from the circling flock and dove toward them. Wayne held out his axe in one hand as he held onto the stalk with the other and waited for his moment of attack. One of the birds approached and he swung – hard.

His axe connected with the bird, and it squawked loudly before smashing into the thick green vegetation and falling toward the earth. Avery struck the second one, while Maddox hit the third with an arrow.

Another bird broke immediately away from the flock and dove toward Wayne. He swung and connected again. Another squawk, and another bird down.

Carma Haley Shoemaker

More birds broke away, and two dove directly at Wayne. He quickly repositioned himself for the incoming attack.

"He can't get them both," Maddox said.

"What?" Jade asked, positioning herself for another attack.

"Wayne can't get both of them at the same time," Maddox repeated himself. Move Jade." Maddox carefully wormed his way around Jade, aimed at one of the birds, and pulled back the string on his bow. Holding his position, he waited for the perfect moment and let his arrow fly. It hit one of the birds with such force, the bird stopped mid-flight and fell out of the sky.

And so did Maddox.

The force of the shot from his bow pulled him forward and he lost his balance. Maddox tumbled headfirst off the beanstalk.

Jade launched herself after Maddox, landing on her stomach. Effy leaped toward Jade and wrapped her arms around Jade's legs to hold her in place.

"Jade stop!" Effy yelled. "Stop! You can't help him."

Jade's upper torso dangled over the edge of the stalk, and she thought she saw Maddox below.

"I see him!" Jade shouted. "He didn't fall all the way down" She attempted to wriggle out of Effy's grip, forcing Effy to move her arms further up Jade's body. Jade pointed down the beanstalk. "Look he's there. Just there. We have to climb down and help him."

Wayne moved next to Jade, pulling her up to ensure she didn't tumble over, too. He wrapped his large arms around her waist and carefully glanced over the side.

"That's not Maddox, Jade," he said firmly. "Your eyes are playing tricks on you. You want it to be him, so that's what you're seeing. I promise you. It's not him."

Following Jack

"Wayne, please ..." Jade pushed and pulled at Wayne's arms, vying for her freedom from his grip. "We can't lose ... I can't ..."

"I know," Wayne said. He pulled her closer and touched his cheek to hers. "I know, Jade," he said softly in her ear. "But if we don't get everyone else out of here right now, we're all going to die. I need you with me, Jade."

Jade pushed on his arms one last time and then stopped fighting. Wayne pulled her away from the edge. Effy barked orders – most of which Jade didn't hear or comprehend. The group fought the predators off until they reached a height where the birds began to retreat. It was only then they allowed themselves a moment to reflect.

***

"We're down two people," Avery said. "How are we possibly going to do this?"

Wayne turned to Jade and offered a prodding nod. She took a deep breath and throught about the conversation she had with her grandfather before she left. His words of wisdom, encouragement, and faith – faith in her.

"Okay, listen everyone," Jade said. "I know this isn't going the way we planned. Avery's right. We're down two people. But I believe in all of you, and I believe in what my grandfather told me before we left. He said to *know* that you will find a way, and the way will find you."

The others nodded and looked at each other.

"And both Dawson and Maddox would want us to go on," Jade added. The nodding continued and they all verbalized their agreement.

"Let's do this," said Wayne.

Carma Haley Shoemaker

***

At last, the group reached the top of the beanstalk. Avery was first, then Effy, Jade, and finally, Wayne. They climbed up and made sure it was safe for everyone else to come up. Jade looked at the map and they followed it to the castle.

***

They ran into a giant couple walking out of the castle.

The giant couple walked over to a tree, where the party was hiding and started kissing. The next thing you know, they were having sex.

Effy tried to watch, and Wayne was embarrassed. Avery closed her eyes and stuck her fingers in her ears.

Yet the giants having sex gave them the distraction they needed, and they were able to sneak over to the door the giants had come out of.

***

There was a piece of rotted wood at the base of the door. Avery and Wayne pulled on it, and the group then crawled under, entering the castle.

***

A short distance inside, they ran into a small female giant sitting on the floor, reading a book. They mistook the small female as a child.

"I'm not a child. I am sixty-two years old. Please don't be like everyone else. They treat me like I'm a freak. They're mean to me, and they kick me around, hit me for no reason, just because I'm small. They call me Litle, but they say I'm

Following Jack

so small I don't deserve two Ts in my name. My real name is Vitta."

Vitta said that she remembered Jack, from when he was there before. She told the group that she never spoke to him, but that she watched him from the shadows as he made his way through Cloud City, taking on her family. His bravery inspired her, and she had always wished for a way to tell him.

***

Continuing with the search, the remaining party members found the egg exactly where Jack said it would be. It was guarded by one single giant sitting in a chair, and he kept dozing off.

Litle walked up to the sleeping giant. "Hi," she said. He jumped, nearly falling off his chair.

"What? huh?" The giant wiped his eye with the balled-up fist. "I wasn't sleeping."

"Of course you weren't," Litle said. She smiled. "But you sure do look tired. I can keep watch for you. I'm not doing anything."

"Yeah, I'm tired." The giant stretched. "But I have a very important job. And I don't sleep on the job. And you're not important enough to do this job." The chair creaked under him.

Litle did not reply. As the giant continued to sit there, she paced the floor and hummed a lullaby.

"Okay, maybe just a little nap," he said, yawning. "Nothing ever happens here anyway. You stay right here, in this chair, and watch the egg. I mean it, Litle." She nodded and acted excited to have such an important job. "But this doesn't mean you're important. It's only because I need a nap."

"I know," she said. "And I promise. I won't take my eyes off that egg."

"You better not," he said, yawning again. He left and walked down the hall. The thud of a big wooden door being closed sounded.

"Come on in," Litle said. "The coat is clearing."

"The coast is clear," Avery said.

"What?" Litle asked.

"It's not 'the coat is clearing,' it's 'the coast is clear.' It's an old phrase used by pirates and smugglers to let them know that the coast was clear of any naval presence such as the coast guard or military personnel."

"What?" Litle asked again.

"Never mind," Effy said. "Thank you so much, Litle. "You did a great job. Now, how do we get inside the cage?"

"Oh, that's easy," Litle said, excited. She grabbed a set of keys off the back of the chair. "With these!" Moving to the door, Litle put a big gold key into the lock and opened it with one try. "Tada," she said, raising her hands.

"Great," Effy said. "But who's gonna carry that thing. It looks heavy."

"I can carry it for a bit," Litle said. "But we need to hurry." Litle grabbed the egg in one hand and shut the door behind her with a light *clang*. The group ran up the stairs and into the great hall where the giants kept their collection of treasures.

Quietly sneaking through the hall, the trio didn't notice a giant walking by, behind them.

"Hey!" the giant yelled.

Effy turned to see him. "I got this," she said. She waved the other two on. "Go, get moving. I'll meet you later. Go! Run! Now!"

Litle and Avery ran out of the great hall, down the

Following Jack

corridor, and out the back gate. They grabbed their gear right where they left it – near the beanstalk, but not next to it.

Securing the egg in the fishing net, they attached the rope, and Wayne and Avery began lowering the egg. Jade climbed down alongside the egg, to ensure it didn't get tangled in the beanstalk or get attacked by any creatures.

***

Litle helped them escape with the egg. She kept the other giants occupied, while the party lowered the egg down the beanstalk to the first point.

"Litle," Effy looked up at the small giant, "can you occupy those two for a few minutes? I have an idea."

"You bet I can," Litle replied with confidence. "They're stupid. It'll be easy."

"Yes! That's great, Litle," Effy said. "Now, can you tell me how to get to the treasure room?"

"Treasure room?" Litle raised her one large eyebrow and looked confused.

"Oh, no, Litle," Effy said. "I'm not going to take anything. I promise. I'm just going to make a really big commotion to draw the giants away so I can get back to my friends."

"Okay, since you promised," Litle smiled. "Go around that corner," Litle pointed, "then go through the double doors and straight down the hall. There's a blue door with an X on it. You can't miss it."

"What about the guard?" Effy asked.

"There is no guard," Litle chuckled. "The giants feel no one is dumb enough to steal from us so they think we don't need a guard on the treasure room.

"That's good for me," Effy said.

Carma Haley Shoemaker

The pair hear the bounding steps of the giants approaching. "Go Effy," Litle said, "Before they see you."

Effy hugged Litle's leg. "We'll never forget you. She sprinted away and jumped into the nearby weed to hide.

The two giants clomped their way out of the door and stopped in front of Litle.

"Hey, you little shit," the dark-haired giant said. "What the hell do you think you were doing?"

:Doing…" Litle said. "Doing when?"

"Just a minute ago," the bald one added.

"A minute ago?" Litle asked. "Where? A minute ago, I was right here."

"Okay," the bald one said, "maybe it was two minutes ago."

"What were *you* doing two minutes ago?" Litle asked.

"Um, well," the bald giant scratched his head and looked at the dark-haired one, who was picking his teeth with his knife. "Uh, two minutes ago? Two minutes ago, I think I was here talking to you."

"Well, then," Litle said, "I guess two minutes ago, I was there talking to you, too."

"Then who was that running down the hall, shitbag?" the dark-haired giant asked.

"When" Litle asked again.

"A few minutes ago," he said.

"Well, it wasn't her," the bald giant said, "because a few minutes ago, she was here talking to me."

The dark-haired giant let out a disgusted huff. "Maybe they're still inside then," he said.

"Maybe they are," the bald one agreed. "We should probably go back inside and look for them."

"You're lucky, shitbag," the dark-haired giant pointed his fat finger at Litle, and the two giants turned and stomped

Following Jack

their way back inside.

Litle turned away from them to hide the smirk on her face. "Yep," she said to herself. "I'm real lucky."

***

Sneaking into the treasure room, Effy's heart raced. She knew she could fill her pockets with gold and jewels and escape with no one – human or giant – ever being the wiser. But that's not why she was there. She had a purpose. A purpose worth more than anything she could steal from this room. She was there to save her friends.

Her eyes scanned the room. "Now," she said, "where are you?" She slowly and carefully slinked throughout the golden statues and diamond-encrusted crowns. "Where are you?" she asked again, in a more sing-songy voice.

Suddenly, a sharp tone rang out. A tone of a harp string.

"Oh," Effy said, thrilled. "Do you want to sing? We can sing – especially if it's going to help me find you." Effy cleared her throat.

> *"Oh, my darling, oh, my darling*
> *Oh, my darling, Clementine ..."*

Effy paused, waited, and listened.

Harp strings echoed her words and her tune. She turned toward the sound and homed in on the location of the item she searched for.

On the top of a small podium sat a shiny gold harp. On the front of the harp was a beautiful figure of a woman who played the magic harp.

"Twinkle, twinkle, little star. How I wonder what you are."

Effy sang another line to a different tune.

The magic harp again echoed her tune.

"There you are," Effy said. "You are so beautiful. Effy rushed toward the harp and snatched her from the podium, putting her arm through the string, and ran toward the door.

The harp gasped. "Are you kidding?" she said. "Why is this happening again? Hello! I'm being stolen again!" the harp yelled. "Help! Help me!"

"There you go," Effy said. "Scream a little louder. Let's get some of these stupid giants to chase us.

"Maybe you idiots should get some better security around here!"

Effy felt the vibrations on the floor. She threw the harp, making the giants run to catch her before she hit the ground. After sneaking through a gap under the door, Effy she made her way to the beanstalk and scurried down.

***

Having lowered the egg to the place on the beanstalk where they last rested for the night, the rest of the group secured the egg, drank some water, opened their packs to eat a bit, and caught their breath.

They heard something above them.

It was Effy.

She caught back up to them, and they all hugged. She was excited to see they had the egg and that everyone else was safe.

***

A little later, they lowered the egg down to the second point, where Dawson fell. The party paused for a moment to remember him.

Following Jack

Wayne took a deep breath and let out a sigh. "He'd be proud of us," Wayne said. Jade hugged him. "And we're not losing anyone else." Wayne pulled a rope from his pack. We're tying ourselves together tonight so I can make sure everyone stays safe". Jade turned to look at Effy, waiting for her to object. She didn't.

"You okay, Effy?" Jade asked. "You didn't object or fight with Wayne or anything. That's not like you."

Effy smirked and let out a quiet chuckle. "You don't see it, do you?" Effy asked. She looked up at Jade. "That boy is the kind of man you keep, like forever. And if he's willing to tie himself to you, to make sure you stay safe at night, well ... fuck girl, just keep him."

"He tied himself to *us*," Jade said, "to keep *us* safe."

Effy chuckled again. "Okay," Effy said, leaning on Jade's shoulder. "Wake up before it's too late, girlie. Actually – go to sleep right now, but start paying more attention tomorrow."

***

After awakening, the party reached the bottom of the beanstalk with the egg. Jade called out to the dragons at once, wanting to show them that she had the egg, and that it was unharmed and in perfect condition.

Not long afterward, the dragon king landed several yards in front of Jade. The wind from his wings blew her long, red hair back from her face. Two smaller dragons landed, one to each side.

They asked her how she came to have this egg.

"My grandfather told me where to find it," Jade replied. "My friends and I set out and retrieved it. We lost two friends doing so."

"I am truly sorry for the loss of your friends," the

dragon bowed to them. "I am King Trenza. And you and your friends have our eternal gratitude for retrieving the Elder Egg. But I am confused as to why would you do this for us?"

"We didn't do it for you," Jade said. "We did it for *everyone*. Your war, it doesn't just affect you." She pointed to the fire in the field and the boulder in the forest of smashed trees. The dragon folded in his wings and lowered his head. The others mimicked his movements.

Jade was in awe. She'd never seen something so majestic and doubted she would ever again.

Standing tall and proud, Jade took a deep breath and gave the king a proper curtsey – just as her grandmother had taught her to do when she was a young girl. And, as this dragon was a king, she was sure to dip as low as her aching body would allow.

"You see, Your Highness, the fighting between you and the giants may happen in the clouds, but it doesn't stay there. It rains down upon all of us, and we're the ones who suffer." The villagers slowly walked out into the field and moved closer. "Please, take your prize and stop the war."

King Trenza agreed. The dragon took a few steps back, lifted his head, and let out a ground-shaking roar. Within moments, dozens of dragons in various shapes, sizes, and colors flew down from the skies and landed, encircling them.

Chapter Three

"Tell me, dear human friends—"King Trenza said.

"My name is Jade Caulder," she interrupts him. "I am

Following Jack

the granddaughter of Jack Caulder."

"*The* Jack Caulder?" A smaller blue dragon spoke up. His wings expanded in excitement. He took several steps forward, looked at the alpha, and scurried back. The large white dragon nodded his head. The small blue dragon continued. "*The* Jack Caulder who went to Cloud City, alone, fought against the giants, and lived to talk about it?"

Everyone, dragon and human alike, looked to Jade to answer.

"Yes," Jade said. She pushed her shoulders back and held her head high. Love and pride made her feel ten feet tall. "Jack Caulder is my grandfather."

"Dear Jade and friends," the king started again, "what can we do to repay you?"

Jade looked at the towering beanstalk, still standing in the distance.

"Dear King," she said, turning her gaze back to King Tenza. "Would you be so kind as to rid us of the beanstalk – but do so in a kind and careful way? You see, my friends … two of my friends … lost their lives on our journey and …" Jade choked up speaking of Dawson and Maddox. "And they may still be among the vines and leaves up there. I ask please, do not simply burn or tear it down. Please, out of respect for them, use care and caution."

"Of course," the king replied.

"And the fires and boulders from the war between the dragons and the giants," Jade continued, "would it be possible to rid the town of those as well?"

"Consider it done, fair lady," the king nodded his head at Jade. "And should you ever find yourself in need of anything – big or small – please do not hesitate to call on us. We are forever in your debt."

"And now, if you will all excuse me, I need to go see

my grandfather. I need to let him know that I've returned safely, and I've returned the egg to you, King Tenza."

Chapter Four

Jade hurried home and ran inside to see her grandfather. Jack was resting quietly. The neighbor who'd been looking after Jack hugged Jade, gathered her things, and left.

Jade tossed her pack aside, hurriedly washed her hands and face, and pulled a chair to the bedside.

"Grandfather," Jade said quietly, taking Jack's hand between hers. "Grandfather, I'm here."

"Jade!" Jack opened his eyes and reached his hand out for Jade. Putting his hand on the back of her head, he pulled her down to his lips and kissed her forehead. "How was your adventure? Did you retrieve the egg?"

"We did," Jade said with pride. "We found the egg exactly where you said it would be, Grandfather. We retrieved it, brought it home, and returned it to the dragons."

Jack smiled so big, his eyes squinted and nearly disappeared. "Job well done, my love," Jack said.

"Grandfather? Are you all right,"

"I'm fine," Jack answered, averting his eyes. I'm just very, very tired."

"I have something for you, Grandfather," Jade said. She grabbed his hand, opened it up, and placed the last remaining magic bean into his palm, closing his fingers around it.

"You didn't use them all?" Jack asked, happily surprised.

"No," Jade said, the corners of her mouth turned

Following Jack

upward slightly. I wanted to save one, just in case. And now I don't need it. You keep it."

Jack pulled his hand to his chest and Jade watched peace envelop him like a blanket. She kissed her grandfather's forehead, mimicking what he had done for her each day of her life. She moved from the chair to the edge of the bed.

"You can rest now, Grandfather," Jade said. "It's okay."

Suddenly, Jade heard the flapping of wings and thuds upon the earth. A gush of wind blew the bedroom window open. Outside, she could see the dragons gathering.

"Grandfather," she bent down and whispered in his ear. "Grandfather, the dragons are here to say thank you. They talk about your adventure to Cloud City, and how brave you were taking on the giants alone. You are a legend to them. They're here to say thank you, and to say goodbye. It's okay, Grandfather. Rest now."

Jack squeezed her hand for a moment and then relaxed. She knew he had gone home to be with their ancestors.

But Jade didn't want him to go. She wasn't ready. She knew it was selfish, but she wanted him to stay with her, to be with her, to continue to guide her as he had always done.

Fighting against the grief, Jade held her breath as long as she could. All at once, with a large huff, her breath heaved, and the tears flowed.

"Grandfather," she cried. She pulled his cold, lifeless hand to her cheek. "Grandfather, please. Please don't leave me. I don't know what to do without you. What do I do?" Tears rolled off her face, leaving dark splotches on the bed sheet. "What am I supposed to do now?"

Jade rested her head on her grandfather's chest and sobbed. She no longer fought back the grief but instead allowed it to envelop her like a blanket.

After a short while, her sobs slowed, and she caught

sight of her grandfather's hand still gripping the seeds.

He wouldn't want me to do this. He wouldn't want me to be weepy and sad. He would want me to move on. To live. To thrive. To keep his name and his legacy alive. He was proud of me. I should be proud of me, too.

Jade leaned forward, kissed her grandfather's cheek, and then stood tall. She wiped the tears from her face with the back of her sleeve.

I am proud.

She walked to the front door, put her hand on the doorknob, took a deep breath and pulled the door open.

Jade walked out the front door and the dragons roared. They roared to honor her grandfather, to honor her, and to honor a sacrifice that could never be repaid.

***

Where the beanstalk once grew, now stands a statue of Jack and a small plaque that reads:

> "Know you will find a way, and the way will find you." – Jack Caulder

Many visit this statue – human and dragon alike – to pay homage to Jack and his lineage for ending the war and being peacekeepers for all species.

Epilogue

After Jade buried her grandfather, she went to visit Wayne. She wanted to visit Dawson's grave, to leave flowers and pay

Following Jack

her respects.

"I'm sorry, but he's not here," Wayne's father said.

"Do you know where he is? I just wanted to see if he would take me to Dawson's grave."

"I don't know what you're playing at, Miss, but I don't appreciate whatever it is …"

"Sir," Jade interrupted, "I'm sorry, I don't understand."

"Dawson doesn't have a grave, Jade."

"Again," Jade said, "I don't understand."

"We don't have a body. He went up there with you, but he never came back. Wayne told us he fell, but his body never …" He paused. "Like I said, I don't know what you're playing at."

"Sir," Jade said, "I meant no disrespect. I promise you I didn't know. No one told me. Please forgive me. I promise you I will find out what happened to your son." Jade shoved the flowers into Wayne's dad's chest. "Again, I'm sorry." She turned and ran off.

What about Maddox? Fuck! He fell. Where's his body? She ran all the way to Maddox's mother's house.

Banging loudly and constantly on the door, she continued until Maddox's mother answered.

"What?" Maddox's mother said, annoyed.

"Oh, shit, I'm sorry," Jade said. "I'm sorry. I know this is going to sound …"

"Oh, it's you." Maddox's mother said. She looked Jade up and down, a sneer on her lips. "What the fuck do you want?"

"Um, I need to ask a question, and it's going to sound awful and horrible and I'm sorry if it comes across as crass, but did they find …"

"No, they didn't find Maddox," his mother replied. "No, there wasn't a body. Yes, I heard that he fell, but he was never found. Is that all? I really can't look at you right now."

"Ma'am, I am so sorry," Jade said. "I promise you I will find out what happened to your son. You have my word."

"I won't hold my breath. Just go the fuck away and leave me alone." She slammed the door in Jade's face.

Jade stood silent for a moment. Turning around slowly, Jade stepped down the walk. *What the hell do I do now? I need to find Avery. To find Wayne. And Effy. We need to figure out what happened to them.*

To the left, Jade heard a barrage of footsteps. Her muscles tightened and hand immediately wrapped around the grip of her sword.

"Jade!" a voice among the foot pounding. She let out a deep breath and her body relaxed. *I know that voice.* "Jade!" She turned toward the noise. It was Effy, with Avery and Wayne running behind her. "Jade!" Effy shouted. "We have a serious problem."

Jade hurried to meet them. "Effy! You'll never guess what I found out!"

"Jade! They fell, but there were no bodies!" Effy said.

"They're not dead, they're missing!" Jade and Effy said in unison.

"Dawson and Maddox aren't dead!" Avery exclaimed.

"Well then we need to find them," Jade said. And we need to find them, now."

The Bank Robber and the Beer Belly
by Marian Gosling

Based on a true story

Chapter I

August, 1975

Bank robberies were more frequent this year...and more dangerous. Nationwide, crooks had shot or held tellers hostage. Even Louisville, Kentucky banks hadn't escaped the trend.

Some Louisville branches had installed bullet-resistant plexiglass between the tellers and the customers. Tellers everywhere were quitting in fear, and fewer people applied to replace them.

New hires had to be above-average in math skills, have an aptitude for seeing details, and a temperament for friendly customer service. But now, they also had to have the courage to face a robbery threat

Marian Gosling

Not everyone passed those tests. The final round of teller training was a tongue-in-cheek session on the "improbability" of being robbed. Applicants were told what to do, and what *not* to do, during the "unlikely" event of a robbery.

For Violet Freeman, the threat didn't seem real, and she was looking forward to a job that offered a step up in weekly pay. It also took her out of the dirt and pressures of being a typist in a dental lab for an abusive boss.

"Ladies and gentlemen, we have tellers who have worked here for over twenty years and never been robbed," the elderly trainer puffed with pride. "However, our legal team and insurance company insist that we provide you with a module on security."

Clara Playforth had been with the bank for over thirty years. She had been a teller, Head Teller, Branch Assistant and Manager. The woman was supremely confident in her ability to orient new tellers into the world of banking. Clara enjoyed this module the most. It was important for her to find that balance between scaring the new hires and making them feel that robbery was an irrelevant issue.

Clara handed out a form with dense writing on the page and continued for the next hour in a monotone. She briefly explained the tricks and tools within the teller cage that activate during a robbery. Clara passed around some red-splattered twenty-dollar bills.

"This is just one of the deterrents to a robber having a successful getaway."

She then leaned forward, placed her hands on the table, and lowered her voice to force them to pay closer attention. It was an old trick used by public speakers.

"Ladies and gentlemen, you should *never* hinder the path or escape of a robber. Your safety is primary. We insure

The Bank Robber and the Beer Belly

the money. Do *not* complicate our lives with any silly acts of heroism."

Playforth tapped her finger on the form closest to her. Two signature lines were at the bottom – one for the trainee to sign, and one for the trainer to sign and date as verification. She waved her hand at the group and frowned. She didn't want them to treat this exercise as totally irrelevant.

"Most likely, the bank will never need this, but I *do* need you to sign off that you *were* trained." A furrowed brow reflected her intensity. "Please sign your name, pass them up to me. I'll sign and turn them in to HR for your personnel files."

Violet Freeman signed with the rest of her small class of six new tellers. She didn't think about it after signing. It was just a "form."

Then, the trainer reminded them that each of them would serve a temporary branch for on-site experience before reaching their official location for daily work.

"When you get to your branch, you'll again be 'sworn to secrecy' on all matters of protocol, dye packs, alarms, cameras, etcetera." Clara giggled, and then her face became smug. "It's not James Bond quality, but we're proud of the equipment installed for your safety.

"One last thing, become aware and report anyone watching your daily routines …especially when you leave for work in the morning."

Taking a satisfied breath, Clara Playforth finished with, "Class dismissed, and good luck to you all."

The class of new tellers left feeling invincible and fully capable of handling the duties.

Violet was thrilled to have passed all the tests and to be hired. Her mom and dad were so proud of her. She walked to her newly purchased, used 1976 AMC Gremlin hatchback.

Violet loved it and called it her "little green tennis shoe on wheels." The bank's salary was more than enough for her $67.86 a month payment (for the next thirty-five months). Even her boyfriend was impressed.

CHAPTER II

The bank hoped, and the local law enforcement believed, that not every robber was actually *good* at planning and executing bank robberies. Yes, the lure of a lot of cash in one place was strong, but the federal penalties, when caught, made *most* crooks think twice.

Violet's friend, a local policeman, had reassured her, saying, "And if he had the 'balls' to use a real gun, and he shot or killed or kidnapped anyone during the crime… Well, buddy, he can kiss his ass goodbye for decades of rotten food, mean cellmates, and meaner guards. That's just the way justice runs."

Only a very desperate person, usually with a drug habit to feed, would take the larger risks of a bank hold-up. If that was the decision, Louisville was an obvious place to try your luck. The four largest, local banking companies operated nearly eighty branch locations within the city and county area.

A bank robber, if smart, chose the branch based on how quickly they could get to a tangle of streets to confuse pursuers, or a pre-chosen place to duck in and hide until the heat wore off. However, that only worked if your addiction wasn't clawing your insides out, urging you to get to your supplier with the stolen cash.

The Bank Robber and the Beer Belly

Unfortunately, some crooks weren't savvy enough and had surprising red dye explosions — ruining their take by marking the cash, *and them,* for easy tracking by the authorities.

CHAPTER III

Eddie Hornback had heard all the stories on the street. They didn't faze him. He had a new heroin habit to feed every so many hours. Coming down made him so desperate, sick, and determined to get that cash to his supplier.

Eddie Hornback was twenty-three years old. He'd had a lousy childhood. Eddie's teachers all agreed that the kid was bright but couldn't, or didn't, *want* to learn his lessons in reading and math. His artwork was beautiful, but school requires more than pretty pictures to pass from one grade to the next. Nobody wanted him in their class for two years running.

Eddie was a "tough case," even though they occasionally felt sorry for the youth.

Eddie's parents never came to the conferences as requested. They never returned the phone calls or answered notes stuck in Eddie's book bag. The teachers suspected things weren't good at home, but by the third grade, the teachers didn't have the patience or time to care. Eddie was just a statistic and endured until "promoted" to the next grade. He'd be their problem.

Eddie's father, Harold Hornback, was a "functioning alcoholic" (which meant that he held on to his job). He was a fermenter at one of the local distilleries. His bosses considered Harold's liberal samplings of finished products as a quality control technique.. Harold had one helluva discerning nose and demanding taste buds for whiskey.

Once home, Harold took out all his work frustrations on his son, Eddie, by using the barber strap to put welts on Eddie's back until he grew tired. Harold threw the weapon against the wall and sent the child away from his sight. He, however, refused to admit he was abusive.

That kid is just useless. I never wanted him, anyway…coming exactly nine months to the day of the wedding. Harold blamed his wife, Diane, for that pregnancy, but he loved her and wouldn't raise a hand to her lovely face. *No, it was better this way. Nobody can see Eddie's back, anyway.*

Diane, Eddie's mom, was emotionally weak and, as usual for a 70s housewife, without a bank account or resources of her own. She needed Harold's pay. Diane was afraid he'd leave if she stepped in against this weekly ritual. Her refuge was in attending the church bingos on Monday nights and bowling in an all-women's league on Friday nights. Harold approved of these "women's things."

Nope, Eddie found very little comfort growing up. Dropping out of school at sixteen was inevitable, and his parents were eager for him to get a job. That was "room and board," he would have to contribute to continue to stay. But already at sixteen, alcohol was an easy get for Eddie. Both of the corner bars knew he was "a chip off ole Harold's block," and what could anyone expect? The neighborhood bar regulars gave Eddie beer, whiskey, and eventually pot as goodwill gestures. The entire neighborhood knew of Harold's abuse… but it wasn't their business.

Fast forward years of Eddie getting larger, until on a hot Friday night, while his mom was bowling, he physically fought off Harold's attack at age nineteen.

The Bank Robber and the Beer Belly

Eddie sadly left his mom but was relieved to leave his tortuous home, moving in with his friend, Tony Spizzirri, to try for a "normal life." He and Tony stuck it out for four years. Each of them worked forty hours, but beer was like water to him. He started showing up drunk for work and lost his job.

Tony finally threw him out when he couldn't pay his weekly rent for three weeks in a row. "Dammit man, what's the matter with you?"

Eddie stole the stereo as he left. *Tony can afford a new one. Besides, I need the money.* Eddie was into new, better drugs. He used heroin to float along in a state of euphoria, and cocaine to feel high-charged joy.

These drugs were gaining ground in Louisville, and Eddie had gotten in early. The bad thing was they were so damned expensive! A regular job just couldn't support Eddie's wide-open habits in August, 1975.

He took Tony's stereo and pawned it for a fancy, little, sawed-off, double-barreled shotgun with a box full of shells. *This is fuckin' cool,* Eddie thought as he looked at the knobbed, wooden rear stock. *I look just like a real pirate with this thing.*

He felt the pangs of his addiction kicking in. It was time to use the gun to get the relief he needed. Eddie wanted to practice with small stuff before he hit a bank. The local dry-cleaning shop was a good place to start.

Chapter IV

Jim Kurtz loved being his branch's manager. Business

was booming, and he had a wide diversity of customers. Corporate judged the success of each branch by its volume of business and the accounts registered as opened and maintained at the branch. It was before the centralization of records on a large database, and each location worked hard to earn and keep customer loyalty.

But more than his job, Jim loved his little family of wife and toddler son… and drinking beer on the weekends. At just thirty-four years old, he had a beer belly of loud burp proportions. Though he was over six feet tall, the beer belly greeted people before his handshake, its protuberance keeping a healthy distance between any bodily contacts.

Jim had inherited the branch from the highly respected Clyde P. Willis when he was (unwillingly) promoted to a vice president position downtown. Jim knew he'd better not mess with the branch's success.

He could sit at his desk and benevolently watch the ebb and flow. He didn't have to exert much energy to answer questions…the "girls" knew everything. (Remember, this was back in the seventies, and stereotypes were still rampant in business.)

Jim was extremely fortunate his assistant manager, Marilyn, had been at the branch prior to Jim's arrival. Mr. Wells had trained her, and *she* was the glue that kept everything running smoothly.

Violet Freeman had served under both managers. It was easy to compare Jim to his predecessor and her fabulous mentor, Clyde P. Willis. She and the rest of the crew missed the older man but accepted Jim as he worked to earn their loyalty and trust.

She often heard Jim joking and laughing with the more prestigious customers about the summer softball league in which he played. His tales also told of the many beers of

The Bank Robber and the Beer Belly

celebration after those games. *It's the 70s, and I guess beer bellies aren't image-breakers for white males in the banking industry,* she laughed to herself.

It was those beers and their very visible effect on Jim that made the crux and danger of this story!

Chapter V

"Damnit, officer. He had a saw-off, double-barrel shotgun," the wizened little man behind the counter complained. "I sure as hell ain't gonna argue with a man holdin' that to my face. I gave him everything in both registers, but he was pissed it wasn't very much. He shot the cash register and then took off out the door."

Donnie wiped his brow, damp with nervous sweat, even though it was now thirty minutes after the incident. "I was too scared to try to see which way he went, and I definitely wasn't gonna try to catch him."

"You did the right thing. I'm also glad you didn't follow him." Officer Patrick Aberli patted the old man's shoulder. "Do you know about how much he got?"

"Yeah, from the receipts, Alma and I figure he only got a hundred and thirty-two dollars total. It's only Monday and we've been slow today." Donnie looked back at the elderly woman sitting down behind him. She was fanning herself with a piece of cardboard, her hand still shaking in fear.

"Officer," she spoke up, "you don't think he'll come back, do ya?" Her eyes were wide with fright.

"No, ma'am. Since he knows y'all don't rake in a lot of cash, I doubt he'll try y'all again."

Marian Gosling

Officer Aberli was right. But Eddie hit a different, larger Parrot Cleaners on Tuesday morning. It was another disappointing haul and he'd been furious. He shot the counter lady in the arm.

And that made him decide to stop piddling around and hit a bank!

Eddie Hornback knew the territory. The Goldsmith Lane First National had multiple getaway paths. He had watched the customers flow through both Monday and Tuesday afternoons (after the heroin had calmed him). He figured all those paychecks required a lot of cash on hand for his taking. And he knew the two police departments would squabble before either of them responded.

It was a perfect target.

Chapter VI

It was after two o'clock that Wednesday afternoon. The (very stinky) Shamrock Quartz employees' rush to cash their checks was over. They couldn't help their odor, and the bank tellers tried hard to not betray their weekly dread.

Marilyn, the assistant manager, having sprayed the branch vigorously with Lysol to lower the stench to a less-than-vomit level, had walked to the back of the branch into the darkened hallway leading to the supply closet and kitchen.

Ginny was smoking her twentieth cigarette for the day. Mary was serenely crocheting at her window. Sandy was quietly rubber-banding bills into the prescribed bundles at her station. Carla was softly singing (off-key) a Conway

The Bank Robber and the Beer Belly

Twitty song to herself at the front drive-thru window. Violet was just waiting for the next customer, who walked through the door.

She didn't get what she bargained for.

"That's weird," Carla said. "That guy who just walked down our driveway has a heavy jacket under his arm. Why would anyone need a heavy jacket in this ninety-degree heat?"

No one answered her. Carla was always making rhetorical remarks. Sometimes her thoughts were funny, sometimes irritating. Unfortunately, almost no one ever listened to her.

The same man stepped into the bank's glassed-in foyer, directly in front of Violet's teller station. She watched in surprised fascination as he suddenly unwrapped the heavy jacket he'd been carrying to reveal a unique-looking gun.

Eddie Hornback looked up and caught Violet's eye. He dropped the jacket, burst through the inner doors, and sprinted to Violet's teller cage, the gun leveled at her face.

The rest of the teller line was oblivious in those first few seconds, but his loud scream of obscenities at Violet startled them into a frozen panic.

"You!" he yelled at Violet. "Don't you pull no fucking alarm, or I'll blow your fucking head off!" he screamed and pushed the shortened, double-barreled shotgun until it was only about six inches from Violet's nose. "Back up, bitch!"

Violet did as she was told.

"All you bitches, back up. Don't you touch anything!" Eddie swung the gun down the line and around to the desk area where Jim stood, his mouth agape in shock.

Marilyn had been in the hallway supply closets, checking on the bank form and paper supplies. The closet was over two-foot deep, and she squeezed into the closet, wanting to crawl up the shelves – out of sight of the vulgar robber. She prayed he wouldn't come down the hallway.

"You get the fuck around here!" Eddie yelled at Jim, motioning with the gun. "You bitches get back, get down to the wall." Eddie surged through the decorative fencing to quickly come behind the teller cages.

Violet hadn't moved and suddenly found herself at the front of the knot of people as they took shelter behind her. Only Jim, with nowhere else to go, stopped …immediately across from her.

Eddie kept the gun on them as he came down to the first three teller cages, pulling wads of bills and stuffing them into a duffle bag he had pulled from somewhere. Violet didn't remember seeing it. Of course, faced with a sawed-off, double-barrel shotgun, who *is* gonna notice an old duffel bag?

Chapter VII

Violet was at the age where life had just begun its wondrous journey of matrimony. New furniture, new husband of just over a year, new vacation plans. She had so much to look forward to. The thoughts of the recent bank robberies suddenly flew through her mind.

Nationwide, there had been two killings of tellers, three more hostage-takings, and one manager maimed for life during the last three months. Robbers were both more desperate and more willing to take extreme measures to escape capture.

Eddie felt desperate enough for any of those atrocities!

The Bank Robber and the Beer Belly

He was getting spooked the longer he was in the building. He *knew* he only had minutes before some alarm would sound.

Eddie worked his way down the line of teller cages, pulling cash, slamming the drawers. When he got to Violet's cage, he saw she was intently watching him.

"Don't look at me, bitch!" he yelled even louder than before.

Violet could feel her eyes widen as she forced herself to look away from the scrawny, scruffy man threatening her. Her eyes dipped downward and across the short distance between her and Jim.

Then it happened. There was the *real* threat…Jim's beer belly!

His breath was coming in panicked gasps. That belly was the shape and exact size of a basketball. It was bouncing up and down as if it were under the expert handling of a Harlem Globetrotter.

Violet's mind screamed at her. *If you laugh, that man will shoot and kill you!*

Violet, in her entire life, had never panicked. In verbal or physical fights, she never lost her concentration. She'd been stoic and clear-headed when she'd fallen out of her favorite climbing tree and broken both bones in her left arm. Violet, strapped in, endured the front of her little green Gremlin being backed over by a school bus. But, she hadn't shed a tear. Her anger kept her together.

She sure as hell couldn't fall apart in laughter at this life-changing moment. Violet swallowed carefully, trying not to draw any attention to the mischief and laughter she knew had flooded her eyes.

"Alright, y'all come with me," Eddie growled at the small group. He backed up and motioned them to follow him out from behind the teller line.

Oh shit! We're gonna be taken as hostages, she thought. Violet realized she was actually more afraid of this than being shot where she stood.

She had no way to know that Eddie just wanted to escape with the money, and he didn't want that fat man or any of those bitches to follow him. "Git down that hallway! No talking!"

Violet led the way, and the rest of the women followed, with Jim (his panic replaced with anger) bringing up the rear. Only when they passed Marilyn, cowering in the closet with her finger over her lips, did anyone blink.

Suddenly, they heard the slam of the glass door as Eddie threw it open and ran out.

The reactions ran the gamut. Sandy peed on herself, Carla nearly collapsed in her fright, and Jim (the big dumb idiot) turned and lumbered out to see which way the insane robber had gone. Not seeing the man, Jim returned and locked both the outside and foyer doors to prevent (or at least slow down) the man's return.

The entire staff (minus Jim) had stayed in the kitchen following Eddie's escape. Marilyn kept watch through the kitchen door's little window. The others sat at the tables, waiting for law enforcement's help to arrive and trying to make sense of the last eight minutes.

Jim came back to check on everyone and was immediately yelled at for his stupidity in chasing the culprit.

"You idiot. You've got a two-year-old son. Being brave won't stop a bullet," Ginny raged at him, her cigarette's ashes falling to the floor as her hand shook.

"I'm fine. I figured he wouldn't look back. Are all y'all okay?" Jim's protective streak was full-blown. He'd done his duty, according to bank policy. But damn, how he had

The Bank Robber and the Beer Belly

wanted to attack that little man.

Jim's still-bouncing beer belly was at Violet's eye level. In her mind, it almost glowed, and she started laughing. Tears came to her eyes as she guffawed into helpless mirth, her coworkers looking at her like she was crazy. Marilyn jumped up and poured a cup of water, but she didn't know whether to give it to Violet to drink or throw it at her.

"Violet, what is the matter with you? There's nothing funny about this," the ever-proper Mary scolded, her voice breaking. The older woman was seriously rethinking her retirement date.

"You guys, you just don't know. I nearly burst out laughing while the robber was right there, just a *foot* away from me." Violet took a huge breath and pointed to Jim's middle. "His belly was bouncing like a basketball! If I laughed, I'd have been a goner!"

The shocked quiet in the kitchen broke into peals of laughter as all the women's eyes fixated on Jim's belly, *still* bouncing. It burst their bubble of fear.

I'm never gonna forget this, Violet thought.

It only took two more minutes for the local FBI to show up. They beat the embarrassed police, who finally showed up thirteen minutes after the call went out.

The FBI agent listened to Violet's story, his eyes twinkling by the end. "Miss, I do believe your restraint may have saved lives."

Violet wasn't so sure, but that beer belly has been a damned funny memory for Violet for over forty years!

Marian Gosling

Epilogue

It only took nine hours for the Jefferson County Police and FBI to converge on the low-cost hotel room where Eddie had passed out from his fix. On the floor lay three bundles of red-stained money, along with more loose bills. He gave them no resistance as they hand-cuffed him.

However, two days later, Eddie found a weak window in the downtown jail, and he escaped. Two hours later, he was recaptured...with a black eye and a suspicious bruise on his chin.

Violet and her coworkers attended Eddie's federal arraignment hearing. It was there that the sheriff explained Eddie would appear in a belly-band chain, ankle-cuffs, and handcuffs, with guards in front and rear. He'd tried escaping (and had almost made it!) again the night before. The slippery, nondescript man had highly embarrassed the jail's guards.

Fast forward two years, Eddie Hornback and two of his fellow convicts escaped from the maximum-security prison in Eddyville, Ohio.

A TV broadcast, at approximately seven-thirty in the evening on the sultry summer night, alerted the Louisville victims of Eddie's prior crime spree.

This time, Violet didn't laugh. She and her husband carefully locked all doors and jammed windows with wooden pieces to make sure Eddie wouldn't pay a visit.

Jim Kurtz was at the softball field, beer in hand, when the alert came up on the concession stand's TV. He couldn't help it. He looked down. His belly was bouncing again.

Eddie was captured three days later near Chicago, at

The Bank Robber and the Beer Belly

a pizza place. The thick pie and pitcher of cold beer were very tempting to his arresting officers. They'd driven several hundred miles on a hot tip to get Eddie, with the permission and helpful surveillance by the local precinct cops.

"Okay, Eddie, take your last bite and last swig of that beer. It's time to go home."

And even though Eddie didn't resist his arrest, the authorities belly-banded him, hand-cuffed his hands and shackled his feet for the ride back to prison. The guards, one who sat with him in the back of the unmarked police car, couldn't imagine how this guy had escaped three times. Or why. He was so laid back and easy-going now that he was clean and sober.

"Guys, you may not see me for awhile, but when I get out, I'll treat you all to one of them pizzas that I was eating ...before y'all spoiled my meal." Eddie held no grudge against the cops.

"Course y'all will have to wait at least twelve years until my parole," he grinned.

Sure enough, Eddie returned to Eddyville prison, endured his next trial for the escape and was returned to the general population.. Keeping a low profile, his beatings from other inmates were minimal. He was generally a nice guy, caused little trouble and found a new passion in reading. The library and book cart became his ticket to a parole for good behavior fourteen years later.

His loyal friend of long ago, Tony Spizzirri, picked him up at the prison gates, once again opening his home to Eddie. They didn't make it to Chicago for Eddie's favorite pizza. They didn't have time to get on each other's nerves like before.

The prison cigarettes kept Eddie from traveling. Lung cancer was the one sentence he couldn't escape.

Publish or Perish
by Alisa Childress

When Caterina first walked this idyllic campus on her orientation tour three months ago, she was anticipating a challenge, but never thought she would feel this far underwater. Her cohorts had been able to devote their adolescence solely to study; most were even able to attend this hallowed school as undergraduates. While she was with her family for her secondary and undergraduate education, she assisted with raising her youngest siblings and working on her family's land. But she always made time to study and was picked to be part of the Intelligentsia. Luckily, this beautiful campus was saved after the Vast Enlightenment Purge, and now she was living her dream.

She was unsure if it was the academic work or the research that was the most time-consuming. She had just released the students of her intro to psych discussion section, sat next to her lectern, and opened her laptop.

Fifth Annual Publishing Olympics Selectees
Portsmouth Research Administrative Offices

Alisa Childress

to Portsmouth student body, Portsmouth faculty

The Dean of the Graduate School and Legacy Foundation would like to congratulate and welcome the following people to participate in the fifth annual Publishing Olympics...

She scanned the list and felt her stomach drop when she saw her name listed fifth out of two dozen names.

Each year, a group of students and brand-new assistant professors raced to see who could publish in one of the sanctioned publications, which, of course, were the most elite journals of each field. The winner was awarded a large cash prize from the think tank benefactor, the Legacy Foundation. The rest were seen as unworthy of this elite university and were banished. Rumors flew about what happened to them, but Caterina thought they were probably sent back home.

Caterina went to her research mentor's office for advice. She knocked on the already open door. "Dr. Thompkins, do you have a minute?" "Of course, I saw the list. I assume that is what you'd like to talk about."

"Yes, ma'am. I saw so many young women in my hometown forced into child-rearing, and I was lucky enough to avoid it by coming here. I planned to use my time to see the effects of this on their psyche. I want to help all the women in their positions."

Dr. Thompkins paused and leaned forward, onto her desk. "That is very noble. And if you have all the time in the world, I would love to see this. But publications don't care about Birthers or Nursers. You will not publish in time. This is far too important. I suggest that you look at the last two years of The Journal of Social and Abnormal Psychology. See what is coming out now and what you can

Publish or Perish

add to the discussion. There has been quite a bit of interest in compassion fatigue. I would start there."

"To be frank, I do not care about how it affects the wealthy to have to see people like me and my family struggle."

"I understand, but if you want to stay here, you may have to. You are a bright woman, and I don't want to have to say goodbye to you. We need more women here."

By the time she attended her classes and graded a third of the essays, it was late in the evening. Caterina went to the library, where she could work in peace. She elicited the help of the staff librarian in pulling recent theses and dissertations, and she grabbed the past two years' worth of every relevant journal she could find.

***

When Amilee saw her name in the e-mail, she knew that it was time to double down on her theory that Truman Capote wrote *To Kill a Mockingbird*. She grew up in their hometown and hoped this would lend some validity and new perspective on this well-worn theory. She could use the cash prize to fund at least three years of work on her Great American Novel. And, while she did not believe the craziest of the rumors about what happened to the losers, she certainly did not want to leave just as her career among the elites was starting.

She sat at a desk in the musty library basement with her well-annotated copies of *In Cold Blood*, *Breakfast at Tiffany's*, *To Kill a Mockingbird*, *Go Set a Watchman*, and her journal. Coming from a dominion without electricity, she was not used to writing on the laptop she was given at orientation. She had come to the library to see what she could find from any of the local papers from her hometown that may have been saved from the purge.

Alisa Childress

In the musty library basement, as Amilee was headed to the microfiche, she spotted Caterina, recognizing her from their orientation tour. As they were the only two women in their orientation group, she was difficult to forget. Even though Amilee knew where the films were located and how to use the machines, she sought assistance from the same librarian whom Caterina had asked for help. If she could slow Caterina down even this much, maybe she could get a jump ahead of her.

***

Philip had taken the week off campus for his CDC work when he got a text from his fiancé and colleague, Mikhel, who had also taken the week off, but was spending it with his ailing mother. "Call me. Important."

He excused himself and stepped outside. "Hey, sweetie. Is your mom doing ok? I knew I should have gone with you."

"No, it's nothing like that. You must not have checked your e-mail recently."

"No. I've been pretty busy. What's up?"

"You are in the Olympics."

"Oh. Shit."

"Yeah, I know. But, if you win, we can afford that house we want."

"And your mom can move in, and we can hire a caregiver."

"And you can have the wedding of your dreams. Mom is calling. I'd better go."

"Give her my love. And tell her I wish I were there with her."

Philip returned to his office and sat at his computer.

His co-worker, Roger, looked up from his work.

Publish or Perish

"Anything wrong? Is your soon-to-be mother-in-law feeling ok?"

"She's fine, thanks. Well, as good as can be expected. Mikhel just wanted to say hi and let me know he got there ok." He hated lying to them, but the university was adamant that outsiders could not know about the Olympics, going so far as to threaten job loss.

Philip was never in doubt that he would publish by year's end. He and his CDC colleagues were studying the effects of various vaccines on Guillain-Barré and how to make them safer from a neurological standpoint. It was just a matter of time before they were ready to publish. Of course, now he had to be the first Olympiad, or he would lose his job. No one really knew what happened to the losers, but he knew he did not want to leave Mikhel and teach somewhere else.

As he walked through the lab, he hid his phone in his pocket, slyly snapping pictures of any document he found sitting out, and the charts hanging over desks.

***

As fall turned into winter, and everyone began a new semester, people were starting to buzz that no one had been accepted to a publication yet. Some even suggested that they should expel the entire crop, as it had never taken this long before. Each competitor was sure that the other had a transcript they were shopping around, and were panicking from the pressure.

Jonathen, in robotic engineering, had been working with the med school on an artificial arm that could respond to brain waves when he got the e-mail last September. They had heard that the arm was possible in the before-times, but the technology was lost during the purge. He had been overjoyed to see that he was number five on the Olympiad list, sure that he would publish by the end of that year, even if it meant publishing on his own before his colleagues from the medical school thought they were ready.

But here he was in January, and he could not get a signal to pass through the long neural path from the shoulder to the fingers. He was, however, able to get it to appear to respond through a series of mechanical switches and pulleys located in the shoulder, elbow, and wrist joints. In his desperation, he thought he could get this to pass as a real arm long enough to get published.

He was testing the movement of the index finger when a surge occurred in the lab. Not only did it knock out power to his lab as well as every room in the building, but it also caused him to burn the joist he was soldering and melt a finger. This was weeks' worth of work out the window. He would now have to remake the hand, ensure everything aligned, and take new data. Assuming that the new one worked at all.

While he could not prove it, he was certain that he was being sabotaged. Any of the other science jocks on the list could be to blame. They all knew what a prime competitor he was and how to knock out the power grid in his section of campus. He combed through his notes on the other Olympiads to determine his biggest competition.

He noted that the astrophysics lab next door and the department's new delicate, high-powered telescope did not lose power, and moved Whyat to the top of his list. Whyat would know that theoretical science did not stand a chance next to what he was doing with its real-world applications. He was helping those in need. Or at least he was before the Olympics caused him to stray from his work with the med school. But he would get back there. His colleagues would

Publish or Perish

have no choice but to forgive him and continue their work once he was published in an elite journal. He made a mental note to look more closely at Whyat's research and to test just how delicate the telescope was.

Since it did not look like the power was coming back anytime soon, Jonathen decided to go home for the night, but saw Amilee walking into the library. He followed her inside, watching her from the stacks. He watched as she took careful notes in her journal from rare copies of books. Books that he would never have a use for. He seethed at the idea that she was getting funding to research something that would have no bearing on anyone. Not like his arm. When he saw her stand and start to pack up for the evening, he bumped into her, causing her to spill her things. Then, as she bent to pick them up, he swiped her notebook from the table.

***

Amilee picked up her things, cursing under her breath at the lack of manners of the young man who caused her to drop everything and then just walked away without helping her to pick them up. *What is wrong with the men here anyway?* She turned to her table and saw that it was empty, and looked around, just in time to see Jonathen give her a finger wave and run towards the door. By the time she got outside, he was gone.

Defeated, she went back inside, where she found Caterina still working at her table. She sat across from her. "Jonathen Sizemore just stole my journal. It had all my work in it."

Caterina looked up from her work. "Huh. He must be more worried about winning than I thought. He always seems so cocky."

"All those science bros are like that. We have to get back at him."

"What do you mean?"

Amilee looked to see that no one was around. "If he is going to come after our work, we need to go after his."

"What do you mean 'we?' I don't recall him coming after my work."

"Come on, have you seen how few women there are on this campus? We are the only two women in the Olympics. We have to stick together. And no one takes our disciplines seriously. How else will either of us win?"

***

Thankful that he took his demonstration pictures before the incident, and that he did not need video proof, Jonathen finished his manuscript in under a week. He then sent it to *Frontiers in Neuroanatomy*, *Anatomic Neuroscience*, and the *Journal of Prosthetics and Orthotics*. He knew that it was bad form to submit to more than one academic publication at a time, but he feared he was already behind, expecting to hear that someone else had been published any day now.

Done with his research, he turned his eye to his competitors. He snuck into the astrophysics lab in the wee hours of the morning and turned the telescope toward the sun, hoping to blow out its eyepiece and internal coatings. He then broke into their computers, tampering with Whyat's research.

***

Seeing Jonathen break into astrophysics, Amilee knew she and Caterina had time. She messaged Caterina, "Meet me at the robotics lab and dress accordingly," hoping that she was

Publish or Perish

still awake and working.

Needing a break anyway, Caterina messaged back, "Be there in 15."

Knowing that the robotics lab had the highest security on campus, Caterina showed up dressed so that, even if they were seen on the security cameras, she could not be identified. "What is your plan?"

"I'm breaking in."

"You know how to do that?"

"They have not been able to use the security locks since the power surge; it should be easy."

Once in, however, they found that all of the lab equipment was locked tightly.

"Well, I guess we need to try something else to get back," Caterina said, relieved, while hurrying out of the door.

When Amilee did not respond, she turned around. "Em?"

Just as she was about to let the door close behind her, Caterina saw Amilee hold a lit candle under a fire detector just outside Jonathen's lab as the overhead extinguishers poured cold rain over her. Thinking of the Great Purge, Caterina prayed this would not destroy too much valuable research.

Horrified and guilty, Caterina returned to her lab, poring over the data from her most recent administration of the De Jong Gierveld Loneliness Scale to undergraduates, who, like her, came from the poorest dominions. Her theory that social isolation was highest among the Breeders and Nursers was beginning to hold merit. Hopefully, despite what Dr. Thompkins said, she would find a publisher. She was certain that she could help people like her and her young sisters.

Amilee returned to her room, removed her wet

clothing, and sat on her bed, spreading her notes around her. She tried to place herself in the world before the purge alongside Lee and Capote. She knew there was some part of history that she needed to solidify if the theory was right or not. She looked at her notes, selectively ignoring anything that pointed to Lee being the author, and focusing on the idea that Capote was Jem. Didn't Capote also break his arm that year? Not finding anything, she began to fabricate doctor reports that showed he did.

***

Jonathen awoke late the following day to banging on his door. As he rubbed the sleep from his eyes, he noticed several missed phone calls from his professor and other students. He pulled on last night's clothes and opened the door as Gerald pushed his way inside.

"What the hell, man?" Jonathen closed the door.

"Where the fuck have you been?! We have all been trying to track you down."

Jonathen held his phone up to Gerald. "The fuck, you say."

"The fire extinguishers soaked the lab last night. We lost everything that wasn't covered up."

Jonathen kept his deceitful arm locked in his cabinet; he didn't want wandering eyes to pry. But he couldn't let that show. "Shit!"

They both ran out the door, stopping in front of the lab. Gerald grasped the handle.

"Prepare yourself, man. It's bad in there."

Jonathen ran to his station to make sure his arm was still there.

"Thank God, I'm safe," Gerald said as he shook his head, looking around at the devastation his friends suffered.

Publish or Perish

Many of them lost months or even years of work.

Jonathen hoped they did not put together that it was because of him. He wondered which of his competitors did this. Having submitted the data and pictures, the actual arm was moot at this point. In fact, it was proof that he forged data. Seeing that the few students left in the lab were distracted trying to save their work, he dropped his arm in water that had pooled nearby. He banged the table in what he thought looked like anger to cover up the noise.

The other students turned around to find Jonathen looking at his arm on the floor and rubbing his hand through his hair. Matthew stopped cleaning his work and patted Jonathen on the back. "I'm sorry, man. I hope this didn't set you too far back in the Olympics."

"Luckily, I already wrote up my data, and I'm starting to submit it. I don't really need my prototype anymore. I just hate losing what I've worked so long on."

"Tell me about it," Christian yelled over the roar of the dryer he was using to save what he could.

"Well, I guess this is useless now." Jonathen tossed the arm in the dumpster with the other ruined robotics on his way out of the lab.

***

Pretending he was taking notes in this month's faculty meeting, Philip was typing up his manuscript. He had been brought into the CDC to recreate what others were doing through simulations with the university software. This provided the conceptual replication necessary to show that their findings were not a fluke. No one could prove that the stolen data wasn't something he developed through one of his simulations. He felt tremendous guilt for stealing their work, but needed to win.

Alisa Childress

Philip had been tuning out the department chair for some time until something he said caught his attention.

"After the misfortunes on the robotics campus, we are moving their researchers in with us. They will be going into the building recently vacated by immunology."

Yeah, immunology "vacated," Philip thought. It was more like they were forced out because no one outside of these walls cared about disease transmission. That was why he must win. Not being tenured, he felt like his vaccine work was next on the chopping block.

Dr. Forrester raised his hand. "I'm sorry, what is happening in robotics?"

Dr. Green started to answer, but Dr. Borden, who prided himself on knowing the goings-on of the university, cut him off. "They are experiencing some sort of electrical trouble. A couple of weeks ago, there was a two-day power outage, and last night, the sprinkler system malfunctioned, destroying all the work in the lab."

"Well, the unsecured work in the lab." Dr. Green corrected. "You should all learn a lesson from that. The students who had the foresight to lock up their work are bringing it to our campus, for the time being. We in applied sciences must stick together."

All of this, coupled with the new telescope being out of commission for several weeks, was too much of a coincidence. He was glad, being the only faculty member, that he was mostly out of the fray. But he decided he needed to double down on his efforts. And to watch his back now that the robotics jocks were on his part of campus.

He had to submit something quickly, even if it meant forging a little data. It should be pretty easy to do, since all of his research was computer modeling.

Publish or Perish

***

Amilee had been stalking her e-mail for the last three weeks, since sending her manuscript to Comparative Literature Studies. She was beginning to regret not sending it anywhere else, as she could practically feel everyone breathing down her neck. But this one was the perfect fit. She just needed to hear back before anyone else did. She opened her computer and breathed a sigh of relief when she saw it in her inbox.

RE: To Kill a Mockingbird Authorship

Comparative Literature Studies Submission Desk

to: Amilee Danza

Thank you so much for your submission. However, we have decided to offer themed volumes for the foreseeable future, and we do not have anything for middle American literature scheduled yet.

Your submission was well fleshed out. While the thesis is not new, your research was original. I am sure you will not have trouble finding a home for it. Please keep us in mind for future submissions.

Sincerely,

Dr. Theo Simpson

"Damn," Amilee muttered under her breath as she pulled out the list of approved journals. She scoured the list for other possibilities, hoping she was not too late. She also perused the Olympiads list, gazing at her competition.

She knew Caterina had not submitted yet. She doubted that Whyat had, because of whatever (or whoever, more likely) happened with that telescope. But she did not know about anyone else. Those robotics folks are super aggressive, so Jonathen was a problem. As was Dr. Philip Grinstead. Being faculty, he probably had more connections.

She thought about how to get to Dr. Grinstead's research, but after Caterina wimped out at the robotics lab, she couldn't count on her to help. It was probably too late anyway. After losing weeks when her notebook was stolen, Amilee had to assume that if she was submitting, most others were as well.

***

"We are going to end class a little early today so that you have time to finish your final papers. And, since some of you said you need a little more time, I am extending the due date until the end of next week. Be sure to e-mail me your papers by next Friday. Any time later, and I will not be able to enter your grades in time. Have a wonderful break. See you next month."

Caterina heard everyone breathe a sigh of relief, but she was doing this for herself. She needed the rest of the period to run a new SaS analysis. And she did not have time to grade until she finished her manuscript.

Her data did not quite agree with her hypothesis. But, maybe if she tossed out the outliers, she could get her p-value under .05. It would still be valid, she thought as she re-ran her analysis. Hitting enter, she got back a p-value of .057. She calculated that she would need to increase her sample size by about 50 to get the value she needed. This meant two more sample groups, assuming they answered

Publish or Perish

like the rest. Time she did not have.

Caterina finished her manuscript barely on schedule, thanks to the dozen or so surveys she filled out. She hated herself for doing it, but told herself that she would have gotten there anyway if she had time to run more groups. She had to do this to save herself, so that she could save those women she left behind when she came here. And at least she did not light a lab on fire.

She had hoped to submit to the *Journal of Abnormal and Social Psychology,* but she did not have time to risk rejection. She would make it there someday. She looked over the approved list and picked the five with the highest acceptance ratio

The following week, sitting down to grade, Caterina checked her e-mail for the papers from her students.

Congratulations to our winner!!

Portsmouth Research Administrative Offices

to Olympiads, Legacy Research Foundation

Portsmouth Graduate School Dean and the Legacy Research Foundation would like to congratulate Jonathen Sizemore for being the fifth winner of the Publishing Olympics. His article "Reclaiming Past Glory: Natural finger movement in an artificial limb" will be published in the October volume of *Frontiers in Neuroanatomy.*

Join us at a congratulatory dinner this Friday, June 18th. If you have any other plans, cancel them, as your attendance is mandatory. Due to financial restrictions, plus ones are not allowed.

Alisa Childress

The rest of the competitors will need to stay after to be introduced to the colleagues at your newly assigned schools. You will be leaving with them, so tie up any loose ends you have here and bring what you wish to take with you.

In an uncharacteristic act of defiance, Caterina forwarded the papers to her chair. If she wasn't going to be here next year, she certainly was not going to be the one to grade them.

***

Philip rushed to Mikhel's office before the e-mail announcing the winner was sent to the rest of the university. He talked him into taking a rare, long lunch in the middle of the day.

After their lunch, they took a walk through campus, noticing the summer flowers. Philip sat on a bench and patted the seat next to him.

Mikhel sat. "What is going on? You have been somber since we left my office."

"Jonathen won the Olympics. They will be announcing it any minute now."

"Oh. What does that mean for you?"

"Next week, I will find out where I am going. And I will be leaving immediately."

"Can I come with you?"

"No. They told us to wrap up any loose ends before then." Tears sprang to Philip's eyes.

"And we are a loose end."

"I'm afraid so. I will miss you so much. I hope you get to have that dream wedding and buy that house we wanted."

Mikhel laid his head on Philip's shoulder as they both cried.

Mikhel texted his chair that he was taking the next ten days off and he would see him on Monday, June 20th.

Publish or Perish

***

Caterina packed up the last few of her books and articles of clothing. She did not have much. Where she came from, they had very few belongings. And she had not acquired much since being here, as attachments to people and things were not encouraged for students at Portsmouth. They were supposed to be only interested in the pursuit of knowledge.

She wondered what her new program would be like. As proud as she was to be among the best of the best, she was relieved to be leaving the grueling expectations behind. She wished that she could visit her family, but the other dominions were not allowed to communicate with the Intelligencia. In her dominion, they were taught that the Intelligencia were elitist and out of touch with them. She wished they could see how she was working to make their lives better.

She made her last stroll across campus to the alumni dining hall, where they served meals to those they wanted to impress. And no one required impressing as much as the Legacy Foundation. Their money alone practically kept the campus afloat.

She entered the Legacy Dining Room and sat next to Amilee. "Any guess who this room is named after?" She laughed.

"Why, you must mean our most illustrious benefactors." Amilee sighed. "I guess it was nice to be amongst the rich while it lasted."

"Yeah. I wonder what is next for us."

Caterina's eyes widened as they brought out the meal. There was more food on each plate than she ate in a week back home.

Amilee looked at the plate placed in front of her. "Let's

worry about that later. First, we feast. At least we will be leaving here in style."

Caterina took a bite. "This is so much better than the cafeteria."

The two women began eating as a man in a dark suit walked onto the makeshift stage in front of them. "It is my honor, as president of the Legacy Foundation, to be in front of so many amazing young minds this evening. The foundation is thrilled to have been able to sponsor the Publishing Olympics for the past five years, and we hope to make this a staple at Portsmouth University for many decades to come."

Amilee looked at Caterina and rolled her eyes. Caterina stifled a nervous giggle.

"At least we won't be here to see it," Caterina whispered.

"You mean you won't miss these hallowed halls, either?"

"I remember when we met that first day at orientation. I was so excited to be here. I just knew I was going to do big things. But this place is bullshit. It's all toxic masculinity."

Amilee faked a gasp. "You can't possibly mean Portsmouth. My friends back home thought I was weird and pretentious before I got here, but I can't hold a candle to these assholes."

"Do you think any of the research they do here is real?"

"I don't know. I just want to go to a place where I can read my books and have real conversations with real people. Without feeling like I don't belong unless I am impressing everyone in the room."

Caterina nodded. "I just want to do real research that helps the women back home. They tried to make me a Nurser there. I watched the children and took care of the land. But I was lucky someone spotted that I was different and brought me here. They made my younger sister a

Publish or Perish

Breeder right before I left. She was only twelve. She cried and clung to me when they took her away."

The women's attention returned to the stage. "Please help me congratulate Jonathen Sizemore as the winner of the Olympics this year. Jonathen, like the four winners before him, will become the newest member of the Legacy Foundation.

"Boy's club." Caterina muttered under a fake cough.

Amilee tried and failed to stifle a laugh. "So, that's where the winners go. What do you think happens to us?"

The men around them glared, so they returned their attention to the speaker.

"Jonathen. Please join the deans and the rest of us Legacy members outside for pictures. As for the rest of you talented young people, just sit tight. Someone will be here momentarily to tell you where you will each be going."

Jonathen and the other suited men left the room. As the door shut. Caterina jumped at the sound of the door locks clicking into place. Minutes later, she and her fellow students began to cough as an odorless gas filled the room.

Pawn to King Four
by Ana Maria Selvaggio

"Don't be such a killjoy! All the girls are doing it. Besides, I can't stand to see you continuing to pine over that private in division. He's beneath you."

Amelia appreciated Lonnie, but her pep talk skills could use some work. "I'm not still pining over anyone." She shot her a glance that was part warning and part smirk.

Lonnie held her arms up in mock defense. "Sorry, sorry! Didn't mean to strike a nerve." Amelia just rolled her eyes at her, and they both laughed.

"Come on, though, seriously. These guys all miss home. They could use a bit of kindness…and it wouldn't hurt if they turned out to be cute either." Lonnie shoved her shoulder into Amelia as they continued to fold laundry.

"Are you doing it? I've never known you to be an avid letter writer."

"No, but…" Lonnie laughed as she ducked a flying towel, "Hey! Hey, okay. I'll do it if you do it. Deal?"

Amelia looked at her best friend of two years and sighed. Lonnie smiled. She knew she was halfway to a win if

Ana Maria Selvaggio

Amelia was sighing. She gave her a minute to come around to the victory.

Amelia had always loved having pen pals. Her father was part of the Army Corp of Engineers so they had moved a lot and it was how she could keep up with her friends, though it was often sporadic, letters having to correct addresses from duty station to duty station till she was old enough to move out on her own and have one solid address. She had made friends all over the world and, years later, still kept in contact with several. Christmas was the only time it was hard to keep up with. Mailing out one hundred twenty-five Christmas cards all over the world could get expensive.

"Okay. Only if you do it with me, though."

"Yay!" Lonnie jump-hugged her, "You won't regret it."

"You have to promise me you will actually write them, though. No sending pinups just to tease them."

"Why I never!" Lonnie let out a Southern-accented gasp, throwing her hand over her heart before falling out into a laughing fit. Even she couldn't dismiss that one. She crossed her heart with two fingers. "Promise."

***

"Bet you get a pretty one. You always do."

"I don't care about that, you know that." Gustav didn't look up from his book. "As long as I can read her handwriting and she can hold an intelligent conversation, I'm happy."

Private Cosgrove stopped reading the letter he was holding and sat up in his bunk. "Now you're just lying," he watched for a smile but didn't get one. "You seriously mean you don't care what she looks like?"

"Nope." Still reading.

"What if she looks like Private Raygun over here…"

Pawn to King Four

Richards, the platoon's resident science-fiction nerd, threw a pillow across the aisle, knocking the letter Cosgrove was reading out of his hand. "Hey! Watch it, Junk Man."

Cosgrove laughed and tucked the pillow behind him, "Hilpany here says he don't care what she looks like long as she's a good *conversationalist*." Cosgrove feigned a fancy hand in the air and stood to turn in a circle. The men in earshot all started laughing.

"Har, har. You know what I mean." Gustav put his book down and leaned back on his elbow, the rain outside was dictating his mood at the current moment. "If she's pretty I wouldn't be upset, but that isn't what matters to me. Not really. Besides, it's just a few letters from home."

"Maybe some photos…" Cosgrove teased his khaki-socked ankle, "And some chocolate chip cookies at Christmas if you play your cards right."

Cosgrove wasn't wrong, Gustav had seen some of the mail coming through. The only sweets Gustav had seen were Hershey's D Ration bars and he admitted he'd kill for some homemade baked goods.

"Well, I can't argue that." Gustav smiled, "Lights out."

"Yes, Daddy," Cosgrove crooned as Private Raygun yanked his pillow out from under him.

Gustav stared at the top bunk above him, then closed his eyes and dreamt of home.

***

Amelia propped her feet up on the desk and grabbed half of her sandwich. She was starving. She gently swore under her breath, almost knocking her thermos of coffee onto the stack of paperwork she'd had to rifle through for the sergeant's request that day. Focused on the handful of gold she was just handed, she almost didn't care.

Ana Maria Selvaggio

***

Dear Amelia,

Thank you for your letter. I'll admit I don't get much mail, so I was a little taken aback you'd actually written.

As you know, my name is Hilpany, Gustav Hilpany. I'm a Private First Class.

I'm glad that you mentioned a love of art. I love art, too, though I don't create any of my own. I appreciate it, though. There is a lot of art over here, some pieces that are really moving, and I worry about its future. Some of us talk about it a lot. We're all just trying to get by from day-to-day, though. It's hard here. Your letter helped.

Maybe when I get back stateside we could catch a gallery. Hope you don't think I'm too forward, only meaning to be friendly.

You're from Ohio originally? I'm from Philly. Sorry, Philadelphia. You pick up bad habits in the military, everything abbreviated. My mom was a teacher, she'd correct me all the

Pawn to King Four

time, "If you have the time to says thanks, make an effort and say thank you." She wasn't wrong.

Food? I won't traumatize you with talk of rations. Being that you work in Boston with them, I'll just say thank you for your "efforts." :)

Do you bake chocolate chip cookies by chance? Inside joke. I miss the pizza back home. We had a couple guys from Italy open a place in Jersey, New Jersey, Nick's. Neither of them spoke English, but they managed to make it work. Guess no one's trying to talk to you with a mouth full of pepperoni. ha

Oh, and the cheesecake. There was this guy there who sold cheesecake out of an alley not far from…that sounded super sketchy to say that out loud (laugh) but, trust me, best stuff on the planet. He's near Reading Terminal Market, another place you should see. One of my favorite hangouts. It's like an outdoor market but all indoors. There's food vendors everywhere, even a few farmers have stalls. There is an Amish family that comes in from Lancaster and (puts hand to heart) they have homemade

Ana Maria Selvaggio

Peanut Butter Pie that...great, now I'm craving it... has brown sugar in it. I got to know them and have been to a couple barn raisings. I started putting on weight despite the hard work. ha

What are your favorite foods? What do you like to make? Have you ever heard of Peanut Butter Pie? Do you like peanut butter?

We weren't originally from Pennsylvania. My grandparents were Irish, settled in Illinois near Chicago. My parents moved to Philadelphia before I was born. Dad was an architect, mom stayed home with me till she couldn't. She got sick. Dad was lost without her when she left us so I can't blame him but, he passed not long after so I joined the Army.

May have lied about my age but it's too late now; what are they going to do, fire me? ha

To answer your question, yes, we have access to books here sometimes. I love to read, too. I've always wanted to write one but didn't know what I'd write about. I have some

Pawn to King Four

ideas now. :) Sometimes I'll get to borrow a book if any of the guys in my platoon get them. I speak a couple different languages (I love words, can you tell?) and picked up Polish quick enough so I can read a bit of what's available locally, too. Hopefully you won't laugh, but I'm reading poetry right now. The guys razz me but I catch them reading over my shoulder sometimes. There's a guy here, underground press stuff, Baczyński.

Who speaks to you, which authors do you like to read?

I'll end this here for now and be patient, though I admit it's hard. Thank you again for taking the time. Stay safe, please.

Your friend,

Gustav

***

Gustav settled into his bunk, the letter having burned a hole in his pocket all day. It was painful to wait. Cosgrove didn't even tease him.

Ana Maria Selvaggio

***

Dear Gustav,

Thank you for your letter, it is so good to hear from you. I am glad that my first letter made it to you safely. I know that things are not ideal there, so I hope you know that you are being thought of and that it gives you a little comfort.

It makes me happy to hear you speak so fondly of art. I feel like art is the best and worst parts of our humanity. I have seen images of breathtaking paintings using a "chiaroscuro" technique where the light seems like it comes from inside the canvas. I could stare at them all day and never see the same thing twice. I fear you would tire of waiting for me at a museum. I usually go by myself so I can take my time.

I would love to take in a gallery with you. There are a couple in Boston as well as museums (my favorite) but, admittedly, I have not taken the time to explore any of them.

I like your mom already. She is right, my mother would agree with

Pawn to King Four

her. "Always take the time," though she was more referring to spending time with people and making them important.

Yes, I bake. Well I am told. I would be happy to send you some, especially with Christmas is coming up. My father is USACE and I know he would help me if I asked. Maybe some for your friends as well if I can.

I love pizza. We have a little place here in Boston that is good. They serve "New York-style" slices. I've not been to New York so I do not have a comparison. These are huge and I can only get through one. My father says I am a lightweight. :)

I am not sure about the cheesecake, I will have to take your word for it. I do not tend to frequent alleyways. :)

Reading Terminal Market sounds wonderful! I love finding new places. And the Amish, I've never met any. You will have to tell me more about them. I have always wanted to travel the world, see new places, meet new people. My aunt travels a lot, all over, and she brings me back books and

Ana Maria Selvaggio

unusual things. She does very little of the tourist-type things and more prefers staying with real families to learn what they eat and enjoy. She tells, told, the most wonderful stories. Sorry, she recently passed and it hasn't caught up with me that she is no longer here. You would have liked her. She was strong, and kind, and funny.

If I send you a package for Christmas, what else could I send you? Maybe a book? Is there anyone in particular's voice you are missing? Please do let me know and I will try to make you something nice to open.

Favorite foods? I do like peanut butter. My mother used to make peanut butter and creamed cheese sandwiches on cinnamon raisin toast. She loved to make bread, she taught me to bake. So did my grandmother. My grandparents lived with us most of my growing up. My father built onto the back of our house - he was in construction, did I mention that before? - and they moved in so we could all look after each other after my mother passed. I miss her. Sometimes it's hard to picture her face in my mind. I take a

Pawn to King Four

lot of photos now to hold space for memories. My father got me a Kodak Brownie camera. He gifted it to me with a copy of a "Brownies" book by Palmer Cox. I am not sure which came first, the camera or the books. Chicken or the egg?

I love poetry. I tried my hand at writing it in college but prefer, please don't laugh, action-adventure comics.

My father got me a copy of a new comic, Wonder Woman, and, I admit, I am hooked. He said she reminded him of me – strong (stubborn) and independent. She is…I won't spoil it in case you have not read it. I will try to send you a copy, if you like comics. You can give it to one of the other men if you do not, I am sure they would appreciate it. She is very caring and supportive…and pretty. :)

Our family likes to gift books at Christmas. My mother used to gift me books on sewing and cooking while, ironically, sliding in the occasional "rebellious" author like Mary Wollstonecraft (feminist). My father got me interested in H.G.Wells, Jules Verne, and Mary

Ana Maria Selvaggio

Shelley (Wollstonecraft's daughter) amongst others. I loved Frankenstein. I loved all their gifts. I read a lot of different genres, it is never boring that way. I like how unique every writer's voice is…

I just realized that I am more than four pages into this letter! It is so easy to "talk" to you. I am a little embarrassed, though, that I have rambled on so long. I hope you do not mind. I can hear your friends teasing you from here.

If they ask…

Yes, I do like you. :)

Your friend,

Amelia

***

My dearest Amelia,

You will never hear me complain about how long your letters are. Each sentence is a long-awaited joy.

As are you.

You got a hoot out of Cosgrove. I'll refrain from telling you the

Pawn to King Four

rest of his commentary. Suffice to say, he's happy for me.

"Frankenstein"? That surprised me. Have you read Stoker's "Dracula," any of Arthur Conan Doyle's work involving Sherlock Holmes (a particular favorite of mine), or White's "The Lady Vanishes"? If I were there now, I would take you to all of my favorite bookstores or, better yet, we would travel and find new ones.

Would you travel the world with me?

Now I am being forward and, I would apologize, but it would be a half-truth and I won't lie to you. Ever.

Sorry this one is shorter than the rest but it's getting busier here. Too many "kids" like Cosgrove to watch out for. (He just hit me and says hello.) I'm looking forward to meeting you in person.

I hope you like hugs.

Yours,

Gustav

Ana Maria Selvaggio

✶✶✶

Dear Gustav,

Tell Cosgrove hello for me. Does he not get his own letters? Should I start including a small note for him as well so you can read in peace? (laugh) I am only joking. I cannot imagine how hard things are for you there. I think about you, all of you, all the time as we hear news come in.

And I love hugs. Sending you one now.

Yes, I have read Stoker, White, and even, of dissimilar genres, Hammett's "The Maltese Falcon" Tolkien's "The Hobbit" – which was lovely but tiring, I am not made for Tolkien I fear – and MacDonald's "The Princess and the Goblin." I love children's books, they are relaxing reads but, most often, end too soon and I become restless for the next.

Not in order are my favorites, "The Hound of the Baskervilles," "A Study in Scarlet," and "The Adventure of the Speckled Band," the latter of which I read first. My father took me to the cinema to see Basil Rathbone

Pawn to King Four

in "The Hound of the Baskervilles" when it came out a few years ago, before all of this ugliness. It was wonderful.

Have you heard of George Méliès? He is a marvel. He is a magician turned filmmaker! No sound, just music, and the loveliest camera tricks. They say his wife is the star in all his films.

Oh, and Agatha Christie. I am particularly fond of her Hercule Poirot books, especially "Murder on the Orient Express." It was the train that pulled me in. I have always wanted to travel on the real Orient Express. I love trains. The rails are like a lullaby. I have only ever been on one, but my grandmother and I used to sit in the park and watch them when I was little. We would have a picnic, usually cucumber or tomato sandwiches in summer, and there was this one tree with a low branch that I could climb up and sit on.

My best friend Lonnie thinks I am boring you. She is reading this over my shoulder - I do not think I am and she needs to mind her own business. (laugh) She is pouting now. She will be fine, I sent her off to get us some

Ana Maria Selvaggio

more coffee.

Lonnie and I have been best friends since my first day in the WAAC, so about two years now. She is trouble and I love her. She has horrid taste in men, though...I told her I wrote that, she just shrugged at me. I'll refrain from the rest of her commentary. (laugh)

I do think of just you most times. I wonder how you are and...I am blushing as I write this...if you think of me. I have an imaginary you in my head reading your letters to me and I often feel like there is a sadness in your voice. Are you sad? I do hope not, but if there is I hope my letters dispel some of it for you.

Please stay safe, and warm, and well.

Yours,

Amelia

***

Gustav winced as he twisted his belt further to tighten the soaked tourniquet just above his knee. He'd bit down on a piece of his shirt, but the pain was too much to bear. He tried focusing on Amelia, her voice that he'd made up in

Pawn to King Four

his head. She'd never sent a photo, but he didn't care. His thoughts were of her last letter as he passed out in the tall grass.

***

Barely lucid, he felt his body drag the dirt, too weak to do anything about it. His shoulders aching, pulled up to his ears, his arms tied awkwardly across his chest as his shirt threatened to strangle him. Eyes closed, lids bright with sunlight, he was unable to block it, his head cradled in his shirt. *Breathe. Just breathe.* His leg throbbing, it felt like a weight had been tied to his ankles. Voices, not quite arguing, but foreign. More dragging. Dimming light. The smell of his mother's chicken soup. Pain in his back as he was rolled. Bumps, thuds, down, darkness. The smell of earth. Cooler. He tried opening his eyes, but his body had other ideas as sleep overcame him.

***

Gustav woke to a gentle hand on his forehead. He'd not meant to startle her when he sat up, panic across her face. She looked around as though to defend herself, but a man was already descending the stairs toward them. The man spoke to him in Polish, putting a firm hand to Gustav's chest to keep him down while softly calming the woman. Gustav could make out a few words aimed at him - "Rest" and "Heal" - so Gustav laid back and let sleep take him. This time willingly.

Ana Maria Selvaggio

***

"*Jesteś bezpieczny, Hill-panya. Obudź się teraz, jedz.*" You safe, Hill-panya. Wake now, eat.

"Hilp…" Gustav, eyes still closed, "It's Hill-pan-knee." Eyes opening, "Hilpany."

The man smiled. "*Mówisz po polsku?*"

"Yes, a little." Gustav was happy to wake to a smiling face and not a German uniform.

"You slept good I think," the man spoke softly, gentle. "I am Jorgen. *Moja żona,* Anna, we take care for you. Hide."

Gustav sat up a little and remembered the dragging, they had brought him to their home and into their basement. His shoulders were sore, he could still feel the aches in his arms. His leg he wished he couldn't feel. He winced when he tried to sit up. Jorgen put a gentle hand to his chest and shook his head.

Jorgen grabbed a nearby sack, folded it awkwardly, and put it behind Gustav head and shoulders so he could raise up a little. Gustav thanked him. His leg had been cleaned and bandaged, his own makeshift bandages blood-soaked and in a pile with his belt nearby. He had lost a lot of blood and, by rights, shouldn't be there. *He shouldn't be there.*

"You saved my life." Gustav tried again to sit up, but Jorgen wouldn't allow it.

"Weak. Rest."

"I don't want to endanger your family."

"Weak. Rest. My Anna make you food. Heal."

The chicken soup smell. His stomach was on Jorgen's side, gurgling loud enough to make Jorgen softly chuckle.

"See, agrees." Jorgen pulled a blanket over him. Gustav was thankful for the gesture, the basement was cooler and he guessed it was probably night. The blanket was rough and still smelled like the horse it had probably been on at

Pawn to King Four

one point, but it was a comfort. Just then, there was a sliding noise and Anna came down the stairs with a small bowl and spoon. She handed it off to Jorgen and gave Gustav a polite smile.

"I'm sorry that I startled her earlier. *Przepraszam*."

"She is good. She care for you, your leg. Stop bleeding." Jorgen pulled an old wooden chair to the side of the bed and sat on it. "Eat."

The smell and steam coming off the bowl was enough. Gustav wished it was a swimming pool. "Thank you but I can…" The groan escaped his lips before he could stop it. Both of his shoulders felt like he'd been broken apart and reassembled.

"No. Rest. Eat." Jorgen spooned up some of the soup and made blowing noises at Gustav to get him to blow on it. Gustav blew a couple times and then almost cried tears of joy as the soup hit his tongue and throat to spread down into his chest. Three more bites and he felt like he could die happy right there.

Amelia.

"I have someone, I need to get to her." Gustav willed himself to stay there. He knew he needed the rest and food to give him back the energy he would need. He looked at his leg, all of the blood he'd lost. He knew he wouldn't get a second chance. This *was* his second chance. He would find a way to get home to her.

"*Moja żona?*"

"Wife? No," it cost him to say it, "but I won't hesitate to ask her if I make it home."

"Home. We help."

Jorgen gestured his other hand around the room. In the dim light, Gustav could make out shelves, supplies, rations next to guns in the corner, and bedrolls. This was not the first time Jorgen and Anna had risked their lives.

"Thank you." Gustav let Jorgen continue feeding him, the occasional sip of water from a tin cup, and a bite of bread, till the soup was gone. "Very good, thank Anna. Tell her it was just what I needed." Jorgen nodded.

"You sleep. Trust you no try to stand?" Jorgen handed him a glass jar. "Use if need. We take care of."

Gustav was embarrassed, but knew he didn't have another choice and awkwardly thanked him, hoping it wasn't Anna who would retrieve it later. He had Jorgen remove the extra blanket and help him turn on his side slightly.

Jorgen left a candle nearby on a stool and took the lantern with him, "*Dobranoc.*"

"Goodnight, thank you again." Jorgen only nodded, ascended the stairs, and Gustav heard the door close, then something slide into place before all was quiet.

Gustav took a moment to just listen. The quiet was deafening but welcome. Blowing out the candle that Jorgen had thoughtfully left within reach, Gustav took three deep breaths and let his body sink down into the bed. He relaxed a little more each time, a technique one of the men in his platoon, one of three from India, had taught him.

"Goodnight, Amelia." closing his eyes, "I'll be home soon."

***

> Gustav,
>
> I have not heard from you in a while. I pray you are well, and whole, and safe. I try to imagine you are off on a secret mission and cannot

Pawn to King Four

communicate, but my heart is worried. It is not like you to not reply. I will stay strong as I know you would want me to be, but please get word if you can. If you cannot, know that I am with you wherever you are.

I miss your words and you.

Yours,

Amelia

PS - Please, if someone other than Private First Class Gustav Hilpany reads this letter, please reply and let me know how he is. Good or bad. Thank you.

***

"She is wonderful. Smart. Funny." Gustav sat in Jorgen and Anna's kitchen. He had been there more than a week, almost two by his reckoning, and he was healed enough to stand somewhat confidently now. They had fed him well and his leg was healing. The bullet had thankfully gone clean through and missed bone. Anna had used herbs and a few things he couldn't identify. It wasn't always pleasant. At first, she'd had to pack the hole with it on both sides, which was a wholly painful experience. Jorgen making him drink something akin to homemade hooch to dull the pain. Whatever it was, he was grateful, though, because it had worked.

"Ah, funny. Good." Jorgen smiled and looked across the room at Anna who was cooking, "My Anna have good humor, she with me." Anna smirked at him.

"She pretty, this your Amelia?"

"She is lovely. I don't honestly know what she looks like, though." Gustav realized he'd never asked her. "The men kept asking me for photos. She never sent any, but I didn't ask." Gustav felt foolish, but only for a moment, remembering the sound of her voice in his head, "She's beautiful, even if I've never seen her."

Anna said something to Jorgen that Gustav didn't quite catch. Jorgen got up and walked to her, kissing her cheek.

"What did she say?"

"You good man."

***

Anna wrapped and packed food into a duffel as Jorgen kept watch out the front window, while handing her things. They were both nervous, but anyone who didn't know them would have just seen two people working in tandem seamlessly. Gustav straightened the shirt they had given him as well as the hat. Anna shook her head and came over to him to adjust it down a little. "Common. Don't be seen."

Gustav knew there was no way he could ever repay them for their kindness, or for the risks they were taking. Anna and Jorgen had put themselves at risk. He was glad they had no children with them, that would have complicated it more. Gustav had learned, though, that she could not carry a child and it made him regret the thought. They had very much wanted to have one and, since they couldn't, found others to look after. They had been doing it since the war began.

Pawn to King Four

He wanted them out and safe. He wanted "his Amelia" to meet them.

Jorgen stiffened for a moment as Gustav heard the noise outside. Still hobbling a little, he knew he wouldn't make it to the basement in time so shifted around to hunch over, like an old man, pulling his hat down further and his scarf up. Anna stepped closer and put her hand on his shoulder as Jorgen opened the door.

The two men whispered in Polish, the stranger nodding to Anna. She nodded back and lifted Gustav's arm to stand.

"You be well, take care your Amelia," Anna's eyes welled up. "Long happy life."

Gustav hugged her, he couldn't help it. Pulling away, he grabbed Jorgen's hand with both of his, "Thank you." He looked back at Anna, "Long happy life." Gustav wondered if he would ever see them again as Jorgen grabbed him in a huge, tight hug.

"This Aleksander, Alek, from the village. He take you to village then there to camp." Jorgen and Alek exchanged a silent look that could only be, *be careful.*

Gustav gave both of them one last look, pulled the bag over his shoulder, and walked out with Alek, doing his best not to limp.

Jorgen had given him a cane, instructed him not to speak - it was obvious, no offense, that Polish wasn't his first language - and to laugh deeply instead "with his belly." They would not be able to use the trains as the occupiers were utilizing them heavily. There had been rumors too hideous to imagine. They didn't speak of it, only sat in silence when news came through from neighbors.

***

Gustav and Alek walked roads only when necessary and took

small paths through wooded areas, slowly, ever watchful. Alek tried to stop for him occasionally, when they could, but Gustav wanted to push on while he was able. When they finally did stop, it was to eat, relieve themselves, and find shelter. They traveled as far as they could each day, taking almost a full two days to reach the village.

Alek patted Gustav on the shoulder, wished him safety, and handed him off to a pair of brothers. Their last name Rudzinski, they had very little interest in talking and started out almost immediately. Gustav thought of Amelia as he watched the brothers quickly repack his bag, give him another jacket, and take his hat. He started to protest but was assured his US Army haircut had sufficiently grown out. He had facial hair hiding him as well now, since he hadn't shaved in weeks. Just to be sure though, one of the brothers "unevened" his hair a bit to look like a shaggy home-cut, gave him a new scarf, and gestured for him to stay between them.

He hobbled along, tired, and without his cane. They had taken it from him, saying it would make him stand out more. The brothers meandered, once feigning drunkenness, then picked up the pace when they were out of town. Gustav did his best to keep up, but would occasionally get an escorted arm hold if he was walking too slowly. Any other time, the brothers would have had black eyes. He wasn't a scrapper by nature but was taught how to end it.

***

The moon was high and full. Gustav was grateful for the light enough to see his footing. They had been walking through the woods for quite a while when one of the brothers put a hand up and the other grabbed his jacket, pulling down. He bit back the pain and squatted down. Voices ahead had

Pawn to King Four

him holding his breath, frozen. He had come so far, closer to her, this couldn't be it.

Just then, he heard a thick Midwestern accent and almost wanted to run toward it. He waited and watched the brothers, though. After a few moments, they stood, gestured for him to, and walked toward the voices.

"*Przyjaciel.* Friend. Friend." The men ahead held their ground, rifles and pistols at the ready.

"Identify," came a firm voice. "*Zidentyfikować.*"

"I hope you boys haven't lost your manners in all this," Gustav smiled, his American accent loud and proud. "Private First Class Gustav Hilpany." Everyone relaxed a little. "These men helped me get here, I was injured."

"Hilpany, you got nine lives. They thought you were dead."

"I didn't think I had enough of a reputation anyone would miss m…" Gustav was interrupted by a hard tackle to the ground. "Sonofab…" He grimaced hard under the weight of an ecstatic Cosgrove.

"Oh dear god you're ALIVE." Gustav could hear his friend's voice hitch.

"Only if you get off me," Gustav sat up and grabbed him back in a quick hug, though, before taking stock of his now re-injured leg. "Ugh. Weeks of healing undone, Jorgen would kill you."

"Jorgen? Oh, sorry, are you…" Cosgrove watched as Gustav stood and almost fell back down. "Damn, I'm sorry. I didn't know. What happened? Where were you?" Cosgrove waived some men over to help steady Gustav. He was so exhausted he let them.

Gustav turned his head to thank the brothers, but they had already gone. Looking around, he picked out the alpha, then stood straight and saluted as best he could.

Ana Maria Selvaggio

"Private First Class Gustav Hilpany."

"At ease. Get settled," then he looked at the men. "Infirmary," before looking back at Gustav "We'll talk later. I'll send someone in to debrief."

Cosgrove was inundating him with questions. Gustav just listened without offering replies until he got the hint. "Sorry, let me get clean and settled first, then we'll talk."

"Yeah, yeah, of course. No problem." Cosgrove grabbed his shoulder gently, though Gustav was waiting for another tackle. "I'm just glad you're here."

"Have you heard from Amelia?"

Cosgrove smiled and pulled two letters out of his shirt. "No, but you have."

***

Gustav, freshly showered and shaved, laid back in the infirmary cot and felt every ache he'd been trying to avoid for the last seventy-two hours. He was exhausted but fed, such as it was. He thought of Jorgen and Anna, and missed them. He imagined them at their little kitchen table eating quietly, their "child" gone, not knowing if he was safe. Jorgen was more like a brother as he thought of it, though. He placed them at slightly older, and on more of an equal, even keel.

He stared at the letters in his hand. Two of them. As elated as he was, he almost didn't want to open them. If he didn't, she wouldn't be heartbroken. If he did, the suspense tightening his chest would be gone. He took three deep breaths, slid a finger into the side of the older-dated envelope, and pulled the letter out.

Pawn to King Four

***

Lonnie had done her best to distract Amelia. Her best friend had been really emotional when she'd gotten word that her guy was alive. She was glad as much for selfish reasons as for Amelia's sake. She'd had to put up with Amelia being chaotically sad, running scenarios past her, and being depressed as hell. Lonnie was glad it was over and they could both move on. She would put up with all of it gladly, though, despite how tiresome it was. Part of her was glad Gustav was alive, too.

"I hope he's healing well." Amelia took another bite of her sandwich. Amelia much preferred the women's mess hall and missed it. With the influx of soldiers, they had gone to a communal mess hall that didn't differentiate between men and women. Their choices were removed, and some of the women had even opted to skip meals to avoid gaining weight for fear of abuse from the men. "I can't eat any more of this."

Lonnie looked around then pulled a shiny red apple from her coat pocket. Amelia took it and slid it into her own. When she was sure no one was looking, she stole several bites and sat back, eyes closed while she chewed. Mouth full, "I could kiss you."

"He's wounded in the hospital and you're already cheating on him." Lonnie started to laugh, but the look on Amelia's face made her freeze. "I'm sorry. That was bad, even for me."

Amelia's voice was low and succinct, "You know. I would never. Even think to…"

"I know, that's more my M.O." Lonnie did laugh this time, but Amelia wasn't smiling. She tucked her apple in a piece of cloth and started to leave. Lonnie grabbed her arm gently.

"Please. Don't go. I really am sorry, sweetie. It was stupid, I didn't think." Lonnie looked close to tears, "I'm so sorry, please stay."

Amelia softened. "It is all a bit raw right now so... apology accepted." She sat and pulled out her apple, "Thank you again."

Lonnie nodded and took a bite of Amelia's rations. The grimace on her face made Amelia smile. She offered part of the apple to her, but Lonnie waved her off. "I'll take my lumps for that comment. Love you."

"You, too."

***

Gustav finished the two letters, he must have reread them at least five times. The last one made him more emotional than he'd wanted to be in front of the others. No one was picking on him, though, and if they'd started, Cosgrove would have made them eat dirt.

"You okay, man?" Cosgrove sat forward in his chair. He'd stayed by him, thankfully quietly, while Gustav re-cooped.

"She was worried sick." Gustav tried to push down the lump in his throat. "She thought I was dead."

"From the sounds of it you would have been if it wasn't for Jorgen." Cosgrove studied Gustav's face, "I'd like to meet him. Thank him."

"Don't go getting all sappy on me." Gustav shot him a wry smile. "I'm okay. There was no way you could have known." He knew Cosgrove, only older by a year, felt like he'd failed him by not being there. They had always had each other's backs, especially when they were in trouble, which was usually Cosgrove's fault. "It's just good to be back."

Cosgrove got up and poured him more water, "Yeah,

Pawn to King Four

it's good to have you back."

***

Amelia waited for the post every day, hoping for a word from Gustav. After almost four weeks from when she'd gotten word he was alive, her waiting paid off. Handed the letter, she tucked it in her pocket and excused herself to the women's bathroom. She waited for a stall, then sat and pulled out the letter. Her hands shaking, eyes already threatening tears.

***

Dearest Amelia,

I am so incredibly sorry that I worried you. Please forgive me. It hurts me to know you were so upset. I could lie and say I was on a secret mission...thank you for thinking me so gallant...but, in point of fact, I was injured.

I am okay or I would not be writing to you.

I was out on patrol and a bullet caught me in the leg above my knee. It missed bone, to which I am grateful, but it was pretty bad. I'll spare you the details.

There was a farm nearby and a man

Ana Maria Selvaggio

in their garden saw me. He and his wife took me in and hid me in their basement till I was healed enough to get back to base camp. They went to great risk to connect me with people that could help me, but I think they had been doing that for a lot of people. It definitely wasn't their first rodeo.

Jorgen and Anna.

They are the loveliest people, I wouldn't be here without them. It is unlikely you will ever get to meet them, but I wish you could. Stranger things have happened. I talked about you the whole time. Anna teased me and said I was oczarowany, "smitten." I couldn't argue.

I won't bother erasing that, but I hope I've not made a mistake.

Cogsgrove just startled the bejesus out of me. He whispered in my ear I should add a little "Do you like me, too?" with a yes or no box. Didn't even realize he was over my shoulder, probably why I got shot. Ha. I hate him sometimes but he makes me laugh and he's the best guy to have on your side.

Pawn to King Four

I have added your name as a friend (they advised me to write fiancée since you aren't family) to my records to be notified if I suffer a worse outcome. I felt bad not getting your consent, I hope you don't mind, but I know what it's like to not know something important. Take solace in the knowledge that Cosgrove is, of course, defending your honor and giving me hell for it. Thankfully privately. He gets it, though.

There isn't anyone else to notify for me back home. I have a cousin but we barely know each other. A couple of the other men here have become good friends, but they would have the information faster than you would. I've been sharing parts of your letters with them. Not all of them, I'm greedy. (In good ways, I'm not the jealous type.) I know they would make sure you knew.

My leg will heal. I am sometimes unsteady and they won't put me back to active duty till I am. Admittedly, I feel useless and don't like it. I convinced the sergeant here to let me at least help around the hospital. Met a guy and his actual wife here.

Ana Maria Selvaggio

Newlyweds, They didn't want to wait till they got back home. I understand why. Life is short, and with the way things go around here, I wouldn't want to wait either. Their last name is Gilbert, they are both part of the medical team here.

Thoughts of you are what got me through. I imagined your voice in my head telling me to keep going, that I was almost home. I hope that doesn't scare you, but I'm grateful for your letters. They have meant a great deal to me. Thank Cosgrove, he tucked them all in his bag and brought them.

I'm going to get some rest now. I start work tomorrow. I can't bend so at least I won't get latrine duty. Small favors.

Ever yours,

Gustav

***

"You should marry that girl when you get home. Cosgrove's not wrong." Gilbert the Female razzed Gustav with a wry smile.
"So he told you, did he?" Gustav wasn't surprised, word got around fast, "All of it I'm assuming?"

Pawn to King Four

"Yes. She sounds sweet on you." Gilbert changed out the dressing on Gustav's leg. "And whatever this Anna of yours did I want to bottle it. You're barely going to have a scar." Gilbert turned his leg over side to side. "Can you bend your leg any better?"

Gustav pulled his knee up, though not without effort. He still had to cup his fingers behind his thigh to do it. "Muscles still not cooperating."

"Well the bullet took part of your quad - quadricep, your major muscle for lifting - so, I won't lie, you may need surgery when you get stateside." Gilbert pulled the gown he'd changed into back over him. "Get dressed. I'm done harnessing you for today."

"Thank you, Doc." Gustav swung his legs over the side of the bed.

Gilbert winced, "Stop calling me that. I'm not a doctor."

"You're the closest thing we have to one right now so get used to it." Gustav smirked at her, "Thank you."

"Go on, get out of here." Gilbert laughed. "And if you happen to see Gilbert the Sexy, tell him I'm snagging lunch in fifteen, he'll have ten."

Gustav laughed, he didn't even want to know what that meant. He had ideas, though, and he almost blushed as Amelia popped into his head. Gilbert the Female must have seen the look cross his face.

"Down boy. Go write her another letter."

***

Dear Gustav,

I am so glad you are able to make friends where you are. I am grateful they look after you. Lonnie looks

Ana Maria Selvaggio

after me as well, though we exchanged a few words today at an ill-timed joke. We are okay, though. She gave me an apple. Can you get fresh fruit there? What did you eat when you were with Jorgen and Anna? I do not know what they eat there, but I imagine it is savory and fresh. I am told they have a lot of gardens there, or did. I do hope that Jorgen and Anna are well and safe.

They have shifted us to a communal mess hall here. I would not have said we were spoiled having our own women's mess hall, but for having now eaten men's rations.

I dream of us having pizza at your Nick's now. I would trade 1,000 apples for it.

And I am not scared. I am overjoyed to think my "voice" had a part in bringing you to safety. If you had gone missing, or worse, I would have found a way to look for you. I would have transferred and found you. I know I am talking foolish but, I would have tried.

I write to my grandmother and include a letter for my father. They

Pawn to King Four

both know about you and are keeping you in their prayers. They ask how you are doing, mostly my grandmother. I think my father is simply checking up on his baby girl to see if "the boy is still around." (laugh) He is a good sort, just protective since my mother passed.

I hope you are healing well. Tell the Gilberts, and of course Cosgrove, I said thank you for being there for you. I wish that I could be, so I write to you thinking of my letters in your hands. It feels so strange to look back before this all started. I can not, not imagine you with me. (How do you write that? I wish my mother was here to ask.) I know that you were not there, that I have never even seen your face, but it feels like you have been beside me my whole life.

Speaking of, Lonnie is chiding me now for never sending you a photo of me. We have never talked about it, and you did not ask, so I did not think of it. I have enclosed one for you now, Lonnie is on the right. I'm the shorter one. I had not met you yet, but I will say now that the *smile in the photo is for you.*

Stay well please, heal and rest. For me.

Ever yours,

Amelia

PS - Cosgrove, make him behave. (laugh)

***

"See, woman knows who's runnin' the show here." Cosgrove stood taller and adjusted his shirt, then proceeded to bust out laughing while Gustav just shook his head, "I can't even say that with a straight face."

"She sent a photo. She's on the left…" Gustav put his hand out and blocked Cosgrove from launching at him. "My eyes first."

"Okay, okay!" Cosgrove backed away and stood at ease nearby, hands in his pockets. "I'll stand guard," he snickered.

Gustav pulled the small photo from its envelope. It was facing away from him, and he almost couldn't breathe. Slowly he turned it and met her gaze. The smile on her face eagerly claimed like a preserver for a drowning man.

Amelia stood arm-in-arm with Lonnie, her best friend posing shamelessly for the camera as she leaned forward to show her chest. Amelia's smile bordered on laughter toward the antics. She was in her uniform, standing straight, staring into his soul. She was like coming home, it was the only way he could think to describe it.

Pawn to King Four

Gustav had been alone for so long that he had learned to default to it. Both of his parents dead, it was easier to stay on the move than to deal with the emotions, so he had joined the Army. In all those years he hadn't thought of settling down once. Then Amelia entered his life.

Home.

Cosgrove put a hand to Gustav's shoulder and didn't say a word. He knew this moment was sacred, and he'd get full-on punched in the throat if he catcalled. After a moment, he chose his words wisely, "The one on the right is a real hoot."

"I'll take your word for it," Gustav didn't move, though there was a slight tremble in his hand. "I'm not looking at her."

"So that's Amelia. She's beautiful. I didn't expect anything less." Cosgrove patted his back. "I won't tell anyone. You couldn't handle all these guys at once."

Gustav knew he was right. One off-color comment about either of the women and Gustav would be in a bar room brawl with half the platoon. He wasn't fully himself yet and wasn't going to risk this new lifeline, Amelia's face, getting damaged. "Thank you."

***

Dear Gustav,

I know I am writing again a bit early, but I wanted to make sure that you got this care package in time for Christmas.

Enclosed are enough cookies for you and Cosgrove to enjoy. I made you a

Ana Maria Selvaggio

scarf, it is not the best, but it is the closest thing to a hug I can give you. I hope you like the colors.

Affectionately,

Amelia

***

My dearest Amelia,

I am forever in your debt. I have claimed your smile as for me and it has tied me to you. Lonnie, per Cosgrove, looks like a hoot. In all honesty, though, I hadn't noticed she was even there until he'd said something. I was too busy staring at you.

I want to stare at art in museums with you, get ice cream and pizza or whatever you wanted. I want to bring you to Poland someday, Anna's cooking is worth the trip. If you allowed me, I would take you around the world in search of new foods, books, and anything you wanted.

Your face is home to me.

Cosgrove is keeping it on the hush

Pawn to King Four

that you sent a photo or I'd end up in the hospital again. He's not wrong. I'd fight the world for you.

Anna's cooking is, I'm convinced, what healed me. She and Jorgen would go out and look through the garden and in the woods nearby. He always took a rifle as she picked. As much for wild boar or wolves as for men. We had boar one night. Though he had a gun, Jorgen refrained from using it when he went hunting for fear of bringing attention to themselves. He and his neighbor's son would hunt together. He preferred a bow and must have been good at it as we never went hungry. Anna didn't flinch field dressing it, she was a marvel. And they used everything. Bones, organs, fur, meat. Bones were for broth and the first thing she utilized. I think the bone marrow was used in part of my poultice. I saw her breaking the bones open and scraping them, next thing there was a new cloth being applied. She is sweet, somewhat quiet, and I can tell Jorgen loves her very much.

I want to look at you the way that he looks at her and get that look in return.

Ana Maria Selvaggio

And I would go to hell and back for you.

...especially after the cookies you sent. The guys got wind so Cosgrove and I had to share. You will be happy to know they've all pledged their undying love. And your scarf is wrapped around my pillow when it's not around my neck. Thank you, I love it. Even more knowing it came from you.

So where would you like to go first when I get home?

All my heart,

Gustav

***

Amelia read and re-read Gustav's letter. The war over, it was just a matter of time before she could meet him, face to face. She spent most of her days jumping up at every car. Her father started calling her "Bean" for jumping beans.

"You getting yourself dizzy every five minutes isn't going to bring him any sooner."

Amelia blushed, she was doing it again. "I'm sorry, Father. I know."

"His letter would have taken about four weeks if not longer to get here and he'll have twice that to get through all the tape." Her father set down two lemonades on the small card table between them and gestured toward the

Pawn to King Four

half-played backgammon game, "Come now, Bean, see if you can beat your ol' dad."

***

Amelia laid in bed with her covers over her head, tears soaking her pillow. She cried as much for the loss as for the realization that her grandmother would never get to meet Gustav. Amelia and her grandmother had been close. She had been the one to smooth things over with her son, Amelia's father, when any discussion of Gustav had come up. She had passed peacefully, and Amelia had been able to say goodbye. Amelia supposed that was all anyone could ask for, to be surrounded by loved ones and leave the world knowing you were loved.

Loved. Gustav.

Amelia sat up and took a deep breath. She felt worn, heavy, and her mind was sluggish. She wanted to lay back down, hide, wait, but she knew she couldn't. The black blouse and pencil skirt she had bought laying across the foot of her bed, she got ready for the service and met her father downstairs.

***

"You didn't have to come but, thank you." Amelia stood over her grandmother's headstone yet to be put in place next to her grandfather's, the ground still fresh after the funeral. There was a welcome breeze under the warm sun and the smell of rain. She couldn't look at the box in the ground, she had faith enough that her grandmother wasn't there, or hoped. She didn't consider herself as religious as others, but if there was ever a woman deserving of Heaven, it was her.

Amelia knew who the man standing at the outside edge

of the funeral was before he'd even approached. He was well dressed in a nicely cut suit, standard military haircut, though she could tell even from there he hadn't shaved in a day or so. He had made sure he was in her line of sight, though, nodded, then stood at ease with his hands in his pockets and just watched her. After mostly everyone had left, he'd walked over. He didn't say anything, just stood by her side and waited for her to acknowledge him. The breeze carried the scent of him across her cheek, spice and a heady musk. In person, he was familiar and admittedly comforting. She had imagined what he would sound like so many times in her head.

"You needed someone. I wanted it to be me."

Gustav reached out and took her hand. He hoped she wouldn't notice he was shaking. It wasn't that he was nervous, to the contrary. He had waited to meet her, to be in close proximity of her for far too long. He was aching to wrap his arms around her tight, protect her, console and comfort her. He held back for fear of frightening her. After all, aside from their letters, he was a stranger.

Amelia smiled at him and pulled her hand out of his, but only momentarily. She laced her fingers back into his in one smooth slide and the world went away. They both exhaled a held breath and visibly relaxed.

Lonnie smiled over at Amelia, then nodded to Gustav, her smile growing wider as she turned to leave. She knew from Amelia's description.

There was no awkwardness between them, it was like coming *home*.

They just stood for a moment before she allowed herself to lean into him. He shifted and put an arm around her shoulders, kissing the top of her head and burying his face in her hair. He just wanted to stand there and breathe

Pawn to King Four

her in for the rest of his life.

***

Amelia stared into the mirror and smoothed her dress. She chose simple and was grateful for it now, a small veil atop her head. Her grandmother in secret had modified her mother's wedding dress to fit the modern 1940s fashion while still keeping all the most important aspects. She knew even before Amelia. She cried when her father gifted it to her almost a month after the funeral. Her grandmother had given him strict instructions to wait, giving Amelia time to decide if Gustav in person was the one she would choose.

There was never any doubt.

Lonnie walked in and shut the door behind her. The look on her face was all Amelia needed to start tearing up again. "Do not start crying, you'll ruin my eyes." Amelia squinted toward the mirror to check her makeup.

"Oh honey, he's not going to know what hit him. You're beautiful." Lonnie took her hand, "He's going to be too busy kissing that face to worry about your makeup."

Lonnie was beyond happy for her. Gustav did everything possible to make sure she was included. He hadn't made her feel like a third wheel, though she was sure he wanted Amelia all to himself. He had even brought Stan along a few times. He was a nice enough guy, but there hadn't been a spark so they'd agreed to just stay friends.

***

Gustav and Amelia had been inseparable for weeks. Cosgrove, Stan, had been too busy setting up shop to feel jealous of Gustav's time. Though, nor would he. He'd never seen Gustav so happy, and Amelia was a doll. She'd made sure to include him in the occasional outing, even tried to set him up with her best friend. She was nice, but he hadn't planned on getting involved with anyone till he had the store set up and working for him.

Stan had been sending money home to his uncle his entire time in service. He and his uncle used to go to yard sales, junk shops, and estate sales on the weekends. They'd pick through to find all sorts of odds and ends, antiques and the like, so it was always his dream to open a little shop when he got home. His uncle's practically had him looking for a place where he could have a shop in the front while he lived in the back of it. His uncle had struck gold, and Stan had a place when he got home.

Gustav was staying with him till he found a house for him and Amelia. He only planned to use Stan's as a kind of forward operating base till he and Amelia left, though. They were going to travel starting with the honeymoon.

Gustav couldn't wait to see the world with her.

"Hold still idiot," Stan tried to straighten Gustav's tie for him.

"I'm a wreck."

"I noticed, I don't know why," Stan took his best friend by the shoulders and forced him to stop fidgeting. "Okay, yeah, I do. She's too good for you." Stan smiled wryly and Gustav pushed him off, laughing.

"I'll be fine." Gustav took in a deep inhale and held it for a moment. "Okay, let's do this." He smoothed his brown tweed suit in the mirror.

"Just remember not to lock your knees."

Gustav couldn't stop kissing her. Their fingers intertwined, he pulled back and gave her a long stare.

"What?" Amelia laughed, but she knew what he was doing.

Pawn to King Four

"I'm just making sure you're real." He smoothed back a curl, tucking it behind her ear. "We're really doing this."

"I've been looking forward to this." Amelia leaned her head onto Gustav's shoulder, the open road map in her lap.

He buried his nose in her hair a moment, "And I will never get us on the road if I keep kissing you so." He gave her one last passionate kiss then straightened and started the car. She laughed and sat up straight. "Where to first, m'lady?"

They had grabbed a slice at Vito & Nick's in the South Side. Gustav and Barraco had crossed paths once or twice but never really got to know each other. He always made a mean pizza, though, so they looked him up when they had decided to start Route 66 officially. The plan was to meander till they reached California. From there they'd fly home to Chicago. Gustav had saved every penny he could so they had a decent nest egg and could enjoy themselves a little while they looked for a house. Stan's uncle, a realtor by trade, was keeping an eye out for them.

Amelia pulled out a journal she'd been making notes in.

Gustav watched traffic, then pulled out onto Jackson Boulevard. Keeping his eyes on the road, he steered with his left and put his right on her leg. He was still marveling at the idea she was real and there next to him. "What do you want to see the most?"

She didn't hesitate. "The historic places, the junk shops or Stan will have our hides," she giggled, "and the Grand Canyon for Dad. I promised I'd take photos." Amelia looked at the camera case on the bench seat next to her. Her father had bought her a million rolls of 120 film and gone in on a new Ensign Ful Vue box camera with Gustav for their trip. She would have to be super selective on what she shot, as there were only twelve images per roll if she was lucky. She couldn't imagine looking at anything through a lens for very long, though, if she were in close proximity to Gustav.

"What about you? I made notes on everything, but what do you want to see most?"

"You. Just you in all those places." Gustav smiled and squeezed her leg.

***

Gustav and Amelia stood on the sidewalk in front of the house to take it all in. Their fingers laced, silent, tears ran down Amelia's face. Gustav wiped them away with his handkerchief and she laughed.

"It's really ours?"

"Yep. Stan's uncle closed on it for us this morning." Gustav wrapped an arm around her and pulled her in. "We're home."

She startled him with a squeal as she ducked out from his arm and ran across the yard to the front porch. "Well come on silly, do you have the keys?"

Gustav laughed and pulled the keys from his pocket, dangling them midair. Amelia ran back to him and looked like a Jack Russel trying to reach a ball. She finally punched him lightly in the stomach and grabbed them while he dropped to the ground in mock pain.

"Lightweight!" she yelled as she raced to the door, knowing full-well he was anything but. He caught up to her and grabbed her around the waist just as the knob was turned.

"Nope! We're going to do this right." Gustav grabbed her up in his arms and princess-carried her into the house. "Welcome home, m'lady."

Pawn to King Four

Amelia opened the boxes and started pulling out kraft brown parcels, marking each with their origin before setting them aside.

"You haven't even unpacked your suitcase, sweetheart." Gustav slid up behind her, wrapping his arms around her waist, and kissed her neck. Amelia didn't turn around.

"I know, but I want to get these all sorted so we can catalog them." Amelia set one empty box on the floor and started to grab another.

Gustav turned her around and held her in a tight hug. "You, my darling, need to settle back in with me first. We can organize everything," he kissed her nose. "Together. This isn't all for you to work." Amelia relaxed in his arms. "It can wait till we've had lunch at least and unpack."

Amelia knew he was right, but she'd spent most of their six-weeks driving planning how she would catalog it. They had mailed things back to Stan's shop, then, when they returned an hour ago, piled it into Stan's truck and unloaded it at the house. Stan had made it known that he should get a purple heart like Gustav's for his unwavering service in not opening anything when it arrived. Amelia had kissed his pained face in gratitude which, according to Stan, had made all the hardships worth it.

"You're right. I'll go make us something to…"

Gustav cut her off. "Nope. Your dad said he left something for us in the fridge. You go sit." Gustav gestured to their moss-green couch that Stan had found for them along with the beautiful mahogany veneer coffee table that fronted it.

Amelia set her marker down and moved to the couch, but not before grabbing her journal and pen. She had taken meticulous notes while they were driving. She'd lost count of how many stops they'd made, but she had taken notes at every stop, leaving space for Gustav to make little doodles of what they'd acquired on each page. They'd come home with three journals full of notes. This one, though, was specifically for her plans to organize the house and catalog everything.

"Here you go, my love." Gustav came in with two plates of food that consisted of cheese, bread, grapes, and some bell peppers he'd cut up. On the side of her plate was some pineapple, on his, an apple. He smirked at her and took the journal and pen from her. She only smiled and relinquished. "Stop. Just for a little bit. Be here with me." He kissed her forehead and sat down next to her, handing her a plate.

"I'm excited, I can't help it." Amelia popped a grape into her mouth.

"I know. Me, too. I'm glad your father built the attic out while we were gone. We're going to need it." Gustav looked at all of the boxes along the walls and in the hallway. "I am also glad I have an organized wife." He had marveled at her bookkeeping skills and was grateful for them. Amelia had cataloged the contents of each box in detail, marking each with a code that coordinated with where it should go. FH for "front hall," which was exclusively for anything outbound. Those boxes would be sorted out to ST for Stan, F for her father, and LG for Lonnie, for her gallery.

Lonnie had surprised Amelia with her dream of opening an art gallery. She'd never once mentioned it, but Amelia would see her sketching things occasionally. She had gotten Amelia her first journal. Lonnie's grandfather had owned a gallery and chose to retire when Lonnie returned and handed her the keys. Lonnie was over the moon, so Amelia made sure to look for frames for her on their trip that she would repurpose. Stan's list was much longer and

Pawn to King Four

more specific, mostly antiques.

The boxes along the walls near the stairs were marked A for attic. Amelia's salt and pepper shakers were in the kitchen marked with a K. The three bedrooms upstairs - theirs, one for guests, and eventually Amelia hoped, a child's room - were all marked and left in the upstair's hallways.

Gustav and Amelia sat quietly, snuggled into one another, and just looked at everything. Gustav would pluck the occasional grape from her plate and feed it to her; she'd return the favor. Gustav kissed the side of her head, "We have a lot of work ahead of us, but you've already made this so much easier than it could have been. You're a marvel. Thank you."

Amelia teared up and kissed him. "Thank you, for writing me." Setting their plates down on the coffee table, she snuggled into his arms.

They were home, and this was only the beginning.

***

"Do you think they will be able to find them?"

"I don't know. My contacts over there said the farm had been shelled, and anyone in the area had moved to the village. I'm hoping they made it." Gustav continued unwrapping the newest batch of pieces that Stan had dropped off.

"Here," Amelia slid her journal over to Gustav with a pen for him to draw the new pieces. After he finished sketching, he measured and made notes on sizes and anything that was visibly noticeable before handing the journal back. She could tell that Gustav's mind was elsewhere, though.

"Let's stop for lunch, are you hungry?" Amelia walked around the kitchen table, kissed him on the head, and took his mug. "Coffee?"

"Please. Thank you." He pulled the last item from the

box, but simply put the empty box on the floor and stared at it.

"They will be okay. They were smart and vigilant from what you told me. I can't imagine them not making it out." Amelia was concerned, but tried not to let it show. The war had done terrible things to Poland but, from what Gustav had told her, Poland's people were strong and resilient. They'd have to be. The Soviets had moved in just as they were rid of Hitler and it took months through various channels to even hope they would get them out, much less to the United States. Their persistence had paid off, though. Finally.

***

Gustav stuck the envelope in the mailbox and put the flag up. He'd have to wait almost a month before he heard back, but it was done. Jorgen and Anna would be coming home.

***

Stan's truck pulled up to the front of the house as Gustav and Amelia stood, his arm around her waist, in front of the porch. He was all nervous energy, so Amelia held onto him tight. This had been a long time coming, tons of paperwork, and they couldn't be happier. Stan hopped out and came around to open the door. A slightly younger-than-middle-aged man stepped down and turned to help a woman step carefully down. Stan started pulling bags out of the back of the truck, yelling, "Delivery!"

Gustav released Amelia and all but ran to them. He grabbed Jorgen into a hug and then Anna. All Amelia could do was stand, grinning ear to ear with tears in her eyes, as her husband found his family again.

"It so good see you. It been long time." Jorgen held him in another long hug, patting his back excitedly. Stan was already loading their things onto the porch.

"It's so good to see you both, please, come." He took both their hands and walked in between them toward the house. "Meet my Amelia!"

Amelia stepped forward and went to shake their hands as Anna grabbed her into a hug and cried. Startled, Amelia wrapped her in a hug, "It's so nice to finally meet you both. Gustav has told me so much about you."

Anna pulled back and held Amelia's waist, "You keep him going when the world was dark." Pulling her into another hug that Amelia returned fully, "I so happy for you both. So happy be here."

Jorgen was grinning ear to ear. Stan patted him on the back and shook his hand. Gustav hugged them both again, thanking Stan and inviting him in for lunch. "Amelia's cooking? Wouldn't miss it."

"This has had to be a big adventure for you both." Amelia shook hands with Jorgen, who clasped hers in both of his, before taking Anna's arm and walking her up the steps, "Please, come inside. Our home is yours now."

***

Laughter filled the living room as they all sat and ate. Amelia had filled the coffee table with fresh fruit, cheeses, homemade bread, a pitcher of lemonade, and some wildflowers Gustav had picked from the backyard. Conversation was light and it was as though the horrors of their past lives had ceased to exist.

"So you drive to California?" Anna sipped her tea and closed her eyes a moment. "*Dziękuję*. Thank you. It is very good."

Amelia smiled, "I'm glad you like it, it is Earl Grey. That is bergamot in the tea, it's a type of orange." Anna looked down at her cup, amazed. "Yes, the trip was long, but it was lovely. So many places to see." Amelia reached over and took Gustav's hand, "We would like to take you sometime, it would be the best way to show you our country."

Anna looked at Jorgen expectantly and took his hand holding her cup close, as though to keep it, "We would like very much. We have find work first though."

Gustav sat forward a little and looked at Jorgen, "I have some ideas on that, for now, if you would be interested. I think it will make the transition a little easier for you."

Jorgen set his plate down and mirrored Gustav.

"Amelia and I have been discussing it and, we would like you to live here."

Jorgen and Anna looked between themselves and back at them. Anna set her cup down.

"We do not want burden for you, you do so much to get us here and," Gustav held up his hand.

"We can give you work, paid work. Stan could use some help at his shop occasionally, maybe he'll take a break," he side-eyed Stan, who was mid-bite into a piece of cheese.

"Yes, I was thinking of hiring in someone part time to help me reorganize." Stan nodded at Jorgen. "I would love to have you there a couple of times a week to start. Anyone Gustav vouches for, you're hired."

Jorgen gripped Anna's hand tight and she covered his with her other hand. "Dziękuję. I start when you need me, thank you." He raised Anna's hands to his lips and kissed them, his smile wide.

"Gustav told me about your garden, it sounded lovely." Amelia smiled at Jorgen, "Would you be interested in

Pawn to King Four

planting a garden here? I am afraid I am not very good with plants. I have a little violet inside that Gustav got me and I'm surprised it has lasted this long. We would pay you, but I don't want you to feel like you are obligated."

Gustav chimed in, "No, no. None of this is obligation. We wanted you here. This is your home now, if you want it, and we just want to help you get on your feet here."

Jorgen and Anna looked at each other for a moment and tears began to stream down both of their faces. "We would love help you. Yes. *Dziękuję, dziękuję bardzo.* Thank you so much."

Gustav put his hands over both of theirs, "We're so happy you are here."

"Would you like to see the rest of the house?" Amelia glanced at Gustav and smiled.

Gustav and Amelia took Jorgen and Anna room by room, Amelia explaining her plans for each along the way. Jorgen and Anna were in awe, commenting on colors and how soft things were. Amelia thought Anna loved the kitchen, but she couldn't read her expression.

"Anna, do you like the kitchen? My family spent a lot of time around our kitchen table growing up, so I wanted a big table we could all sit around."

Anna leaned into Jorgen and spoke in hushed tones, she looked embarrassed and apologized.

"No, no," Amelia felt bad for putting her on the spot. "I'm sorry, I shouldn't have singled you out. I know that you are just getting used to things here."

"She did not know how to say." Jorgen held Anna's hand, "She think it is dream. We did not have things like this back Poland." Anna whispered again, "She always see photo of modern kitchen in old magazine, always want but feel bad for want."

Ana Maria Selvaggio

Amelia reached out and took Anna's other hand, "My Gustav told me how hard you worked. He told me about the wild boar you made for dinner, I couldn't do that." Amelia laughed, "You deserve to have rest and beautiful things around you that can help you."

Jorgen translated and Anna's eyes welled up with tears.

"Gustav," Amelia looked at him and nodded, "I think it's time."

Stan nodded as well, "I'll go get their things."

Stan walked to the front foyer and got Jorgen and Anna's bags, then took them outside. Jorgen and Anna watched, then turned to Gustav and Amelia, apologizing profusely.

"No, no, no." Amelia laughed, "I'm so, so sorry. Please, come with us." Gustav held the door open for all of them. Jorgen and Anna, very confused, followed them outside and around to the right to a little cottage. Stan was waiting there with their bags.

Gustav turned to them and held out a set of keys. "This is yours. *Home.*"

Jorgen and Anna looked at each other, then at Stan, then Amelia, and back to Gustav.

"Thank you for let us stay. We no make mess."

"No. Home. This is your home. This was ours, but we have the house now." Gustav closed Jorgen's fingers around the keys as Amelia took Anna's arm. "This is yours, we want you to have it."

Anna began shaking and grabbed onto Jorgen's arm as the tears came for both of them. Anna grabbed Jorgen into a hug and then hugged everyone, including Stan. Jorgen could only stare at the house.

Gustav put a hand on his shoulder, "You okay?" Jorgen didn't answer, but turned and hugged Gustav tight.

Pawn to King Four

"You good man," patting him on his back. "Good man."

"You both must be tired, let's get you settled. Jorgen, would you like to do the honors?" Amelia gestured toward the door.

Anna took his arm to steady him, and they walked the last few steps to their front door. Jorgen fumbled a little with the key till Anna put a hand on his. A turn of the knob and the door swung open into their new life. Stan followed with all of their bags, then Gustav and Amelia. There was a basket of bread, salt, coffee, and a beautiful throw blanket on the coffee table as well as a vase of wildflowers.

Amelia took Anna's hand and led her straight to the kitchen. "You deserve," was all she said as she guided Anna to a chair at the small kitchen table. "And there's four chairs, if you would ever like to have company."

Anna was silent for a few minutes, just looking around the room, then she whispered, *"Dziękuję bardzo,"* and held Amelia's hand to her cheek. "Thank you more. This change every thing. All this."

Amelia and Anna just sat quietly while Gustav and Stan helped Jorgen get their bags where they needed to go and gave him a tour.

"Stan is helping get Jorgen settled, we should go." Gustav kissed the top of Amelia's head, "Let's let them rest, they've had a hard journey." Amelia agreed.

"We are right next door. You have a phone here," pointing to the light, pistachio green phone on the wall next to the door. "You just pick up," she demonstrated. "Push these numbers," pointing to the phone number printed on the scrap of white paper taped to the side, "and wait till we pick up."

"Or you can just come knock on the door." Gustav

laughed. "We'll let you both get some rest." He squeezed Anna's shoulder and led Amelia out into the hallway as Stan and Jorgen came out from the bedroom.

"Anna is sitting in the kitchen, I think I might have overwhelmed her, I'm sorry." She put her hand on his arm, "We're just so happy you are both here and safe."

"Cannot say thank enough. I go to her." Jorgen shook her hand, then Gustav's and Stan's, before going to the kitchen to join Anna.

"Successful mission I'd say." Stan smiled, "I think they are both a bit shell-shocked."

"Yeah, this is nothing like their home back in Poland," Gustav glanced around the pretty little cottage they'd called their first home, "I can understand. Everything here is new to them. I hope they like it."

"I left them instructions on the counter for the toaster, Gustav even drew pictures." Amelia smiled at him, "I'll explain the rest later. Right now, they need sleep."

Gustav took Amelia's hand, "We all do, but this is a whole new life for them."

Stan said his goodbyes as Gustav and Amelia went inside the main house.

***

Unseen from below, a curtain in one of the closed, attic windows moved.

***

Sunlight dappled the garden through the trees, a light breeze flowing over them. Amelia sat back in the chair Anna had brought out for her and placed next to the garden. Anna had been making sure Amelia got time in the sun every day

Pawn to King Four

for herself as well as the baby. Amelia closed her eyes and lifted her face in the sun, and just enjoyed the warmed air moving over her skin.

"What want…boy, girl?" Anna was sitting on the ground near Amelia's feet, snapping green beans into a bowl in front of her.

Amelia rubbed a hand over her belly. "Honestly, just healthy. But I would like a boy for Gustav. I feel like he is a boy."

"Let see?" Anna set the bowl aside, smoothed her apron, and gestured to Amelia's left hand. "Ring?"

Amelia pulled her ring off and Anna dug in her garden basket for a piece of twine. Stringing the ring on the thin sliver of string, she took Amelia's hand and placed the string between her thumb and forefinger. She stilled it, "Hold over belly. Think of baby."

Amelia held the string as still as possible over her belly and thought of how the baby felt kicking inside of her. As she did, the ring began to swing. Only slightly at first until it started to form a very distinct circular motion. Amelia watched it move, fascinated.

"You get wish. It boy." Anna made a circular gesture in the air. "If straight line it girl. Circle, boy."

Amelia smiled so hard her face hurt and slid the ring back on her finger, giving the strong back to Anna, "Thank you." Anna nodded and smiled.

"Hello, my sweet boy."

***

"Anna, come quick!" Amelia shouted from the kitchen door. Anna and Jorgen were outside tending the garden they had created up behind the two houses. Anna jumped up and stripped off her dirty garden gloves. She stopped at the step

Ana Maria Selvaggio

Amelia was standing on, holding her belly.

"Time?"

Amelia smiled and laughed, "No, no. Not yet. Feel, he's kicking…" She took Anna's hand and held it against her belly. A moment later, two kicks met Anna's palm. Anna cried and laughed. "Jorgen! Come here!"

Jorgen stood and removed his gloves, "Gustav might not…"

"Oh don't be silly, he's kicking, feel." She grabbed Jorgen's hand and placed it on the other side of her belly just in time to feel a little foot kick. Jorgen laughed and pulled his hand away. Anna placed her other hand where it was and laid her head on Amelia's belly, when she nodded to go ahead.

"He is going be strong." Jorgen laughed and smiled as Anna closed her eyes to listen. The baby kicked her cheekbone. Anna pulled away and laughed. Amelia loved seeing her smile, she was like sunshine when she did.

"Well, he better be, or all this extra food I'm eating is just going to my hips!"

They were all standing around laughing when Gustav came through the house behind Amelia. "What did I miss?" Gustav kissed her on the neck and she turned.

"Feel. He's been kicking for the last ten minutes."

"Hey you, be good to your mama." Gustav bent down and spoke toward her bellybutton like it was a microphone. Laying his head against her belly, he was rewarded with a kick to the ear. "Whoa!"

Jorgen laughed and nodded, "Strong."

Gustav nodded and rubbed his ear before kissing Amelia. "I better treat you good, or he's gonna beat me up when he's out." Amelia laughed and snuggled into his arms.

Anna walked back to the garden and pulled a fresh

Pawn to King Four

carrot and handed it to Amelia, "For eyes," pointing at her belly, "make good, strong."

"Thank you, that little garden of yours has been a wonder. I'm so happy for this. You will have a little helper soon, too." Amelia tapped her belly with the long, leafy carrot greens, "I want him to know all about how to garden. I'm hoping he won't inherit my black thumb."

Anna tapped the green carrot tops. "Soup," then tapped the orange body. "Eat raw…or soup. Can all-so eat green top. Wash, eat. Or," she paused a moment to think, "dry in sun, mix," and made a shaking movement, like over food.

"Oh! I always just cut them off. Thank you. Will you teach me?"

Anna grinned wide, "Yes, yes. Thank you."

Gustav took the carrot, washed it off, and brought it back to Amelia. "You heard the woman, eat Bugs." Amelia laughed and held it up like a cigar before taking a bite off the tip.

"Bug? No bug." Anna looked at the carrot, then back at the garden.

Gustav laughed, "No. Bugs Bunny. Cartoon. You know, 'What's up Doc?'" Amelia laughed, his impression was awful.

"Oh!" Jorgen shook his head, "Bug Bunny."

Amelia pulled off part of the green carrot top and ate it. "Oh, it's almost like pepper. Here," she pulled off part of it and handed it to Gustav, "I could make those like Swiss Chard. Thank you, I never knew. I feel so wasteful now."

"You can eat most every part of garden," Jorgen gestured toward the plot of dirt they had nurtured and worked over the summer. "Most, not all, we teach."

Gustav and Amelia were both thankful for the giant

trees in the back that allowed for some shade, even in the summer months. The plants got plenty of sun and it wasn't as hard on them to be out there.

"Thank you. This is a treat…" Amelia leaned into Gustav, "I need to sit down I think." She waved him off when he started to fuss, "I'm okay, just tired all of a sudden." Gustav led her to the chair as Anna came in and Jorgen fetched their harvesting baskets from the garden.

"I cook dinner, rest." Anna wouldn't take no for an answer, and Amelia knew better than to argue. It would be three against one.

"Thank you." Amelia sat back and Gustav set a large glass of lemonade in front of her with another glass full of water, before kissing her temple and helping Jorgen in with all the baskets.

"Let me know what you need, Anna." Gustav rolled up his sleeves as Jorgen sorted out the contents of the baskets between the two houses. Anna had him clean a few odds and ends, then showed him how to cut them up for her.

"Better than mess hall duty." Gustav stole a berry and Jorgen laughed when Anna held up a wooden spoon at him, "Maybe just as dangerous, though!" They all laughed, and Gustav stole another one, handing it this time to Amelia.

"I feel spoiled. We're so blessed." Amelia rubbed her belly and closed her eyes, savoring the fat, fresh blackberry in her mouth. She let out a happy sigh and watched everyone in the room working side by side harmoniously.

"I can't wait to meet you, little one," she whispered. "Oh what a family you have."

***

Gustav took a look at the scratches on Michael's back. "Do they hurt?" Amelia asked as Gustav pulled his shirt back

Pawn to King Four

down.

"Only a little, don't be mad at him." Michael picked the cat up and held it in his arms, "I know he didn't mean to do it."

"I know, sweetheart, we aren't mad." Amelia smoothed hair away from Michael's face and tucked it behind his ear. Amelia looked up at Gustav.

"Try to get some sleep, okay?" Gustav tucked him in. "Do you want him to stay with us tonight?"

"No, it's okay." Michael settled in and tucked the cat under the covers with him. "He won't do it again." Amelia and Gustav didn't have the heart to move the orange tabby and thought Michael might actually be safer with him.

"Okay, sweetheart. I love you. We're just down the hall if you need us." Amelia kissed his forehead and stroked the cat's nose, "Sleep well."

"Night, Mama. I love you."

"Night, buddy." Gustav scruffed his hair, "Love you more."

"I heard that, Gustav Hilpany." Amelia waited at the door for him.

"Oops! In trouble again," they laughed. "Night." Gustav turned out the light.

Amelia stood and watched him a moment, then left the room, worry on their faces.

***

"We can't keep saying it's the cat. He'll wonder why we aren't getting rid of it if it's hurting him all the time." Gustav ran his fingers through his hair.

"Have you had someone come in and bless the house?" Stan looked at them over his coffee cup.

Amelia watched Michael and Anna in the garden pulling

weeds through the screen on the back door.

"Here we go again," Gustav gently laughed it off.

"Look. I know you don't believe in this kind of stuff," Stan set his cup down, "but it is real. I've seen things with my own eyes enough to know it would be good to rule it out."

"He's right, sweetheart. And what would it hurt?" Amelia put her hand on Gustav's, "Please. We've tried everything else."

"Okay, but I don't want him here for it."

"Deal." Stan looked at Jorgen, "Did you say you had a priest at your church who could do a house blessing? Would they be able to handle this?"

Jorgen nodded, "Father Santos."

"Could you tell him our concerns, what has been going on, and ask if he could come by?" Amelia glanced at Gustav, "He can come while Michael is at his tutor's, that should be enough time."

Gustav kissed her cheek and walked out to the garden.

"I will smooth it over with him, he will be fine." Amelia watched Michael show off the vegetables they were growing to his father. Anna laughed as Michael gestured with wide arms about the vegetables like he was telling big fish stories.

"He's always been a stubborn skeptic." Stan got up and washed his cup in the sink before setting it to dry on the rack. "I'm gonna head back, good luck." Stan gave Jorgen a quick pat on the shoulder, then took Amelia's hand and kissed it with a squeeze.

"Thank you, Stan."

"Anytime. You know where I am if you need me."

Jorgen got up, washed his cup in the sink, and set it aside before nodding to Amelia and walking out to the garden.

After a few minutes, Gustav came back into the house and walked around behind Amelia's chair, hands on her

Pawn to King Four

shoulders. She leaned her head back into him. "I hope this works."

"So do I." Amelia laced her fingers into his, on her shoulder, "So do I."

***

Gustav and Jorgen returned with Father Santos to Amelia and Anna both sitting on the porch waiting for them. Michael was at a friend's house for a sleepover so they would have the house to themselves. Jorgen introduced Anna and Amelia, then they all went into the house.

Father Santos prepared his vestments on the porch and lit a censer on a chain before entering the house.

The moment he entered the front foyer, everyone was hit with a gentle humming, almost tinnitus in nature but at a lower frequency. Not quite a growl but not friendly.

"There is definitely something here." Father Santos gently swung the censer and walked around the main floor of the house. He was drawn to the basement and the upstairs. Investigating the basement, he felt as though he was being watched, but that it was not with ill-intent. Moving upstairs, he was pulled to Michael's room and spent more time there, blessing the room and paying careful attention to the window and doors.

Entering the hallway again, he passed through two more bedrooms including Gustav and Amelia's and a guest room, before hesitating at the end of the hallway. Stopping then taking a step back at the door, he moved the censer around it. "This is the source."

Gustav prepared Father Santos for the attic, explaining that their collection was there, most items surrounded with salt. They had had very little issue with the items and Michael was not allowed in the attic simply because it was their work.

Ana Maria Selvaggio

Their personal collections were around and throughout the rest of the house. Anything in the attic was being processed, restored, and on its way out to a museum or private collector. He, Amelia, and Michael had traveled the world for several years in search of artifacts or varying type; everything from books and toys, to knick knacks and pieces that had gone missing during the war.

Gustav didn't talk about the war very often, but he never failed to talk about the art he had experience while he was overseas.

Gustav unlocked the door to the staircase for Father Santos. Telling the others to wait for him, Santos started up the stairs by himself. Halfway up the stairs he acted as though he were struggling to move. Even the smoke from the incense in the censer seemed to pause.

Father Santos crossed himself and backtracked a step then stumbled. Gustav went up to meet him and felt a push on his chest. Both men backed slowly to the bottom of the stairs, looked at each other, and Gostav locked the door.

Father Santos was the first to speak, "Keep this door locked, it is not safe." He looked down the hall at Michael's door. "If your son is being attacked, we need to make his room a sacred space where nothing can enter." He looked to Jorgen and Anna, then Amelia. "I can give you protection charms, the Saints will watch over him. They are to be left in his room and above on all the sills of the doors and window. I will return with others when I can."

"He won't understand. We can't do this." Amelia stood staring out the kitchen window, holding the countertop to keep the world from spinning.

"I don't want this but…I don't know what to do. The scratches are getting worse."

Gustav's voice was shaking, something she was

Pawn to King Four

unaccustomed to in all the years they'd been together. She turned to him and wrapped her arms around him.

"He'll have a good education, and we have friends that can keep an eye on him." Gustav pulled her in tighter, "He's not safe here, and I won't make this decision without you."

Amelia lifted her head from his chest to look him in the eye. The despair in her eyes was almost more than he could bear. He kissed her to close them. They were standing like that, in each other's arms, when Michael arrived home from his tutor's.

***

"I won't go." Michael stood with his hands fisted by his side, tears running down his face. "We were going to Scotland next."

"I know, I know." Amelia was doing her best to stand her ground, even though she wanted to protest with him, "We'll get to see England, though, and that's close!"

"Yeah, and then you'll DUMP me there." Michael broke, "What did I do?"

"Oh honey, sweetie," Amelia scooped him into her arms, "you haven't done anything, you hear me." Amelia pulled him away from her and took his face in her hands, "Nothing."

"Then why?" he looked at Gustav. "Why?"

"We want a better education for you than you will get here, and we need to travel for work." It wasn't a complete lie. There had been several galleries, museums, and collectors that had been inquiring about their collection and curation services again. He still felt the villain for saying it, though.

"But I've always gone on those trips with you. Why can't I go now?" Michael looked between Gustav and Amelia, visibly confused and hurt. It was more than Amelia could bear.

"I'm going to go make us some lemonade and let you two talk," she stood and did her best to keep from faltering till she got to the kitchen. Anna, who had been pulling muffins out of the oven, took one look at her and left everything on the counter, grabbing her into a tight hug. Amelia buried her face in her neck and sobbed as quietly as she could. It wasn't quiet enough.

"Mom, are you okay?" Michael put his hand on her shoulder. Amelia tried to regain her composure, and Anna handed her a dish towel.

"Yes, baby, I'm fine." Amelia reached over and pulled him close. He was only eleven and almost as tall as her now.

Gustav came into the kitchen behind him and Michael turned both barrels on him, "This is your fault. Why can't I go? My grades are good, and I always do what you ask. This is bulls…"

"Watch it," Gustav warned. "I know you're mad, you've got a right to be, but it's not forever. It's for your own good." Gustav pulled a chair out and sat down, motioning for Michael to sit.

Michael shook his head no. "Staying here, with my family, is for my own good," and with that, he stormed out the kitchen door and headed for a spot in the back corner of the yard. Gustav stood and started toward the door. Amelia caught his arm.

"No, let him be for a few minutes." Amelia softened her grip on his arm and smoothed his shirt.

"Miss Amelia, I would like talk to him in few minute." Jorgen looked to Anna, who nodded at him, "I can talk him understand better. I can help."

"Thank you, I don't know what else to do."

Pawn to King Four

***

Michael was sullen the entire time they were in England. They had gone everywhere he'd wanted. Amelia had made lists in the travel journal she had made for their trip and knew all of the places he had ever wanted to visit. To him, none of it mattered now, though. He was convinced that his father no longer wanted him and was forcing his mother to send him away. And he still didn't know why. She was obviously upset about it, Michael had caught her crying on more than one occasion.

Despite even Amelia's gestures, Michael pulled away more, isolated himself. Better to be prepared for the break. His anger toward Gustav got him in trouble more, so he just stayed quiet; mostly answering only Amelia, sometimes answering no one.

***

The second week they were there was all about him settling into his new home. They did a tour of the boy's school and got him set up in his dorm. The boy he would be sharing the room with hadn't arrived yet, and Amelia was almost happy he would have the place to himself to acclimatize first, alone.

Alone.

Amelia got busy to avoid thinking, "Is there anything you need, sweetheart?"

"You know what I need." Michael saw his mother's eyes start to well up and immediately felt bad, then angry, "I'm sorry. I know this is hard on you. I love you, I'll be fine."

"Promise to write me, I want to hear all about everything." Michael could tell she was trying to be sincere, but he knew his mother's voice and could hear the underlying desperation she was trying to hide. "There are envelopes already stamped in your bag. I will send more for you before you run out."

"Mom, I'll be fine. I'm sorry," Michael wrapped his arms around her waist and held her tight. "I'm sorry."

Amelia pulled him in tight and just stood there with her face buried in his hair for a minute, eyes on Gustav. "You will make me cry and mess up my makeup," pulling back, "I love you, more than the world. You make me proud here." With that, she stepped back and handed Michael's hand to Gustav. He promptly dropped it.

"We love you. You'll do well here. You'll be safe."

Michael noticed his father's choice of words but was still too angry to care. "I was safe at home, but whatever. Go have fun. Make sure Mom has time to write me."

"I know you hate me, I wish you wouldn't." Gustav put his hand out to Michael, offering a shake. "I don't want to leave with us like this."

Michael turned his back on him, with a "You should have thought of that before," muttered under his breath.

Gustav put his hands in his pockets and looked at Amelia. "Goodbye, Son. Make sure to write your mother or she'll worry. You can call, too." Amelia started to step toward Michael but Gustav shook his head. "Okay then, we'll leave you to it."

Michael turned around and they were gone.

***

"Remember, testing begins next week, so review your notes. I'll be out of the office for a couple weeks, so Professor Gardner will be standing in. Do not think this gives you an advantage, he's been briefed." Student reactions were mixed between groans and laughter, "Have a good week next week! Make me proud."

Professor Michael Hilpany slid his lecture notes into his

Pawn to King Four

filing cabinet in the corner, locked it, and grabbed his duffel out from under his desk. Turning off the lights, he locked the classroom on his way out. He had an hour before he needed to be at the airport but had brought everything with him so he'd already called for a taxi to meet him outside. It was almost two hours from the University to London Heathrow. He'd packed snacks for the drive but planned to sleep away most of the nine-hour flight to Chicago.

Michael was torn. England had become his home, but now he questioned just how much he had let it actually *be* home. He'd stayed mostly to himself, not wanting to get attached to anyone for the most part. Michael had dated a few girls over the years, but nothing serious, and even male friends were scarce. He studied, advanced, and succeeded at everything he set his mind to in life, except actually living it.

And now he was headed somewhere that made him question all of it.

Reaching into his messenger bag, Michael pulled out a brass coin and rubbed his fingers across it. It had been his good luck charm, something his mother had given him. It always helped ground him when he was anxious. Michael stared out the window and watched the English landscape go by, wrestling with the thoughts in his head.

When he got there, he'd meet with this Gilbert guy about the estate, Frank, if he remembered right, and sign whatever he needed to sell it off. He had two weeks to sort it out or hand it off. Either way he wasn't staying.

Home?

He didn't have one.

About the Authors Of the Marathonarium Anthology Volume II

In alphabetical order by last name, your Marathonarium Anthology, Volume II authors are…

Clayton Barnett

Having never written fiction before, a middle-aged Clayton stumbled into NaNoWriMo 2014 and created a book which, over the next eight years, became the first of the multi-volume future history of Machine Civilization, a world set from now to a hundred years hence. So far.

Clayton works a part-time job to pay for copyediting, cover designs, and his liquor bill. He is a misplaced Texan currently in Ohio with his wife of thirty years, three dogs, and a cat who thinks he's a dog. Both of his daughters are grown and out and about in the wide world.

Clayton's website is https://machciv.com/

His blog is https://machciv.com/

Follow him on Amazon at https://www.amazon.com/Clayton-Barnett/e/B01LZZBEQ2

Kathy L. Brown

Kathy L. Brown writes speculative fiction with a historical twist. Her hometown— St. Louis, Missouri, USA—and its history inspires much of her fiction.

The haunted 1920s world of the Sean Joye Investigations book series was conceived in a creative writing workshop. The idea wouldn't go away, and Kathy published two Sean Joye novellas while working on her first novel, *The Big Cinch*, released by the Montag Press Collective in December 2021. The Big Cinch won the 2022 Imadjinn award for best urban fantasy novel.

After spending the pandemic editing and publishing a secondary-world young adult fantasy, Wolfhearted, Kathy is preparing the next Sean Joye novel, The Talking Cure, for publication late in 2025.

Learn more at kathylbrown.com.

Abigail Christine Cahoe

I guess the best way to do this is to start with the basics. I was born, raised, and live in Louisville, Kentucky. I am 43 years old. I love everything to do with history but my focuses are United States and European History. It amazes me, how many patterns there are when you look over a specific time period. Anyways, for someone that hated English and Language Arts in school, how in the world did I become a writer? It's a good question that perplexes me to this day.

I guess the main reason I started writing was to create a world where I was living as my true self because I am Transgender, and my first ever stories that I wrote were about me walking up one day to find myself magically turned into a girl. Then I found others like me that were writing stories along Transgender themes, and loved a series by a good friend of mine so much that I started writing fan fiction filling in gaps between his/her books. That is how I found this wonderful group of Creatives here at Imaginarium. I am so pleased to say that my first published piece is here in this second anthology of stories, and I hope you enjoy it.

Alisa Childress

Alisa Childress writes creative nonfiction, fiction and personal essays. She has an MS in clinical psychology and now works as a case manager for persons with developmental disabilities. A proud nerd, multi-hobbyist, and empty nester, she lives with her husband and animal menagerie in Louisville, KY. Her essays have appeared in the *Potato Soup Journal, Adult Children: Being One, Having One & What Goes In-Between A Wising Up Anthology, Open Door Magazine, Mother Egg Review,* and several Medium publications. Her debut fiction piece, Second Chances, appeared in the *2023 Marathonarium Anthology.* Follow her on Facebook, Instagram, Threads and BlueSky @ authoralisachildress. And check out her website and blog at www.alisachildress.**com**

S.D. Croft

S. Donovan Croft and SD Croft are pseudonyms for the writer and publisher of the novel *Shadows of Carath* and other upcoming Science Fiction/Fantasy stories within the "Weapons of Legend" universe. His upcoming novella, *Day*

Zero: Catalyst Crew, will be available in 2025. He contributed to Quanta Publishing's Sci-Fi/Fantasy anthologies *Stranded, Amazing Robots,* and the upcoming *Noblesse Oblige Stellaris,* edited by Page Zaplendam. Croft also contributed to the Lemur Thone's Sci/Fantasy anthology *Tales from the Lemurverse: In the Midst of a River,* edited by Clayton Barnett.

Croft served twelve years in the Army National Guard and is a decorated Veteran of Iraq and Afghanistan. He is a former Corrections officer who works in Law Enforcement, serving a combined twenty-seven years. Croft has been married to the same amazing woman for over twenty-nine years, and they have five wonderful children. He currently resides in South Carolina.

Marian Gosling

Marian Gosling's short stories of romance, humor and crime are featured in Kentuckiana Romance Writers and Imaginarium anthologies. Her upcoming debut novel, *Trudy's Bizarre Legacy,* captures strip mall drama and humor in Panama City Beach, Florida. She also is a published poet in Words of the Heart.

Marian lives in Louisville, KY with her husband of forty-five years. They enjoy three adult children and seven grandchildren. Marian loves swimming, reading all genres, dreams of more horseback riding, volunteers for the annual Imaginarium Conference, and is an avid animal lover-serving the family's rescued cat and dog.

Follow Marian on Facebook as www.facebook.com/mariangoslingauthor or email her at www.mariangoslingauthor@gmail.com

Grathew

Grathew has reached a fair degree of education, culminating in a Bachelor of Science in Computer Science. During this time, he picked up tabletop role-playing games and started building worlds for them. After getting a boring day job in business software, he returned to inventing worlds,. After sharing them online, he was heckled into putting stories in them.

Joseph M. Isenberg

Joseph Isenberg received bachelor's degrees in History and Political Science as well as a master's degree in History from Iowa State University. His research emphasized medieval and ancient history in Iowa State's Agricultural History and Rural Studies program. He earned a law degree from the University of Iowa College of Law. He practiced law for a number of years.

He resides in central Iowa where he regularly participates in miniature wargames and role-playing games with the alumni of the Iowa State University Guild of Wargamers and Roleplayers. He has had a couple of role playing modules published in Chaosium's "Call of Cthulhu" contest volumes. In 2021, he published his first novel, *Hot Halcon Nights: A Tale of the Pan-Galactic Empire*. He has published a number of short stories in anthologies with Quanta Publishing (*Amazing Robots*, and *Stranded*, as well as *Noblis Oblige Stellaris*, forthcoming), *New Myths* (The Growers, forthcoming), Three Ravens' Publishing (*Face the Storm*, forthcoming). Together with Clayton Barnett, S. Donovan Croft, Grathew and Page Zaplendam, he contributed to *In the Midst of a River*, the first Lemur Throne anthology.

His novel, *Hot Halcon Nights*, is available on Amazon

Teri Kay Jobe

Originally hailing from the forests of Pennsylvania, Teri Kay Jobe has always had a love of stories. As a child, she would perch on top of her father's chair and listen to him read to her. This fed an imagination that hasn't slowed down since. From playing Dungeons and Dragons, to narrating audiobooks, to writing her own stories, she is seldom far from fantastic worlds. Even her day job as a park ranger lets her tell the true stories of history to anyone who is willing to listen. When she's not traversing the far-off worlds of fantasy, Teri can usually be found enjoying the company of her husband and their feline fur-babies.

Lisa Mildon

Lisa Mildon is a freelance copy editor and entrepreneur, CEO of Coffee House Writers, founder of Creatively Caffeinated and her own editing and writing business at lisamildon.com. She is currently pursuing a Master of Fine Arts at Southern New Hampshire University. Her work has been published in *Marathonarium Anthology: Volume 1* and on various technology websites. Along with writing and editing, Lisa loves arts & crafts, playing PC games, and camping with her hubby and their two Rat Terriers.

Anette Miller

Annette Miller grew up in Baltimore and married an Air Force man, getting the chance to see Germany and most of the United States. Always a fan of superhero stories, science fiction, fantasy, and horror novels, she didn't discover romance until her oldest son was two. Then, she couldn't get enough. After getting introduced to tabletop role playing games, her and her husband's characters began to develop their own stories, which obviously needed to be written. Soon, her imagination took over, and she combined her two loves. Because she loves the woods, she tries to work in a little magic and new takes on fairy tales in her stories.

Randi Perrin

Randi doesn't take herself seriously, and neither should you. Depending on the day, she'll claim to be a beach girl (not a lie, that's where she grew up) or a little too country (not really a lie either, she lives in Kentucky). She's a perfectionist (a blessing and a curse), a little bit obsessive-compulsive about grammar, a lot neurotic about stupid things like eating cake, and is too sarcastic for her own good. She has too many dogs, a handful of cats, and a kid to keep her busy. She'd much rather be curled up with a dog, a book, and a glass of Moscato than going out and doing stuff because introverting is cool. (And adulting is not.)

Zevon Price

Zevon Price is an author of fantasy and horror. She grew up in the coalfields of Appalachia, where she spent the entirety of her youth making up stories and grand adventures while trying to avoid all the ways Mother Nature has tried to kill her. Today she resides in Kentucky, where she wrangles three rescue dogs and continues to write offbeat fantasy stories. She will scare and delight you, and maybe even gross you out a little:

https://zevonprice.com/

Brian Ronk

Brian is a Christ-following writer, programmer, and coffee-holic from North Central Ohio, where he lives with his wife and kids. He works as a data cowboy (according to his wife) wrangling other people's data, and has experience in the print industry as well.

With a librarian for a mother, it was no wonder that he grew up with a healthy love of books. Brian could often be found with his nose buried in one as a child, and that love has not lessened. His first book was fan fiction about a favorite cartoon series in elementary school, which still sits on a bookshelf. And like a certain hobbit, Brian longs to see the mountains and find a quiet place to finish a book.

When he isn't reading or writing, Brian enjoys spending time with his family, and playing games.

Facebook: https://www.facebook.com/BrianTRonk/

Website: https://briantronk.com.

Ana Maria Selvaggio

Under the name Renmeleon, Ana Maria Selvaggio has been an illustrator, writer, designer (graphic, book, game), and "Instigational Motivator" since 1986. Specializing in playing muse, she has worked with independent authors since the mid-90s and continues to mentor.

Selvaggio is the owner of Dragonfly Press Publishing, the founding Captain of the Kentucky Browncoats, and the steering committee lead for the global fan group, Can't Stop the Serenity.

For further information on Renmeleon, please visit: http://www.renmeleon.com

Carma Shoemaker

Carma Haley Shoemaker is an International best-selling writer of Candy Cornered, Code Red, and Sage and Time. Winner of Best Romance for Sheltered and Family Recipe, Carma has currently published 27 books. Her latest book – *What's Left, Poems of Heartbreak, Loss, and Mourning* – is a collection of poetry dedicated to her oldest son, Alec, who passed away unexpectedly on May 29, 2024.

Starting her career as a non-fiction writer and editor for iParenting.com. She moved to a freelance career writing for various print and online publications such as *Women's Health, Men's Health* and *Fitness, European Homes and Gardens, Parenting, Health, Baby Years,* and *Fit*. Her writing now consists of mixed-genre writing where her characters are put through hardships, trials, and heartbreaks. But she still believes in fast-love, true romance, and HEA endings – however they may come about.

Before jumping feet-first into the inkwell, Carma worked in the medical field, starting as a nurse's aide at 15, and moving her way up to an LPN in 1999.

Carma currently lives in Ashland, Ohio with her mini-panther, Mystic. When not writing, she enjoys filling her days with baking, Supernatural reruns, and dancing in the living room like no one is watching.

If you'd like to keep in touch, feel free to do so:

FACEBOOK – https://www.facebook.com/carmicwords

TWITTER – https://twitter.com/TheGingerScribe

PINTEREST – www.pinterest.com/thegingerscribe

INSTAGRAM – https://www.instagram.com/thegingerscribe/

AMAZON AUTHOR PAGE – http://www.amazon.com/author/carma

GOODREADS – https://www.goodreads.com/gingerscribe

R.N. Warren

R. N. Warren is a fantasy author with a passion for crafting enchanting worlds. Warren graduated with history and creative writing degrees at the University of North Texas, which basically means they're professionally qualified to make things up — as long as they sound historically plausible. Drawing inspiration from travels across more than 30 countries, Warren brings depth, and weaves wondrous landscapes into every adventure. When not writing, Warren continues to explore new places and perspectives, always seeking the next story waiting to be told.

Website: www.rnwarren.com

About the Editor
Stephen Zimmer

Stephen Zimmer is an award-winning author, editor, podcaster, and publisher based out of Lexington, Kentucky. A writer in several genres of speculative fiction, Stephen currently has 33 books in print. The editor-in-chief of Seventh Star Press, a small press with multiple imprints, Stephen founded and co-directs The Imaginarium Convention, a 12th year annual convention held in Louisville, Kentucky for writers and storytellers of all genres.

Stephen is also the co-host of the weekly Star Chamber Show live podcast, hosted on PodBean.

He is an active member of the Bluegrass Writers Coalition and the Chicago Writers Association!

Find Stephen online at:

Website: www.stephenzimmer.com

Facebook: www.facebook.com/stephenzimmer7

X: @sgzimmer

BlueSky: https://bsky.app/profile/stephenzimmer7.bsky.social

Instgagram: https://www.instagram.com/stephenzimmer7

Threads: https://www.threads.com/@stephenzimmer7

TikTok: https://www.tiktok.com/@stephenzimmer7

LinkedIn: https://www.linkedin.com/in/stephenzimmer7/

Substack: https://substack.com/@stephenzimmer

The Imaginarium Convention

The Imaginarium Convention, now in its 12th year, is a unique event for writers and storytellers of all genres, including authors, filmmakers, game developers, artists, musicians, poets, publishers, editors, cosplayers, and many other creatives, and their fans.

The convention features three days full of extensive panel and workshop programming, an expo, a film festival, live entertainment, literary and film awards, cosplay, and much more!

A broad array of over 200 professional guests and panelists are featured in the programming, including authors, editors, publishers, filmmakers, screenwriters, game designers, comic creators, artists, actors, poets, and many other working creatives.

The home of the Imadjinn Awards, Michael Knost Wings Award, and Imaginarium Convention Film Festival Awards, The Imaginarium Convention is also the home of the Imagination Hall of Fame. The inaugural Imagination Hall of Fame 2025 Inductee Class will be celebrated and formally inducted at Imaginarium 2025!

The Imaginarium Convention hosts an inclusive and welcoming environment that enables networking, learning, professional opportunities, promotional opportunities, and other benefits to independent creatives.

Visit the official website for details at

https://www.entertheimaginarium.com/.

Made in the USA
Middletown, DE
01 July 2025

77699865R00273